Aurora's Journey

What she found
and lost along the way

Rosina Vigil-Armon

Editor: Annette Byrd
Book and cover design: Debby Schoeningh/The Country Side Press

Published in LaGrande, Oregon and printed in the U.S.A.

ISBN: 978-0-9963131-4-8
Library of Congress Control Number: 2022912078

VIGIL FAMILY TREE

Pedro Vigil (v-hill) – Margarita Lucero

Manuel A. Vigil – Isabel Lucero

Maria Telesfora
Maria Rufina de la Cruz
Jesus Maria Severo
Juana Maria
Maria Guadalupe
Santa Cruz
Flavio
Maria Hilaria
José de Jesus
José Lonsequin
Margarita Portana
Manuel Antonio
Francisco

Esquipula Vigil – Josefa Pino

Andres Mariano
Santa Cruz
Doloritas
Maria Aurora
Rita

Family Ties

Flavio Vigil
Son of Manuel Vigil

Aurora Vigil
Daughter of Esquipula Vigil. Flavio and Aurora were cousins.

Telesfora Vigil
Flavio's oldest sister, married to José Pino
José was a brother to Josefa Pino-Vigil, uncle by marriage, to Aurora

Rufina Vigil
Flavio's sister – first marriage to Rafael Luna
Rafael's son, Melquides, was Rufina's stepson

Melquides Luna
First married to Margerita Vigil – Flavio's sister
Melquides later married Aurora Vigil-Debaun

Map of New Mexico

Prologue

When I started searching for my family's roots, I had no idea how tangled they were. I knew that his name was Flavio Vigil, and that he died at an early age. Other than that, I knew nothing about my great-grandfather. The census records from the 1800's revealed little more. It wasn't until I went back to New Mexico that I unraveled the story of my family's tragic past. The complex puzzle only began when my great-grandfather died. It was after his death that the journey of my great-grandmother, Aurora, began.

Aurora's family lived near the Rio Grande River on land granted to her mother's family by the Spanish Government. Long before that, the families lived in northern New Mexico on land granted to them by the king of Spain. Aurora's father, Esquipula Vigil, and his brother Manuel built a cluster of small adobe fortresses in a small settlement called La Parida. These compounds assured that if the Apaches raided there would always be help nearby.

Esquipula, was married to Josefa Pino, Aurora's mother. Euipula owned rich farmland along the river. He devoted himself to his land and his family.

Manuel Vigil married Isabel Lucero. They named their seventh child Flavio. He was born next door to his cousin Aurora. Manuel's house was the largest. It too was a fortress, built with rooms on three sides. A stable and heavy gate enclosed the fourth side. Manuel sold some of his land and bought a mercantile and saloon in Lemitar, north of Socorro. He built gristmills in Lemitar and Socorro. Eventually, Manuel purchased land for cattle and sheep ranching.

The nearest town was more than five miles away, so the extended families only had each other to rely on. The cluster of their adobe *haciendas* skirted the *bosque* , a green ribbon of land along the slow-moving river. The Rio Grande provided irrigation for their fields. By 1858 the Pinos and the Vigils had lived on this land for almost thirty years.

Flavio

Aurora strained to look out the window. Was the dust coming from the road? She balled up her fists. *Flavio should be here with me. Tio Manuel had no business sending him to Mesilla. Who would be headed toward Snake Ranch at this time of day?* Aurora clutched her chest.

"Rita!" yelled Aurora. "Where's my son?" Aurora pulled Manuelito toward her. She waved to her sister, Rita. "The Apaches are coming! Close the shutters! Are the rifles in the chapel?"

Rita ran to the kitchen and peered out the window. Seeing nothing, she rolled her eyes and tried to calm her sister. Aurora struggled away from her. She whirled toward the windowless chapel at the far end of the house. Rita trailed behind her. Manuelito's fat little legs pumped to keep up with the women.

"I don't think it's Apaches," Rita argued. "They wouldn't be on the road."

Aurora bolted the heavy wooden door, then pressed herself against the wall behind the altar. She put one hand on her back and the other across her swollen belly. Then she frantically waved for Rita and Manuelito to join her.

"It's probably Papá bringing the grain for the horses," said Rita.

Aurora tiptoed across the room and put her ear to the door. Manuelito crawled over a bench. He toddled toward the wooden santos flanking the lace-covered altar. Rita lunged and caught him before he grabbed a hand full of altar cloth. With the two-year-old in tow, Rita put her arm around Aurora and led her toward a bench.

"Here, take your son," she panted. "I'll get the rifle."

They huddled in silence that only lasted a few minutes. The rumble of wagon wheels echoed against the door. Aurora held her breath and glared at Rita.

"You go," Aurora ordered. "Take the rifle just in case."

The heavy door creaked opened and Rita squeezed through it. She crept past the bedroom, rifle in hand. Rita breathed deeply. As she strained to hear voices, she remembered that they were alone at the *rancho*. She lifted the rifle a little higher.

"*Mijita, Mijita,* where are you?" Esquipula's familiar voice filled the adobe house.

Rita put down the rifle and ran into the kitchen. "Papá, Aurora thought you were Apaches!" She giggled and dismissed the idea with a wave of her hand. "Aurora jumps every time a rabbit hops across the yard."

Rita fell silent as she looked past Eequipula to the frozen figure in the doorway. It was Manuel, Flavio's father. His face was set in ashen sadness, his dark eyes fixed on the floor. Rita backed away from Esquipula, questions forming like thunder clouds.

"Where's Aurora?" Esquipula asked gently.

"In the chapel. I'll get her," whispered Rita.

Esquipula drew his adopted daughter to him. "No," he sighed, "I'll get her."

Rita turned to Manuel. "*Tio* Manuel?" She pulled a chair away from the table and motioned toward it. Manuel didn't seem to notice. He was slumped against the door, his tears dropping onto the wooden floor.

Aurora peeked out of the chapel with little Manuelito struggling to break free of her grip. She saw her father in the dimly lit bedroom and flung the door open. "Papá!" she wailed. "I thought the Apaches were. . . . "

Esquipula scooped up Manuelito with one arm and enfolded his daughter with the other.

"What's wrong, Papá?" Aurora asked anxiously.

With head bowed, Esquipula led his Aurora to the edge of the bed. "*Sentate, Mijita*. Sit down my little girl. Something has happened to Flavio."

Aurora's breath caught in her throat. Her unborn baby lurched against her heart. She gazed at her father with an open mouth. Manuel and Rita appeared at the door. Manuel stumbled across the room and collapsed next to his daughter-in-law. He covered his face with his giant, worn hands and began to sob.

"Papá!" Aurora's eyes darted from one man to the other." Please, *Dios Santo*, what?"

Esquipula wiped his own tear-stained face on his sleeve and took a ragged breath. "Flavio's been shot," he managed before he was overcome with another sob. "*Esta con Dios, Mija*. He's with God." He cradled Aurora's face in his calloused hands and looked into her glazed eyes. His words drifted past her.

"No," she muttered.

The image of the men beside her blurred and floated into mist. When she opened her eyes again, Aurora was lying on the bed. Manuel held her hand while Esquipula gently wiped her forehead.

Aurora began to tremble. "No, no, no!" she screamed. She grabbed her father's sleeve. "What do you mean, he's been shot? Who? Why?" Her shaky hands curled into fists as confusion descended into anguish. Folded between the two men who had protected her all of her life, Aurora felt alone. Pain filled the room like a dark veil threatening to overwhelm them all.

Rita sat at the kitchen table rocking Manuelito. Her hot, silent tears dampened his soft black hair. *This is a dream, brought by the devil to take away the peace of God. Flavio can't be dead. He's only lived for twenty-two years. He was so happy that Aurora was giving him another child. And Aurora, only eighteen years on this earth, with a child not yet born.* She kissed Manuelito and held him even tighter.

Manuelito screamed, "Mamá!" Stretching out his arms, he squirmed out of Rita's embrace. He darted toward the bedroom with Rita on his heels.

She managed to snatch him up before he got across the threshold. He twisted and kicked as Rita carried him out the door. Outside, Manuelito's fit subsided. The November wind soothed his troubled little body. His dog, Chapo, came bounding toward him and he grabbed the shaggy dog's ears. The mutt shook his head and the chase was on. Rita sank onto the wooden step. *He doesn't know,* she thought. Unending sobs rolled over her. *He'll never know his father.* Rita looked toward the house and the ghostly figures inside.

Unable to speak, the three huddled together and rocked. Aurora kept shaking her head. Words formed, then disappeared into darkness. Her head pounded. The room began to spin and her morning meal violently erupted onto her lap.

Esquipula ran to the kitchen. He wet the corner of a rough linen towel and ran back into the bedroom. Manuel was holding Aurora up, struggling to remove her soiled skirt. Quickly Esquipula started wiping his daughter's mouth and hands.

Bracing Aurora under each arm, the men lowered her back into bed.

"*Ay, Santa Maria,* what are we going to do now?" Esquipula pleaded to an invisible saint.

No one was willing to leave the cool darkness of the room. Aurora began to moan again. Manuel retreated to a corner chair and Esquipula busied himself with gathering up Aurora's soiled clothes. The afternoon slipped away with the three lost souls wrapped in grief. There were no more words to say; no way to make things better.

✳✳✳

Outside, Rita still sat on the porch hugging herself. Her shivering masked spasms of tears. She slipped inside and grabbed her shawl and a jacket for Manuelito. As she stepped back outside, Rita left behind a trail of soft moaning. She wanted so much to be with her family, but she knew that her place was out here, keeping Manuelito from getting underfoot.

The cool air cleared her thinking. *How could this be true?* What happened? *When? Why?*

Only this morning the two step-sisters were washing Manuelito's baby clothes, getting them ready for the next baby. When they made the noon meal, they had laughed as Manuelito toiled at rolling out tortillas with his mother's *rodillo*. They had giggled over their childhood memories; swimming in the Rio Grande and chasing boys with cattails. Aurora always stopped short when it came to hitting Flavio. Rita knew that Aurora had always loved her cousin. They were supposed to be together forever.

As Rita walked slowly toward her little charge, she went numb again. This couldn't be happening. Manuelito pulled himself up Rita's skirt. His lower lip was trembling. Chapo had long since escaped to the barn. Rita wrapped Manuelito in her shawl and walked toward the water tank under the windmill. The creaking of the windmill caught Manuelito's attention for a moment, but he soon began to buck against her and point toward the house. The sun had gone behind the hill and Rita knew she couldn't keep Manuelito away from his mother any longer.

A gust of wind followed Rita into the kitchen. She instinctively walked to the cook stove, expecting the comfort of its warmth. Instead, the feel of cold metal told her that the fire had long since gone out. Manuelito struggled out of her arms and into his grandpa Esquipula's.

Manuel took the kindling from Rita and started a fire in the cook stove. He nodded toward the bedroom. "You go in," he said to Rita. "*Ya no puedo*, I can't anymore."

Rita looked from one father to the other. In the dimness, they looked like hollow shadows floating through the room. She left them sitting at the table, silently keeping each other company.

Rita pulled the blanket under Aurora's chin. Aurora lifted her pale hand and Rita pressed it to her heart. Aurora's lip began to tremble. Rita put her hand on Flavio's unborn child and pushed out a ragged sigh.

Esquipula tiptoed into the bedroom and built a fire in the little potbelly stove. Rita rocked Manuelito to sleep, put him in his cradle, then crawled in next to Aurora. She could hear the two fathers whispering in the next room. From the sounds of their pacing, Rita knew that sleep wouldn't touch them.

Rita tossed and stirred in her sleep. When she awoke in the morning, she found Aurora gone. As she slipped into the kitchen, she wasn't surprised to see Aurora and Esquipula at the table. He was holding his daughter's hand as he gazed into her heart-shaped face. Her eyes were swollen; her hair hung in ragged strands.

Aurora grabbed her father's arm. "What happened? Tell me what happened. You said that Flavio had been shot? That can't be true."

Esquipula dropped his gaze. "Tomorrow, *Mija*, when you're feeling a little better."

Manuel came in with an armful of wood. "I think I hear a wagon. Maybe it's your mamá."

Manuelito cried out and Aurora automatically hurried into the bedroom and lifted the two-year-old out of his cradle. She used to love the mornings with Manuelito half asleep, cuddled against her and his unborn sister or brother. Somehow the baby knew its brother was near and would tickle him with muffled kicks.

Aurora put him down on the floor. He reached up for her, but she turned away. With one arm, Rita gathered Manuelito up. With the other arm she led Aurora back into the kitchen.

Manuelito ran to the window. He tugged on Manuel's pants leg. His grandpa lifted him up to see what was making all the racket. Manuel was relieved to see his oldest daughter, Telesfora. Her husband José had been driving the horses hard. Huddled in the wagon were Manuel's four oldest children.

Aurora slowly lifted her head and look toward the door. "Mamá!" she cried. The door opened and Aurora raced toward it, but it was Flavio's sister, Telesfora, who gathered her up. Telesfora glanced toward Esquipula. "Josefa stayed with Isabel. So many are hurt by Flavio's death. We're all trying to take care of each other." Telesfora folded Aurora against her heart until Aurora's sobs turned into gulping breaths. "We've come to take you home," she said.

Then Telesfora pulled Manuelito into her arms. She wrapped him in her shawl and kissed him fiercely. Her eyes darted to her father. "He doesn't know?" she whispered.

Manuel closed his eyes and shook his head. "How can he know? He's only two years old." He swallowed a cry, then slowly moved toward the little knot of family that had gathered on the *porche*.

Manuelito tried to wiggle out of Telesfora's arms, but she held him tight. "Don't worry, *Mijito*, I'll take good care of you."

A cold wind pushed the family toward the Lemitar cemetery. With a brother at each elbow, Aurora led the procession. The long slow walk halted when Aurora's numb mind descended into darkness. Her brother, Andres, lifted her from the ground. With Esquipula's help, Aurora was placed on the bed of the wagon that trailed behind the funeral procession.

Rita climbed aboard, wrapped her sister in a blanket, and held her tight. The family stopped to rest often. Each time they did, another *descansado* was placed in the ground. Each little cross had Flavio's name written on it.

The family made the sign of the cross and the procession moved on. The creaking of the wagon that carried Aurora's beloved husband shook her out of her trance. She pushed Rita aside and scooted off the wagon. She ran to Manuel and tore at the sleeves of his coat.

"Let me see my Flavio!" she screamed. "I have to see him one more time!" Flavio's father, Manuel, held her fast until her body stopped shaking.

"No, *Mijita*," Esquipula whispered, "I told you. It's better to remember him the way he was."

The funeral procession veered off the dirt road and gathered under a cottonwood tree. Telesfora guided Aurora to a fallen tree and gave her sips of water. Aurora slapped away the offer of a tortilla.

Flavio's mother, Isabel, closed her eyes and wrapped her arms around herself. She pushed herself away from the tree and drew Aurora to her.

"They tell me the same thing. I don't want to believe that I can't see Flavio again, but I know it's better this way." She put her hand on Aurora's swollen stomach. "You have to get through this day so things can start getting better for you and Flavio's children."

"Things will never get better!" Aurora wailed. The baby's kicking beneath her ribs made her stiffen. "What am I going to do now?" she moaned. For the first time in days, Aurora looked around for Manuelito. Out of the corner of her eye, Aurora saw her little son nestled in Telesfora's arms.

Again, Isabel pulled her little daughter-in-law toward her. "You're coming back home. We'll be together like we've always been."

When they reached the cemetery, the priest's words drifted past the numb family. Before climbing into his buggy, Father Martinez gave a gentle handshake to Manuel and Esquipula.

The final leg of the family's journey was to Manuel's house where the warm smell of *pozole* and *frijoles* enveloped the family.

Like shadows, people filed past Aurora, picking up her limp hand to give her their condolences. Aurora finally gave in to her exhaustion. With her mother's arms around her, she slipped into the darkened bedroom. She closed her eyes to shut out the spinning room and finally drifted off to sleep. When she woke, Aurora cried out for Rita, but she was gone.

✳ ✳ ✳

Esquipula had taken Rita and two of his men back to Snake Ranch to gather Flavio and Aurora's belongings. As Rita began packing things away, she thought, *they only lived here for a short while, not long enough to call this place a home. Now here we are taking Aurora's things back to her father's house.* Rita's tears fell on Flavio's clothes as she put his shirts and pants into the trunk that the young couple had brought to the ranch after their wedding. Aurora's dresses were lovingly folded on top of them. Rita carefully packed Aurora's wedding dishes into a barrel.

She hoped she would overhear the men talking about what happened to Flavio, but she only caught bits of their conversation; shot him... for no reason ... *gringo* ... on his way to Mesilla. When the men noticed Rita listening, they fell silent.

Rita gave up trying to find out what had happened to Flavio and finished the packing. After the wagon was loaded, they began the long journey back to La Parida. Rita let the rocking of the wagon lull her to sleep.

When they reached La Parida, the gate was opened to let the wagons into the little courtyard. The men unloaded trunks and crates into the room where sacks of grain were stored. The room next to it was made ready for Aurora with a bed and cradle. The small domed fireplace in the corner was brought to life. Rita ordered the men to put Aurora's trunk and Manualito's crate beneath the window. She rolled out a worn rug to soften the dirt floor. Then Rita brought in bedding and made the room ready for her stepsister.

When she finished, Rita crossed the *plazita* and ducked into the large main room. The dome shaped adobe fireplace on the far wall

15

heated the room. On the other end was a wood cook stove. In the center of the room sat a long table where the family took their meals. Ristras of chili and dried corn hung from the *vigas* that held up the sod roof. Telesfora was busy grinding corn on a *metate*. Manuelito lay in a little hammock nearby.

The rhythmic sound of stone against stone had lulled him to sleep.

Josefa glanced at the sleeping child. *"Graciasa Dios*, Thank God," she said to Rita. "He doesn't know what happened."

Rita replied, "Yes, all he knows is that he's here with his family, safe and loved." Her hand flew to her mouth. Her words threating to start tears flowing again and with them a torrent of Josefa's tears as well.

Rita picked up a wooden bowl and started making the ground corn *masa* for tortillas. The women spoke in whispers, careful not to wake Aurora and Isabel, sleeping in the next room. Soon the women in the kitchen heard soft whispers coming from the bedroom. Isabel cuddled Aurora, wrapping her and Flavio's unborn child in her arms. "He's gone, *Mijita*, and there's nothing we can do." Isabel smoothed Aurora's hair. "I know you want to go with him, but you have Manuelito and this baby to live for. You know my pain is as great as yours and I would go with the saints to find him, but I have twelve others to live for. We have to go on."

❋❋❋

The celebration of the *Santo Niño* passed without Aurora noticing. The family didn't attend midnight Mass. There was no *pozole* or *empanadas* to welcome the family home. The day after Christmas, Telesfora brought Manuelito back to visit his mother. Her husband, José, handed Aurora a small cotton bag. She looked from the bag to José.

"For the boy," José urged.

Aurora gave Manuelito a bag filled with an orange, and ribbon candy. Manuelito grabbed a piece and stuffed it in his mouth. Sweet goo ran down his chin as he tore the wrapping from the gift at the bottom of the bag. His eyes widened when he saw the little wooden pony that *Tio* José had carved for him. Aurora smiled and slipped a broken piece of candy into her mouth. Sweet peppermint washed across her tongue. It was the first time she remembered tasting anything since Flavio's death.

✳ ✳ ✳

Now that the frosty air kept them inside, women worked at their looms, at grinding corn, and endless cooking. When Aurora ventured out of her room she sat staring at the wall until her mother handed her a sack of beans to clean. Without a word, Aurora did as she was told.

When Telesfora brought Manuelito to see her Aurora went through the motions of caring for him: a hug, a word, a cloth to wash his face. But when he didn't appear at her knee, Aurora didn't notice.

Every evening Telesfora bundled Manuelito up and took him home with her so she could cook José's evening meal. In the morning she walked up the hill from her house and brought Manuelito to his mother. With no children of her own, she treasured the time she spent with Flavio's son.

Telesfora remembered when her brother Flavio was born. It had been a hard birth and her mother, Isabel, was in bed for weeks. The fifteen-year-old Telesfora had cared for her little brother as if he was her own. Now, with her hand wrapped around Manuelito's chubby fingers, she knew that a part of her beloved Flavio was still with her. When she had lit candles and prayed for the children that never came, Telesfora had no idea that God would send her Flavio's child instead.

✳ ✳ ✳

A few days later Aurora awoke early with the baby kicking her full bladder. With her hand on her back, she started the little fire in her room, then hurried across the *plazita*. She found her mother stirring the pot of *atole*. Rita was setting the table. Josefa turned and inspected Aurora's bulge. The baby had dropped.

"Today we'll get the baby's clothes ready," Josefa said.

Aurora looked down at her swollen body. "It's not time yet. It's only December,"

Her mother put both hands on Aurora's swollen belly. "It might come sooner," she said. "Look what you've been through."

Rita was sent to Lemitar to tell the curadera to be ready. The old woman who had brought Aurora into the world began brewing healing herbs that would help Aurora through the birth. La Señora didn't have long to wait. Five days later, Aurora's father, Esquipula, put on his sheepskin jacket and drove his buggy to Lemitar. The journey was slowed by darkness and blowing snow.

17

La Señora swung the door open before Esquipula knocked. Her bundle was sitting on the table and she was fully dressed.

"I knew the baby would come tonight," said La Señora, pointing out the window. "The moon is full."

Esquipula looked from the moonlit window to the old woman. He started to shake his head in disbelief; then he remembered the time that La Señora had knocked on his own door minutes before his wife, Josefa, felt her first pain.

Aurora's second baby boy entered the world the next afternoon. The tiny bundle felt like a feather in Aurora's arms. She looked down at his little round face, tears dropping on his soft cheeks. She whispered, "He looks just like Flavio."

Josefa took the baby from her arms. "Rest now, *Mijita*."

"Stay with me, Mamá. I don't know how much more I can endure."

Rita and Telesfora helped La Señora clean up the rags and bloody sheets. The fresh linen felt cool against Aurora's fevered shoulders. She scooted over enough to let her mother slide in beside her.

-4-

News of Flavito's safe birth reached Lemitar and pots of beans, *rellenos*, and *sopas* began to fill Josefa's kitchen. The women who brought them spoke in whispers.

"He's the size of a rabbit," said Rita, "but his cry is strong. Flavio's sister, Maria, still has her baby at her breast, so she can help if Aurora can't nurse."

All the women in the kitchen turned toward the bedroom. With knitted brows, they nodded.

The day after Flavito's birth Manuel brought Isabel to see their grandson. She tiptoed into the darkened room. Aurora opened her eyes and reached toward the mother of her beloved Flavio. The bed springs squeaked when Isabel sat beside her daughter-in-law. Aurora's hand felt like a ghost. Tears filled Aurora's eyes. The ceiling evaporated into a blur.

Isabel caught her own tears in her handkerchief. She rose and gazed into the basket. "He's so small," she sighed. "He's going to need you even more than Manuelito does. *Ay Mijita,* I know you don't want to see another day, but Flavio's still with you." She lifted the baby toward Aurora. "Love his sons like he would have loved them."

Isabel laid little Flavito in Aurora's arms. The baby squirmed and squeaked. She folded the blankets away from his little face and saw her son as if for the first time. Aurora managed a quivering smile. "Flavio," sniffed Aurora.

Isabel nodded, "Flavio," she agreed.

Tiny Flavito was baptized that afternoon. There was no clinking of wineglasses or hearty *"Salud"*. After holy water was sprinkled on the baby's head and a blessing prayed over him, the priest shook Esquipula's hand. He buttoned his coat, opened the door and pushed against the cold wind. All the way home Father Martinez prayed for God's tiny child.

❋❋❋

In the month since he was born, Flavito's translucent skin thickened a little. Wisps of eyelashes now framed his hazel eyes. He could be picked up without fear of harming his thin limbs. Josefa kept him in a basket by the fireplace. It was too cold for Aurora and the baby to stay in their room across the *plazita* so a bed was set up in the corner

"Can I hold him?" pleaded Santa Cruz.

"Not today," answered Aurora. She touched her little brother's shoulder, "He's too little, maybe in a few weeks."

Telesfora and Manuelito had been on their way to Esquipula's when she spotted the men on the roof. She quickened her steps. By the time she reached Esquipula's she was puffing out frosty little clouds that evaporated in the chilly air. She swung open the door and snow drifted across the floor. Telesfora handed Manuelito to Josefa and stomped the snow off her boots. "It's getting deeper," she huffed. When she looked up and saw Aurora at the table, Telesfora brightened. "So, you're feeling better?" She threw a hopeful glance at Josefa.

"A little," answered Aurora; it's warmer in here to feed the baby."

"Good, good," said Telesfora "A little at a time, that's all you can do."

Manuelito tugged at his mother's skirt. She took his fat little hand and smiled. Telesfora helped him onto his mother's lap where Aurora folded him into her arms.

José finished feeding the horses and ran in from the stable. When he saw Aurora holding Manuelito he raised his eyebrows and shot a look at his wife.

"I'll take you both back on my horse," he grunted to Telesfora. "You better not plan on bringing Manuelito over tomorrow. It looks like the snow isn't going to stop."

"Manuelito can stay here," offered Josefa.

Aurora's eyes widened. "It's too soon," she pleaded, shaking her head.

Josefa broke in, "Well, it isn't good for Telesfora and Manuelito to come over in this storm."

José threw his hands into the air. "There you go; he can just stay with us."

Telesfora looked pleadingly between Josefa and José. "He's happy at our house."

Josefa squinted at Aurora. She was pale, with dark circles under her eyes. With her elbows propped on the table, she held her head in her hand. "A little longer," she moaned.

Manuel lifted his chin toward Telesfora. "We'll take the buggy." José breathed a sigh of relief.

The crowded table echoed with voices. As Aurora slipped toward the rocking chair, she picked up her baby and rubbed his downy hair. Manuel looked toward her. A wave of sadness and pain washed over him. *Mijita*, he thought, *the gringo who took our Flavio will pay for this.*

✳ ✳ ✳

José rode his horse behind Manuel's buggy. Manuel dropped Telesfora and Manuelito off while José took his horse to the corral. Then he climbed into the buggy next to Manuel. Manuel snapped the reins and turned toward Lemitar. José poked his finger at the air and started to rant.

Manuel interrupted, "I know, José; the women, all they can do is cry. I'll do something about the man who killed my son."

"He was an *Americano*," José hissed. "You know they won't do a damned thing to him."

"Then it's up to me," answered Manuel, snapping the reins again. "I'll send one of my men to find out who he is."

José scooted closer to Manuel and began to spit out words that Manuel had heard before. "The *Americonos* have taken our land. They've taken our government and now they've taken your son!" He flung his fist into the air. "They flood our towns with their stinking saloons and whores and set up shops to sell things to our women; things they don't need. The law means nothing to them. They have to be stopped."

Leaning away from José's anger and spittle, Manuel's thoughts began to drift. His head pounded as he thought about his decision to send young Flavio so far away from the ranch.

Flavio had ridden to Mesilla to sell his father's cattle and to pay the vaqueros who had driven them to the livestock yards. He had taken his friend, Roberto, leaving the women alone at Snake Ranch. The only man left at the ranch was Juan who was bringing the sheep down from the hills.

Manuel shook his head and grunted. He realized that ranching hadn't been easy for the newlyweds. Flavio had known little about the cattle business, only what came from his father's ledgers. Flavio's aching back and the blisters on his hands reminded Manuel of when he first started ranching.

Pulling himself back from his painful memories, Manuel hung his head. He swallowed his guilt and pushed his horses forward. "This one will be stopped," he vowed to José.

When they reached Lemitar, darkness was draped over the town.

"I'm going to stay in Lemitar tonight," Manuel said. "I want to keep the fires going at the store." He turned to José. "Drive over and tell Isabel that I won't be home."

Manuel went into the store and sat in the back room. The oil lamp flickered, casting shadows across the white-washed adobe walls. Here, alone, he wept for his son and tried to make sense of what had happened.

Flavio had made a good deal for Manuel and was ready to celebrate. He wrapped his arms around his friend Roberto's shoulders as they headed toward their horses. Roberto had jumped at the chance to travel south with Flavio. He had spent his childhood in Mesilla where many of his friends still lived.

The two young men were riding back toward Mesilla when they stopped at Roberto's friend's house to celebrate. Felipe offered them a glass of his homemade wine. When Flavio told them that his wife was expecting their second child, Felipe slapped him on the back and poured him another glass of wine.

Knowing that they had to reach Mesilla before nightfall, the two men set off again. They were almost there when they stopped to rest at the home of another of Roberto's friends.

"I grew up with Edwardo," Roberto sighed. "Who knows when I'll be back this way." Flavio looked toward the sun dropping closer to the mountain. "Alright, but just another hour," he grunted.

When Edwardo heard about the cattle sale and the coming birth of Flavio's child, he brought out his good Mexican wine.

Sunset was fading by the time the men left Edwardo's house. Flavio was singing and talking about getting back to his Aurora when he saw two men coming toward them. Flavio automatically had lifted his rifle and supposedly shouted

"*Quien vive*, who lives or maybe, who wants to live?"

Manuel spat at the wood pile and hissed, "That's what the *gringo* said. What if Flavio was saying *quien viene*, who's coming?" Manuel started pacing. "That *gringo* shot my son for no reason. He just shot him! I'll send my man Soto to Mesilla as soon as the weather calms down. He'll find out who this *gringo* is." He swallowed the last gulp of whiskey and fell into bed.

❋❋❋

Manuel's son, Severo, finished shoveling the snow from the steps of the store. He glanced at the empty road, then opened up the store. He started a fire and set the coffee pot on top of the stove.

When the smell of *piñon* wood and strong coffee reached Manuel, he was lured out of the back room. Severo jumped when he saw his father.

"You look like someone who crawled out of the grave," Severo said, handing his father a mug of hot coffee.

Severo laid a blanket over his father's shoulders and motioned to the chair near the potbellied stove. He unwrapped the tortillas, then opened his round lunch tin. Severo poured beans and *carne asada* into a little pan and put it on the stove. From the back room Severo brought out two tin plates.

"Eat. You won't be able to do anything about Flavio if you get weak and sick."

"I can't eat. I don't sleep. When the man who killed my son is put in the grave, then I'll sleep."

Severo reached to embrace his father, but Manuel pushed him away.

"Let the women cry. I'm going to find the man who killed my son and put an end to him."

Manuel stared out at the gray sky and set the plate on his lap. "When is this snow going to end?"

January brought bone chilling-cold, but more snow didn't come with it. Josefa put the crying baby in Aurora's arms every morning and brought her into the big room to sit by the fire. As Flavito suckled, Aurora looked down at him and tried to smile. She changed his diaper and bundled him up again. He made little cooing noises and nuzzled as Aurora patted his back. She closed her eyes and pressed her face against his softness. She found herself singing, "Flavito, *Mijito, como te amo, mijo de me.*" As Aurora sang to her baby, she looked out the window, but didn't seem to notice that the weather had changed.

✳✳✳

Josefa was grateful when February broke the bitter cold. She had to tip the canister to scrape out enough flour to make tortillas. Her bean supply was getting low too.

"My knees hurt in this cold weather," she said to Aurora. "You want to go with your father to get supplies?"

Aurora looked down at her wrinkled dress. It hung on her like the cast-off dresses that her mother used to give her to play with. She touched her matted hair. "No," she muttered.

Josefa nodded toward Rita. Aurora's sister dragged in the galvanized bath tub, filled it with snow, and set it next to the fireplace. Bubbling pots of water steamed up the windows. As Rita poured boiling water over the snow in the tub, Josefa took Flavito from Aurora and nudged her with her elbow. "It's time you started looking like the living."

Aurora jerked away and stomped back to her room but, by the time the bathwater was heated, Aurora reemerged with a soft dress and a flannel blanket in her arms.

Josefa bolted the door and helped her daughter into the tub. She gently washed her thin arms. The bones of her back bumped against the wash rag. When her long black hair was washed, the water turned a grayish brown. Aurora pushed the scum away from herself and slipped out of the tub. Her mother wrapped her in the flannel blanket and rubbed her all over, then guided her gently to the rocker.

Rita dried Aurora's hair and Aurora reached up and patted her face. As Aurora lifted her arms to slip on a clean dress, she noticed her pale arms. She studied her bony fingers.

Her hand flew to her mouth. "I look like my *abuela*!" she cried.

Aurora turned to her mother, her brows knitted, "Where have I gone?"

Josefa pulled her close. "You tried to follow your Flavio, but we wouldn't let you go. Manuelito and Flavito kept pulling you back too. Today you will start down a different path."

Aurora rested her head on her mother's shoulder and let Josefa rock her. Then Aurora turned the chair toward the fire and shook out her hair.

Rita ran her fingers through it. "Do you want me to braid your hair and put it up?"

Aurora shrugged, "Maybe."

Rita and Josefa exchanged a hopeful smile.

❄ ❄ ❄

Esquipula waited for the day to warm a little before getting out the buggy for the trip to town. Aurora wrapped a soft wool blanket over Flavito. She put a pair of Rita's long underwear beneath her dress and slipped on her wool coat. Josefa handed her a newly woven *mantilla* to wrap around her head.

Josefa and Rita followed Aurora to the buggy. As Esquipula started down the lane, Aurora looked up at the flawless turquoise sky, the first sky she had noticed in months. Esquipula started humming to the rhythm of the swaying buggy. Aurora scooted closer to him and lifted her face to the sun.

When they arrived at Lemitar, Aurora strolled through her father-in-law's mercantile, touching bottles and jars. She brushed her hands over colorful bolts of cloth without saying a word. José scurried around gathering the things on Josefa's list.

The little bell over the door tinkled, making Aurora jump. Aurora's friend Agnes, and her children, rushed into the store. She was busy making her children stomp the mud off their boots when she spotted Aurora. She started toward her with a smile as big as the sun, but the look of Aurora's gaunt face stopped her. Aurora frowned at her childhood friend as if inspecting a stranger.

Agnes took a deep breath and walked slowly toward the woman she had grown up with. "Aurora, finally I get to see you and your baby."

Agnes motioned to her children and they gathered around the stove. The old men, who usually occupied these chairs, rose and shuffled toward the back room. Putting an arm around her friend's shoulder, Agnes invited Aurora to sit and visit. Aurora unwrapped little Flavito and presented him to her friend. Agnes looked from the baby to Aurora and her face broke into a wide grin. "He's beautiful," she sighed. "Can I hold him?"

Flavito scrunched up his face and arched his back in a long-awaited stretch. Agnes started babbling, her words tumbling over each other. "I'm so sorry. I wanted to come and see you, but the snow. This is the first time I've come to town."

Aurora shook her head and smiled. "Some people never change, *Graciasa Dios*." Yes, thank God, she thought, *I've been like a spirit who drifted away from this world, but it's still here. They're all still here.*

With one hand intertwined in her friend's, Agnes rocked Flavito in silence. She thought of the hard winter, with her children cooped up in the house. Her husband had gotten grumpy because he had so little to do. Agnes wanted to gossip, but her friend's sunken eyes stopped her. Agnes had never been without words before, but today she found none. They sat in silence watching the other customers.

Suddenly a quick smile flashed across Agnes' lips. "Remember when we were kids? The boys used to run after us whooping like Apaches. I was so scared."

Aurora frowned as long-ago memories fell into place. Flavio had never actually seen a real Apache, but the boys were always leaping from behind mesquite bushes and jumping from the roof of the chicken coop. War cries and feathers tied to their hair made the little ones scatter. These sudden attacks were enough to keep the children from roaming the sage- covered hills near La Parida. By the time Flavio was twelve years old, there were five other little brothers and sisters to torment.

For Flavio, the next best thing to scaring the little ones, was sneaking along the irrigation canals to spy on his cousins. The boys built a fort among the brambles at the edge of the wheat fields. Flavio scampered up a cottonwood tree and whistled three short chirps. When his brother Severo returned his signal, Flavio climbed down the tree and dove under the sagebrush. Hunching low, he rendezvoused with the other boys. After making elaborate plans, the boys descended upon the unsuspecting girls with war whoops and wooden tomahawks.

Aurora and her sister Rita had set up house in a lean-to built near the fort. When the war party attacked, most of the girls ran screeching into the house, but Aurora stood and fought.

She came out swinging a cottonwood branch. Rita circled back and began to deploy an arsenal of rocks that she had stashed behind a mesquite bush. With blood dripping from a cut above his eye, Flavio ran home threatening to tattle on the girls. Aurora waved her club and yelled, "You do, and we'll tell on you." That ended the war against the girls.

As Aurora grew, her little lean-to was abandoned. Soft dresses and ribbons took the place of tattered pinafores and scuffed up boots. When she outgrew her dresses, they were passed on to Rita; the little Navajo girl who had been adopted into the family three years before. Someone from Magdalena had found her, lost or abandoned, and brought her to the Vigil family. She was quickly folded into the sisterhood of Aurora and her cousins. But as she grew, Rita spent more time in the kitchen helping Josefa and less time primping with her stepsister, Aurora. Rita was only fussed over on Sunday morning. The girls were always properly dressed when the Vigils paraded into Mass at Lemitar.

After church, the families of La Parida had always gathered for a meal. The half-grown boys huddled in the corner of the *plazita*. The girls helped put the food on the table and kept up a noisy chatter. Flavio followed their every move. When they turned to go back into the house, he darted toward the table hoping to grab a tortilla before they were devoured by the pack.

Aurora saw him and gave chase. Flavio held the tortilla above his head. Aurora jumped for it, but it was out of reach. She balled up her fist and punched Flavio in the chest, turning his snickers into a choking cough. He stiffened and put his arms up in defense. When he put them down, Aurora looked intensely into his hazel green eyes, eyes that she had never noticed before.

✳✳✳

Agnes finally broke the silence. She leaned in close to Aurora. "What can I say? How can I help?"

Aurora hadn't thought about being helped. She opened her mouth to speak, then just shrugged. The little bell above the door of the mercantile rang and the door swung open. Severo rushed in stomping the snow off his boots. In the afternoon shadows, Aurora

29

thought she had spotted her Flavio. Her breath caught in her throat. Then Severo slipped behind the counter. The light from the window fell on him and Aurora's hopes faded.

Agnes' little boy bolted from his chair and ran toward the candy jars. "Stop!" Agnes yelled.

Aurora's thoughts snapped back to her friend. She stared at Agnes. *How can I help you?* Aurora remembered Agnes asking. Suddenly the world of this little store became too much for Aurora. She took Flavito, pressed her cheek to Agnes' and motioned to her *Tio* José. She gathered up her packages and led Manuelito out the back door. She thought about Agnes' questions all the way home.

❊❊❊

Josefa unwrapped the store goods, handing out the peppermint sticks that Manuel always included for the little ones.

"How did it go?"

Aurora brushed past her. "I'm tired," she answered. "There were so many people in the store. Oh, I saw Agnes, but I didn't really want to talk to her. She kept talking about when we were children. Then I started remembering." Aurora shook her head.

Aurora changed Flavito's diaper and went into the bedroom to feed him. She propped herself up on pillows and fell asleep with her baby at her breast.

Aurora awoke to the smell of venison and potatoes frying on the wood stove. The voices of Esquipula and Josefa seeped into her awareness.

The squeak of the bed springs had stirred her. Josefa was taking the baby from her limp arms. Josefa smoothed Aurora's hair the way she did when Aurora was a little girl and came in crying with a skinned-up knee. "Maybe you weren't ready to go into town yet," whispered Josefa.

Aurora put her head in her hands. "Agnes asked me what she could do to help and I didn't know what she was talking about. I haven't been in the world for so long, I can't even think."

"It's alright. It takes a long time to come back from your loved one's grave. The people around you sometimes think that you can just cry and get over it, but I know they're wrong. A few steps at a time. Do as much as you can today. Tomorrow God will strengthen you so you can do more." Josefa pulled the covers over Aurora's shoulder.

"Rest," she whispered, then she tiptoed into the kitchen.

Esquipula glanced at his wife.

"She wasn't ready," Josefa whispered.

"She has to be pushed a little. What about her children?" Esquipula snapped.

"She's getting better, a little at a time."

"I'll kill that *gringo* son-of-a-bitch!" Esquipula stormed out, slamming the door, leaving only silence behind.

Josefa gathered the children around the table and sent Rita to get Aurora. "Come and eat," Rita whispered.

Aurora moved her head from side to side to work out the stiffness. She smoothed her wrinkled skirt and shuffled to the table. The air around the table was heavy with silence.

"Agnes was at the store," Aurora said.

All heads turned toward her, then back to Josefa. It was Rita who embraced Aurora's words. "Oh, I haven't seen her in so long. We've been stuck in the house for the winter. I bet baby Juanito is getting big."

"I didn't notice, but I think she said she would come and see me. She said that Flavito looks like his father."

Rita braced herself for Aurora bolting from the table, but she was smiling. Rita turned toward Josefa who raised her eyes to the heavens. She passed a plate of tortillas to Aurora and the chatter of the family filled the room.

Aurora had barely noticed the noisy gaggle of children that now occupied her father's home. Since her brother, Andres, moved his family back from Magdalena, Josefa and Esquipula's house was full of grandchildren. Josefa had encouraged the move because Rita had gone to Snake Ranch with Aurora and Flavio and the house suddenly seemed empty.

Andres and his wife, Barbara, had converted the family chapel into their living quarters while they built their house in Lemitar. Josefa relished having her grandchildren underfoot, but now that Aurora and her baby needed her, the house seemed too small for all of them.

❄ ❄ ❄

At daybreak, when Esquipula saddled up his horse to ride to the grist mill, Josefa followed him into the stable. "While you're in Lemitar stop by Agnes'. Tell her that talking to Aurora made a difference. Tell her that she should come to see her and bring her children. Telesfora can bring Manuelito over to play with them."

Esquipula shook his head. "You women are like a bunch of chickens, always pecking and squawking about each other."

Josefa stiffened. She crossed her arms. "You're the one who said Aurora needed to be pushed. Seeing Agnes will help."

Esquipula waved her away, but he did stop at Agnes' house and asked her to visit. The following Sunday, after church, Agnes and her husband Rafael drove their wagon to La Parida. The sunny day did nothing to ease Rafael's uneasiness. Flavio had grown up with him. They had played together in the schoolyard at Lemitar. They swam in the ditch and got into trouble for stealing watermelons from old man Torres' garden. What was he going to say when he walked into the room where now only Aurora stood?

Esquipula met them on the porch. He slapped Rafael on the back and said he needed help in the barn. Agnes grabbed her husband's arm and pulled him toward the door. "At least say hello and give her your condolences."

"Of course," he answered. Rafael took off his hat as they walked through the door. He released a slow breath and moved toward Aurora. She was sitting in the rocker feeding Flavito. Agnes' two children scrambled toward the table.

Agnes rushed toward Aurora and kissed her forehead. "It's good to see color in your face," she said.

"It's the fireplace," Aurora answered.

Agnes peeked at the baby and pulled up a bench. Rafael stood, weaving a little, his hat gripped tightly in his hands.

"Aurora," he said softly. "*Lo siento*, I'm sorry. Whatever you need, we will do."

A heavy weight suddenly pressed against Aurora's chest. Hearing Rafael's voice caused old memories to come flooding back. She was a child again, being chased by Flavio and Rafael. A ragged sigh escaped from her. She choked back tears and nodded. "You were so mean to us girls."

"I had to be. You threw rocks at me and tried to push me in the river."

"I don't remember that, but I do remember you and Flavio chasing me around with the bloody chicken head."

Rita shook her finger at Rafael, "Yes, and you threw it at me."

"Yeah," smiled Rafael, "and you got me in trouble for it."

He shook his finger at Rita and she shook her head in denial. The sadness that had smothered the room was overtaken by laughter.

"I have to go help Esquipula." With that, Rafael escaped and the women settled into gentle conversation.

Josefa boiled water for fresh coffee. The children gathered around the table where Rita served them warm *atole* and sticky *molletes*.

By the time Agnes and her family left, Aurora felt more like a human than a wandering spirit. "They're all still here," she said. She lowered her head, ". . . almost all."

Rita put her head against Aurora's shoulder, reassuring her that she was not alone.

Josefa stopped wiping the crumbs from the table and took Aurora's hand. "A little at a time. You'll see; the snow has melted and the sun will help us grow a new garden. Do you need to rest?" Josefa asked.

Aurora took a deep breath. "No, I think I'll give Flavito a bath now that the room is so warm.

Rita placed a small tub of soapy water on the table, and the three women fussed over Aurora's son. Flavito blew bubbles. He kicked and waved his arms, glad to be out of the confinement of his blankets. Rita let his cousin, little Amalia, have a turn at washing Flavito's tummy. Aurora looked around for Manuelito, then remembered that he was still at Telesfora's. She closed her eyes and sighed, then turned back to Flavito.

When the snow melted off the roads, they soon turned to hard packed clay. Manuel's hired man, Soto, had just gotten back from Mesilla. José stopped stacking bags of flour in the store room behind the grist mill. He put his ear to the door. José heard the name Montgomery, then El Paso. As Soto and Manuel went out the door, José strained to pick up more information. He caught the words, "Cattle drive."

When Manuel had heard that the roads were good to the south, he had sent Soto to Mesilla to ask the whereabouts of the cowboy who shot Flavio. Three days later Soto had found out that the cowboy's name was Montgomery. He was headed to El Paso to join a cattle drive.

"Maybe they'll drive the cattle to Magdalena," said Soto, "and we'll be waiting for him."

José followed the men across the yard, straining to listen. By the time he reached the corral, Manuel and Soto had disappeared into the stables. José grinned and slapped his hand against his canvas overalls. He threw his jacket over his shoulders and saddled up his horse. "Wait 'till I tell Telesfora the news." He pointed his steed toward La Parida where he knew a hot meal would be waiting for him.

When he arrived, he swung open the door and swiped off his hat. Telesfora jumped and raised her eyebrows, "What's going on?"

José shrugged his shoulders. On the ride home, the more he had thought about telling her, the more he wasn't sure he should. He remembered how women talk. Would they want revenge as much as the men did, or were they just busy praying and taking care of Aurora?

He knew that Telesfora only wanted to be a mother hen to Flavio's little boys. When she played with Manuelito at the table, she said silly things like, "I remember when your papá was your age. You know, I took care of him when he was born because our mamá was too sick." Then she would start crying again.

No, thought José. *It's better not to tell the women.*

José smashed his potatoes into his beans and wrapped his noon meal in a tortilla. "I have to get back. Manuel wants me to take a wagon load of flour to Socorro before the sun goes down."

Telesfora shook her head and turned to wipe Manuelito's face. Before she could wave goodbye, José was back on his horse and riding off.

✳ ✳ ✳

When Manuel spotted José trotting toward him, he steeled himself for another unending rant. "You're one of the lucky ones," blurted José. "You got to keep your land-grant up north." He pounded his fist in his hand. "Now the *gringos* want to come and take everything from us, even our sons."

"It wasn't luck," snapped Manuel. "Me and Esquipula had to fight hard for it. The *gringo* judge tried to tell us that the land given to our family two hundred years ago wasn't ours because we didn't have the right papers. I'll never forget the way that judge treated me. "From the cottonwood trees at the edge of the *bosque* to the red hill. What kind of legal description is that?" he mocked. Well, that bloated frog wasn't laughing when I showed him the surveyor's report that my father drew up when the Mexicans tried to pull the same shit on us. They didn't take away our land then, and neither did the American government."

José slapped a sack of grain onto the wagon. The boards groaned and dust flew. Then he launched into another tirade of how the people of El Norte took care of the Mexican governor, Perez, when he tried to overtake them and change everything.

"Now the *gringos* are here like fleas, and look what happened to Flavio."

One look at Manuel's clenched jaw and José's words trailed away like dust.

Manuel turned and stomped toward the store. "I'll take care of this!" he shouted.

The Rio Grande was swollen with melted snow from the mountains. The willows along its banks sprouted pale green leaves. The fields were too wet to plow, but the warm New Mexico sun would soon dry them out.

Manuelito had spent the night with Aurora, but now she wanted to go into town with Josefa. Aurora dreaded the thoughts of Manuelito riding in the back of the wagon with her little nephews. Would they watch him or push him out of the wagon?

Aurora walked down the road to Telesfora's house. Before she left, she hugged her mother. "He'll be safe at Telesfora's. My life would be over if I lost Manuelito too."

"Yes, but don't you think he's spending too much time with her? He's starting to call her Mamá."

Aurora whirled and her eyes burned a hole through her mother. "It's too much—the baby, and losing Flavio, and Manuelito, and these noisy children always underfoot. Don't you understand? I'm trying as hard as I can."

Josefa tried to embrace Aurora, but she twisted away. Aurora rolled her eyes. "Go to church," Aurora mocked. "That's all I hear from Telesfora. 'God will help you.' Why should I pray to a God who was cruel enough to take my Flavio? What do I have left?"

"Look in your arms," Josefa said softly.

Aurora hugged her baby close and gritted her teeth. Josefa slowly raised her head. "You think I haven't had my heart torn out? Flavio was like a son to me. He was always at our house with your other cousins. And before that, I lost a child before he was born. I've lost my father and my mother. The flood washed our fields away and we had nothing left. You're only eighteen. I know you don't want to hear this, but by the time you're as old as I am, you'll know more losses."

Josefa rested her hand on Aurora's arm. "But, after the bad times, come the good. I know it doesn't feel like that now, but your heart will heal and you'll need your children's love as much as they need yours." Josefa looked out at the weeds sprouting between the sagebrush. She took a deep breath and shook her head.

The bumpy trip to Lemitar was traveled in silence. Josefa's thoughts tumbled and worry gripped her chest. *Did I say too much?*

Have I been too hard? Aurora is just beginning her journey to womanhood. When I was her age, I never thought there would be unhappy days. The old women would talk, and sometimes cry, but they never told me why. I had to learn on my own. Maybe, thought Josefa, *this is how it should be. If we knew what was coming, we would never be born.*

She turned to Aurora. *"Lo siento Mija.* I'm sorry my daughter. I wish life had been kinder to you, but you have all the Vigils and the Pinos. Your whole family will help you through this. You will, I promise, feel the weight of your sorrow lift."

Aurora slouched back on the buckboard and stared straight ahead.

Josefa parked the wagon behind Manuel's store and the women slipped into the back room. Aurora made a little nest of blankets on the cot for Flavito. He had grown chubby since the cold winter day he came into the world. His black hair was thick and his eyes were turning green like his father's. As soon as Manuel heard voices, he ran to the back room.

The bell above the front door tinkled and Manuel glanced toward the store.

"I can help you a little bit," said Aurora," but I can't leave Flavito for long or he'll roll off the bed."

"You don't have to worry about that," Manuel grinned. He lifted up Flavito and strode toward the circle of old men to introduce his grandson. When the baby let out a screech, Manuel passed him back to his mother and pointed to the back room. Aurora heard the buzz of voices through the door as she sat on the cot to feed Flavito. The mercantile was crowded with men buying their spring planting seeds. Their wives had come with them, anxious to escape their winter confinement.

Aurora opened the door slightly and peeked into the store. "Maybe I should stay back here with Flavito," she said to her mother.

Josefa opened the door and swished past her. As she emerged from the open door, every woman in the store turned toward the back room.

"Aurora came with me," she told them, "and of course she brought Flavito. Oh, he's getting so big."

One by one the women knocked gently and asked to come in. There were no *"Lo sientos"* this time. They just wanted to see Aurora's beautiful baby. Aurora sat in Severo's swivel chair with Flavito. She held court, telling them that she was feeling a little better and how glad she was that Flavito looked so much like his father. She was surprised to hear, over and over, the same thing that her mother had said. "Your heart will heal a little at a time, and this one will help you heal it."

When the last woman left, Aurora changed Flavito and put him in his nest on the cot. She ambled into the store where she was welcomed with Manuel's big bear hug. "Pick out some cloth and make yourself a dress," he said. "You're as skinny as a snake. Make something that will fit."

She ran her hand across a bolt of sky-blue cotton with a field of tiny yellow flowers. Then she looked down at the black dress that hung from her bony shoulders.

Manuel glanced at Josefa's frowning face. It *hasn't been a year since we lost our Flavio; Aurora's still in mourning*, he remembered. He pulled out a bolt of black linen with tiny sprigs of faded gray leaves.

"This will be close enough," he sighed.

Aurora looked up at her mother, a smile replacing her frown.

Her sour expression returned, however, when she admitted, "I don't sew too good."

Josefa and Manuel exchanged a glance.

"Isabel makes her own dresses. She can help you and she would love to see more of the boys," suggested Manuel.

Aurora had almost forgotten about her mother-in-law. "I don't know if she would want to see us. Wouldn't it bring her more pain?"

Manuel smiled, "To have a part of Flavio to hold would only bring her joy" He wrapped up eight yards of linen fabric.

With the children gathered into the wagon, Josefa and Aurora clattered back to the little cluster of houses at La Parida.

Manuel leaned against the porch, waving as Josefa's wagon left the yard. His eyes were fixed on the little hunched figure clad in black. Manuel swallowed his sadness and returned to the back room. He caught his reflection in the dusty mirror that Flavio had nailed to the wall.

A quick smile touched his lips as he remembered the day, long ago, when Flavio saw Aurora skipping into the store. Flavio was helping his father stack crates in the back store room. He had caught his reflection in that faded mirror and quickly combed his wavy black hair with his fingers. He leaned in closer and rubbed his finger across the downy shadow of his mustache. Flavio brushed the straw and sawdust from his shirt before going into the front of the store.

Aurora no longer wore her hair in braids. Now that she was growing into womanhood, she twisted her locks into a bun at the nape of her neck. Wisps of dark curls brushed against her soft oval face.

Aurora had helped her *Tio* Manuel gather supplies while Esquipula sat with the circle of old men, a fixture in Manuel's store. Esquipula hadn't noticed that his daughter was more excited than usual to go to her uncle's store.

Flavio had slipped behind the counter and reached for the lantern oil just as Aurora took her hand away. The tips of their fingers touched and both of them quickly looked at the floor. He leaned across the counter and slipped a pouch of tobacco into her basket.

"Are you going to Telesfora's wedding?" she asked, eyebrows raised.

Flavio brushed the floor with the toe of his boot. "I don't know. I guess the whole family is supposed to go to my sister's wedding. If you're going, I'll be there for sure." His smile flashed across the room.

Esquipula had gathered their baskets. Aurora sauntered toward the door and glanced back. Flavio's eyes were fixed on her.

Manuel shook his memories away and turned the dusty mirror toward the wall. Then he busied himself with unpacking crates of lamp oil.

❊ ❊ ❊

As Aurora and Josefa caught sight of their house Aurora announced, "All the women thought Flavito was beautiful. Next time I go to town I'll bring Manuelito so everyone can see him too."

Josefa inhaled deeply. The corners of her eyes crinkled with a smile. Aurora turned to face the sun.

When they neared Telesfora's house, Aurora straightened and jutted out her chin. "Manuelito can stay home with me from now on. Now that it's warmer, maybe we can move back into our rooms. If we move the loom to the corner of the weaving room, Manuelito will have a place to play."

Josefa made the sign of the cross on her forehead, grateful that Aurora was coming back to them. As they turned the wagon into Telesfora's yard, however, Josefa's joy turned to worry.

"What do you mean, he's going to stay with you now?" Telesfora

39

exclaimed. "You can't just take him!" She braced herself against the table, glaring at Josefa and Aurora.

"You're forgetting who he belongs to," countered Aurora. "Did you think I would just let you keep him forever?"

Telesfora twisted her hands. "No, of course not," she stammered. "I just meant that this is so sudden. Give me some time to pack his clothes and talk to him about going back." She picked up Manuelito and started swaying and choking back tears. Manuelito clung to her neck.

Aurora started to reach for Manuelito, but Josefa pulled her back. "Perhaps she's right. Telesfora can bring him over in the morning."

Aurora huffed. Josefa tightened her grip. In the end, her mother's tight-lipped determination convinced Aurora to let Telesfora have her way. She gave Manuelito a kiss on the cheek.

"I'll see you in the morning," she said. "All of your cousins want you to come and play with them."

Telesfora's lips were drawn into a thin line as Aurora marched out the door.

-8-

The fields finally dried enough for Esquipula to plant his corn and wheat. When Aurora took Manuelito to feed the chickens he jumped up and down and waved at his grandpa. Aurora sat sunning herself on the bench. She leaned against the warm adobe wall and watched the men fixing the irrigation canals and getting the horses hitched up to the plow. *The canal*, she thought. *Papá used to get so mad at me and Rita for playing in it. We were making mud pies to throw at Flavio and the other boys.*

She caught Manuelito and carried him, kicking and screaming, into the walled *plazita*. "We're going to see your *abuela* Isabel," she said. "Today I'll start sewing my new dress. Maybe now I'll have enough patience to learn how to sew." Aurora wrinkled up her nose at the thought of it.

With Flavito in one arm and Manuelito grasped firmly, Aurora walked down the path to the next house. The big wooden gate creaked when she pushed it open. The wall enclosing the patio kept Flavio's little brothers and sisters safe. The herd of children played underneath the mulberry tree in the center of the *plazita*.

Flavio's little brother, Francisco, grabbed his nephew. "Come over here," he said. "We're digging holes to put grasshoppers in." He handed Manuelito a sharp stick. Manuelito plopped down and started poking at the dirt.

Aurora went into the big room that was much like her mother's. Isabel was planted in front of the stove, where she always seemed to be. She set a pot of *chili* on the warming shelf and rushed to hug Aurora and the baby.

"Let me see him!" She looked from Flavito to Aurora and tears welled up in her eyes. "He looks just like my Flavio." She sank onto the bench and rocked him gently.

Aurora reached to take Flavito from her. "I was afraid this would hurt you,"

"Oh, no!" Isabel wiped her face on her sleeve. "Having Flavito means that I will always have part of my Flavio. Where is Manuelito?"

They went out to the *plazita* where Manuelito was already encrusted with dirt. Isabel sniffled, then laughed. She passed the baby to Aurora and picked up Flavio's oldest son. "And you," she said, "you look like your *Abuelo* Esquipula." She kissed his dusty little nose. He wiggled and kicked, anxious to get back to his digging.

Isabel lured him inside with the promise of mint tea and a licorice stick. The rest of the children stood with their lower lips out. "You can all come in," she laughed. "We'll have a little *fiesta* for my grandsons."

The younger ones didn't know what their mother was talking about, but it didn't matter. They were all going to get a licorice stick. They devoured their treats and started clambering away from the table. With sticky hands and faces wiped clean, the children were sent back outside.

Isabel wiped off the table and spread the dark cloth across it. She took out her worn cloth measuring tape and began to measure Aurora. A soft "Oh no," escaped her lips, but she quickly hid her concern with a crooked smile.

❄❄❄

Aurora wore her new dress the next time she went into town with her father.

"I have a lot to do," Esquipula announced. "Why don't I take you to Estella's. I have to wait until the freight wagon comes in to get the barbed wire for my new fences. It's not good for you to be at the store today. Manuel's cattle are in the corrals. The *vaqueros* will be drinking at his saloon."

Aurora leaned her head on her father's shoulder and wrapped her arm in his. "I can't remember the last time I went to Estella's and, you know, my friend Gloria lives in Socorro. Maybe this summer I can go visit her."

Esquipula patted his daughter's arm. "Manuel can take you in his buggy when he goes to check on his grist mill. This is a busy time for him and that's good. You haven't seen him when he thinks no one is looking."

Aurora fell silent. *Where have I been? How could I not remember that Manuel has lost his son?* She loosened the blanket from around Flavito and kissed his little round face.

Esquipula covered Aurora's hand with his own rough hand and squeezed. "You go visit and forget for a while."

After Esquipula dropped Aurora and the boys off, he took his wagon to the freight station, then walked to Manuel's store. He was surprised to find Severo behind the counter. "Where's your father?" Esquipula asked.

Severo lifted his chin toward the saloon next door.

Esquipula frowned. "Manuel? At this time of the day?"

"The *vaqueros* are talking. They know things all the way from Texas. One of them might know where this Montgomery is. I heard Soto talking to the man who brings freight from back East. By the end of the summer, every *Hispano* from Santa Fe to the big river will be looking for Martin Montgomery."

Walking into the saloon, Esquipula let his eyes adjust to the smoky dimness. He spotted Manuel and joined his brother at the bar. Manuel leaned in close. "I got word that Montgomery was seen near El Paso working at a ranch. I'll go to Socorro next week when the cattle buyers come in from the East. I'm going anyway, with my cattle. I'll see what they know." Manuel turned to José who was draining the last sip of his beer.

"Let's go," he ordered. "Today is freight day, and there'll be a lot of people in the store. Send Severo to the freight station."

"I'll go with him." said Esquipula.

As they walked down the slope to the freight station, Severo kicked a pile of dried horse manure. "We'll get him. Papá knows a lot of people. Montgomery doesn't know what a mistake he made. He shot the wrong Mexican."

Esquipula's chest began to tighten. Would his words turn Severo's anguish to anger? He swallowed hard and stuffed his shaky hands into his pocket. "Severo, I know that your pain has hardened into anger. I understand that. But will killing Montgomery bring Flavio back?"

Severo froze. "You don't think that the killing of my brother should be avenged?"

"Would killing another man help heal your heart?" Esquipula put his arm on his nephew's. "Or would it blacken it?"

On the way home Esquipula was grateful for Aurora's chatter. Her words softened the memory of Severo's twisted glare.

9

The thick adobe walls that surrounded the *hacienda* kept the warm morning air from penetrating the rooms that Aurora had claimed for herself. A beam of dusty light drifted across the room as she opened the door and looked outside. Manuelito shivered and pulled away from his mamá. He dodged past her when she stepped outside to gather kindling for the fire. When Aurora looked back to check on him, Manuelito had joined his cousins in a game of chase the rope.

Aurora glanced at the gate to make sure it was bolted, a child-hood habit. With the wooden plank in place, she knew Manuelito would be safe.

Aurora stirred the coals and topped them with kindling. She wrapped herself in her shawl while the fire came to life in the dome-shaped fireplace. Satisfied that the fire was ablaze, Aurora skipped across the *plazita* to her mother's kitchen.

Telesfora was sitting at the kitchen table. She reached for Aurora. "Let me take Manuelito back with me while you finish fixing up your rooms." She looked past Aurora, "Where is *Mijito*?"

"He's playing in the yard with Anna and Pedro. It's good that he's out in the sun. He'll be alright here with me. Mamá can help me with him," answered Aurora without looking at Telesfora. She grabbed the broom and hurried to her rooms without a backward glance.

With an old rug covering the dirt floor and the shelves dusted, Aurora was ready to take back her rooms.

In the next room Andres grunted as he heaved the big wooden loom into the corner. The burlap sacks of yarn were hung on pegs that jutted from the walls. Manuelito peeked in and jumped onto the packed dirt floor.

"Look, *Mijito*, "Aurora encouraged, "you can play in here when the sun gets too hot."

The rest of the children tumbled inside. "Let's go get our sticks. We can play in here."

Aurora grabbed Pedro. "Not today," she said, "The sun is out and you've been cooped up in the house all winter."

A loud knock at the gate startled all of them.

"I'll go!" shouted Anna. She bolted, but Aurora swung out her arm.

"No *stupida*, you don't open the gate until you know who's on the other side. Mama!" Aurora yelled, "There's someone here."

Her mother had peered out the little window in front of the house when she heard the wagon coming. "It's La Señora. Let her in," she shouted.

Andres lifted the wooden plank and opened the door that was cut into the big gate. As Josefa and La Señora hugged, Aurora retreated to her room. She put her hand over her mouth. The room began to spin and she shuffled to the edge of the bed. Memories flooded back. Not in words or pictures. It was feelings- the fear of having only the protection of the chapel door between her and the Apaches, the relief of her father's voice, then the hit in the pit of her stomach, then numbness.

How, she wondered, *can I be happy to see the sun? How could I be excited about fixing my room. Flavio is gone.* There was a lump in her throat and numbness began to creep back, but it didn't penetrate far.

Andres banged on the door. "Mama wants you," he hollered.

Aurora started then drifted across the room. She shaded her eyes against the piercing sun. As she stepped into the *plazita*, Aurora stepped out of her hurtful past into the present.

"*Buenos dias Señora,*" greeted Aurora. "No one is sick in the house?" Aurora turned toward her mother. She tilted her head and searched her mother's eyes.

"No, no, no," the midwife declared. "I delivered a baby in Socorro last night and was going home, but the journey is so long. I thought I would stop and rest before going on to Lemitar.

Josefa warmed up some tamales and stirred the beans. As La Señora told Josefa about the birth, Aurora sat with her elbows resting on the table. Their gossip began to pull her into their conversation.

"Can I see Flavito?" asked La Señora. "How is he doing?"

Aurora nodded and looked at the old woman as if for the first time. "I barely remember when you helped me with Flavito's birth."

La Señora patted Aurora with her leathery hand. "You were lost in your grief, but I can see by the roses in your cheeks that you're coming back."

Aurora looked from Flavito to the woman who had brought him into the world. She whispered, "He's growing and sucking me dry, and laughing. He's beautiful, like his father, but now he's going to sleep." She put her finger to her lips.

Flavito made suckling sounds in his sleep. La Señora gently brushed her hand across his thick black hair. She folded her hands as if in prayer. "*Dios mío*, he looks just like his father. You know, I brought him into the world too."

"And me," Aurora chirped. "We all came into the world in your hands." Somehow this idea made Aurora feel like Flavio was still a part of her.

La Señora took Aurora's hands, "*Mija*, I know about more things than are in this world. Your Flavio, his *espíritu*, is with the angels, but it's with you too. Don't you feel him sometimes?"

Aurora shrugged. "What are you talking about?"

"Has the pain begun to let go of you?"

Aurora nodded. "A little; I'm moving back into my rooms and Manuelito is going to stay with me, but I'm afraid if I let go of my sorrow, I will betray my Flavio."

"No, *Mija*, your sorrow was meant to go away so you can live in this world until you join Flavio in the next. Every time you hold your children remember where you belong, and remember that Flavio is still here, in your heart."

Aurora put her hand to her lips. "It's alright to be happy for a little while?"

La Señora nodded and patted Aurora's hands. "Come on. I smell your mama's tamales."

10

The quiet village of Socorro swelled with drovers and cattle buyers. Manuel decided not to ask the cattle buyers about Montgomery. He would let his men ask around. The questions would get mixed in with all the trail gossip. While his men poured into the saloon, Manuel and the other cattle buyers took over the back room of the hotel. This was the first time he had seen some of the ranchers since Flavio had been killed. He dreaded the pity and the questions. His cousin, Diego, from Magdalena was the first to talk to him.

"I know you're looking for the *gringo* who killed your boy."

"I'm taking care of it," Manuel growled. "It's too hard to talk about."

"I know. It was the same when my father lost all of our land to the *Americano* judge with all his papers. They were written in English so my father couldn't read them."

Manuel patted him on the back and nodded.

Diego lifted his chin toward a group of cigar-smoking cattle buyers. "McCutcheon is building another gambling hall in Socorro. He wants to build one in Magdalena, but we're trying to stop him. Pretty soon it won't be safe for our women to go out of their houses."

Loud voices and clinking of glasses used to invigorate Manuel. Now the noise closed in and began to smother him. He waved Diego away and hurried outside. He got back in his buggy and rode to the cattle yard. On the way he thought of the son who should have been sitting beside him.

He looked out at the cattle milling in the corrals. Then his gaze fell on the ruddy faces of the young American cow hands. *All the faces used to be brown,* he thought, *and I knew the names of their fathers.*

Manuel closed his eyes for a moment. He remembered how hard he had fought to keep his land near Taos. Sometimes he felt guilty because so many of his neighbors had lost everything that the King of Spain had granted them.

Then, with no say from the people of El Norte, the land belonged to Mexico. His father had fought against the Mexican governor who changed the laws to suit himself. He and his father had joined the rebellion against the new government.

Then Manuel went south with the promise of the Socorro land-grant. Life had been good to him there. His family had grown along the Rio Grande, but today, none of it mattered. *I fought so hard for what I have*, he thought. *I was going to leave it all to Flavio and Severo. I knew they would help their little brothers along the way.* He glanced up at the cattle milling about in the corrals and shook his head.

Manuel walked behind the corrals. He leaned against a cotton-wood tree, trying to untangle his feelings. In the silence, his thoughts began to fall into place. *My son is gone.* He wiped a tear from his cheek and his vision cleared. *But the others are still with me.* He looked toward the distant mesas. In the stillness, his thoughts began to change.

Manuel had watched the families in El Norte turn against each other. Some joined the rebels who fought against the new Mexican laws. Others thought they should comply. The rebels took over, and communities were split apart. He heard men talking about getting even for the wrongs their neighbors had done to them. The next day those neighbors would retaliate, and the hatred grew. The bitterness began to rot the heart of the community. He knew little about the world then, and couldn't understand why the fighting wouldn't end.

Bile rose up in Manuel's throat. He took a deep ragged breath. Then he thought about Severo, willing to work harder than expected. He thought about his other sons who were growing out of childhood, and his daughters who were marrying fine young men. He thought about Aurora and Flavio's little sons. His hand flew to his mouth, sti-fling a sob.

Manuel pushed himself away from the tree. Still thinking about the family that relied on him, he spit the bile on the ground. *Isn't it better to let Montgomery go than to allow him to rot my family with hatred?* He turned away from the corrals and let the tears roll down his face. Then his eyes turned upward. *There will come a day when Montgomery will be punished for what he did.*

Manuel hopped into his buggy and rode through the *bosque* un-til his pain subsided, then he blew out a long breath and headed back to town. *No matter how much my heart is torn,* he thought, *I still have to sell my cattle.* When he got back to the hotel, he spoke quickly and made hasty deals with the Eastern cattle buyers. The journey home passed without notice. Severo opened the gates and Manuel's little flock of children came running toward him.

"What did you bring us Papá?"

"*Lo siento*; I had a lot of business to do in Socorro. I'll bring you back something from the store tomorrow."

Dejected, the children shuffled away, but not before Manuel ruffled the hair or patted the bottom of each of his children. He blinked away the memory of the son that was no longer there.

11

Manuel wasn't looking forward to his next trip to Socorro. He didn't really want to take Aurora to the growing town. It had changed so much. There were so many men living on their own. The miners from Kelly, and drifters, lost after the Civil War. He wouldn't dare take her when the cattle drovers were in town, but today he was going all the way to Magdalena. While he was selling his sheep, Aurora could visit with her friends. Manuel dropped Aurora and Rita off at his daughter, Rufina's, house. She hadn't seen Flavito yet and was anxious to cuddle her little nephews.

With one eyebrow lifted, Manuel glared at Rufina, "Don't let Aurora go out by herself," Manuel cautioned. "You know how excited she gets when there's a lot going on."

Rufina flashed a look at Aurora while trying in vain to keep Manuelito away from the dog. "Don't you think she's changed?" Rufina asked. "Life does that to you."

Manuel looked at his daughter-in-law, so frail now, the laughter gone out of her eyes. He grunted, remembering the young woman who danced at his daughter's wedding.

Aurora had waltzed into Rufina's reception wearing a purple satin gown. Her black hair was bundled on top of her head, secured with a tortoiseshell comb.

Flavio was clustered with a group of his cousins at the back of the hall. His eyes kept darting toward the door. When he spotted Aurora, he drew in a breath that didn't escape his throat. He seemed to be permanently affixed to the floor.

Aurora swished past him, leading a group of friends to the center of the room. Flavio willed his feet to move, but they weren't fast enough. Before he could reach her, Fernando swept Aurora up and danced her across the floor. When the lively music finally stopped, Flavio pushed through the crowd.

He stood behind Aurora watching her gather an audience, ready to hold court. Flavio elbowed his way toward the front of the crowd. He tried to make his lips move past an awkward grin but, when he opened his mouth, only a little grunt escaped.

"So, you decided to put on some clean clothes and join us?" Aurora teased.

Flavio blushed amid the laughter of his little group. His cousin Vicente slapped him on the back and snapped him out of his spell. The music started up again and Flavio shouted over the noise.

"How could I pass up the chance to see all of you dressed up like a bunch of stuffed monkeys?"

Vicente joined the laughter and tried to nudge Flavio toward the food table, but Flavio shook him off. Before he could reach for Aurora's hand, Martina Garcia grabbed his arm and pulled him toward the dance floor. As the swirling crowd glided in a circle, Flavio's eyes fastened on Aurora. Every time he caught sight of her, she was glancing back at him.

Manuel climbed back into his buggy. "Life," he huffed, "it changes us all."

✳✳✳

Rufina took Flavito from Aurora. "Let's go in the house. It's cooler in there."

Indeed, the little adobe, with its narrow windows, was a welcome respite from the early summer heat. Rufina dipped a tin cup into the bucket of water that was tucked into a shady corner.

Aurora took two long gulps and gave the rest to Manuelito. "I didn't remember Socorro being so far away." She rubbed her bony hips.

"You don't have enough meat on your bones to pad your bottom," laughed Rufina. She swatted Aurora on the bottom.

She offered Aurora the only upholstered chair in the room. Rufina sat beside her, making silly noises that made Flavito's fat little legs fly. Every time he giggled Aurora smiled a little.

"God has blessed you with two healthy sons," said Rufina. "Flavio would be proud of them."

Aurora cocked an eyebrow and let out a breath. "Everybody tells me that they will help me get better."

Rufina reached for Aurora. "You are getting better. You're here, aren't you?"

Aurora leaned toward Rufina. "Everybody looks at me with those big sad eyes. They whisper when I'm around. I'm tired of it." She put her hands on her hips. "I've moved back into my rooms, and Manuelito is with me. Some days I don't think about Flavio all day long. I came to see you because I wanted to think about something besides my sadness. I don't want to hurt anymore."

"Good, we won't speak of things that have passed. I have enough news to tell you." Flavio's older sister rolled her eyes and let out a mischievous laugh.

Flavito arched his back and let out a screech stopping Rufina in mid-sentence. She looked up at Aurora for the first time since she started talking. Aurora lifted the baby and pointed toward the bedroom.

Aurora tiptoed back to the parlor door and began rolling her shoulders. "I'm tired. It was such a long ride. I think I'll rest with Flavito. Tomorrow, I want to go see Gloria. Rita can tell me the rest of your news on the way there."

✳✳✳

The sun warmed Aurora's back as the wagon bumped toward the foothills of Socorro. Gloria's house was nestled among the cottonwoods that grew around the springs. The lane curved and Gloria's adobe house appeared. On the *porche*, Gloria was jumping up and down and waving. Without thinking, Aurora broke into a grin. Gloria rushed toward her friends before the wagon stopped. Aurora hopped off and the two old friends hugged and giggled like little girls.

Rita climbed down the wagon wheel carefully, cradling Flavito in one arm. When she came around the horses, Gloria threw out her arms. The three of them swayed, cheek to cheek.

"Come in! Come in!" Gloria laughed.

The thick adobe walls offered welcome coolness to the dimly lit room. "Let me look at him." Gloria took Flavito and stood him on her lap. He looked around and puckered up his lips. His crying stopped when he spotted his mother, and Gloria was forced to give him up.

Gloria folded her hands to her chest and looked at Aurora. "He has his father's eyes."

She began to stammer. *Should I pretend that this is just another visit?* Manuelito decided for her. He was crawling onto the table and Gloria's little girl was trying to push him off.

Gloria scooped him up and sent the children out to play on the back porch. When she came back in, Gloria poured each of them a glass of cool spring water with a sprig of peppermint.

"It's been so long," Gloria began. She reached out and squeezed Aurora's arms. "Is it getting any easier?"

Aurora took a deep breath, "A little. . . at least I feel like getting out of the house."

Aurora stuck out her chin. "I don't think some people want me to get better. You should have seen the tears when I took Manuelito from Telesfora. Did she think I was going to leave him with her forever?" Aurora shot a quick glance at Rita. "She's only Flavito's *tia*; I'm his mother."

Rita leaned forward and raised her eyebrows. "Anyway, tell us about Socorro."

That was the invitation Gloria was waiting for. She began telling them what had gone on in Socorro when the snow fell, then melted away. Rita laughed and asked more questions. Aurora found herself smiling and shaking her head. Gloria noticed Aurora shoulders dropping a little and the veil clearing from her eyes.

While telling about the cowboys shooting up the streets in Kelly, Gloria stopped in mid-sentence. She jumped up and slapped her face with both hands. "Oh no, what time is it? I can't believe we've spent all morning talking. The men are here to eat."

Gloria dashed to the stove and started heating up last night's pork stew. She was glad she had made extra tortillas the night before because she knew her friends were coming to visit. She had also prepared a big pot of red *chili*.

Aurora started setting the table. Her stomach tightened when she thought about Alberto coming home to his wife. She started at the sound of men's voices. Her mind went back to that day at Snake Ranch when she heard about Flavio. She had thought she was safe when she heard her father's voice. What came instead was a blow that she didn't think she could recover from.

"I'll go get the little ones," she said. Aurora scampered out the back door and pressed herself against the wall. Her heart pounded. She had to lay her hands against the wall to steady herself. *I don't want to go back in,* she thought. *Maybe I can tell them I'm feeling sick.* She took a couple of deep breaths, yelled at the children to come in, then slowly opened the door.

Aurora had just stepped inside when Alberto swept her up and twirled her around. He couldn't believe how light she was. He sat her down gently. "It's so good to see you," he smiled. Then he ducked his head. "*Lo siento.*" As quickly as his wide smile had disappeared, it reappeared, "But you're here with us today. This is good."

The memories that had washed over Aurora vanished with Alberto's embrace. While they ate their noon meal, Alberto joined in the news about the *ranchos* and the village of Socorro. He bounced Flavito on his lap and rode Manuelito around on his shoulders. When he put him down, Alberto turned to Aurora.

"We're not that far from Lemitar and Manuel comes to Socorro all the time. We'll see each other often."

With hugs and promises to return, Aurora and Rita loaded the boys into the wagon. On the ride back to Rufina's Manuelito stretched across his mother's lap and slept. Rita took the reins and Aurora cuddled Flavito tightly.

"It was so good to see our friends," Rita began. "I like this time of the year. Everyone's getting out after they've been stuck inside, and before the farm work begins."

Rita's soft humming and the rocking of the wagon almost put Aurora to sleep. In the hazy time between sleep and wake, Aurora looked across the distant *mesas*. The lavender hills were sprinkled with silvery green. "Winter doesn't kill the sagebrush," she said to the air. "It always comes back."

Rita squeezed her arm and kept humming.

12

Manuel came in late that evening, tired and sore from the long trip to Magdalena. He unwrapped a set of silver *concha* buttons that the Navajos had brought into the general store. These he handed to Rufina. Then he unfolded a length of soft velvet to make a quilt for Flavito.

"I've never seen this color." Rufina brushed the deep blue cloth against her cheek.

"I'll have to order some for my store," Manuel said. "The wagons will move out next week." A rueful smile spread across Manuel's lips. "I don't know where I'm going to put all the new merchandise." He raised his eyebrows and shrugged.

Then Manuel put his finger to his lips and glanced around the room. "Oh, I forgot that Aurora always wanted to go back East with me."

Rufina gestured toward the bedroom. "It's alright. Aurora's resting with Manuelito. I kept supper warm for you Papá."

Rita joined Rufina and Manuel at the kitchen table to hear about Manuel's trip.

"There were more sheep ranchers there so the prices were down a little. Oh, and Julian Chavez was there. I remember him from Toas."

"What was he doing clear down in Magdalena?" Rufina asked.

Manuel frowned, "*Pobresito*, poor man. Julian said that after most of his land was taken by the *Americanos* he had to move to Belen with his uncle."

"Oh, but that's not so bad," Rufina said. "There's good land at the *bosque* and his uncle owns quite a bit. The *gringos* weren't able to take the Mexican land grants away so easy, but how did he end up in Magdalena?"

Manuel crossed his leg and took another sip of coffee. "His uncle had enough help on the ranch. He has a brother in Magdalena with sheep, but he's getting old, so Julian went up to help him."

No one noticed when Rufina's husband, Antonio, slipped through the back door. He cleared his throat and everyone flinched. "Oh, *Dios mío*," Rufina slapped at her husband, "don't sneak in like that."

Rufina's husband moved away from the door and gave his father-in-law a rough handshake. He started to raise his voice. "They didn't get my father's land either, at least not all of it." He stifled his curses, remembering that his children were in the next room. He poured himself a cup of coffee and stomped to the table.

Manuel was relieved when Rufina set the food on the table. As Antonio droned on, Manuel remembered the bitterness of his own youth. He had seen his relatives and friends destroyed by their losses. He became more determined to let the changes move him forward, instead of burying him in the past.

✳ ✳ ✳

When Manuel's wagon stopped behind the store, José ran out to greet him. "How did it go?"

"I got a fair price for the sheep. There were a lot more ranchers there yesterday. Oh, and I saw Julian Chavez."

"Julian? From El Norte? You know the *Americanos* stole his father's land too."

The minute he mentioned Julian, Manuel regretted it. José didn't wait for him to finish recounting his story before he started fuming.

"Pretty soon there won't be any *Hispanos* left in New Mexico. First it was Mexico. Governor Perez trying to take away our laws, but we took care of him. When we sent his head in a basket to Santa Fe I thought we would be left alone." José spat a long string of tobacco juice. "Mexico just sent another governor. Then they sold us." He shook his fist. "They sold us to America."

"We fought hard to keep those *Americanos* out, remember?"

Manuel busied himself unloading the wagon, but José didn't seem to notice. He waved his arms and raised his voice.

"Then big General Kearny came with his American army." José spat and wiped his mouth on his sleeve. He raised his fist. "We fought against them, but there were too many." José spat again.

"Then the lies started." José's voice rose to a high pitch. "We could keep our land! Their laws would protect us! Nothing much would change!" José kicked the dirt. "Are there any *Hispanos* left in El Norte?"

Manuel started unhitching the horses. One of his men rushed out to help.

"No, no, *Señor* Vigil, let me do this," he said.

Manuel pointed to the other horse while he kept working on the horse on his side. He took his leather case out of the wagon and his hired man led the horses into the corral.

56

Manuel brushed past José and his cursing tirade. In the back room, Severo was bent over the ledger book. When he saw his father, he drew a line beneath the last entry, and stood.

"Papá, how did it go?"

Manuel told him how many sheep were born in the spring, how many the coyotes had gotten, and how much he made on the sale of the remaining ones.

He started to tell Severo how much Magdalena had grown, but he noticed that his son kept glancing back at the books. Manuel patted Severo on the back and dropped heavily onto the squeaky chair beside the desk. Severo laid his pen down when he noticed his father's big frame sag and his voice go silent.

Severo sat up straight. "Montgomery, has anyone heard where he is?"

Manuel shook his head. "Not with the sheep men."

Severo dipped a cup into the galvanized water bucket. "Some water Papa?"

Manuel drank the water in one long gulp. Silence filled the room and Manuel's mind began to wander to José and his talk about El Norte. Manuel had witnessed the killing of Governor Perez and been caught up in the rage that drove his neighbors to fight and kill. By the time General Kearny's army came, Manuel was tired of the fighting.

Manuel jumped at the chance to spend the summer with his uncle in Santa Fe. He had helped his uncle Pedro fill his store with goods brought from the American East. *Americanos* traded with *Hispanos*. Men in suits and women in fine dresses shopped in *Tio* Pedro's store.

"Change is coming," *Tio* Pedro had said. "We can either fight against it and lose, or change with it and win."

After he came home from Santa Fe, Manuel listened more carefully to his neighbors. They threw rocks at their friends who sold land to the *Americanos*, land their families had lived on for two hundred years. Manuel began to think about what his uncle had said. He knew that his life couldn't get better when the people around him clung to their bitterness. If he wanted to start a new life, he would have to move south.

One of Manuel's cousins had moved down to Belen when the Mexican government handed out land grants along the Camino Royal. The *camino* was a well-worn trail that settlers used to travel back and forth between Mexico and the northern Territory of New Mexico.

In the central part of the territory the Camino Royal had little protection from the Indians. In return for rich farm land along the Rio Grande, men would serve in the militia to protect travelers.

Manuel settled even further south in Lemitar. He had land beside the river, good *bosque* land. He sold some of his land and built a store. His uncle helped him to fill it with merchandise and set up the books. From this start Manuel had bought cattle and sheep, built gristmills, and found his Isabel. His brother, Esquipula, joined him and started farming the rich soil of the Rio Grande Valley. José had stirred up all of Manuel's anger and regrets of his youth. *Where would I be if I had stayed in El Norte?* Manuel mused.

✳✳✳

The little bell jingled as *Señora* Romero hurried into the store. José scurried to fetch a sack of flour for her. He slapped it onto the wagon bed and handed her the receipt without saying a word.

When he came back into the store, José spit into the brass spittoon and wiped his mouth on his sleeve. *"Que se va al diablo,* she can go to the devil!" He shook his fist at *Señora* Romero.

"What happened?" Manuel looked toward the wagon moving into the street.

"Señora Romero," José huffed.

"They're good people," Manuel said. "Don't tell me she said something that made you mad." Manuel was standing over José with his hands on his hips.

"Good people, ha! The whole family can go to the devil."

Manuel looked at the ceiling and rubbed his neck. He knew he would regret asking about *Señora* Romero's transgression. He also knew that José wouldn't stop ranting unless he could let off steam. With his hands in the air, Manuel nodded.

José recognized the signal and begin his litany. "I can't believe that Felipe Romero let his daughter marry a *gringo*, a *gringo*! What does he want with Adelina Romero? She looks just like her *abuela*, skinny and pale." José shook his finger at Manuel. "You know what that *gringo* wants. He wants that good *bosque* land near San Acacia."

Manuel blew out the breath that he'd been holding. He waved José away and hurried out the back door. Leaning against the stable wall, José's bitterness rang in his ears. *If he would just let go of the past.* Manuel looked up and spotted the horseshoe Flavio had nailed above the stable door.

13

Aurora and her mother took Esquipula's wagon to Lemitar. They rode past fields awakening with pale sprouts. The back of the wagon was full of Aurora's little nephews and nieces. She kept glancing back to make sure that Manuelito was in the center of the wagon.

Josefa felt her old muscles being healed by the sun. She let her shawl slip from her shoulders. "You can visit with Estella while I get the supplies. Maybe you can take Luzita with you. She always takes good care of Manuelito."

Aurora shifted closer to her mother. *Had Luzita taken good care of Manuelito,* she wondered? Lines formed on her forehead. She hadn't paid much attention to the little flock of children occupying the *plazita*. She clutched her mother's arm.

"Are you alright?" Josefa asked.

Aurora held her head high. "Keep bringing me back. Don't let Telesfora take Manuelito. Put me to work. Make me take care of my sons, and don't let me sleep the morning away."

"I can do that," Josefa laughed. "I could use the help."

The road curved and Lemitar came into view. Josefa turned the wagon onto the dirt road just past the church. Estella's house was the last one on the road. Estella came around the corner. She swept a strand of hair away from her eyes. Her sleeves were rolled up and her apron was wet. Her frown turned into a wide grin when she saw who her visitors were.

"Oh, Aurora!" she shouted. She waved them toward the porch. As Aurora and the children unloaded, Estella wiped her hands on her apron. She dashed into the kitchen and asked the cleaning girl to fetch some water for her guests.

Josefa whispered to Aurora, "Maybe we shouldn't stay. Estella is doing her washing today."

Aurora looked up and saw the galvanized tub sitting on a low table. She yelled at the children to wait, and hurried toward the house. Estella met her at the door.

"You're washing. We'll come back some other day."

Estella glanced at the steaming tub and waved Aurora's suggestion away. "I was almost finished and the white clothes need to soak. It's so hot out here. I'm ready for a *refresco*."

She motioned Aurora to the bench and waved goodbye to Josefa. Her two little girls darted out the door and the pack of children ducked underneath the mesquite bush where they had built a fort.

A thin Navajo girl brought out a tray with two glasses of water. A lemon slice adorned the rim of each glass. Aurora raised her eyebrows and daintily took the glass.

She lifted it to her friend, "*Dona* Estella," she mocked.

Estella stood and curtsied like a lady; then both of the young women burst into laughter.

"I treated myself to a lemon when I went to Manuel's store," said Estella. "They came all the way from California. Have you been to the store lately? He has things that I've never seen before. His wagons just came back from St. Louis." Estella clapped her hands excitedly.

Estella's stories drifted past Aurora until she forced herself to hold onto a word or two. Estella slowed down when she saw Aurora squinting. She lifted her glass and took a sip. "Anyway, you should go when you're feeling up to it."

"I'm alright," Aurora said, "I saw some blue glass in the store window. Maybe I can talk Mamá into buying a vase for the spring flowers."

Aurora bit into the lemon and scrunched up her face. She cleared her throat and began telling Estella what stories she remembered from Socorro.

"My cousin Antonia is getting married at the end of the summer," said Aurora. "Of course, I probably won't go, but I know you'll be invited. Ernesto, her beloved, is your cousin.

Estella flashed a toothy grin. "When Ernesto was helping fix the back fence, he was whistling and smiling. There was no one there. He turned red when I came up behind him with some water. So, it's Antonia."

This time the mention of two people in love didn't send Aurora to another place. She was happy for them. Only a little sadness tightened her throat. *We were happy too,* she thought, *but it's over now.* Aurora stood up and started walking toward the children.

✳✳✳

The next week Aurora planned to go to Lemitar with Telesfora. She slipped on the dress that she had worn last summer. She ran her fingers along the lace collar. When she looked down at the field of tiny pink flowers, she smiled. The cotton fabric was soft and it floated when she walked across the room. She didn't notice her mother leaning against the door.

Josefa handed her a black dress. "It hasn't even been a year. What will people say?"

"I just wanted to see how it looked," Aurora answered. "Estella reminded me of it last week." Aurora slipped off the dress. It smelled like sunshine. She folded it and put it back in her trunk. Her mother helped her button the black dress.

"Mamá, I don't want to feel sad anymore." She smoothed her skirt. "When I wear this, people treat me with pity and I remember. I don't want to remember anymore. It felt good to joke with Estella and to talk about our friends. I'm going into town to see all the new things in *Tio's* store. Estella was so excited about them."

"Well go, but with respect for Flavio."

Aurora tightened her fist. "I don't want to think about him. It hurts too much. Don't you understand? Going into town makes me forget for a while. What does it matter what I wear?"

"Putting on a black dress doesn't mean you can't begin to live again. It's just a sign of respect."

Aurora huffed. She thought about her old *Tia* Manuela who had worn black for the rest of her life. She thought of her as *La Viuda*, The Widow. Aurora eased herself onto the bed.

"But I'm not old. Do I have to wear black dresses for the rest of my life like *Tia Manuela*?"

Josefa chuckled softly, "No, but at least for a year to show your respect."

"And my sadness," finished Aurora. "I feel like I have to put it away sometimes so I can keep going."

Josefa put her arm around Aurora. "This life is hard. We all have a bag full of misery that we carry with us, but there is joy too – the laughter of your little boys, your family, your friends."

The clatter of Telesfora's wagon brought them out of their conversation. A child's scream sent them scrambling out the door. Manuelito lay sprawled on the ground with little Francisco on top of him.

"Mamá!" Manuelito wailed.

Telesfora leaped from the wagon and flew to the child. "He ran right out in front of the horses when he saw me!"

Telesfora and Aurora picked up Manuelito in a tangle of arms.

"Is he hurt?" Telesfora cried.

Aurora wiped the dirt from Manuelito's face.

"I think he's alright," panted Francisco. "I knocked him out of the way."

Telesfora whirled toward Aurora. "What was he doing out here by himself? He's just a baby! I don't know why you don't let him stay with me."

Telesfora's words hit like a blow to Aurora's chest.

Telesfora scooped Manuelito up and took him into the house. She washed his face and dusted him off. When she hugged him fiercely, Manuelito struggled to get away. He cocked his head and looked from one mamá to the other. Then he took a small step toward Aurora. The other children crowded at the door, letting the heat and dust float into the room.

Aurora choked down a sob and reached for her little boy. "Oh, Manuelito, where have I been? I don't want Telesfora to keep you, but I'm not even watching you."

Manuelito fell against his mother and wrapped his little arms around her neck. Aurora sat cross-legged on the floor and rocked her son. Josefa shooed the other children outside, then took Telesfora's arm and led her to the porch.

Aurora could hear Telesfora and Josefa talking over the top of each other. She caught a few words and her shoulders tightened. *Just because Telesfora doesn't have any children of her own doesn't mean she can take mine.*

When the two women came inside, Aurora glared at Telesfora. She was just about to tell her cousin that she didn't want her to take care of Manuelito anymore, when Telesfora reached down and gently helped Aurora to her feet.

"*Lo siento*, I'm sorry," she said. Telesfora wiped her eyes on her apron. "I know what you've been through. I was just trying to help."

Manuelito reached for Telesfora and Aurora let him go.

"I know things are getting better for you." Telesfora wiped her eyes again with a shaky hand. "You just tell me when you need help. I love you and Flavio like you are my own children."

She took a deep breath as she stepped outside. She climbed back into her wagon. "We'll go to the store tomorrow."

Josefa nodded in agreement and slipped back inside. She poured two cups of coffee. Josefa waved Aurora to the kitchen table and laid a gentle hand on her daughter's arm. "She was here when no one else had the strength to do the things that needed to be done," said Jose-fa. "Why don't you go lie down for a while. Flavito is sleeping. What happened today could have happened to anyone." Josefa draped a quilt over Aurora and made the sign of the cross as she slipped out of the bedroom.

Aurora breathed deeply and closed her eyes. She folded her hands and prayed. "Help me find my way back." She started to drift into sleep, but awoke with a start. Instead of curling into a ball, Auro-ra sat up and planted her feet firmly on the floor.

"What can I do to help?" she asked as she strode back into the kitchen.

Rita and Josefa looked at each other, eyebrows raised. Rita shrugged and stammered, "I was going to get some water, but. . ."

Aurora grabbed the bucket from her and marched to the pump. Josefa and Rita watched her through the window.

"Maybe she's back," Rita whispered.

Josefa squeezed her arm and went back to her *metate*. As she rolled the grinding stone over the corn, she began to whistle *Las Mañanitas*, a little song Aurora had always known.

Aurora set the bucket on the low table in the corner of the kitch-en, then crossed the *plazita* to her rooms.

"Maybe I better go help her," Rita said. She ran across the packed dirt court yard. "Do you need some help?"

Aurora looked at Flavito's cradle. "It's hard to take care of his bed-ding," she said. "The covers have to be changed every morning. Now that it's summer we should put the mattress in the sun to air out. She started lifting it out of the cradle and Rita rushed to help her. They draped it across a wagon wheel that leaned against the fence.

"I'll go get the fresh linens for the cradle," Rita said, "and a blan-ket. It still gets a little cold at night." She rolled up the damp bedding and turned to go out the door, but Aurora took them from her.

"While you're getting the blanket, I'll put these to soak. Who does Telesfora think she is? I can cake take care of my children."

Rita bobbed her head and skipped back to the cooking room. "*Santa* Maria!" she squealed. "Aurora is putting Flavito's bedding to soak. We put the mattress to air out."

She grabbed Josefa and the two women danced around the room like children. Andres looked up from the wood pile. He scrunched up his face. Josefa cupped her son's cheeks. "Oh *Mijito*, you don't know what this means!"

Rita dug out the little blankets from the trunk and started back to Aurora's rooms. Josefa hung onto the open door, tears silently running down her face. She dabbed her nose with her handkerchief. *Wait until I tell Esquipula,* Josefa smiled.

Esquipula couldn't wait to tell his brother what had happened at home. He felt like a sack of grain had been lifted from his shoulders. Manuel slapped his brother on the back.

"Bring her to town next time you come," Manuel said. "I brought her something special from St. Louis. Oh, and bring the boys too." He shook Esquipula's hand and invited him to the saloon for a celebratory sip of whiskey. They both let out a long sigh.

14

Esquipula wiped his forehead with his tattered bandanna. He closed his eyes and let the sun soothe his aching back. Then he surveyed his *chili* fields, just waking with new sprouts. Leaning against his shovel, he let his mind wander back to a time when Manuel had come to talk to him in these same fields.

As the fields of *chili* had turned shades of red, Manuel had known that he needed to talk to his brother. He drove his buggy along the canal and waved his hat at Esquipula. They met under the cottonwoods that grew along the river. Esquipula dipped his hat into a bucket of water, shook it off and plopped it back on his head. Then he offered his brother a drink of clean water from a big pottery crock.

"So, you came to help me pick *chili*," Esquipula had laughed. "I bet you wouldn't last an hour in this heat." Esquipula lifted his hand and let it go limp. "I bet you wear gloves so your hands won't get dirty while you're counting your money."

Manuel had laughed and slapped his brother on the back. He took out a clean handkerchief, dipped it into the bucket and offered it to Esquipula. As his brother wiped his sunbaked face, Manuel sat on one of the stumps that served as a resting place for the field hands.

"Have you noticed that Flavio is spending a lot of time at your house lately?" Manuel asked.

Esquipula shaded his eyes with his hand and turned to Manuel. "Yeah, him and Santa Cruz and Aurora walked down to the fields last evening. Oh, and Flavio said he wants to help pick when the *chili* is ripe." Esquipula furrowed his brow. "The other day I saw them down by the river." He straightened and turned toward his brother; his chin tucked into his chest.

"You know, now that I think of it, it was just Flavio and Aurora."
Manuel gave him a sideways glance.

"No!" Esquipula shook his head. "They're always fighting. I remember when Aurora busted his head with a rock!"

"*Hombre*, that was years ago. In case you haven't noticed, they're not children anymore."

"How could Aurora be interested in Flavio? The other day she was talking about going back to St. Louis with you; you know, when you take your wagons for supplies. Josefa told her that she couldn't go without a chaperone and she started yelling that no one ever lets her do anything. You know how she gets."

Esquipula had watched his daughter grow past childhood into a beauty. Whether in Lemitar or La Parida, Aurora gathered the other young people around her. She would waltz into Manuel's store talking about some big idea or fancy plan. Before anyone knew it, Aurora would have given everyone a task and she was left with nothing to do but soak up all the credit. The next week it would be something different.

Esquipula shook off his memories as he picked up his hoe and trudged back home. He looked toward the sky and prayed that the girl who had been full of laughter and sunshine had come back to him.

❋❋❋

When Esquipula got home he found a gaggle of women sitting in the *plazita*. Margarita ran to Esquipula. "*Tio!* she squealed, embracing the uncle that she hadn't seen in months. "Let me get you some water." Margarita took Esquipula's arm and led him into the house. "I came to see my sister, Telesfora, but I had to see Aurora first."

She put her hand on her chest. "Oh, *Tio*, it's hard to see Aurora so thin. I'm so glad I came to see her while we're in town. Los Lunas is so far away. I haven't been here since Flavio's, uh, Mass." Margarita folded her fingers around her uncle's rough hands. "I wish I could have been here more."

Esquipula rubbed her hand. "Don't worry about it. It's just going to take time, and she's getting better. Did she talk much today?

Margarita nodded. "She was just telling us about Gloria."

"That's good, for a long time she couldn't even hear what people were saying. She's coming back to us. I'm glad you were here today. Now she can talk and laugh with you."

"But she's not the same," Margarita whispered. "Remember how she was always the center of attention? When Manuelito was born, you would have thought she was the only woman to have given birth. I thought she was going to wear the baby out passing him around. She was so proud of him." Margarita's voice faded. ". . . they both were."

"It's only been a few months," sighed Esquipula. "I hope you never have to feel the pain she's going through."

Margarita lowered her eyes. "Oh, I know. I guess I forgot for a

66

while. I was just so glad to see her." She handed Esquipula a glass of mint water and they stepped into the sun.

Esquipula spotted a dust cloud on the road. He tapped Margarita on the shoulder and pointed. "Melquides," he nodded. Margarita helped Josefa take the dishes into the kitchen. When Melquides arrived, Margarita was waiting for her husband with a basket of quince preserves from Josefa's cellar.

Melquides tipped his hat and started gathering his family. He glanced at his wife. "*Lo siento*, Margarita, I have to get back with the supplies."

"Do you have to go so soon?" pleaded Aurora. "It's been so long since I've seen you." Aurora brushed a kiss against Margarita's cheek. With the promise of another visit next month, Margarita waved goodbye.

Esquipula raised his eyebrows when he saw Aurora chuckling. His stomach tightened as he gathered the courage to ask her what she was laughing at.

"Oh, I was just remembering what Margarita was saying about Elena. There's as much gossip in Los Lunas as there is in Lemitar." Aurora turned toward the house. "I think I'll go to church next Sunday. Maybe I'll get a chance to tell Estella about Margarita and Elena."

Esquipula turned to Josefa. Her eyes were closed and her hand was over her heart. A thin smile touched her lips.

❋❋❋

Aurora pulled her black dress out of the trunk and gave it a hard shake. She threw it on the bed and began fixing her hair. She gently held the tortoiseshell comb that Flavio had given her. When memories crept back, Aurora stuffed the comb into her hair. She slipped on the black dress, but didn't turn back to the mirror.

Back in her mother's kitchen, Aurora's attention turned to her baby. She and Rita gave him a warm bath in the little tub. She brushed his black hair and pulled a soft cotton gown trimmed with lace over his head.

Rita tilted her head. "Why are you dressing him up?"

"For church; it's been too long. Go get Manuelito so I can give him a bath."

Rita was fixed to the floor. "You didn't say anything about going to church yesterday."

"Yes, I did." Aurora shrugged. "I told somebody I was going," she snapped.

Rita ran outside and cornered Manuelito. He kicked and squealed in protest.

"We're going to give you a bath," Rita ordered. She turned to the other little ones. "And the rest of you, go in and get cleaned up for Mass." She stood at the door until all of the children straggled into the house.

Rita handed Manuelito his little wooden horse and he stopped screaming. Aurora plopped him down in Flavito's bath water. He had the same black hair as his brother, but it was curly like his grandfather's. His eyes were the same dark brown too. "When did you get so big?" Aurora wondered out loud.

Manuelito threw his hands up. "Yesterday," he answered.

Aurora tickled him and he wiggled and splashed. She dressed Manuelito in short pants and the new shirt that Telesfora had made him. None of the children were allowed outside until the wagon was ready to leave.

As usual, the Vigil family filed into church just as the singing began. People turned and whispered as Aurora walked by. Estella reached out and touched her hand. Aurora wanted to lean down and embrace her, but her father hurried her along.

As the priest performed his rituals in Latin, Aurora breathed in the familiar scent of frankincense. Then her gaze fell on the statue of the Blessed Mother. Was Flavio being cared for by the woman who had lost her beloved son? She tightened her hands around the pew in front of her when the priest's voice stopped. In the stillness, one simple word entered her mind, yes.

When Josefa nudged her, Aurora started. People were standing. Their muffled voices filled the little church. Aurora crowded into the aisle with the rest of the parishioners. The light of the open doors drew the crowd outside.

Everyone milled around the churchyard after Mass. They were anxious to catch up on their neighbor's gossip. At first people shied away from Aurora or passed by quickly with a *"Lo siento,"* and a pat on her arm. This all changed when her friend, Dolores, came out of the church. She rushed toward her childhood friend and squeezed her.

Aurora covered her mouth to suppress a squeal. Dolores held Aurora at arm's length. "You look better than they said," she laughed.

Aurora shook her head. "They probably got me mixed up with the *viuda* Manuela." They tapped their heads together and stifled a giggle. Dolores glanced toward the priest, then at her mother-in-law. Neither were watching, so they turned their backs to the crowd and laughed out loud.

Dolores took Flavito and caressed his round cheeks. When Estella spotted Flavito in Dolores' arms, she led a covey of women toward Aurora. They all took turns holding Flavito and waving people over to see the baby.

"I had a lot of help," Aurora sighed. She put a hand on Josefa's elbow.

"*Como no,*" uttered Josefa, "of course." The village women nodded with understanding.

The men were bringing the wagons around, so the little knot of women drifted apart. Aurora handed Flavito to Rita before climbing into the wagon. Aurora's cheeks were aglow.

"Everyone loved Flavito," Aurora chirped, "and they all think he looks like his father."

Rita put her arm around Aurora and waited for the tears to flow. When they didn't come, she glanced at her sister. Aurora was looking toward the horizon, a smile turning up her lips.

15

As August began to sizzle, Aurora rolled up her sleeves and helped Rita with the washing. She took over making tortillas when her mother was busy in the garden. One morning, while she formed the little balls of dough, Aurora remembered how much she had missed her mother's kitchen when she went to Snake Ranch. She was glad that Rita was there to help, but it was so quiet. The L-shaped house stood in the open with only a barn to keep it company.

Aurora never felt safe without adobe walls to protect her. Flavio used to laugh when she flung her arms around him at night. "You're home!" Aurora would cry. "I thought I saw some Navajos on the hill."

Then Flavio would pick up his little bride and twirl her around laughing. "Forget about the Navajos. I'll take care of you." He laughed again as he lifted his chin toward the bedroom. Aurora would always struggle free and thump him on the arm in mock protest.

A lump rose up in Aurora's throat and she forgot about the tortillas. A familiar flutter tightened around her heart, then fled.

Rita came in with a basket of eggs. She stopped and looked, wide eyed, at her sister. "Aurora, what's happened?"

Aurora shrugged. "I was just remembering."

Rita poured water into a pan and washed the eggs. While Aurora finished making tortillas, Rita called the children to wash up for breakfast.

Rita spooned a big lump of lard into the skillet and started frying eggs. With the little pot of *chili* bubbling, and potatoes sizzling, Rita and Aurora glanced at each other and sighed. Aurora took the pile of tortillas to the noisy pack of nieces and nephews. She smoothed Manuelito's hair and tore him off a piece of tortilla.

✳✳✳

Josefa brought in a basket of fat green *chili*. She sent Rita to start a fire in the *horno*. The little domed oven in the corner of the *plazita* was started with slivers of *piñon* wood. Josefa dreaded roasting *chili* in the outdoor oven. Every time she pulled the flat stone away from the opening, a wave of heat threatened to singe her face.

"I wish we could roast the *chili* on the stove," she said to Rita, "but the house is already too hot."

When the first batch of *chili* was brought into the house, it was wrapped in a damp towel and set in a big bowl. Aurora moved to the table with Flavito on her hip. She sat him on the floor and he crawled to the bench. With one hand on the bench, he grabbed his mother's skirt and tried to crawl onto her lap. Josefa squatted down and held out her hands. Unwilling to let go of his mamá, he buried his face in Aurora's skirt.

"This is such a hard time with the little ones," Josefa said. "They're not old enough to go outside with the others, but you can't put them in a basket and get your work done." She put both hands on Rita's shoulders. "I say a little prayer every night for you. You are such a help."

Aurora plopped Flavito in the corner and gave him a wooden spoon and the silver rattle Manuel had bought him. She yelled out the door for Antonia to come in and keep Flavito busy. Then she sat next to Rita and fanned herself.

It had never been her job to peel *chili*. Aurora had washed her baby's clothes and helped Rita cook and clean, but the other chores had always been done for her. Now she started to pick up a wilted *chili* pod by the stem.

"No!" yelled Rita. "Your hands will be on fire for the rest of the day and when you touch Flavito, he'll burn too."

Aurora dropped the *chili* and washed off her hand.

"Why don't you get the dried clothes from the line?" Josefa suggested. "You can fold them in your room."

There was a time when Aurora would have rebelled against her mother's orders, but today she was glad to feel like part of this workforce.

✳ ✳ ✳

Telesfora's wagon rattled into the courtyard. Aurora nodded toward Telesfora as she walked to her room with the clothes basket. Telesfora lifted a hand and waved to her.

Aurora quickly folded clothes, anxious to get back to the kitchen. The week before, Telesfora had begged to take Manuelito to see his *Tia* Rufina. Surely, she would bring back news from Socorro.

Luzita and Guadalupe helped Telesfora carry two baskets of green *chili* into the house. The girls grumbled on their way back outside. They had been recruited to keep the *horno* going and to bring the *chili* in when it was roasted.

On the way back to the house, Aurora passed Ernesto, who was

71

trying to keep the little ones away from the hot oven.

"Manuelito, go play under the tree," Aurora commanded.

Manuelito turned toward his mother and stuck out his tongue. Aurora froze. Her little boy had never done anything like this before. Hurt mixed with anger. She dropped the clothes basket, grabbed his arm and swatted his behind. "Don't you ever do that to me again!" she shouted.

Manuelito melted into tears. Aurora looked up at the other children. "Who taught him this dirty thing?"

The children scattered.

"If I ever see any of you sticking out your tongue, I'll cut it off!" she yelled.

Telesfora ran outside. "What's happening?"

Manuelito ran to her and hid behind her skirt. As Aurora told her what had happened, Telesfora knelt and wiped away Manuelito's tears. "My sweet little boy, you know that was a bad thing to do, especially to your mamá."

Manuelito looked from his mother to Telesfora and clung tighter to Telesfora.

Heat rose from Aurora's chest. "He's not your little boy," she hissed through clenched teeth.

Telesfora stiffened. "Someone needs to take care of him," she spat. "You don't even know where he is most of the time. Two days ago, he walked to my house by himself. I brought him back. I would have told you about it, but you were sleeping with Flavito."

Aurora's lips drew into a thin line. She wrenched Manuelito away from Telesfora and stomped to her room. The bed springs protested as she rocked her little three-year-old son. Her anger ebbed and flowed. It was mixed with guilt and confusion. *For a long time*, she thought, *I didn't know anything of my children or anything else. But that was a long time ago. Now I know where Manuelito is. He's with his cousins while I'm busy helping Mamá.*

She hadn't thought much about Telesfora's offer to take Manuelito to Socorro. He loved going in the wagon and Telesfora was his favorite *Tia. When had he become her little boy?*

Manuelito wiggled out of her arms. Aurora knelt beside him. "I love you *Mijito;* you're mine. Give your mamá a kiss."

A wet little kiss was planted on Aurora's cheek. It was returned with kisses all over Manuelito's face. He giggled and Aurora laughed as she opened the door. "Don't go near the *horno*. It's hot!"

She handed him a wooden spoon to dig in the dirt with. Aurora shook her finger at the other children. "Stay here in the shade and play and, you older ones, watch Manuelito."

When Aurora stepped into the kitchen, the women stopped talking. She took Flavito and sat in her father's leather chair.

After loosening their collars, the women went back to their *chili* peeling in silence. Telesfora stood and took a few steps toward Aurora.

"*Lo siento*," she said. "I know you've been through a lot, and I'm sorry I spoke to you the way I did. I've only been trying to help. . . "

Aurora cut her off. "You're right, or at least you were. I was lost for a while after. . ." She took a long breath. "But I'm better now. I thought Manuelito was safe playing with the other children. I'll watch him closer from now on." She pulled herself up and met Telesfora's gaze. "He's mine."

16

The cottonwoods turned golden as the *chili* turned red. Telesfora and Antonia watched the little children while everyone over the age of twelve harvested the *chili* that had been left to ripen. Josefa wanted Aurora to stay and help with the children, but she marched to the fields with the rest of the family. She tore off *chili* pods and threw them in the basket, only stopping to stretch and rubbed her aching back.

Andres and his wife, Barbara, were picking in the row next to Aurora. She caught sight of Barbara out of the corner of her eye. Barbara stood in the middle of the field inspecting Aurora as if she had rattles on her tail. Then Barbara turned to Rita and whispered.

Rita threw down her basket and shouted, "I keep telling you, she's changed!"

Aurora brushed between the *chili* plants. By the time she reached Rita, Barbara had moved to another row.

"What was that all about?" questioned Aurora.

Rita's lips were twisted into a grimace. "She was surprised that you weren't picking at the edge of the fields where it's easier to slip away and sit in the shade."

Aurora bolted toward her sister-in-law. Rita grabbed her arm. "Leave it. You know what a silly cow she can be. Besides, it's time to stop and eat."

Aurora growled under her breath as she walked toward the cottonwoods.

❋ ❋ ❋

Long tables had been set under the trees at the edge of the river. At noon, people ate cold tamales. Meat and potatoes were wrapped in tortillas and brought to the table in enamel tubs.

Aurora took the bandana from her head and wiped her brow, then splashing her face with cool water. She sat far away from Barbara. Rita pointed to a knot of older girls who were giggling and flirting with the boys. She elbowed Aurora. "You weren't any older when you married Flavio."

Aurora stared at the red-faced girls. It seemed like a hundred years ago since she had been that young. Their voices drifted away as memories enveloped her.

She had always hated the backbreaking job of picking *chili*. The sun turned her pale skin dark and rough. She groaned at the memory of putting on a veil to go to church. When Flavio had seen it, he stepped back and wrinkled up his nose.

"Why are you wearing that?" he had asked. "Are you planning to marry someone else today?"

"Oh, no," Aurora stammered. "My face is as brown as a bean and I didn't want my friends to see me like this."

Flavio had snatched the veil from her head. "You think you're the only one who's been baked in the fields. Take a good look at your friends. We're *Hispano* farmers. If I had wanted to marry a white ghost, I would have gone back East and found someone in St. Louis."

Flavio tried to embrace his little wife, but Aurora twisted away. She climbed into the buggy and turned away from her husband. Flavio followed her. He slapped the reins and pointed the buggy toward La Parida.

"I didn't mean to hurt you, *me amor*. I was just teasing."

Aurora turned her face away, not to hide her pain, but to bury her shame. "I don't know why I do things sometimes," she whispered. "I just want to be beautiful for you."

Flavio had pulled her toward him and kissed her on the forehead. "You'll be beautiful to me until we're both dried up and planted behind the house."

Aurora relaxed her shoulders. She slid close and wrapped her arm in his.

The women's conversation slowly seeped into Aurora's awareness. Rita handed her a cup of water and asked, "Where were you?"

Aurora shook her head. "I was just remembering how silly I used to be when I was first married."

Aurora stood and rolled her aching shoulders. "It's time to go back. Maybe we can get this field done before the sun scorches the hair off my head."

Rita pulled Aurora away from the table and they plodded toward the field.

17

Josefa always welcomed the first dusting of snow. Winter was a time to rest. The store room was full. The *chili ristras* had been hung to dry on the *vigas* above the stove. Aurora and her little boys were tucked away in their rooms.

Josefa jumped when Aurora burst through the door. Manuelito flew past her. "I won, I won!" He giggled.

Aurora put Flavito down and plopped Manuelito on the bench. She mixed some *atole* with a little cold water so the boys wouldn't burn their tongues. Flavito waddled on unsteady legs toward Rita and lifted his arms. Aurora took a step toward him, then decided it was alright for Rita to change his diaper while she cooked and mashed up some eggs for her boys.

After the morning meal, the children were sent outside to play. The women and older girls sat in a circle around the fireplace. Josefa sewed the sleeves on a new wool shirt for Esquipula while Aurora hemmed her new black dress. The old one had gotten too tight.

With the hem finished, Aurora snuck a peek at her mother. Satisfied that Josefa was busy at her sewing, Aurora sewed three small, black, faceted buttons on the front of her dress. What could her mother say? The dress needed buttons. She had to have this tiny bit of sparkle to remind her that she wouldn't wear black forever.

✳✳✳

Manuel drove into Esquipula's yard as the sun was rising over the *mesa*. He wrapped Aurora in a wool blanket. She was afraid that Manuelito wouldn't stay in his blankets, so she left him with Josefa. Aurora rode to Socorro with Manuel to visit her sister-in-law, Rufina, and her friend Gloria.

While Manuel locked up his mill for the winter and delivered his flour to the stores in Socorro, Aurora could catch up on the news of Socorro.

After supper Aurora helped Rufina wash the dishes while Manuel and Antonio sat in the parlor. When Aurora hung the cast-iron skillet on the hook, she heard Flavio's name coming from the next room. She stood by the door, craning to hear more. Her sister-in-law cleared her throat and waved at her to come away.

"They're talking about Flavio. I've heard the men talking about him before, but when they see me, they all stop talking." Aurora looked anxiously at Rufina.

"Papá tells me to leave the men alone," warned Rufina.

"Something is going on and I want to know what it is," Aurora whispered.

Rufina took hold of Aurora's arm. "You don't need to know. You have enough on your heart."

Aurora tipped her head sideways. "Do you know what's going on?"

"All I know is that Manuel found out the name of the man who shot Flavio. He's looking everywhere for him. Please don't let your thoughts rest on these things. Take care of your little boys and treat yourself with kindness." Rufina pulled Aurora close. "Leave the revenge to the men."

Aurora hadn't thought much about the man who had taken Flavio from her. Now her stomach tightened and flipped. She steadied herself with her hands on the back of a chair.

"You see," Rufina said. "This is no business for you to even think about."

Aurora's brow knitted. "Maybe you're right." She sat with her head cradled in her hands while Rufina showed her the tablecloth she was embroidering. She examined the delicate stitches and told Rufina that her mother was teaching her some new stitches. Turning slowly from the parlor, Aurora said, "I'm, um, trying the stitches on Flavito's new gown.

❋ ❋ ❋

Manuel listened for the women's soft voices then leaned closer to Antonio. Manuel squirmed, then shook his head. He lowered his voice. "I've sent men to Santa Fe to ask everyone coming south on the trail. I've set men toward Texas where the cattle come from, but now I don't know about this."

Manuel rubbed his forehead and sighed, "What if they find him? Will the soul of one of my men be stained with Montgomery's blood?"

Manuel picked up his cold pipe. He started to put it in his mouth, then threw it across the room. Antonio pressed himself into the chair, his eyes wide. Manuel glanced toward the kitchen and walked to the front door. "Will the death of Montgomery bring my Flavio back? If it could, I would kill him myself, one hundred times over." Manuel stepped onto the porch, gulped down unspent tears, then turned.

77

In a shaky voice he whispered, "Nothing will ever take away the pain of losing my son." He looked toward the dim light of the kitchen. "But I have other children . . ."

Antonio stood, weaving back and forth. He was used to the strong man that stood up against everything that threatened to break him. *How could Manuel stop looking for Montgomery?* Antonio pushed against the squeaky screen door. He had expected to finish his conversation, but he saw that the light had gone out of the big man's eyes, so he stepped back inside and tiptoed to his room.

Manuel saw lamplight coming toward the porch. He pushed himself up and took the lantern from Aurora.

Aurora kissed Flavio's father softly on the cheek. "I'm going to bed now. Flavito is already asleep, but he wakes up early."

"Good," answered Manuel, "I need to get back to Lemitar early and make sure the wagons are loaded with the grain going to Santa Fe." Manuel kissed his daughter-in-law on the cheek and started into the house.

The next morning, during the long ride home, Aurora hummed softly. Manuel swayed back and forth, letting the past fade into the future.

18

Rita gathered up her skirt and ran to the wagon. "How was Rufina? Did she tell you about Cecilia's wedding?"

Aurora pulled off her coat. She answered her wide-eyed sister's question. "Of course, all the Lunas were there from Los Lunas, and the Griegos from San Antonio. Some of the Pinos were there too."

"I wish I could have been there, just to see Cecilia in her wedding dress," Rita twirled around, "and to watch everyone dancing."

Rita followed Aurora into the kitchen. Aurora moved to the stove to warm her hands. "Where's Manuelito?"

Josefa ducked her head and answered, "Telesfora took him to spend the night."

Aurora pulled the door open. "Wait!" Aurora yelled at Manuel. "Don't leave! I have to go get Manuelito."

Manuel turned the wagon around and helped Aurora aboard. Telesfora's house was just down the road, but the wind was biting and Aurora wanted to get there as quickly as she could.

"Come in," Telesfora said to Manuel.

Manuelito burst out of the house and Aurora lifted him into the air.

"What did you bring me from Socorro?"

Aurora laughed, "I brought you your little brother."

Manuelito pouted as Aurora hurried him into the house. "Your surprise is at home. *Tia* Rufina sent you something."

Manuel already had a cup of steaming coffee in his hand when Aurora came through the door. Telesfora handed Aurora a cup and motioned for her to sit. "It's getting cold sooner this year. The trip to Socorro must have been hard." Aurora sat on the edge of her chair.

Telesfora leaned in. "What about the wedding?"

Manuelito tugged at Aurora's skirt. "I want to go home!" he wailed. "I want to see what *Tia* Rufina made for me."

Aurora passed on the highlights of Cecilia's wedding with the promise of a visit later in the week. She shushed her son.

"Alright, we'll go. I have to get back to the baby anyway."

Aurora breathed a sigh of relief as she gathered up her son. As soon as they got in the house, Aurora gave Manuelito a piece of Rufina's homemade caramel, then turned to Josefa.

"Why did you let Telesfora take Manuelito? I don't want her telling me that I should take better care of my sons. The only reason I left him was because it's so cold, and you wanted him to stay at home."

Josefa looked up from the bowl of dried corn she was scraping off the cob. "She made Manuelito a shirt and pants and wanted him to try them on. Manuelito always wants to go with her."

"Because she spoils him," Aurora spat. "You should have seen the way he acted when I went to get him. He wanted to come home and get *Tia* Rufina's gift. He wouldn't even let us talk."

Josefa glanced at Rita. "Alright, I won't let him go with her again."

Aurora flung her coat on the bench. She took Flavito into the bedroom to change him, then strode back into the big room. "I'll take them with me everywhere from now on."

Josefa and Rita stopped scraping corn. Only their eyes moved toward each other. Then Josefa's body softened. She looked toward the heavens and sent up a silent prayer. *Aurora is back,* she thought.

While Flavito was nursing, Aurora told her mother about the wedding. She took Flavio's picture from the table. Her eyes dropped to the floor.

"We loved to dance at weddings and fiestas." She touched the photograph gently. "I'm glad I didn't go to this wedding. I would have been sitting in the corner with the rest of the widows watching everyone having a good time. All I do now is hear about other people's happiness. My story is too sad for anyone to talk about, and now winter is coming again. We're all going to be stuck in the house."

Rita threw a kernel of corn at her. "*Tio* Manuel goes into town every day and you can always go with him."

"And do what?" answered Aurora, "Sit around the stove with the old men?"

"No, *Tio* Manuel says that the storeroom is full, but he doesn't have anyone to help him unload the crates and put things out. Why don't you go help him? The boys would be fine playing in the back room."

Aurora's eyes lit up. "Do you think he would let me? I could go over to his house in the mornings with the boys. That way Isabel could see them for a while. I could wash things off before I put them out. *Tio* Manuel and José aren't very good at that. But what if he doesn't think it would be proper for me to be at the store?"

Josefa smiled. "You would be in the back room. I'll have Esquipula talk to Manuel about it?

Rita winked, "You can bring me all the gossip."

"There wouldn't be any gossip in the back room and *Tio* José would make sure I stayed there."

"You would have to come out to rest once in a while. Besides, *Tio* José doesn't own the store. You wouldn't have to go every day, just once in a while, to get out of the house."

With the boys bundled between them, Manuel and Aurora took the buggy to Lemitar.

"I have to come home early this afternoon, so if you don't like working in the storeroom, I can bring you home."

Aurora frowned. Manuel never went home before dark, but she didn't say anything. She wasn't sure about this either. How was she going to work and take care of two little boys? When she and Flavio used to help in the back it was always fun. Aurora would wind the pretty cloth around herself and Flavio would waltz her across the floor until José barked that they were ruining the goods.

Aurora looked out at the snow-covered sagebrush. *Maybe this wasn't such a good idea,* she thought. *Would the back room hold too many memories? Would Manuelito be satisfied to stay in the storeroom or would he be pestering Severo? Would it be safe for Flavito to toddle among the crates and straw?* Aurora gripped Manuel's arm, "Maybe I shouldn't go."

"We're almost there. I don't have time to take you all the way back. What's wrong?"

"I just thought about the boys. I don't know if I can keep an eye on them while I'm working."

Manuel gave Aurora a sideways glance. "You didn't think about that before we started out?"

"Well, I did, but I wanted to get out of the house and I have to do something besides pass on gossip."

Manuel slapped the reins and the horses sped up. He drew a breath and let it out slowly. "We'll just have to see."

He shivered, not because of the chilly air, but with the memory of another buggy ride. When the wheat had been stored in the mill house, Flavio had asked if he could ride back to the store with his father.

"What's wrong with your horse?" Manuel had questioned.

Flavio loved to race his horse to town with the wind in his face and the sun on his back.

"I'm almost twenty years old," Flavio stammered. "You were about my age when you married Mamá, and built your house in La Parida." Flavio didn't move. Only his eyes darted toward his father.

Manuel prodded the horses to a trot. "I've been thinking about that too," answered Manuel. "I saw the way Catalina Garcia was looking at you at Telesfora's wedding. She comes from a fine family." The corners of his lips turned up. He had hoped that the beautiful Garcia girl would turn Flavio's eyes away from Aurora.

Flavio tightened his lips and clinched his jaw. "Papá, it's Aurora."

Manuel twisted around, eyes wide, mouth agape. "Aurora, what does she know about keeping a house? Would she be able to have a meal on the table when you come home at night? Would your clothes be clean when you leave the next morning?"

Flavio glanced at his father. His lips began to quiver. "I thought you liked Aurora. I know we're cousins, but we won't be the first cousins to marry. Besides, what did my mamá know about these things when you first got married?"

Manuel wiggled, trying to get comfortable. "Your mother had been helping her mother since she was a little girl. I see Rita and Josefa working while Aurora sits laughing with her friends. She's too busy planning what to wear to the dance to learn from her mother. Does she even know how to make tortillas?" Manuel let the silence fall between them. He turned just enough to see Flavio's shoulders slump. His son let out a soft groan.

"*Lo siento*, I'm sorry son. I've said too much."

Manuelito broke the silence when he squealed, "We're here! We're here!"

Manuel shook away his memories and helped Aurora from the buggy. She still had a frown on her face. He led her through the back door. "Don't worry about the boys. You know how much everybody loves Manuelito. If Flavito needs to sleep, you can put him on the cot in Severo's office. Besides, I'm not going to stay all day. Let's see how it goes."

Aurora waited for Manuel to go in with her, but he waved her on. "I'll be there as soon as I put the horses up." He wanted to clear his thoughts before he went into the store. *I have a chance to help Aurora get back into life . . . but the boys. If only she would leave them with Telesfora.* He sucked in a deep breath and helped take the harnesses off the horses. By the time he led them into the stall, Manuel was feeling a little calmer.

When José spotted Aurora, he dropped the flour sack he'd been carrying. "Where's Manuel? Is he sick?" When he saw the boys, his face softened. José tossed Manuelito into the air. He turned toward Aurora. "What are you doing here so early? Why didn't Manuel take you over to Estella's?"

Aurora took off Manuelito's coat and unbundled Flavito. This gave her time to find the right words. "Oh, I thought you could use some help unpacking the crates. *Tio* Manuel told me that there was too much for you to do. Besides, it's only for a few hours. I'll keep the boys with me."

José put his hands on his hips. "Manuel really let you do this?"

Aurora started stammering out an answer when Manuel came through the door. José stared at Manuel and jerked his head toward Aurora.

"It's just for a while," explained Manuel. He took his son-in-law by the arm and ushered him into the store. "It's been a long time since she has wanted to do anything. You know how she gets when she doesn't have something to keep her busy."

José started to protest, but his voice wavered when he saw Manuel's downcast eyes. He threw his hands into the air and slipped behind the counter.

Manuelito started to follow Manuel, but Aurora cut him off and coaxed him into the storeroom. As soon as they stepped through the door, Aurora found the peppermint sticks and gave one to each of the boys, as promised. The first hour went well. The boys played in the empty crates and their *Tio* Severo brought them warm cups of *atole*. Then Flavito needed to be changed.

When Aurora took the baby to the cot, Manuelito escaped into the store. "Oh no!" yelled Aurora. "Please Severo, go grab him! Flavito is messy. I have to change him."

Severo looked up from his ledger and the situation slowly sunk in. He threw down his pen and ran into the store. He found Manuelito holding court in front of the old men.

"Come on Manuelito," begged Severo, "You have to go back with your mamá."

Manuelito stomped his foot. "No!" he yelled. "You go back!"

Severo lunged for his nephew, but was stopped by the cane of *Señor* Griego. "Leave him alone. Manuelito can sit here and tell us the truth. It will be a welcome change from all the lies I've been hearing around here." At that, the other old men pounded their canes and jeered.

Severo looked at his father. Manuel lifted his chin and Severo slid back into his office. Manuel carried Manuelito to the counter and sat him down.

"*Mijito*," he started, "you don't talk to your *Tio* like that. You have to do what he says."

Manuelito stuck out his lower lip, a tantrum forming like a thunderclap. His grandfather's strong grip changed his mind.

"But I don't want to go back!" he screeched.

"Well, you go say *lo siento* to your *Tio* Severo and ask if you can come back. If your mamá says it's alright, you can sit with the *viejos*. You'll be good for them. Laughter makes the blood circulate and they need that."

Manuel swung Manuelito to the floor and led him back to the storeroom. Aurora had unpacked the box of little wooden spinning tops. Flavito giggled every time his mother sent a top spinning across the floor. Manuelito stopped in his tracks when he saw the top, and sitting with the old men was forgotten. He made a grab for the top and Flavito squealed in protest.

Manuelito pressed the top to his chest and ran toward the door with Flavito toddling behind him. Aurora blocked their escape.

"Manuelito, I was showing the top to Flavito. Give it to me."

"No, I want it!"

Aurora put out her hand. "The top belongs to your *abuelo* , I was just showing it to your brother."

"No, it's mine!"

Aurora yanked the top from Manuelito's hand. His high-pitched wail echoed his brother's. She shut the door and put Manuelito over her knee. After the third swat, she sat him down firmly. "You're not going to act like this when I bring you to the store. I am not *Tia* Telesfora. I won't let you get away with everything."

Fat tears rolled down Manuelito's cheeks. Flavito's eyes grew big as he clung to his mother's skirt. His lip began to quiver. Aurora clinched and unclenched her fists, then she knelt down and embraced her little boys. She wiped away Manuelito's tears and kissed them both on the cheek.

"I love you both so much," she said softly, "but when we come to the store or go to someone's house, you have to behave. Do you understand?"

Manuelito's curly hair bounced as he nodded his head. He hugged

Flavito and said sternly, "We have to behave."

When the screeching began, José had marched to the back room. He listened, then tiptoed away, anger welling in his chest. *That ungrateful girl,* he thought, *those boys would have had no one if it wasn't for Telesfora. Why aren't they with her today?*

Aurora smiled and embraced the boys again. She set some toys out for them to play with. When the novelty of the toys wore off, Manuelito pushed on the door that led to the store. Aurora picked up Flavito and took Manuelito by the hand. *"Portase bien,"* she warned. "Behave yourself."

Manuelito ran to Manuel and showed him the top, a torrent of excited explanation pouring out.

At the counter *Señora* Gavaldon was waiting for Manuel to wrap up her packages. She looked down at Manuelito, then at Manuel with her chin tucked into her chest. She raised her eyebrows and withdrew the coin she was offering for her purchases. "Who is this child?"

"This is my grandson," Manuel answered, "Flavio's little boy."

She looked from Manuel to Aurora, a red hue rising in her cheeks. "Oh," she stammered, looking at the floor. *"Lo siento,"* she whispered.

Aurora quickly chimed in. "He's not used to being at the store for so long. He's used to having his *abuelo* all to himself.

Señora Gavaldon patted Manuelito's head. "He'll learn," she said in a high-pitched voice.

Before Aurora could continue her explanation, *Señora* Gavaldon gathered her packages and swooped out the door.

Aurora turned to Manuel. "He's just a little boy and he will learn, or maybe it was a bad idea for me to come to the store with them."

Manuel put his arm around Aurora. "Don't worry about *Señora* Gavaldon. She would squawk if you gave her a free chicken. I'm getting hungry. I'll send Severo to the saloon for burritos de *carne adobada* and some *frijolitos* for the boys."

After they ate at the little table in the office, Aurora took the boys back into the storeroom. They played with the crates and toys while Aurora unpacked oil lamps and cast-iron frying pans. Flavito finally settled onto a pile of straw. His eyes were drooping but, every time Manuelito scraped the little wooden cart across the floor, he sat up.

"Go sit with the old men," Aurora whispered to Manuelito. She changed Flavito's diaper and fed him. He was asleep when she laid him on the cot in the corner of the office.

With Flavito tucked away, Aurora took the new merchandise into the store. Most of the *viejos* had gone home to nap. The two younger ones were conversing with Manuelito as if he understood everything they said. Manuel, and even José, had to laugh at the three separate conversations that were going on.

"When Flavito wakes up, we can go home," said Manuel.

"I can get another crate unloaded, the one with the wool jackets."

"Good. I know they'll sell well this winter."

Aurora worked quickly. She shook out the jackets and brought them into the store, one armload at a time. Manuel stacked them on the shelf behind the counter.

"What else do you want me to bring in?" Aurora followed Manuel into the storeroom and he decided on some buttons and ribbons. Aurora took her time going through them. She put aside the ones she wanted for the dresses she planned on making. *Maybe I better not show these to Manuel*, she thought. *They're not black.* She put them on a high shelf and took the rest into the store.

Flavito started to stir as Aurora slipped past him. "He's waking up," she told Manuel.

He sent José to hitch up the horses. Aurora bundled up her children in heavy quilts. She wrapped a quilt over her head and huddled against Manuel. Manuelito was asleep by the time they dipped across the first arroyo. The rhythmic spinning of the buggy wheels lulled Flavito back to sleep. When their house was in sight, Aurora dared to ask, "How do you think it went?"

"Maybe the next time you can leave the boys with Telesfora." He put his finger in the air. "Or, how about *Tia* Juanita in Lemitar? You could go to your *tia's* when the boys get tired or you need to feed Flavito."

"I know I would get a lot more done without the boys, but *Tia* Juanita has enough children to look after." Aurora lifted her chin. "And I don't want to burden Telesfora. She's done enough for me."

✳✳✳

Aurora's heart sank a little. *Maybe my place is in my home,* she thought, *but that's just it, I don't have a home anymore.* A heaviness settled in her chest, as unwanted memories unfolded.

What had happened to her dreams? They were going to leave Snake Ranch next summer. Manuel had bought a ranch in Mesilla. Flavio was going to run the ranch and pay his father back for it. Aurora was looking forward to finally having her own home. She loved her *Tio* Manuel, but the ranch near Socorro was his. Flavio was just working the land.

In Mesilla, she would be in charge of her own home. The summer before she became a widow, Aurora and Flavio made the two-day trip to see the ranch house at Mesilla. Aurora refused to get out of the wagon when she first spotted it. Two adobe rooms melted into the earth. The windows were broken and the doors were ajar.

"What have you brought me to?" she had screamed. "I can't live in a place like this. Is this where you expect me to raise your son?"

Flavio sprinted between the house and the wagon waving at Aurora and pleading, "*Calmase*, calm down Aurora! I swear, I didn't know it would be this bad!"

"But Manuel did. He came down here to buy the property."

Flavio threw his hands in the air. "Maybe we're at the wrong place."

Aurora stopped talking in mid-sentence. Flavio turned the wagon around and headed toward Mesilla. They had gotten to town late that evening and hadn't asked for directions.

"I thought this was the right place," Flavio said. "I was going by the map Papá gave me, but I should have asked *Señor* Griego. He sold the land to Papá."

Three miles down the road they stopped at a faded sign tacked to a fence post. It read Griego Ranch. Flavio turned down the rutted road. The adobe house was snuggled against a knoll, cottonwood trees almost hiding it from view.

"There, you see. The house must be near a spring or there wouldn't be any trees. Papá said he bought the ranch because there were springs along the hills so there would be plenty of water."

Aurora craned her neck to inspect the condition of the house. It was large, with a gate in the adobe wall. "This is what I expected," she announced. She waited, with her chin in the air, for Flavio to help her down. A short, round woman came to the gate before they reached it.

"Hello, I'm Flavio Vigil. My father bought the property next to. . . "

Before he could finish, the door was flung open by a tall man holding a rifle. He looked at both of them and broke into a smile.

"Oh, yes, yes, Manuel wrote and told me you were coming. Did you find the place?"

Aurora broke in, "I thought this was the place."

Señor Griego shook his head, "No, this is my home."

Aurora leaned forward and raised her chin a little more. She opened her mouth to speak, but *Señor* Griego interrupted. "Where are my manners? Come in. My wife will fix you something to eat."

He led them across the *plazita* and into the house. While *Señor* Griego was introducing his grown children, Flavio told them that they couldn't stay. They were just looking for directions to the ranch house.

"We found a house, but it was almost fallen in." Flavio glanced cautiously at Aurora. "I thought we had gone down the wrong road. Could you give us directions?"

Señor Griego shook his head. "No, no, you were on the right road."

Aurora huffed and started to turn away.

"Wait," said *Señor* Griego. "That wasn't the ranch house. Keep going over the hill. The house needs some work," he chuckled, "but it's a lot better than my *abuelo*'s old one."

Aurora let her shoulders drop. She smiled and thanked *Señora* Griego for the water. The old woman's face crinkled into a smile. She wrapped her hands around Aurora's.

"It will be good to have another woman nearby. Do you have children?"

Señor Griego put his hand on his wife's shoulder. "They're in a hurry to see their new home," he said. "Why don't you come back and have the evening meal with us." He drew his wife closer. "Then we can talk."

As they left, Flavio gave Aurora a sideways glance. To his relief, she was nodding and smiling.

Flavio turned the wagon around and headed back toward the road they had first discovered. It curved, then slanted downward. Against rose colored cliffs stood a neat little *hacienda*. It was made much like her childhood home, three sided, with a stable across the fourth side. Flavio helped Aurora down from the wagon, then opened the heavy gate. The windows were dusty. Cactus and weeds had sprouted in the little *plazita*. Tumbleweeds that had been trapped in the small courtyard blocked the entrance to the house. Flavio slashed his way through the weeds with a stick and pushed the door open. Aurora stepped inside and turned to Flavio. After a quick look into every room, Aurora announced that it just needed a good cleaning. "I think I can live here," she said.

Flavio broke into a smile and a song. He grabbed Aurora and danced her across the floor, sending up a cloud of dust and laughter.

Aurora pushed the Mesilla ranch back into her memory as they neared her father's house.

20

While she chopped potatoes, Aurora asked Josefa what had happened to all the furniture she had bought for the house at Mesilla.

Josefa stopped rolling her tortilla and studied Aurora. "What made you think of that?" she asked.

Aurora shrugged and said, "I was just thinking how much I was looking forward to having my own home. We were so happy. Now I'm here, back in my father's house. Sometimes I feel like a swallow without a nest. I thought helping *Tio* at the store would make me feel like I was part of life again but, with the boys, it was no good. Now where shall I go?"

Josefa put another tortilla on the griddle, giving herself time to search for an answer. "*Mija*, this is your home. You don't have to go anywhere else."

Aurora threw down the knife and crossed her arms. "No! It's your home and I don't belong here. I belong with my husband, but he's gone. So now where do I belong?" She went to the window and peered down the road.

Rita put her hand over Aurora's. "You have to stay with us for a while. You can't manage by yourself, especially in the winter."

"You don't understand," snapped Aurora, "I know I have to stay here, but I don't want to. I want my own house." She bounded across the room and dropped onto her father's leather chair.

Josefa scooted the tortilla off the stove and knelt in front of Aurora. "Today you're with the people who love you most. Right now, this is where you need to be." Josefa stroked her daughter's hair.

"You'll see," chimed Rita. "Tomorrow you'll feel better. You know, I watch you like a little hawk. What I've seen is that you're having more good days than bad. I was so glad you went to the store with *Tio* today. So what if it didn't go so good? It was your first try. It'll get better." Rita winked at Aurora. "Remember the first tortillas you made. They were supposed to be round, but yours looked like a herd of old cows."

The sisters hugged and went back to the table. "Tell us what happened today," said Rita.

"Well," sighed Aurora, "*Señora* Gavaldon was at the store."

Josefa slapped her cheek. "Oh no," she laughed.

Aurora told them that *Señora* Gavaldon didn't like Manuelito being there. "I said I was sorry, but that's the last time she'll hear those words from me. The store was partly Flavio's, and that makes it partly mine. I can be there anytime I want to."

Josefa raised her eyebrows and smiled at Rita.

❈❈❈

After *Señora* Gavaldon left, José had slid toward Manuel and nudged him. "I don't know about Aurora working at the store. She's still in mourning. What will people say?"

Manuel put up his hands in a helpless gesture. "She was working in the back room. We just have to find a way to keep the children out of the way."

José stroked his chin. "Maybe you're right. Aurora likes being in charge of things. It's good to see her interested again, but the boys." His voice sank to a whisper. "You know Telesfora would gladly take care of them." José started to say more, but stopped when Manuel raised his hand.

Manuel took a sip of coffee and braced himself. He knew that when José got started, nothing could stop his long-winded sermons.

José began to pace. He shook his finger and moved close to Manuel. "Maybe it isn't safe for Aurora to be at the store. There are more *Americanos* coming in every day. They ask me if there's any land for sale and I always tell them no; they're not welcome here."

Manuel turned to José and pursed his lips. He encouraged José not to worry so much. "You know that there isn't any land for sale around here. So, they come and go."

"Yes, but there is property for sale in Socorro."

Manuel nodded in agreement. "Oh, I heard that Adolfo Torres is moving his family from Magdalena because it's getting too rough there. He's going to build a store across from the plaza. One more *Hispano*, and he's a strong man. We'll be able to help each other."

"I hope that's true," said José, "because every time I go to Socorro there's a new gambling hall or saloon. I told my sister that she shouldn't go to town without one of her hired men. It isn't safe for decent women." He leaned closer and whispered. "Don't let Aurora go alone."

Manuel sighed and nodded, then put his cup on the shelf and opened the door for *Señora* Baca. Four children trailed in behind her. Manuel hurried to gather the items on her list and handed out candy

92

to the little ones. José rolled his eyes and threw his hands into the air.

"Sit over here," he commanded. "You have to eat your candy sitting down." He leaned toward Manuel and growled, "Why do you give them candy? They put their sticky hands on everything."

Manuel grinned. "I know," he winked. "I don't want you to run out of things to do. So now you have a reason to clean things up."

José scrambled into the back room waving his arms and complaining. "Maybe it wouldn't be so bad to have Aurora here to help me," he grumbled.

21

Aurora rushed out of church on Sunday. She had spotted her friend Estella. "There you are," she smiled. The two friends embraced. Estella's husband, Juan, gave Aurora a quick hug and joined a knot of young farmers.

His friend Melquides grinned. "I see the hens ran you off."

Juan shrugged his shoulders. "When Aurora shows up, I know it's hopeless to try to talk. At least when Flavio was alive we could leave them to their gossip and talk about important things."

Melquides put his hands in his pockets and kicked the ground. Their silence was broken when Esquipula joined the group. "I think it'll be a good year for the cattle." Aurora's father said. "It's almost the end of November and the grass is still green."

While the men talked about their hay crop and how many piglets had survived, Melquides' eyes kept moving toward the women. His wife, Margarita, was holding Aurora's hand. It looked like they were huddled together in sorrow, Margarita for her brother Flavio, and Aurora for her husband.

The two hadn't seen each other in months. Melquides' land was far north, near Los Lunas. It took every waking hour to coax a living from it. Melquides knew his wife missed her family, but most Sundays were spent cooking and cleaning instead of helping him with the farm.

He had planned to go right back to Los Lunas, but seeing the two women together, he knew that this afternoon would be spent at La Parida.

Manuel motioned for his family to load into the wagon. He asked Melquides to bring Margarita and the baby to the house. "Isabel worked all day yesterday. She wanted the food to be ready in case you could stay."

When Melquides saw Esquipula walking toward his wagon he quickened his steps. He didn't know if he should ask about Aurora. Now that they were alone, he took off his hat and shrugged. "How is Aurora doing? It seems like the light has come back into her eyes."

Esquipula glanced toward his daughter and smiled. "She's starting to tell everybody what to do, and she doesn't want to live in her mother's house anymore."

William

22

"I don't know about selling Eaton the land north of Socorro." Esquipula wiped his brow on his sleeve.

Manuel raised his hand. "It makes sense. It's only fifty acres. Eaton needs that slice of land to get his cattle to the river. We can get a good price for it."

Esquipula spat into the brass spittoon. "Why should we sell to the *gringos*?"

"Because," snapped Manuel, "with that money we can buy the Romero land along the river. It starts at Polvadera and goes almost to Socorro. The territory is growing whether we like it or not. It won't be long before the *gringos* are paying top dollar for land that we can't feed a jackass on."

Esquipula's family sat around the fireplace. Aurora sewed the hem of her new dress and listened to her father discussing the land deal with his brother.

Esquipula threw his hands up. "If you think it's a good deal, I'll go to Socorro with you tomorrow and sign the papers."

Aurora's eyes lit up. She put down her sewing and turned to Josefa. "Maybe I could go with them and take Rufina the corn we promised her."

"We're going to meet with some *gringo* lawyer to fill out the papers. We won't have time to take you to Rufina's house." Esquipula glared at Aurora. "You can stay home and help your mother scrape the rest of the corn off the cobs."

Aurora's lips tightened into a thin line. "Rita can help her. There are still crates to be unloaded. I was going to the store tomorrow, so it doesn't matter if I'm gone."

Esquipula tucked in his chin and stared at Aurora under heavy brows. "The boys don't need to be cooped up in the back room all that time, and your mother needs your help."

"Do this, don't do that. I'm treated like one of the children," Aurora mumbled as she stomped across the *plazita* to her little rooms. *All that beautiful furniture that we bought for Mesilla just stored away. Maybe I can fix up Tia Juanita's old place.* She looked into the next room, crowded with the old loom, two beds, and her wooden chest. *I'll talk to Mamá tomorrow.*

✻✻✻

Manuel picked up Esquipula as the rooster began to crow. He wanted to be at the lawyer's office when it opened, then deliver Esquipula's flour to the stores and check in on his gristmill.

William De Baun's office was at the end of a long adobe building between the park and the road to the San Miguel church. William welcomed his new clients with strong coffee.

The young, fair-haired lawyer stacked the papers on his desk into a neat pile, then drew a document out of his drawer. He offered the Vigil brothers his newly purchased leather chairs.

"I'll have you sign the transfer of deed for the fifty acres. My partner, Jonathan, is going to see Mr. Eaton on some other matters on Friday. He can take this over with him. We'll get it signed and I'll record it." William slid the paper across the desk and rose, ready to shake the hands of the Vigil brothers.

When Esquipula leaned back in his chair, William twisted his mustache and smiled nervously. He resisted the temptation to bow. He had heard about the Vigils from Lemitar and was anxious to bring them into his circle of influential clients. "Is there something else I can do for you?"

"You will probably see us again in a few days," Manuel announced. "With the money from the Eaton sale we're going to buy some land in the *bosque*." Esquipula described the flat farmland that ran toward Socorro.

"You mean the Romero land? Holm Bursum tried to buy that stretch of land. Mr. Romero ran him off."

Esquipula's shoulders heaved as he snickered. William sat and leaned closer to the brothers. He told them about the rumor that the railroad was coming to Socorro. He said that the flat land near the river would be a great place to lay the tracks.

Manuel caught Esquipula's eye. They raised their eyebrows at the same time. "Who else knows about this?" whispered Manuel.

"My law partner told me and warned me to keep it quiet but, since you're buying this prime stretch of land, I thought you should know. Mind you, it's only a rumor. There's a lot to do before the rail line reaches us. Socorro has never been incorporated into a legal town. That has to happen in order for the railroad companies to do business with the local merchants and farmers."

William slid out of his chair and raised his hands. His words tumbled over each other. "Just think what this will do for our community. I'm learning about all the regulations and procedures to get us incorporated." He started pacing as if his small office couldn't contain him.

William turned to Manuel and Esquipula and stepped closer. "This is where I could use your help."

He explained that the first step was to sponsor a petition. "The sponsors have to own land in Socorro," he said.

"If you own land in Socorro, and I think you do, you could be the first to sponsor the petition and get this started."

The Vigil brothers sat in De Baun's office for another hour asking questions and discussing the lengthy procedures of incorporating. In the end, both Manuel and Esquipula thought incorporating would benefit everyone. They shook William's hand, agreeing to help *Señor* De Baun with the incorporation.

The sun was fading by the time they reached the *bosque* . Esquipula threw a sheepskin over their laps and Manuel shared his wool blanket. Both men were hungry and tired, but Manuel turned his buggy toward Pablo Romero's farm. When they arrived, Amalia Romero was putting supper on the table, so Manuel quickly sealed the land purchase with a signature and a handshake. As Pablo walked Manuel to his buggy, Manuel promised to stop by later in the week. "There's something going on that you should know about."

Manuel heaved a heavy sigh and turned to Esquipula, "This means another trip to Socorro so *Señor* De Baun can register Pablo's sale at the courthouse." Manuel wasn't looking forward to another bone-chilling trip, but the brothers didn't want anything to hold up the sale.

23

The sun seeped through the wavy window glass, making ghostly patterns on the packed dirt floor. Aurora opened her eyes to find Flavito beside her bed reaching for her. He raised his arms. "Mamá?" he pleaded.

Aurora let out a deep breath and pulled her son into her bed. *If I cuddle him next to me,* she thought, *he might go back to sleep.* But when her arm reached around his soggy diaper, she knew that morning was upon her. As Aurora reached for a diaper on the shelf, she discovered that Manuelito wasn't in his bed. She grabbed Flavito, ducked out the door, and ran to her mother's. "Manuelito?"

Josefa turned from the water bucket. "Shush, you'll wake up the others." Manuelito was sitting underneath the table doing battle with two wooden horses.

Aurora plopped Flavito down and pulled Manuelito from under the table. With his arm gripped tightly in her fist, she cried, "You don't ever leave our room without telling me, you hear?" She started to shake him, but his big brown eyes filled with tears and Aurora released her grip. His lip began to quiver as he shrank away from his mother. Josefa's firm hand on Aurora's arm stopped her from dragging Manuelito back to his room.

With her fists clenched at her sides, Aurora turned to her mother. "He scared me. I couldn't live if I lost him too." Aurora turned her back to her son so he wouldn't see her tears.

Josefa put down her pail and wrapped her arms around her daughter until her sobbing relented. "I'll have Andres fix a latch on your door. Sit *Mijita.*"

Aurora shuffled to the stove and poured herself a cup of coffee. Before she set it on the table, she remembered that Flavito needed to be changed. She clenched her teeth. "I can't even wake up before I have to start taking care of my boys. I love them, but sometimes I just want to run away." She looked at the floor, then peeked up at her mother. "What's wrong with me?"

Instead of the stiff glare Aurora expected, Josefa was smiling. "Why do you think I get up early in the morning, before everyone else wakes."

As she changed Flavito's diaper Aurora looked around the room.

The only sound was the rattling of the wooden horses. While Josefa peeled potatoes, Aurora rocked Manuelito. She tried to explain to the three-year-old why he shouldn't leave without telling her. The toddler wiggled out of her arms and Aurora started chopping onions for the *chili*.

"Mamá, I was thinking. Maybe I could move into *Tia* Juanita's old house. It would be my own, and it's close."

Josefa let a potato slip into the pan of water. "Oh, I don't know. With you living at home we can all help each other."

"I know, but I want a place of my own," Aurora groaned. "Papá got so mad at me the other day. Maybe he's getting tired of me and the boys living here. I should have been on my own by now."

"Papá wasn't mad at you. He has a lot on his mind. He and Manuel are selling a piece of property to buy some land near Polvadera. It's good farmland, near the river. Oh, and they think that the railroad might come to Socorro." Josefa's hands flew to her mouth. "Oh no, I wasn't supposed to tell anyone!"

Josefa wrapped her hands around her coffee mug and leaned toward Aurora. "Anyway, a lawyer named De Baun told them about it. Your papá doesn't trust the *gringo*, but Manuel likes him. Papá thinks that Manuel is getting too tied up with the *gringo*s."

Aurora had listened to *Tio* Manuel and the other men at the store. A lot of them didn't want all these changes. They said that the *gringos* were trying to wipe them off the land that their families had owned for hundreds of years. But *Tio* Manuel kept saying that the United States had laws to protect their land and the men were fools if they didn't change with the times.

"*Tio* José gets so mad at him but I think *Tio* Manuel is right," continued Aurora. "No one is going to put the silver back in the Kelly mines. No one is going to send the sheep and cattle back to Mexico. No one is going to tear down the new courthouse in Socorro. Things are changing."

Josefa raised her hand, "Enough! I hear enough about this when the men sit on the porch after supper. By the end of the day, I just want to sit and listen to the crickets. If I had a little more help, maybe I wouldn't be so tired."

The women exchanged glares as Aurora's brother, Andres, pushed through the kitchen door. Esquipula stood and stretched in the doorway of his room. When he saw Aurora, he turned to Josefa and raised his eyebrows.

"Yes, I came in early. Manuelito ran over here before I was awake."

Esquipula ruffled Manuelito's hair, smiled at Flavito and accepted the coffee that his wife offered. Aurora started to ask about the land sale, but decided against it. Instead, stirring the *chili*, she asked Josefa how much more corn had to be husked.

"If we start after everyone is through eating, we'll be done before I have to start the noon meal."

Aurora grunted. *Is this what my life is going to be?* she thought. *Will the sound of crickets at the end of the day be the only thing I have to look forward?*

✳ ✳ ✳

Manuel's buggy clattered into the *plazita* and Esquipula sopped up the last of his eggs with a piece of tortilla. Manuel stomped his boots on the porch, then stepped through the door. He gave everyone a quick nod and headed toward the stove to pour himself a cup of coffee. He patted Aurora on the shoulder and hurried past her.

Giggles erupted from beneath the table. A small hand reached out and plucked at its *abuelo's* pants. The big man contorted himself to play peek-a-boo with his grandson. He straightened with a groan. "Well, Esquipula, are you ready to go?"

Aurora started to ask Manuel about the sale of the properties, but one glance at her mother's tight lips and big eyes warned her against it.

Esquipula pulled his hat over his ears. He waved toward the door. "We better go before it starts snowing. I want to get Romero's deed transferred as soon as we can. De Baun said he would open his office early for us."

As soon as the two men climbed into the buggy Manuel asked why Aurora was up so early and helping Josefa.

"Manuelito came over without telling her," Esquipula answered, "and it scared her. She keeps talking about wanting to move into *Tia* Juanita's old house. Maybe what happened this morning will make her realize that she still needs to be at home."

Manuel clicked his tongue and shook his head.

✳ ✳ ✳

Manuel wove through the narrow streets of Socorro and pulled his buggy behind the long adobe structure. The small sign on the door read: *William Tell De Baun and Jonathan Dougherty, Attorneys at Law.*

101

Manuel pounded on the door and waited with his arms wrapped around his chest. A tall unshaven young man emerged, raking his fingers through his blonde hair.

"Mr. Vigil, and Mr. Vigil," he stammered. "I didn't expect you so early."

Esquipula looked at the sky. "The sun has been out for two hours. It's not early."

Manuel grimaced, but said nothing. He just elbowed his brother and pointed toward the door.

William ushered the men into his office. He opened the shutters and started to sit behind his desk. "Oh, would you like some tea or coffee? I'll have to make it, but it won't take long."

The Vigil brothers shrugged at the same time and William disappeared into the room behind his office. When he came back, his suit jacket was on and his pink cheeks glowed with a quick scrub. Cups rattled as he set the tray on the edge of the desk.

"I have the transfer of *Señor* Romero's deed ready for you to sign," William said. "I'll file the papers this morning."

William put the paperwork in his leather briefcase and set it aside. Then he laid out a document and drew in a deep breath. "I've drawn up the petition for the incorporation of Socorro." He wore a wide grin as he handed Manuel the pen. Each of the Vigil brothers signed on a line, then shook William's hand.

William touched his finger tips to his forehead in a mock *Salud* and escorted the brothers to the door. "I'll keep in touch with you about the petition," William smiled.

Esquipula didn't return his smile. Manuel tipped his hat and ducked out the door.

Stepping into the buggy, Esquipula whispered, "I don't trust him. Why is he so anxious to help us?"

Manuel steered the buggy toward the gristmill. "We'll lock up the mill, then come back to the courthouse. I'll check to make sure the papers were recorded and our names are on the new deed."

Esquipula nudged his brother with his elbow. "I feel like we might have put one over on the *gringos*," he said with a satisfied smile.

Manuel's brow knitted. "What are you talking about?"

Esquipula sat up straight. "Well, you know, the Romero property? I'm glad we found out about it. It's one less piece of land the *gringos* will get their hands on." Esquipula slapped his knee. "And the railroad might be going through it."

Manuel took out a cigar and lit it. "You're beginning to sound like José. Besides, Pablo Romero wouldn't have sold to the *gringos* for any amount of money. You know what his family went through up at Taos. He only wanted to sell because his vineyard flooded again last year. He's had enough. He wants the money to buy more cattle for his land on the other side of the river. His son is old enough to run that part of the ranch."

"Nepolito Romero?" Esquipula huffed, then fell silent. "I guess he is old enough, and the Romero land is not too far from La Parida. The Romeros are good people and Nepolito is about the same age as Aurora."

Manuel gave his brother a sideways smirk. "You're thinking too hard again. You better talk to Aurora before you have the priest send out the *bandos*."

Esquipula raised his eyebrows and twisted his mouth. "You're right, I don't know what I was thinking. Nepolito is too young for Aurora; besides, he has his mother's big nose."

The brothers shared a hearty laugh, then wrapped themselves in their own thoughts until the road dipped across the arroyo.

Esquipula helped Manuel heave sacks of flour onto the wagon and secure all the doors at the mill. They started back toward town in silence. Manuel tied his buggy in front of the new courthouse and hurried inside. The two-story brick building loomed over the squat adobes encircling it.

Esquipula gazed up at the court house tower. He jumped down from the buggy and looked toward the plaza. Wooden storefronts surrounded it, and people bustled in and out of stores. He drew in a deep breath. *What happened to all the little adobe houses?* He felt a tightness in the pit of his stomach. *I guess Manuel is right. Things are changing.*

Esquipula walked around the park and peered into shop windows and still Manuel didn't emerge from the courthouse. The sun was dipping close to the mountain. Esquipula took out his pocket watch. He started up the courthouse stairs as Manuel came bounding out.

They hadn't gotten past the park before Esquipula cleared his throat. "I had time to think while you were checking on the papers. I'm starting to feel bad about this deal. Shouldn't we tell Romero about the railroad?"

Manuel gave his brother a sharp look, but Esquipula pushed on. "Aren't we always talking about how we *Hispanos* should stick together, especially against the *Americanos*?"

Manuel groaned. "Look, we didn't know about the railroad when we agreed to buy the land."

Esquipula fixed his eyes on his brother until Manuel relented.

"I guess you're right, especially after what I found out. I checked with *Señor* Baca at the assessor's office. He knows everything that's going on around here. He said he couldn't tell me for sure, but you know, the closer to the river, the flatter the land."

"What do you mean?"

"The flatter the land, the cheaper it is to lay railroad tracks, but I guess the *gringos* don't know about the floods, and who's going to tell them?" We'll stop by Pablo's on the way home."

Manuel pushed his horse to a trot and reached the Romero farm before the sun slipped behind the mesa. With their hands cupped around steaming coffee mugs, the brothers told Pablo what they'd found out. Manuel assured Pablo that they would back out of the deal if that's what he wanted.

"I thought you wanted the land for your farm." Pablo looked at Esquipula. "If it doesn't flood in the spring, you can plant corn, but it was no good for my vineyards."

Pablo's wife, Amalia, put her stout hand on her husband's shoulder and cleared her throat. "We are going to your store tomorrow. We'll let you know what we decide." As Manuel turned the buggy around, he heard loud voices coming from the house.

✳✳✳

The next afternoon, Pablo Romero stepped into the mercantile with his hat in his hand. Manuel pointed his chin toward the back room. Pablo wiped his forehead with his sleeve. He sneaked a quick look at Amalia to make sure she was busy ordering José around.

"I finally convinced her that selling the land was for the best. I've already sent for the cattle, and I don't really think the railroad would build that close to the river. Some *gringos* know what they're doing," he smiled a crooked smile, "and some *gringos* don't."

Manuel sat forward and offered Pablo some pipe tobacco. Pablo waved the offer away. Manuel let his hand rest on his neighbor's shoulder. "I think you did the right thing." He again assured Pablo that he knew nothing about the railroad when he first came to talk to him.

104

"I just thought that since your land was close to Esquipula's, it would be a good chance to add to his farm." They shook hands, and slapped each other on the back.

24

Aurora lifted the heavy *chili ristra* off the rusty hook and handed it down to Rita. When she twisted to lift it over the hook, her back caught, sending searing pain up her spine. Josefa and Rita helped her off the stool. Her mother rubbed the muscles of her lower back. Aurora stood up slowly and breathed deeply. The pain began to drain as her mother helped her to the bench.

"It's time to rest a little," Josefa said. With a nod from her mother, Rita soaked a cloth in cold water. Aurora put it across her forehead and over her eyes.

Josefa lifted Aurora's blouse and rubbed her back with one of La Señora's salves. The scent of *rosa de castilla* couldn't overcome the odor of *pegapega*. Aurora peeked from under the cloth and looked at her mother. She opened her mouth to complain about all the work women had to do, but Josefa's words stopped her.

"Rita, you can finish. I have to start heating up the food. The men will be in from feeding the cattle soon."

Aurora's lips quivered and she sucked up a sniffle. She peered up at Rita with pleading eyes. Rita patted her hand. "I know it isn't easy, but we would have been doing the same thing at Snake Ranch. What did you think your life would be like? You were married to a rancher."

Aurora put her hands over her mouth to stifle a moan. "I guess I didn't think about anything but marrying Flavio. I thought you would take care of the house while I played with the babies."

"I was there to help, but I wasn't there to do it all. Your mother should have made you do more when you were home, learn more, so you would know what your life would be like when you got married. And don't go saying that you want to move to *Tia's* house by yourself. I can't be much help. Andres is almost finished with his house. With him and Barbara gone, I'll have to help Mamá even more."

Aurora pressed her lips tight so the words, "Remember your place." wouldn't be spat out.

Voices coming from the road brought Aurora's thoughts back to the damp cloth on her forehead. She stood, rolled her shoulders, and realized that the pain in her back was gone. She put the damp cloth around her neck and followed Rita to the stove. Soon the room was filled with sweaty, weary men.

She looked at her father as if seeing him for the first time. His elbows rested on the table and he held his head in his hands. Aurora handed her father the damp cloth and started passing out dishes heaped with steaming food.

While Rita washed the dishes and Josefa swept the floor, Aurora gathered up her boys and slipped out the door. "I'll be back after they fall asleep," she said.

Neither woman acknowledged her empty promise.

Aurora lay on the bed next to Flavito. His soft slumbering usually put her to sleep, but today her mind kept tumbling over the never-ending washing, cooking, and caring for children . . . her mother's life. She curled up into a ball and whimpered. How long before her hands were as rough and red as her mother's? At least with Flavio, there was laughter and loving and her own house in Mesilla to look forward to.

Aurora moved to the rocking chair and gazed at the bare branches of the cottonwoods. They bent in the wind and took her thoughts with them. She had imagined herself living in Mesilla as the head of the household, with servants to order about.

She looked down at her rough hands. It was more likely that she would have been the one who washed the baby's clothes and Flavio's filthy pants. Her shiny hair would have dulled as she beat the dust from the rugs. Rita's words suddenly stung her ears, "I can't do it all." When, Aurora wondered, had her life turned into her mother's?

❄ ❄ ❄

With the bleak winter in retreat and before the planting began, the women had a little time to sit by the fireplace in the afternoon. When Manuel sent word that the freight wagons had come in, Aurora jumped at the chance to escape the boredom of embroidery and family gossip. The next morning, she was waiting for Manuel on the porch. She tucked her mother's supply list into her leather bag and loaded her baskets into the back seat of the buggy.

Manuel ruffled Flavito's hair and wrapped Manuelito in his quilt. Then he squeezed Aurora's hand. "Wait until you see what came from St. Louis."

Aurora leaned forward, as if doing so would push the horses faster.

With Manuelito settled in the corner of the storeroom, Aurora got to work unloading crates that were filled with treasures from the

107

East. She was balancing an armload of fabric when she bumped into a solid block of a man. She looked up into eyes the color of the sky.

"Pardon me, ma'am, let me help you with these." William took the bolts of cloth from Aurora and looked around, trying to decide where to put them. He looked down at Aurora for an answer, but she was fixed to the floor.

"*Señor* De Baun," Manuel greeted. He took the fabric from William and plopped it on a pile of shirts. "We were going to see you next Monday. You sent word that we had to sign another paper, something about the petition."

William nodded. "*Señor* Romero has to sign it too, so I decided to come to Lemitar and get all the signatures at once." He nodded. "It'll save you a trip to Socorro."

Manuel touched William on the back. "Thank you. Let's go into my office."

Aurora didn't move as the men brushed past her. She took a deep breath and rushed to José. "Who is that?"

José looked up from wrapping *Señora* Montoya's package. He grunted, "That's the *gringo* lawyer that's helping Manuel and Esquipula with their big land deals." He spat into the spittoon and handed *Señora* Montoya her goods.

"What am I supposed to do? I shouldn't go through the office. They're doing business, but my boys are back there."

"Go!" José waved both arms. "Manuel won't care. It's not like you're disturbing the Pope. De Baun just handles the papers."

Aurora tapped softly at the door and tiptoed into the room. "*Perdón Tio*," She whispered. She began to disappear through the storeroom door when her uncle caught her arm. He stood and bowed slightly at the waist. "*Señor* De Baun, this is the daughter of Esquipula."

William stood and touched his hand to his forehead. "A pleasure to meet you, ma'am."

Aurora stretched to her full length and tipped her head. "*Señor* De Baun." With that, she turned and slipped into the storeroom. As she closed the door an unobstructed smile spread across her face.

What seemed like an instant later, Manuel swung the door open. "I told *Señor* De Baun you could take the papers to your father to sign. He'll pick them up on his way back to Socorro."

Aurora looked around at the crates and dry goods strewn across the floor.

"Leave it. You can come back tomorrow if you want to. If you don't, José will finish up. Take the buggy. I'll ride back with *Señor* De Baun. Oh, and stop by my house and tell Isabel that we'll be having a guest for supper."

William started to object, but Manuel waved his objection away.

Aurora pried her boys away from their toys. With peppermint sticks in hand, they were loaded into the buggy. Before it rumbled past the last house, both boys were asleep. The rattle of wheels brought Aurora's thoughts back to the road. She laughed to herself. "I'm glad you know the way," she said to the horse. When she spotted Manuel's house, she shook off the thoughts of the blue-eyed man. *What am I thinking? I'm going to Flavio's mother's house.*

The blare of children's' voices woke both boys. Before they knew it, Manuelito and Flavito were swept into the pack of Flavio's little brothers and sisters.

"No, no, no!" shouted Aurora. "They need to go in and see their *abuela*, then they can play." She marched the boys into the big room and found Isabel sitting with a basket of clothes in front of her.

Isabel put down her mending and rushed toward them with open arms. "Come and see your *abuela*." She scooped Flavito up and looked from him to Aurora. "He's getting so big. He's not a baby anymore, and Manuelito, he's almost four years old. You need to bring them to see me more often."

Aurora flinched and looked at the floor. "I want to, but there's always so much to do."

Isabel raised her hands and looked to the heavens. "I know, I know."

"I'll bring them over every Sunday afternoon." Aurora sucked in a breath. "That way I can help you with the cooking."

Isabel raised her eyebrows and tilted her head. "Won't your mother need you?"

"Rita is there and Andres is moving his family to their new house. Besides, we don't have to stay all afternoon. We don't usually have our big meal until evening."

Isabel put Flavito down and chased Manuelito to the door. She managed to give him a big squeeze before he escaped to the *plazita*.

Isabel poured two glasses of cool water. She flavored each with a sprig of peppermint. As Aurora took a welcome sip, Isabel set her rough hand on Aurora's face. "You look so much better," she said.

Aurora blushed. "You were right when you told me that it would take time." She blew out a deep breath. "Time, there doesn't seem to be enough of it in a day."

The women shook their heads and laughed. Aurora's tight shoulders dropped as she started telling Isabel all the gossip from the store. "

"Oh, I almost forgot, *Tio* Manuel is bringing home the lawyer that's helping him with the papers for the petition."

"What?" Isabel stood and looked at the stove. "Does that man expect me to pull food out of the sky?" She lifted the heavy lid of the storage box. With her hands in the air, she trotted to the back room. "I have some *carne adobada* and plenty of potatoes." She swung open the door and ordered Lupita to bring in a basket of *calabazitas*.

"What time is it? I'll have to make extra tortillas. Oh wait, he's a *gringo*. I wonder if he'll eat what we eat."

Aurora looked up and saw that Flavio's mother's face was drawn. Her eyes were brimming with tears.

"A *gringo* sitting at our table. Why did Manuel do this?"

"Oh, I met him at the store. He seems like a nice man." Aurora brushed crumbs from the table, not daring to look at Flavio's mother. "I'm sure *Tio* was only thinking about feeding him before he traveled back to Socorro. I can stay and help for a while."

Isabel shoved more wood into the stove and slammed the cast-iron pan on it. She combed her fingers through her hair. "Well, you could put the dishes on the table, but Lupita and Guadalupe can help me. He's only one man. There won't be that much extra food to cook. It's just that he's a lawyer and a *gringo*, but I guess we have to get used to them." She made the sign of the cross on her forehead and asked Saint Michael to protect her family.

"Tell the children to go to the pump and wash up," Isabel ordered, "and they better come in and change their clothes." Lupita pushed open the door with her foot and brushed past Aurora with her basket of squash.

Aurora hugged Isabel good-bye and slipped out the door. She herded the children toward the pump and gave them their orders. Amidst much squawking and a little kicking fit, Aurora managed to gather her boys and start home.

Aurora sat back in the buggy, passing houses without noticing them. Before she had talked to Isabel, she couldn't wait to tell Rita about the tall blue-eyed *gringo* she met at the store. Now she knew that she wouldn't say a word about him.

25

Esquipula saw the buggy in front of his house and quickened his pace. "Where's Manuel?" he asked as soon as he pushed through the door.

Aurora stopped chopping potatoes. Her hand went to her mouth. "Oh, I almost forgot; I drove *Tio's* buggy back. *Señor* De Baun will come by so you can sign some papers. He's going to eat with Tio Manuel, then I guess he'll be here afterward."

Esquipula grunted. He poured warm water into a bowl to wash off the grime of the day. He picked Flavito up and swung him around, then chased Manuelito around the table. Flavito squealed and jumped up and down until his uncle Andres gave chase too.

"Enough!" Josefa shooed the children out the door. Esquipula gave her a pat on the bottom. She slapped his hand away in mock annoyance.

Aurora watched from the table. *How many times*, she thought, *had her father picked her up and twirled her around? How many times had she seen that special look between her parents?* Then her smile turned upside down. *How many times had she and Flavio swung Manuelito between them as they walked to the barn? How could these memories have faded so soon? What's the matter with me? I won't even speak to De Baun when he comes in.*

When Manuel and William De Baun arrived, Esquipula introduced Josefa. She nodded stiffly, eyes on the floor. Rita turned from the table and looked at Josefa. Unable to catch her mother's eye, she scraped leftovers into the dog's bowl and handed the dishes to Aurora. Aurora poured hot water into the galvanized tub. When Josefa turned away from the men, she spied Aurora scrubbing and rinsing. Stunned into silence, Josefa shrugged and retreated to her sewing basket.

Aurora didn't have to avoid the visitors for long. Esquipula poured wine for Manuel and William and invited them to sit on the *porche*.

William tipped his hat, "It was nice to meet all of you."

Rita stopped sweeping and stared at the tall stranger. Josefa gave him a thin smile. Aurora didn't turn away from her dishes.

William pulled his jacket tight and drank his wine quickly. With the papers signed, he steered his buggy toward Socorro.

After the dishes were put away, Aurora went outside to the porch. Her boys ran ahead to their room, but she lingered, leaning against the post and fanning herself.

The brothers stopped talking and fixed their eyes on her.

"Is it dry enough to plant?" She asked her father.

"*Segudo*, for sure" he answered. "With the men I've hired, I'll have the seed in the ground by the end of the month."

Aurora wanted to ask about the land they bought and the incorporation of Socorro, but she knew that neither man would talk to her about it. She took a few steps off the porch, and simply asked Manuel if he needed her at the store tomorrow.

Manuel looked from Esquipula to Aurora. "I could use a little more help, but why don't you leave the boys with Telesfora. You know she would be happy to take care of them, and you would get your work done faster."

"She only wants to help," added her father.

Aurora huffed and looked back at Manuel. "I guess it would be alright." Aurora set her jaw. "Then I could be back in time to help Mamá feed the hired men." She shuffled toward her room with the two men watching.

"She's doing a lot more around here," Esquipula sighed. "Thank you for letting her help at the store once in a while."

Manuel crossed his legs and poured himself another glass of wine. "She's coming back, but I'm not sure she wants to be stuck at La Parida."

Esquipula shook his head. "It's been almost two years. Now she's talking about wanting a house of her own. I don't know if this is a good or bad thing."

"She has a home and a family, Flavio's family." Manuel stuffed his hat on and strode to his buggy. "What else does she need?" He gave his brother a backhanded wave. "I'll see you tomorrow."

"I'm glad we're done with the Romero deal." Esquipula yelled. "Maybe we won't have to see that *gringo* anymore,"

Manuel rolled his eyes before stepping into his buggy. "They aren't going away and, as much as I hated looking at those blue eyes, De Baun isn't the man who killed my son. Besides, there aren't any *Hispano* lawyers. I had to use him."

Esquipula took a deep breath. He started to say, "but you didn't have to bring him to our homes." He stopped himself before the words escaped. He knew that his brother felt the same way he did. Why add to his pain?

✳✳✳

Manuel hopped down from his buggy and slapped his hat against his leg. Fine white powder filled the air. His face was covered with a dusting of flour. When Josefa saw him, she put her hand over her mouth to hide a grin. Rita dusted off his shoulders. "*Tio*, you look like you just came in from a snowstorm," she teased.

"I had to help at the mill," he answered. "Most of the men are in the fields helping with the planting. I've been so busy that I forgot to send the second page of the petition to the lawyer." He moved toward Aurora. "José said that you were going to Socorro on Sunday. You can take the paper to *Señor* De Baun."

"Me?" Aurora's eyes grew wide. "Why can't *Tio* José take it?"

"You know how he feels about *gringo*s. I don't have time to argue and listen to another sermon on how our land was taken away. The church is just up the street from his office. Just walk over with Santa Cruz and give it to him."

Manuel shoved the envelope into Aurora's hand and returned to his buggy. Aurora surveyed the envelope. Her chest tightened.

✳✳✳

The day before, when Aurora had picked up the boys, Telesfora had invited her to ride to Socorro on Sunday. Her sister Maria's granddaughter was being baptized. "I knew you would want to go, and we can show off your two beautiful boys. Everyone will be surprised at how much they've grown."

Aurora had smiled. "Will Gloria be there? It feels like I haven't seen anyone in Socorro for years. All I do is help Mamá. When I help *Tio* at the store, I barely have time to stop at Estella's before I have to go home."

Aurora looked into the kitchen where the boys were busy dunking *bizcochitos* into sloppy mugs of milk. Telesfora gathered up the clothes she had washed for them.

"I hope you don't mind," she smiled. "I made them some new shirts. Look, they match." She smiled down at curly black halos of hair and kissed each boy on the head. "They are beautiful," she said to no one in particular.

Aurora twisted one of Flavito's curls around her finger. She smiled in agreement. "We better go so I can help mamá with the evening

114

meal."

"I'll pick you up after breakfast on Sunday," Telesfora said.

With kisses and endless hugs, Aurora managed to escape Telesfora's embrace. The ride home wasn't long enough to unravel her thoughts. After the dishes had been washed, and the dry clothes brought in from the line, Aurora finally got to sit on the *porche* with her mother and Rita.

"Telesfora really seems to love the boys," Aurora whispered. "Maybe I was wrong about her."

Josefa rubbed her daughters back. "Remember, *Mija*, what you were going through."

The women watched the evening sun light up the new leaves on the sage brush. They chatted about the people who came into the store. Aurora wanted to ask what they thought about the fair-haired lawyer who had come to their house, but she remembered how her mother had spat into the stove after he left. So, she just sat listening until the crickets started their evening songs.

❋❋❋

Aurora dressed her boys in their matching shirts and velvet pants. Before they wiggled away, she held each of their faces between her hands and gave them a soft kiss.

"Oh, good," she sighed, "Telesfora and José are here. You won't have a chance to get dirty." She took both boys by the hand and marched them to the wagon. On the way to Socorro, Aurora told the boys who lived in each farm house they passed. When they could see the roofs of the houses in Socorro, Aurora remembered the envelope.

"*Tio* José, *Tio* Manuel asked me to give. . ."

José waved her away. "I know. He shouldn't have asked you. You can't see a single man by yourself. I'll have to go with you."

Aurora's chest tightened. She hoped she could win this argument. "Maybe Santa Cruz can go with me. It will just take a minute. I won't even have to go inside."

José grunted. Telesfora quickly filled in the silence with a song about a little bean plant that wound its way around the window. Aurora sat back and breathed in deeply. She shot a glance at Telesfora to make sure she hadn't noticed how anxious she was.

After the baptism, Aurora and Santa Cruz found the lawyer's office door with a little sign next to it. Her brother pushed her aside and knocked. After a moment, William pulled the door open. Shading

115

his eyes with his hand, he peered out to see who was knocking on a Sunday.

Santa Cruz nudged his sister. "My *Tio* Manuel sent me with the second page of the petition," Aurora said. "He forgot it."

"Oh good," smiled William. "I thought I'd have to go clear to Lemitar to get it. Won't you come in?"

Santa Cruz tipped his hat and turned to leave. "We can't. We have to go to *Tia* Maria's. Come on Aurora."

She looked back as they hurried away. William was still in the doorway watching them trot down the road. Aurora wanted to scold her brother for being so rude, but she was afraid her voice would be shaky. The fluttering in her chest seemed to have a mind of its own.

❄❄❄

"Aurora, where were you?" asked Maria. "It's so good to see you. I haven't seen you in so long."

After the cousins hugged, Maria took Aurora by the hand and led her into the crowd. Telesfora was in the center of a circle of women who were cooing and vying for a chance to squeeze Flavito's little round cheeks. When Manuelito saw his mother, he made a dash for her. She took his hand and led him to a cluster of cousins.

Maria tapped her on the shoulder. "Come and see the baby. She's so tiny."

Aurora glanced back at the children and decided it would be alright to leave Manuelito for a few minutes. She picked up Flavito and followed Maria. Flavito touched the newborn's nose then reached to grab her. Aurora pulled him away. "No, no, *Mijito*! She's too little for you to hold."

Aurora carried Flavito back to the children. Standing beside Manuelito was *Tia* Telesfora. She tapped Aurora's shoulder, then reached for Flavito "You go enjoy yourself. They'll be alright with me."

Aurora looked from her children to the crowd of familiar faces. She finally dropped her shoulders and joined the young women who had gathered on the back porch.

"Where were you?" They all asked at once.

"I saw Telesfora with your boys, but you weren't with her. I thought she had brought them and you weren't coming," said Dolores.

"Oh no, I came with her, but Papá wanted me to take some papers to the lawyer De Baun. It only took a few minutes."

"What?" her cousin, Dolores, giggled.

The women were looking at each other with wide grins.

"What's going on?" asked Aurora, "I had to go! *Tio* sent me, and Santa Cruz went with me." The redness in Aurora's throat crept into her face.

Dolores swiped the air. "It's alright. Don't worry. It's just that we've all been watching him. He's so handsome."

"Yes," Hilaria broke in, "and my father says he's one of the good *gringo*s, as far is he can tell."

"And you've met him and talked to him?" Bernarda chimed in. "I don't think he's much older than me. You know, he doesn't have a wife."

The women erupted in giggles.

"Now I know why you made so many visits to the church," Hilaria teased Bernarda. "His office is just around the corner."

"He lives on the same street as you do. Is that why you take so many evening walks?" countered Bernarda.

This time it was Hilaria's turn to stammer and blush.

Aurora stood aside from her young cousins. She rolled her eyes. "You girls. He's a *gringo*. What would your fathers say?"

The women fell silent, but the smile that crept across Aurora's face gave her away. With all eyes on her, she had to admit, "Alright, he is handsome."

Bernarda squeezed her hands together. "So, you've talked to him?"

"Only for a minute, and I doubt if I'll ever see him again."

As the afternoon waned, Aurora learned that Dolores was going to Lemitar the next morning. Aurora slipped into the circle of older women sitting in the parlor. Tapping Telesfora on the shoulder, Aurora drew her into a quiet corner.

"There's so much news. I want to hear it all. Mamá and Rita will want to know what's happening in Socorro." She squeezed her hands together like a child begging for candy. "I'd like to stay here tonight. I can ride back with Dolores in the morning."

Telesfora was quick to agree. "I can help Josefa feed the planting crew." She lifted her chin. "I'll take the boys back with me. That way you can have a good visit with the girls."

Tio José began leading the boys out the door. Aurora stepped in front of him.

"No, I want them with me. They can play with Dolores's girls."

As Aurora picked up Flavito and grabbed Manuelito's hand, a tight-lipped glare passed between José and Telesfora.

26

The next morning William gathered up his petitions and strode with his law partner toward the court house. "I'm glad Esquipula's son and his wife brought me the last of the paperwork," said William. "I didn't want to waste the day going back to Lemitar."

"I'm surprised that Esquipula could spare one of his sons. They're all busy working in the fields."

"This was yesterday. He said they were going to the church. Maybe it was Esquipula's daughter and her husband." William rubbed his chin. "He looked a little young for her."

As they crossed the plaza, Jonathan stopped and turned toward William. "Esquipula's daughter? You mean Aurora?"

"Yeah, I think that was her name. I met her the other day at Manuel's store."

Jonathan made a grumbling sound. "Aurora isn't married. That must have been one of her brothers with her."

As they climbed the courthouse stairs, Jonathan's words sunk in and the corners of William's mouth turned up.

While Jonathan held the door open, he said, "Don't go getting any ideas. There's bad blood between that family and us *Americanos*."

Before William could ask why, Jonathan rushed into the assayer's office and William went down the hall to file the petitions.

✳✳✳

Dolores had to make a stop at the Torres Mercantile before they left town. The fabric for her dress had come in.

"I think I'll stay in the buggy with the children." Aurora said, "They'll all cry for candy and they had enough at the baptism."

"I'll just be a minute. *Señor* Torres has my things ready for me."

Aurora's gaze wandered toward the beautiful courthouse. The two-story brick building, with its towers, shown like a diamond in the mud. *Socorro is getting to be quite a little town*, she thought.

She didn't notice William walking across the plaza until he stopped in mid-stride. He changed directions and came toward the buggy.

"Good morning, Miss Vigil."

Aurora sucked in her breath. "*Señor* De Baun."

William reached over and tickled Flavito. You have quite a handful. Are these all your cousin's children?"

Aurora managed a shaky smile. "This is Flavito my youngest son." She drew Manuelito to her, "And this is my other son Manuelito."

William dropped his head and managed to close his mouth. He looked up and down the street, trying to give himself time to unravel his confusion. He looked at the four-year-old climbing over the wagon seat.

"Manuelito, so he was named after his uncle?"

Aurora started to say, "and my husband's father," but she didn't think William would understand. "Yes," she answered.

"So, you work at your uncle's store?"

"Only when the freight comes in." Aurora was grateful for the chance to take a good look at William. She liked the way his full mustache twitched when he talked. She looked away when he caught her staring at the blonde curls brushing his collar.

William shook off what Jonathan had said. He must have been mistaken about Aurora being single. "And your husband, does he work with your father on the farm?"

Aurora's breath caught in her throat. Everyone knew what happened to Flavio. She had never had to explain to anyone. "I, uh, he's. . . " Her hands began to tremble. She could feel the blood draining from her face. "He's no longer with us. He's in God's hands now."

Williams swayed backwards. "Oh, I'm sorry. I didn't mean to upset you."

Aurora looked toward the store. She closed her eyes and let out a breath between her teeth. She was grateful that Dolores was walking toward her with arm full of supplies. William tipped his hat and started to reach for Aurora's hand, then quickly changed his mind.

"Again, I'm sorry. I hope to see you. . . and your family again."

Dolores climbed into the wagon and craned her neck to see who Aurora was talking to.

"We can go now!" Aurora commanded.

Dolores' brow knitted, "Aren't you going to introduce us?"

Aurora twisted around to face her cousin. She wanted to say. "You know who he is," but instead, she softened her features and said simply. "Dolores Baca, this is William De Baun, my father's lawyer."

William stepped back and allowed the wagon to ease into the street. Neither woman looked back or said good-bye.

"So that's *Señor* De Baun," Dolores grinned. "My father says he's trying to make a lot of changes in Socorro. He says that maybe it's time to start accepting that the world has changed. The *Americanos* are here to stay and Socorro has grown so much since they came."

Aurora was glad she didn't have to talk. Looking at the new Chambone Hotel, she knew that Dolores' father was right.

Aurora changed the direction of the conversation. "So, you like living in Socorro? *Tio* José is always worried when I come to Socorro. 'Don't go past the gambling halls by yourself. Make sure there aren't any miners or stinking cowboys on your side of the street.' Don't you feel afraid sometimes?"

"Well, I just don't go down Manzanares Street and I go to town with Sinforosa or *Tia* Manuela." She elbowed Aurora. "You know how your Tio José is. He never sees the good in anything. Never mind him," Dolores smiled. "So, what do you think of *Señor* De Baun?"

Aurora's throat tightened. She spoke slowly, "Oh, he seems alright, but he asked me about my husband. I didn't know what to say."

"Why would he ask about your husband?"

Aurora shrugged. "I just thought he was asking about my family. I couldn't think. I was too busy trying to find an answer. You know, that was the first time I had to tell anyone about Flavio." She put out her hand. "I'm still shaking a little. Let's talk about something else. I don't really care about *Señor* De Baun."

Dolores put her arm around her cousin and drew her close. "You're right, we're almost out of town." She pointed toward the north. "Look how the *bosque* has turned green and the air is warming up."

Aurora nodded. She gave Flavito a little hug and tried to shake off Socorro and *Señor* De Baun.

❋ ❋ ❋

The summer heat had brought ripe gardens and deep house cleaning. Manuel didn't have time to take Aurora home in the afternoon, so she rarely went to the store. She washed bedding and swept off the *vigas*. As she helped clean out the cellar, the memory of *Señor* De Baun began to fade.

27

When the evenings began to cool and the fields were put to rest, Aurora's family breathed a sigh of relief. They looked forward to the *Fiesta* de San Miguel in Socorro. Held the first week of September, it was a welcome celebration. But when Esquipula learned that his sister's house was full, he threatened not to go.

"Whoever heard of staying at a hotel?" he huffed. "I don't care if Manuel is throwing his money away at the Grand Hotel. We can sleep in the back room at the Pino's."

Aurora tightened her fist, "Papá, *Tio* Manuel has stayed in hotels in the big Eastern cities. He's used to hotels and restaurants. All we women know is working from sunup to sundown, then dragging into the house to make supper."

"And the food you make for supper was put there because I worked from sunup to sundown. You're the daughter of a farmer, not some fancy city lady. We'll stay at your *Tio* Vicente's house. It's right behind the church so we can walk to the fiesta."

Esquipula slammed his hand on the table, stuffed on his hat, and stormed out the door.

Aurora, her lips in a pout, looked from her mother to Rita. Josefa turned to the stove and Rita finished folding the clothes.

"Get me some water." Josefa handed Aurora the bucket and started measuring the flour for tortillas.

When Aurora came back in, Josefa said, "Don't be so mad at your father. The family will make room for us. That's the way it's always been. I wouldn't know what to do in a hotel with all those strangers."

Aurora glanced at Rita who just shrugged. She shook her head and handed the basket of clothes to Aurora. Then she started rattling the plates and silverware onto the table.

Carrying her folded clothes to her room, Aurora welcomed the chance to escape the women. The harvest is done, the fruit is drying, the *chili* has been hung, Aurora thought. *Maybe it's time for me to spend a few days at Gloria's. I'll talk to Papá about staying with her. That way they'll have more room at Tio Vicente's.*

✳ ✳ ✳

It was Manuel and Isabel who took Aurora and the boys to Gloria's. Her sister and family were there from Magdalena so Aurora had to share a bed with her boys in the *casita* behind the stable. She looked around the adobe room filled with worn furniture that no longer served in the main house.

"We could have stayed at the Grand Central," she said to Manuelito.

He skipped toward the door. "Can I go outside?"

Putting Flavito down, she dropped her bag on the squeaky bed, took out her new dress, and spread it across the headboard. She sat for a while with her head in her hands, then heard laughter coming from Gloria's house.

Her mood changed the moment she stepped into the house. Aurora was swept away with the stories the women were telling and the laughter that filled the room. As soon as the sun dipped behind the mountain, everyone clambered into wagons and buggies and headed for the churchyard. Patricio played the guitar and Aurora allowed herself to join the singing. At first, she was startled to hear her own voice. *How long has it been since I have sung?*

They heard the *fiesta* before they saw the canopies and tables. The band was already playing lively *rancheritas*. Aurora had to hold on to Manuelito to keep him from jumping off the wagon and joining the children who were circling the dancers.

Manuel waved and pointed to the table he was saving for them. Aurora squeezed through the crowd. She handed Flavito to Isabel's outstretched arms.

"Come here to your *abuela*," Isabel cooed. She bounced him up in the air until he was bubbling with laughter.

Aurora put her arms around Isabel and gave her a kiss. She looked around at all the familiar faces. Then she saw a table full of strangers at the edge of the canopy. The *Americanos* were laughing and talking just like the people she had grown up with. When a new song started up, couples swirled onto the dance floor and everyone in her little group clapped to the music. Aurora looked from the dance floor back to the *Americanos*. There was William clapping and tapping his foot. As much as Aurora wanted to look away, she couldn't.

Aurora shook her thoughts of William away. She was brought back to her group when Gloria poked her and pointed to her sister. Aurora threw back her head with laughter. Gloria's sister and her husband were high-stepping around the dance floor, elbows flying.

She clapped her hands, then Aurora' smile faded. *At least I can watch the dancing.* she thought, as memories of her Flavio flooded back.

Aurora spotted Rita out of the corner of her eye. She was signaling for Aurora to join her. Aurora pushed through the crowd and the pain in her chest didn't complete its journey to the pit of her stomach.

When they were away from the crowd, Rita put her arm around her sister. "I saw the sadness fill your eyes. I hope this isn't too much for you."

"Flavio used to love to dance." Aurora whispered.

"I know *Mija.*" Rita squeezed Aurora's hand. "Maybe we can go back to *Tio*'s house for a while. We can say that Flavito is getting tired."

Aurora nodded. "Every time I forget a little, something hits me over the head and reminds me."

Then Rita looked up and caught a glimpse of Josefa waving frantically. "Rita, Aurora, we need more plates!"

Aurora released her memories and made her way to the makeshift kitchen that was set up behind the dance floor. She took a stack of plates out of a crate and started toward the tables.

The music started up again. Gloria and the others clapped along to their favorite song. Aurora looked at them and frowned. She slammed the plates down in front of them, but they didn't notice.

"I can't even enjoy the *fiesta* without having to serve," Aurora pouted.

"Oh, you poor thing," Gloria teased. "You're almost finished with the plates." She nodded toward a cluster of young men. "Maybe someone will ask you to dance."

Aurora tightened her lips and stepped backwards. "Oh no, no, I'm past dancing!"

Gloria stopped clapping. When she turned to face her friend, her eyes were brimming with tears. "Aurora, you're only twenty years old. Quit talking like you're an old lady." She put her arm around Aurora. "Yes, I know you're a widow, but you're still so young."

Gloria didn't have time to say more. Josefa and Isabel nudged her out of the way and set platters of steaming tamales on the table.

Aurora and Rita started passing them out, but Manuel's chair was empty. Josefa shrugged, then pointed with her chin toward the crowd. Aurora plopped a tamale on his plate and continued around the table. When Aurora looked up, she saw William following her uncle to their table.

"I told *Señor* De Baun that I had to get back to my table because I saw the tamales." He gave José a quick glance. "He said he'd like to try one." Manuel signaled for Josefa to put a couple of tamales on a plate, but she just stood, her hand in midair.

José stood so quickly that his chair threatened to topple over. Manuel squinted and excused himself. He grabbed José's elbow and pulled him to the edge of the crowd.

"What could I do?" Manuel shrugged. "He's trying to be part of the community. And he helped me with the land deal. Let him have the dammed tamales and we can get back to enjoying the fiesta." Manuel made his way back to the table, but José disappeared into the crowd.

At the table, the laughter and talking had stopped. All eyes were fixed on the tall *Americano*. Manuel cleared his throat and broke the silence by introducing the family.

William's head bobbed as Manuel rattled off names. Finally, William shook his hands in the air. "Stop, *Señor* Vigil; I can't keep track of who's who!"

Manuel laughed and slapped William on the back. "Well, maybe you'll stay in Socorro long enough to figure us all out, but I doubt it."

Aurora stood in front of the surprise guest with a tamale limp in her hand. She picked up a plate, plunked the tamale on it and handed it to him without a word,

He started to say, "*Gracias Señora* Vigil," but stopped before he made a mistake. Instead of going back to his table as expected, William took an empty chair and placed it next to Esquipula. The family took silent bites of food between sharp glances at William.

As more food was passed around, William began sorting out the people at the table. Manuel was married to Isabel. Esquipula was Manuel's brother. Aurora was Esquipula's daughter, but William thought he heard her being called *Señora* Vigil.

He shook his head. Vigil was Esquipula's last name, so how could she still be Vigil when she had been married?

William looked around. Manuel had turned his back to him and was laughing with a circle of men. He heard bits of Spanish words above the music. Now was not the time to ask. William stood, tipped his hat and thanked the women for the food.

The sky darkened and the wind picked up, but the dancers kept twirling. Aurora and Rita retreated to a circle of young women with babies. They caught up on all the news from San Antonio to Magdalena. Flavito lay asleep in her lap. Manuelito forced himself to stay awake on Rita's lap despite her soft swaying.

Aurora wrapped her shawl tighter and asked Gloria if she was ready to go.

"Hours ago, but my sister won't stop dancing." Gloria rubbed her swollen middle.

Aurora gave Gloria a little hug. "Oh, I almost forgot that another little one is on the way."

Aurora was about to suggest that they take the children to the wagon when someone sat in the chair beside her.

"Good evening *Señora* Vigil."

Aurora drew in a breath. "*Señor* De Baun."

William leaned over and wrapped one of Flavito's curls around his finger. "What a beautiful little boy you have there. Your father must be very proud of both of them."

Aurora looked at Rita, eyes wide. "Well, thank you. They're both so tired. I was just about to take them to our wagon. I hope Gloria's sister is ready to go. All the children are getting tired."

William stretched and took a deep breath. "It's about time for me to turn in too. I tried to find your uncle to tell him how much I've enjoyed the evening, but he's nowhere to be found. Please give him my adieu."

A breeze swept through the crowd and Aurora caught the scent of William's cotton shirt and a hint of the cigar he'd been smoking. She caught herself leaning forward and tilting her head to see the curls on the nape of his neck. She straightened up and looked around. People were either leaning on tables, eyes half closed, or dancing.

"I'll tell my uncle you said good-bye."

"Good night, *Señora* Vigil. Maybe I'll see you sometime at your uncle's store."

William pushed his chair in and started walking away. Aurora sat back and waited for him to disappear into the darkness before she stood and motioned for Rita to follow her to the wagon.

As they stumbled through the darkness, Rita was grinning from ear to ear. She giggled and pointed at Aurora. "Bernarda," she teased. "Oh, he's so handsome, and those eyes."

Aurora twisted and cocked her head. "What are you babbling about? Have you gone crazy?"

"Oh, don't think I didn't see. You almost fell off your chair, you were leaning so close."

"What are you talking about? I was not leaning. You watch what you say and don't go talking to anyone else. It was bad enough that he came and sat down by me. Thank heavens no one seemed to notice."

Rita slowed her pace, distancing herself from Aurora. She swallowed the words she wanted to say. Then she mouthed to herself, "So what if you like him."

By the time they reached the wagon, the heat had drained from Aurora's face. She laid Flavito on some blankets and climbed into the wagon. Rita handed Manuelito to her.

With the boys wrapped in their little cocoon of blankets, Aurora and Rita sat curled up on the wagon floor sharing Aurora's big shawl.

Aurora pulled it away from Rita. "I'm still mad at you."

Rita tugged back. "Would it be so bad to love again?"

Aurora gasped "How could I? Besides, he's a *gringo*."

Rita looked up at the stars and rolled her eyes. "I hear and see more than people think. The men are saying good things about *Señor* De Baun. He wants to help Socorro grow and he's willing to help the *Hispanoes*. He's not like some of the other *gringos* who think they're better because they brought their big ideas to New Mexico."

Aurora just shrugged, her thoughts twisting like a rattlesnake.

28

Late the next morning Manuel and Isabel gathered up Aurora and their two grandsons. When they got to Socorro, Manuel turned onto Manzanares Avenue.

"Where are we going?" asked Aurora.

Manuel just smiled. The buggy stopped in front of the Grand Central Hotel.

"We should have a meal before we go back to Lemitar." He turned and wrapped his arms around the boys. "We're going inside to eat. *Pórtarsen bien*, behave yourselves."

His stern look convinced the boys that he was serious. They nodded their heads in unison. With Manuelito at her side, Aurora trailed behind her uncle as they entered the hotel restaurant. Aurora strolled into the room with her chin in the air. *Finally*, she thought, *I get to sit and have someone serve me*. Manuel took the menu out of Aurora's hand and ordered for the family.

"Is this what the Eastern hotels are like?" Aurora asked, looking around at the heavy drapes and fine china.

Manuel huffed out a deep laugh. "This is nothing. They're ten times as big, and the menus, who knows what to order?" Manuel swept his hand across the room. "The tables even go outside."

Aurora's eyes got big and began to sparkle. "I wish I could go with you, just once."

Isabel patted her on the hand and gave her a sympathetic smile. Aurora's face twisted into a pout. She looked down at all the forks and spoons that sat on linen tablecloths.

"Will it ever happen?" She asked in a soft voice.

Manuel grabbed Flavito and sat him on the chair. "Maybe when the boys get older."

Aurora shook off her disappointment and decided to enjoy her first restaurant meal. She watched Isabel unfold her napkin and lay it on her lap. As she did the same, Aurora looked toward the table that Manuel was waving to.

William waved back and Jonathan touched his fingers to his forehead. Aurora sat up a little straighter. Then she remembered her conversation the night before.

"Oh, *Señor* De Baun wanted me to tell you that he enjoyed the fiesta and to say adieu, whatever that means."

"Who knows?" shrugged Manuel. "They don't speak the King's Spanish. You just have to keep your mouth shut and pretend you understand them."

The waiter arrived with an armful of plates heaped with thick slices of bacon, fried potatoes, and eggs. A tower of toasted bread was set in the middle of the table along with a crystal jar of raspberry jam.

Aurora put Flavito on her lap and Isabel scooted Manuelito close to her. When the meal was finished, Isabel spooned jam from the crystal jar on bits of toast and delighted her grandsons with the treat. Aurora chatted about the people she had seen at the fiesta. She thought if she kept talking, her mind wouldn't keep floating back to William.

The lawyers stood and sauntered over to Manuel's table. Manuel stood. Looking at Jonathan he said, "Let me introduce my family." When he got to Aurora, he said, "This is my daughter-in-law." He ruffled Manuelito's hair, "and these are my grandsons."

William cocked his head. His mouth gaped open a little.

"*Señor* Vigil," stammered William. "Did your niece, uh, your daughter-in-law, tell you how much I enjoyed the fiesta?"

Manuel put down his napkin. "*Seguro*, for sure. I'm glad you enjoyed it."

Isabel looked up. "Are you a member of San Miguel?"

"No, no, I'm not, so I didn't understand a lot of the prayers and rituals. It was all in Latin. Did you understand it?" he asked, looking at Aurora.

"Of course I did. I've been hearing the Mass of San Miguel since I was a child."

William swallowed a nervous chuckle and nudged his law partner. Jonathan took the hint and they said a quick goodbye.

The lawyers walked up Camino Royal Street toward their office. Before the men went their separate ways, William asked the question he'd been holding onto since last night.

"I'm so confused about the Vigil family. I can't understand who's related to who."

Jonathan laughed, "Get used to it. They're all related."

William scrunched up his face. "Yeah, I'm beginning to realize that, but it's Aurora I'm wondering about. She's Esquipula's daughter so she's Manuel's niece, but he just introduced her as his daughter-in-law."

Jonathan pointed toward the office. "This may take a while. Let's have a cup of coffee and I'll tell you all about it."

With the men sitting on the back porch, Jonathan began. He explained that Aurora married Manuel's son Flavio. They were cousins. He was shot and killed down in Mesilla. The man who shot him was a cowboy from Texas.

"I'm surprised Manuel is so friendly. The locals don't exactly welcome us with open arms, and that family has a reason to hate our kind," snorted Johnathan."

William swirled the coffee in his cup. "So that's why Manuel had a chip on his shoulder when he first came into the office. I thought his arrogance was just that old Spanish family attitude. He softened up when he thought I knew what I was doing. And, of course, I treated him with the utmost respect."

Jonathan took another sip of coffee. "You better; he owns a lot of businesses, and that brother of his, he owns some of the finest farmland around here."

"Yes, that brother of his, Aurora's father, he hasn't softened up."

"You haven't been here long enough to know the history of these people. Their families go back generations. It wasn't until 1824 that New Mexico became part of the United States. They did a little stint with Mexico but, before that, they were under Spanish rule. This is their country and they're not willing to let it go to us Johnny-come-latelys."

William's brow knitted. "It's been part of the United States for over fifty years. We're not Johnny-come-latelys."

Jonathan laughed, "In their eyes we are."

Jonathan took a puff of his cigar and squinted. "You know, William, it's best if you stick to the Anglos in the community. My niece, Nancy, wants to introduce you to some of her friends."

William let out a long, slow grunt. "I have enough to do with my work. Besides, if you believe what you're saying, why did you invite me to go to that church thing?"

"I want them to know that we consider ourselves part of the community. It's good for business, but your personal life is something else." Jonathan shifted in his chair. "Surely, you're not interested in Aurora?"

William shook his head. After a long pause, he told Jonathan that he just wanted to untangle the relationship.

Jonathan put his empty cup on the table and stood. "She's a pretty little thing, but I would stay away from her if I were you."

William looked across the *plazita* and nodded absentmindedly.

29

"I'm so glad you came." Gloria hugged her friend. "My sister will be here when the baby is born, but I'm glad you're helping me get ready instead of her."

Aurora raised her eyebrows.

"Oh no," stuttered Gloria, "I only meant that when she comes, she'll bring all of her children. I don't get much rest with all their commotion."

"Well, it's only me and my boys. You can rest while I'm here."

The next day, Gloria sat on the *porche* crocheting a baptismal jacket for her baby while Aurora scrubbed the little clothes that were worn by the last two babies. She looked down at her hands and remembered how she had teased Rita about her rough hands. Now she couldn't tell the difference.

When she was hanging out the little clothes, she noticed that there weren't many diapers and some were frayed.

"Tomorrow I'll go to Socorro and buy some muslin." Aurora held up one of the tattered squares. "We can hem them while I'm here."

Gloria put her hand on her back and rose stiffly. "Oh, thank you. I've been meaning to do that but there never seems to be enough time."

❋ ❋ ❋

Aurora was grateful that she found a place to hitch her buggy beneath the trees that circled the plaza. As she walked back to the buggy, she spotted a new bakery next to the bank. The smell of freshly baked bread drew her toward it. She had to giggle to herself. *Imagine, buying bread and pies. I think I'll like this new Socorro.*

She glided out of the bakery. Her hands were wrapped around a warm bag of little rolls smothered with maple frosting and cinnamon. Aurora was still smiling as she crossed the park. She was thinking about how delighted the children would be with her treat.

"*Señora* Vigil."

Aurora turned to see that the familiar voice was coming from William.

"I see you've discovered Simon's bakery."

Aurora's head turned from side to side. Satisfied that no one was around, she took a step closer to William. She smiled and took a big whiff of her treats. "Don't they smell good?" She raised the bag.

William sniffed and agreed. "What brings you to Socorro?"

"I'm helping my friend Gloria get ready for her baby." She nodded toward the buggy. "We're going to make some diapers."

William blinked. "I see," he said slowly. "Before you start your task, would you like to join me for a cup of tea at the Grand. I'd like to know more about you. I mean your family."

Aurora smile faded. She started shaking her head before she spoke. "Oh, I couldn't. Gloria is waiting for me. We have a lot to do before the baby arrives. *Adios*, I mean goodbye *Señor* De Baun."

William moved into step with Aurora. "Well, maybe I'll see you at your uncle's store. I'll be in Lemitar next week. I want to talk to him about the incorporation process." As they walked, William told her about Socorro and how much it was growing. He told her about the mining and the talk about the railroad coming. "Socorro needs to be a legal town."

William stopped talking when they reached the buggy and saw Aurora's knitted brow. "I'm sorry; I'm probably boring you. I'm sure you need to get back with Gloria's diapers."

Aurora tossed the packages into the buggy and whirled around. "I know what you're talking about. My father and uncle were talking about Socorro the other day. We're just as interested in what's happening as you are."

As she stepped into the buggy, William's hand slipped under her elbow to help her. Aurora jerked it away.

"I can't take any more time to talk to you, *Señor* De Baun. I have to go make diapers." She snapped the reins and turned the buggy around.

William stood, swaying a little. *What set her off?* When he got to the office, William walked past the noise Jonathan was making. As soon as he sat at his desk, Jonathan was at the door.

"Didn't you hear me? There's going to be a town meeting next week."

William looked up from his papers. "What? I was thinking of something else."

Jonathan dismissed him with a swat to the air. "Or someone else, judging from that silly grin on your face."

William's smile faded. "No, I was just. . . " By the time he thought of the right thing to say, Jonathan was no longer in the room.

30

The two friends were sitting on the porch, Gloria's crocheting in her lap. Aurora's brow creased as she took uneven stitches in the muslin. They watched the children crawling onto an old wagon, claiming it as their new fortress. The women sat in silence for a while until Aurora put together words that she could safely say.

"I saw that *Señor* De Baun again this morning." She glanced at Gloria out of the corner of her eye, ready to assess her reaction.

Gloria finished a row of crochet. With a sly smile, she turned to Aurora. "Hmm, I saw you talking to him at the *fiesta* dance too. What does he want with you?"

Aurora shrugged. She let Gloria know that William was just asking about her papá and *Tio* Manuel. "He had some papers for them to sign when they sold some land." Aurora shrugged again. "*Tio* Manuel seems to like him."

Aurora looked toward her friend, only to be met with silence. She told Gloria about incorporating Socorro. "He wants Papá and *Tio* Manuel to help him."

Gloria finally put her crochet hook down. "And what do you want?"

"What do you mean?" Aurora stammered. "Ouch! You made me poke my finger."

"What do you want with him?" Gloria cocked her head.

Aurora couldn't untangle her words. She felt like a little girl chasing a boy with a stick because she liked him. She wanted to blurt out that she couldn't stop thinking about him, but was confused because she shouldn't be thinking about him. *What about Flavio and the sadness I thought I would carry forever? What would people say? What would Gloria think? He is an Americano.* Aurora looked up at Gloria then looked down at her sewing.

Gloria clapped and smirked. "You like him!"

Aurora let out the breath she'd been holding. "No, well, I don't know. I don't think I'm supposed to like anybody else, and he's a *gringo*. "*Tio* Manuel seems to think he's alright, but Papá doesn't feel the same."

Aurora put her sewing in her lap and told Gloria about the argument she overheard. She told Gloria how mad *Tio* José had gotten because *Tio* Manuel was doing business with a *gringo*. *Tio* José reminded him that a *gringo* had killed his son.

"I could hear them in the storeroom. *Tio* José was crying. He said he was sorry he was talking about Flavio and he didn't mean to hurt *Tio* Manuel." Aurora went on. "I've never seen *Tio* Manuel raise his hand to anyone, but he swatted at *Tio* José and ran him out of the store."

Aurora walked to the end of the *porche* to give herself time to straighten out her feelings. She remembered that *Tio* Manuel's voice sounded quiet and far away. "He said that he was trying to forget what happened to Flavio and remember that it was only one man who took his son from him. He had even said that he was tired of looking for the *gringo* that killed him. He said that killing Montgomery wouldn't bring Flavio back."

Gloria held back words that might wound her friend. *Manuel had every man in the territory looking for Montgomery. How could he just stop looking?* While Aurora went to check on the children, Gloria thought about Manuel. The slump of his shoulders and the bend of his head made him look old and tired. *Where was the strong, proud man that she had looked up to all her life?*

Aurora sank onto the bench and Gloria reached for her hand. "Your *tio* carries a heavy burden, but it shouldn't be yours to carry too. So, this *Señor* De Baun, what do you think of him?"

Aurora breathed out slowly. "Well, I don't really know him. Maybe I just like the way he looks. You know, I have never really looked at blue eyes before." She picked up her needle and started sewing again. "Listen to me. I'm acting like a silly girl. He's just talking to me to find out about *Tio* Manuel. I probably won't see him again."

Aurora scrunched up her mouth and concentrated on the monotonous needle work. As she stitched, her thoughts settled, and she remembered what William had said. "I just want to get to know you."

She finished the diaper she was working on, folded it and put it in the basket. When she reached for the next piece of muslin, she couldn't remember folding the last one.

❇ ❇ ❇

Manuel sent word to Aurora that he wouldn't be back to Socorro until the next Tuesday when he would attend the town meeting. When Gloria took the note, she breathed a sigh of relief. Aurora would be with her for a few more days.

135

"Your *Tio* Manuel said he would be here for the town meeting so, if you want to, you can stay."

Aurora gave Gloria a tight hug. The work was the same, but being away from her family was a relief. When Gloria's husband, Alberto, came home, Aurora would retreat to the *casita*. Somehow it felt different from her rooms at home. She had made it her own with a colorful quilt that Rita had made. A vase full of wild flowers brightened her little table.

Aurora lay on the bed and closed her eyes, but her respite didn't last long. She sat up when she heard Gloria's husband, Alberto, riding into the yard. When Aurora saw him running across the yard, she forgot about her nap and chased after him.

Alberto swung the door open, talking as he tromped through the kitchen. "There's going to be a meeting next week to make Socorro an official town in the territory. *Señor* Armijo is going to let us off early so we can go. He said we all need to be there. He said that Socorro might become the county seat someday."

Aurora's eyes widened. "Can I go?"

Alberto's mouth opened, then snapped shut. "Why would you want to go? This is a meeting for the men."

Aurora's fists flew to her hips. "Why shouldn't women go? It's our territory too!"

Alberto let out a tight groan. He pointed to his pregnant wife. "You have better things to do."

Aurora marched out the door. Her feet made little puffs of dust as she scurried to the *casita*.

Late that evening, Alberto banged on Aurora's door. "The baby, it's coming! I'm going to get La Señora."

An hour later Alberto held on to La Señora's bony elbow as she let herself down from the wagon. He tried to keep up with her as she made a beeline for the little storage-room behind the house. As she moved through the door, she sent up a quick prayer.

The neighbor's wife was holding onto Gloria as she clung to the birthing rope. Aurora swabbed Gloria's forehead with a damp cloth. She kept fanning the door to regulate the temperature of the room. It was past midnight before Gloria's third child came into the world - a tiny girl, pink and soft as cottonwood fluff.

31

Gloria's sister, Catalina, arrived the day after Gloria's third baby was born. She wiped her hands on her apron and grabbed the broom out of Aurora's hand. "You can go home now," she announced. "I'll need the *casita* for me and my kids."

Aurora and Gloria shared a wide-eyed glance. "Well, maybe you can ride to Socorro with Alberto tomorrow afternoon," Gloria stammered, "You know, when he goes to the meeting."

Alberto helped Aurora load her belongings into the back of the wagon. Before Aurora left, she squeezed Gloria and promised to visit again soon.

Alberto kept his eyes on the distant mesa. Aurora watched the road in front of her. Rufina had sent word that the boys could stay with her while Aurora attended the meeting. When they got to Rufina's, Manuel's wagon was in the yard. Several of *Tio* Manuels's workers sat in the back of his wagon.

Aurora handed Manuelito and Flavito down to *Tia* Rufina.

"I'm glad you came early," Rufina said. "I think every man in town is going to be there." She moved closer to the wagon. "Your *tio* didn't want you to go, but I told him that I had signed the petition, and so had you." She threw her hands up. "So, why not let you go? You can tell me all about the meeting without all the huffing and puffing the men are going to do."

Aurora winked and scooted away from Alberto. Alberto shifted in his seat. "You'll probably be the only woman there," he grunted. "You can sit in the back row.

Aurora didn't flinch. "Oh no; everyone is supposed to be there," she stated. "This is an important meeting."

With the boys safely in the back yard, Alberto headed toward the Garcia Opera House.

Aurora waved to *Tio* Manuel as they climbed down from the wagon. He strolled over and offered her his arm. They walked through the crowd to the front row of chairs. Aurora was surprised to see so many women mingling with the men. The *Americanos* settled on one side of the room and the *Hispanos* on the other. Aurora spotted some of her friends, but didn't want to squeeze back through the crowd to get to them.

At exactly seven o'clock, Judge Salomón Pino gave everyone a start by pounding his gavel. Muttering voices stopped. Four men joined Judge Pino on the stage. Among them was William De Baun.

Aurora forced herself to breathe as William stood, cleared his throat, and started speaking.

"I've drawn up the petition to incorporate Socorro into a town of the territory of New Mexico. Some local land owners have sponsored the petition. This is just the first step," William continued. He explained that people would have to go door to door and get the petition signed. Then there would be another meeting to approve the petition.

The floorboards began to creak with the shuffling of feet. People looked at each other, hoping that the person next to them understood the English words of the American lawyer.

Aurora leaned forward. William's words were caught in the net of her excitement. *I could stay at Gloria's, no at Rufina's, so she could watch the boys.* She held onto the arms of the chair to keep from leaping forward and shouting, "I can help!"

William patiently answered questions until everyone seemed to have a trifle of understanding. Then William stepped off the stage and Manuel pressed toward him. Aurora tried to follow, but the crowd pushed her back. When she worked her way to her uncle's side, she heard *Tio* Manuel telling William that he was proud to be one of the sponsors. As they were shaking hands, William spotted Aurora watching him.

His voice caught, and he couldn't force his eyes back to Manuel. Manuel stopped talking too. He looked from William to Aurora. The moment seemed to be frozen. Aurora broke the spell by offering to help circulate the petition. When she looked up for her uncle's approval, he was glaring at her with a furrowed brow.

"We'll talk about this later." Manuel nodded his good night to William. He grabbed Aurora by the elbow and whisked her out the door as she waved good-by to Alberto.

"This is not for you," Manuel stated as they rode to Rufina's. "This is man's work. You can't go all over town knocking on strangers' doors."

Aurora sighed, "I guess you're right. I just got so excited about helping. You know, I listen to you and the men talking at the store. I think all the changes are exciting. I don't see why women can't help too?"

Manuel moaned. "I'll give you two reasons," he snapped. "Who would take care of Manuelito and Flavito? Would you drag them around with you?"

As soon as the words left his mouth, Manuel was sorry he had spoken to Aurora so harshly. He didn't understand why his niece had never been happy just making a home and caring for her children. He thought that in time she would settle down with Flavio, but that was not to be. He had tried so hard to be patient with her, but this was too much.

As they turned the corner onto Mount Carmel Street, Manuel patted Aurora's folded hands. "I'm sorry I snapped at you, *Mija*. I know you want to be right in the middle of all the changes, but you have to be careful. Socorro isn't the same as it was when you were a little girl. The miners and cowboys are bad enough, but the drifters scare me the most." Manuel cleared his throat. "When Socorro is a legal town, we can start making laws, real laws to keep us safe."

He gave Aurora's hand a squeeze. "Your place is in La Parida with your children. What if you help me at the store every Wednesday?"

Aurora didn't answer. She slipped into her cousin's house while Manuel put the horses in the stable. By the time he crept into the house, Aurora had gone to bed.

Manuel stayed up later than usual, talking to Rufina and Antonio about the petition and the changes coming to Socorro. When Rufina mentioned William, Manuel suddenly remembered the look on his face when he saw Aurora. *He held her hand a little too long. And now she wants to help him.* Rufina had to nudge Manuel back to the conversation.

Manuel went to bed thinking about the long ride back to La Parida. Should he say something? Did he imagine things that weren't there? He woke up with a start in the middle of the night. He was dreaming about his Flavio at the ranch. When Aurora opened the door to greet Flavio, it was William who embraced her. Manuel shook off the terrible image. The dream probably came from the excitement of the evening and missing his son in the presence of all those young men.

32

William couldn't think of an excuse to stop by Esquipula's on the way to see Manuel so when he saw Aurora behind the counter of her uncle's store, he quickened his step. As soon as José spotted him, he sprinted to the back room and bellowed for Manuel. William shook Manuel's hand and begin speaking quickly, hoping to remain near Aurora but Manuel jerked his chin toward the back room. He turned and dashed away with William trotting after him.

Taking the bitter coffee he was offered, William delivered the petition. He wanted Manuel to keep it in the store so people coming from Socorro could sign it. William told Manuel that several men had already signed and they would probably get enough signatures by the end of the month.

"I really appreciate your help. I'm anxious to get this done before winter sets in," said William

Manuel looked over the petition. He glanced at the back door, thinking about ushering William out that way. Then he remembered that William's horse was tied up at the front of the store. As William strode toward the front door, Manuel placed himself squarely in front of Aurora.

She peeked from behind her uncle and stepped sideways. "How long will it take to make Socorro a legal town?" Aurora asked.

The old men who huddled around the stove turned in unison. William started explaining how there must be a public vote. Then a mayor and city council would be elected. Aurora kept nodding while he was talking. William's voice got louder. He began to speak faster, encouraged that someone was interested enough to ask questions. He finished by saying that it would probably be next summer before the process was completed.

Aurora raised her chin. "I want to help, but *Tio* Manuel said that it wasn't safe for a woman to go from door to door."

William agreed. "But we'll need people to verify the names on the petition. Maybe you can help with that."

Aurora's eyes glimmered. "I'll be glad to, if I can find someone to take me to Socorro."

❋❋❋

The next month Aurora sat in the clerk's office at Socorro bent over stacks of signatures. Her cousin Benito called out each familiar name as she checked them off the list. William stopped by every day after court. He put a gentle hand on Aurora's shoulder. "With your help, we'll be done in no time."

Aurora was staying at Rufina's who agreed, against her husband's protest, to watch the boys for two hours every afternoon. By the end of the week all the signatures were verified. To celebrate, William invited Aurora to dinner.

Rufina's son-n-law Domingo, cleared his throat. He had been sent to fetch Aurora every afternoon. He stood next to Aurora, tugging her arm. "Who's going to escort you?" he asked, tight lipped.

William looked at Aurora then back to Domingo who was standing ramrod stiff. Crimson flashed across Aurora's cheeks, her glare burning a hole in Domingo.

"Well, I would love for you and your wife to join us," William stammered

Domingo turned toward the buggy and reached to help Aurora. "We'll see," he grunted.

Without taking a step, Aurora turned to William. "I'm sure we'll have dinner with you. Where would you like to go?" She nudged Domingo. "We'll meet you there."

Aurora didn't wait for Domingo to turn the buggy around before lashing out at him for acting like a burro and embarrassing her.

"You're really going out in public with that *gringo*?" Domingo stopped short at reminding Aurora that a *gringo* had killed her husband.

"That *gringo* is making Socorro into a legal town so it can grow and prosper. What's wrong with wanting to help?" Aurora twisted and looked out at the passing houses.

Domingo slapped the reins, jolting Aurora forward. She gasped, then drew herself up. "I suppose you think like Tio José, that every-thing should be like it was for our *abuelos*. Well, like it or not, things are changing and I'm going to help."

❋❋❋

Aurora fed the boys and put them to bed early. She tucked strands of hair into her hat and took one last look in the mirror. When she heard the buggy clatter into the yard, she skipped to the door. She stopped short when she saw who was in the buggy. Instead of Domingo and his wife, Maria, Aurora saw only Louis, Domingo's younger brother.

"Domingo couldn't go," he announced with a frown. "He sent me to escort you."

"Why, what's happened?" Aurora asked. "I thought Maria was looking forward to finally going to a restaurant."

Louis just shrugged and looked into the distance.

Aurora breathed a soft "Oh no, well, maybe I shouldn't go either." She started to go into the house, then turned back to the buggy. "No, I better go. What will *Señor* De Baun think? He's expecting us."

She climbed aboard the buggy and sat as far away from Louis as possible. Both of them looked out at the stores that lined the narrow streets, until the Grand Central Hotel finally came into view.

When they entered the hotel lobby, Louis lagged behind. Out of the corner of her eye, Aurora caught him gawking at this wondrous place. He was inspecting the mahogany clad room with its plush furniture and crystal chandeliers. Aurora slowed her pace, remembering the first time she saw this room.

They entered the dining room through huge French doors and were greeted by a maître d'. Aurora told him that they were dining with Mr. De Baun. Louis walked rigidly by her side, twisting his hat. He tried not to be obvious as he gawked at the other diners.

William stood and reached for Aurora's hand, squeezing it for an instant. Then he turned with a frown to Louis.

"Oh," Aurora explained, "this is Louis, Domingo's brother." She cocked her head and waited for Louis to speak.

Louis looked at William's outstretched hand and slowly reached for it.

"The others couldn't come because. . ." Louis stammered, "Well, I came instead." He threw back his shoulders. " Aurora mustn't be seen without a family escort."

Aurora looked at Louis. A hint of a smile tugged at the corners of her lips as he struggled to make excuses.When they sat down, his sharp glare clipped Aurora's chin.

William cleared his throat to conceal a chuckle. He was sure that reminding Louis that this was 1880, not 1580, would not be appreciated by her chaperone. He took his cue from Aurora who seemed perfectly at home with the situation.

As they were waiting for their food, William learned how seriously the *Hispanos* value their honor and respectability. Louis talked about the saloons and gambling halls. He told William about the fight he had with a drunken miner who had mistaken Louis's horse for his own.

William had to agree that there were some changes that weren't so good. He leaned toward Aurora and began to reach for her hand, but remembered Louis and pulled it back.

"Don't you see? That's why it's so important to make Socorro a legal town. After it's incorporated, we'll have a sheriff and laws. We'll be able to clean up this riff-raff."

Aurora sat listening, grateful for the chance to study this lawyer with his slender hands that drew pictures in the air when he spoke. While they ate, William tried to fit Louis into the tangle of Aurora's relatives. Soon the serious talk of incorporation melted into family stories and a bit of laughter.

When the waiter brought little cakes piled high with strawberries, Aurora asked William about his family. He told her that his father was a farmer on the plains of Iowa. Aurora tried to imagine flat land that stretched to the horizon. A little shiver rippled through her.

William laughed. "I know what you're feeling. I thought New Mexico would be just like Iowa, all flat desert. But it's beautiful; the colored mountains, the green valley, even the cactus flowers."

William went on to explain that after the Civil War he came out West because he wanted to be part of the country that was new and growing. "I couldn't see spending my life behind the plow after I heard about places that were just coming into their own. I wanted to be part of all that."

Aurora recognized the faraway look in his eyes. She had the same look when she listened to the men who drove the wagons back from St. Louis, Missouri.

When William gently nudged the conversation back to her, Aurora only told him what he already knew. She put her napkin on her plate and pushed out a little sigh.

"I worry about my sons growing up without a father. Yes, they have two grandfathers and a whole family that loves them, but I think they're getting spoiled."

She glanced at Louis. He was propping up his head with his hand.

"I think it's time to go," she said. "I'm sure both of you have work to do early in the morning."

Louis came alive, gathered up his hat and jumped out of his chair.

He was halfway across the carpeted dining room when he realized that Aurora wasn't behind him.

William's hand slipped into Aurora's. "I'd like to see you again."

The temperature in Aurora's chest began to rise. She looked around the half-empty dining room.

"Perhaps you can come to Lemitar next Sunday and go to church with us. I'll ask my father if you can come over for a meal afterward."

William groaned. "Well, you see, I'm not a Catholic."

Aurora leaned backwards.

William had seen this stance before and scrambled to put things back in order.

"Oh, but I've been wanting to learn more about the faith. Perhaps this would be a good opportunity to start learning."

Louis gave Aurora a sidelong glance and hurried her to the buggy.

William strolled back to the little room behind his office. The evening had been nothing like he expected. He poured himself a glass of whiskey and stepped into his backyard. He finally tore his glaze away from a yucca silhouetted against the sky. He shook his head, took another sip, and wondered what he was getting himself into.

33

On the long ride home, Aurora finally had a chance to think about William. A knot gripped her stomach. She would only have a few days to muster the courage to tell her parents that she had invited William for a visit. She shook off her worry. *I'll just tell them that I want to find out more about him. Who knows? Maybe after Sunday, I won't want to see him again.*

Aurora waited until Saturday. After supper, she slipped onto the bench where her father sat watching the sunset. Esquipula put his arm around his daughter and looked toward the peach-colored mesas. "This is my favorite time of the week. The work is done and tomorrow I can rest." While he lit his pipe, Aurora thought about the endless ways she could tell her father about William's visit.

Aurora twisted her handkerchief. "About tomorrow. . . I've invited *Señor* De Baun to go to church with us and come to our house to share a meal." She squeezed her eyes shut and waited for her father's thunder.

It came slowly. "Does your mother know about this? She's the one who has to prepare extra food." He turned toward his daughter. "Why didn't you ask us before inviting this *gringo* into our home?"

"Well, I was helping with the petition, and he was grateful for the work I did. He took me and Louis to the restaurant to thank me. I guess I just got excited."

Aurora stood and started pacing. "Maybe I can send word. I can tell him that it is not a good day for us to have visitors." She stopped pacing and sat back down. "I just thought he could tell you how the petition was going and how you can help. You said you would help."

Aurora let her words settle while Esquipula puffed his pipe to life.

"Manuel has told me about how you look at each other." Esquipula peered at his daughter from beneath furrowed brows. "I didn't expect you to stay unmarried forever. You're a young woman. You should have a husband and a home." He stood and leaned against the post. "I just thought you would marry someone from Lemitar, from a family that we know. What do you know about his family? Where does he come from? We don't even know who he is."

Aurora stopped herself from saying that William was from Iowa and that his family had farmed the land since his grandfather was a boy. She knew that Esquipula didn't want an answer to his questions.

"Papa, I didn't say I want to marry him. I need to find out more about him. I'm just asking if we can share our Sunday meal with him."

Esquipula sighed deeply. "Let's go talk to your mother."

When Josefa heard the news, her jaw tightened. "What do you mean, he's coming to church? Is he a member of our Holy Catholic Faith?"

"Well, no, but he said he would like to learn about our faith. I asked him to come over after church. He could talk to Papá about the petition and everything that's going to change when we incorporate Socorro."

Josefa's mouth twisted into a tight little pucker. "Incorporate Socorro. Aurora, this is the business of men. Your business is here, taking care of your two little boys."

Aurora clicked her tongue as she stood. "I know where I belong, but can't I be interested in anything else besides changing pants and making tortillas?"

It was Esquipula's turn to stand. He didn't have to say a word.

"I'm sorry Mamá. I didn't mean to disrespect you. I just want to visit with *Señor* De Baun and to have us get to know him. He seems like a good man." She wanted to say, "I'm not asking the priest to send out the *bandos* announcing our wedding." But she tightened her lips to stop herself from raising the ire of her parents again.

Esquipula raised his hands in helplessness and let them fall against his dusty pants. "It's only one afternoon," he sighed.

✳✳✳

Every time the bright light of the doorway was darkened by a silhouette, the people in the adobe church craned their necks. It seemed that everyone in Lemitar had heard that *Señor* De Baun would be attending. When the Vigils took their places in the front pew without William, the women of the community were disappointed.

William slipped into the church just as the tower bell rang. He sat in the last pew. It took all his concentration to mimic the kneeling, and standing, and repeating of chants. He swiped his hand across his chest every time the others made the sign of the cross. Nothing in his Baptist upbringing had prepared him for this.

When people rose and started making their way to the altar, William looked over the shoulder of the man in front of him. The priest was holding up a little white disk.

Some people were filing into the aisle, some were staying in their seats. William decided to stay and observe. *Communion, this is communion.* In the silence of the church, he was struck by the reverence of bowed heads and folded hands. He felt the sting of being an outsider who wanted in.

The thick adobe walls softened the chanting, wrapping everyone in a serenity that William had never felt before. He was almost lulled to sleep by it when people started shuffling into the aisles and moving toward the door. William tried in vain to spot Aurora. The man beside him gave him a nudge and forced William into the little walled courtyard.

He backed up against the wall, hat in hand. Bernarda smiled and started toward him, but was stopped by her mother's hand. Some of the men tipped their hats. José stood at the edge of a cluster of men. He leered at the pale visitor.

The Vigil family was almost the last to emerge. William let out the breath he'd been holding. He knew the law and the business of Socorro, but the world of these native people was as foreign to him as another country.

William offered his hand to Esquipula before he greeted Josefa and Aurora. Each man tried to make conversation about the crisp fall days. The tension ended when Manuelito ran in front of his *abuelo*. Esquipula grabbed his arm. Manuelito giggled and tried to wiggle away.

Aurora's cheeks warmed. She shook Manuelito and knelt down. "*Portarse bien*, behave. We're at the church."

The four-year-old looked up at his mother who was holding him tighter than usual. He shot a look at his grandfather. Esquipula's stern face let him know that his game was over.

William wanted to reach for the chubby little boy who was now hanging on to his mother's skirt. He glanced at Josefa who stood with her arms crossed and decided that to touch Manuelito would be a mistake.

Instead, William put his hand out and said, "Good morning, *Señor* Manuelito. I'm *Señor* De Baun."

Manuelito puffed out his chest and shook the stranger's hand. Aurora smiled at William with gratitude and relief.

Esquipula took a step toward the gate then turned, "*Señor* De Baun, would you join us for a meal before you return to Socorro?"

"Thank you, *Señor* Vigil. Maybe after we eat you can show me your farm. I've been told that you have one of the best vineyards in the valley."

Esquipula started leading his family toward the wagon. "We're harvesting the grapes now. You will be able to taste last year's crop. The wine is my best yet."

William handed the boys up to their young uncle. "Oh, I met you a while back. You were with Aurora when she brought me the petition papers."

Santa Cruz nodded and turned back to the business of getting his nephews to sit down. Rita held Flavito on her lap, with one arm around Manuelito.

✳✳✳

William never got tired of the smell of *piñon* wood that greeted him when a door was opened. The aroma in Josefa's kitchen mingled *piñon* with roasted pork that had been marinated in red *chili*. The table beside the stove was laden with bowls and pots covered with damp linen cloths.

Esquipula settled himself in the leather chair near the fireplace. He pulled a chair away from the table for William.

"The food will be ready soon," said Esquipula. *Then you can be on your way*, he thought. He didn't offer his pipe tobacco, or a cup of coffee.

Aurora stepped into the room taking off her hat. "Excuse me, I have to get my boys out of their good clothes before they're ruined." Aurora pulled Manuelito along as she hurried across the *plazita*. She wondered what she was thinking when she invited William to her Sunday dinner. She forgot about having to get the boys changed and helping Josefa and Rita with the meal. She had only thought about William meeting her family and praying that they would like him. She tugged the clothes off the boys and wrestled them into their old pants and shirts. Shoes were forced onto little feet and they were sent out to play. Normally, Aurora would change too, but today she ran back to the house.

She was met by William and her father standing on the *porche*. Her father was sweeping his arm over the land to the east, his land. She only heard a snippet of his words. "This land was part of the Socorro land grant."

Aurora stood between them. She slipped her arm around her father's and gazed at his fields. When she dared to peek at William, her amber eyes caught the golden light of autumn. William's eyes captured the blue of a cloudless sky.

Esquipula's words floated past both of them and the moment vanished into thin air.

"I have to go help Mamá put the food on the table. "*Perdoname*, Papá. Excuse me." She made a small curtsy and stepped inside.

William sat next to Esquipula with Josefa across from him. Aurora snuggled next to her mother. No one spoke as the platter of *carne adobada* was passed around. The beans and corn were ladled into children's bowls by the nearest adult. Manuelito shook his head vigorously at the chicos, but Aurora put a spoonful of corn in his bowl anyway. "Just taste it," she pleaded.

When all the platters were laid back on the table, everyone bowed their heads. Esquipula said grace. With a nod of his head, silverware rattled and voices rose.

Josefa laid her fork down and looked up at William. "You went to church this morning. So, you are a member of the Holy Roman Faith?"

Chili dripped from the spoon that Aurora held in midair. Her breathing stopped. She didn't dare look at William.

"No, ma'am, I was raised a Baptist and, I must say, I didn't understand much of what was going on." William looked around the table. Even the two little ones had put down their spoons. All eyes were on him.

"I would like to know more about the Catholic religion. Maybe you, uh, or, Aurora can teach me." *The jury has shifted*, he thought. *What can I do to get them back on my side?*

"When I came out west, I didn't know anything about New Mexico. I didn't understand that it belonged to families who had lived here for hundreds of years. It didn't take me long to realize that I was an outsider in a place that wasn't mine."

William leaned back in his chair. He knew that his next few words would win or lose his case. He looked at Josefa, then Esquipula. "There are two sides to the West. Those of us who are building a life in a new place, far from home and family. Everything is so new to us. We left our customs and religion back home. Then there are the people who have lived here for generations. Their roots are deep and their lives are solid. They know who they are. We newcomers are trying to find our way in a world that we know little about."

William glanced around the table. He realized that he had finally put into words what he had felt since he got off the stagecoach at Santa Fe. He wanted to say more. He wanted to thank Esquipula for protecting his daughter, for helping her raise her sons. He wanted to say that he admired the strong ties that the families had to this land, and to each other. However, a lawyer knew when saying more would be too much.

He took a drink of water and looked directly into Esquipula's eyes. "I truly respect you, sir, and admire you and your family."

Esquipula put down his fork, his mustache jerked to one side. Little beads of perspiration formed on William's forehead. *I've gone too far,* he thought. *This man thinks I'm a buffoon, a carpetbagger.* William took another bite of the *chili* that threatened to paralyze the back of his throat. Then he dared to glance at Aurora.

Her chin was tucked into her chest and she was smiling. *Oh, good Lord,* he thought. *Does this mean she thinks I'm a charlatan, trying to sell the family a bill of goods?* He tried to take another bite and realized that his hand was shaking. William decided to eat quickly and rid these people of his pitiful self.

He took another gulp of water and wiped his mustache. He wanted to dab his forehead with Josefa's linen napkin, but he thought that it might offend.

"This food is so delicious, *Señora* Vigil. Once I got used to the fire on my tongue, I couldn't get enough of it."

Josefa straightened a little and smiled. "Who cooks for you?"

"Well," William answered, grateful that the conversation had turned away from his ill-fated attempt to impress the family. "I eat at the Grand Hotel sometimes, but my housekeeper, Antonia Torres, takes pity and shares her food with me."

"Oh, Antonia, she's a good cook. Her mother taught my mother how to make *pozole.*"

William didn't know what *pozole* was so he just nodded and smiled. He dropped his shoulders and asked for another tortilla. When William raised his eyes to Aurora, she gave him a head-tilted smile.

Esquipula stood and put a gentle hand on Josefa's shoulder. This signaled that the meal was over. Andres shoveled the last few bites into his mouth. He and Santa Cruz stepped over the bench and headed for the door as Rita and Barbara picked up the dishes. The little ones were captured and wiped clean. William reluctantly put down the last piece of tortilla and wiped the butter off his hand and wrist.

Esquipula was holding the door open for him. William thanked the women for the tasty meal. When he attempted to shake Josefa's hand, she just looked from it to her husband. William puffed out a bit of nervous laughter, touched his forehead and escaped outside. The women burst into giggles as soon as the door was slammed shut.

"I didn't really want him to come to my house," Josefa laughed, "but it was worth it to see the *gringo* sweat."

Aurora slapped a towel at her mother in mock reproach. "He was trying so hard."

"A little too hard," snickered Rita.

She took a cast-iron kettle from the stove and poured steaming water into a galvanized pan. As Josefa loaded the dishes into it, the three women grew quiet. Aurora wanted to ask what they thought of William, but she decided to untangle her own feelings first. There would be plenty of time for discussing his visit.

Aurora was sure that William's visit would be the topic of conversation for days. Her stomach suddenly tightened when she realized that William's visit would become the talk of Lemitar. She remembered the look that *Tio* José and *Tia* Telesfora had exchanged, and how she made the sign of the cross as they left the churchyard.

Aurora grabbed a soapy cloth and wiped the table. It would give her a few minutes to think about how, or even why, she should protect her interest in William.

As Esquipula showed William his vineyards and fields, William enjoyed the smell of ripe purple grapes and the rustling of dried corn stocks. He told Esquipula that he too was raised on his father's farm and this time of year always made him homesick.

"It's in October that I always feel guilty about leaving home to go West. I know my father could use my help, even though three of my brothers are still on the farm." William tried to describe the flatness of Iowa. It was so unlike the rolling hills and soft mesas surrounding La Parida.

By the time they got back to the *plazita*, Esquipula was using a softer tone of voice. He shook William's hand firmly, but didn't invite him to sit on the *porche*. William looked toward his buggy, then decided to risk another indiscretion.

"I'd like to thank your wife again for that wonderful meal, and to say goodbye to Aurora." He waited until Esquipula nodded, then knocked on the door.

The women were drying dishes and stacking them on a shelf next to the stove. William held his hat in his hand. He bowed slightly and thanked Josefa, Rita, and Aurora for their hospitality and dinner.

"I hope to see you soon," he said, facing Aurora. "There's a lot more to do for the incorporation."

Aurora shot a pleading glance at her mother. Josefa issued a quick nod. Aurora hoped that William hadn't heard Josefa grunt. The movement of Josefa's head was barely perceptible, but Aurora knew it was a signal that she could walk William to his buggy.

-34-

The November winds were blowing before William was able to go to Lemitar again. He needed to tell Manuel that the petition had gathered enough signatures to continue with the incorporation. Now Manuel and Esquipula could sign its approval. The rest of the process would go quickly.

When he got to Esquipula's, he was met with the familiar smell of *piñon* coming from the chimney. The table was set with a platter of licorice flavored cookies and a pot of strong coffee.

William folded his long frame onto a bench and joined Aurora's family with a little more ease. While the *bizcochitos* were eaten and coffee sipped, William told the family about cattle drovers who had flooded Socorro. They had started harassing some of the town's women. "Of course, the men of Socorro took offense. It almost led to bloodshed."

William turned to Esquipula. "We really have to get Socorro incorporated so we can put firm laws in place."

He glanced around the room filled with various relatives and noisy children. He gave up hope that he would have Aurora to himself. Finally, he said that he had to get Manuel's signature and get back to Socorro before nightfall.

Maybe she can at least walk me outside. He began to untangle himself from the bench. Josefa tilted her head toward the stove. Rita filled a napkin with *bizcochitos*. She passed them to William without saying a word. Josefa busied herself with the dishes. Andres gathered his children by the fireplace and begin strumming his guitar.

William settled back down. He was the only one left at the table with Aurora. He leaned forward so his voice wouldn't be overheard. As Aurora leaned in, he touched her foot with the toe of his boot. With Josefa only three steps away, they talked only about the boys, and how the snow would soon keep them all at home.

William asked for another *bizcochito*. Their fingers touched when Aurora passed the plate. It sent a shock wave through both of them. William looked around the room.

Josefa and Rita had settled themselves near the fireplace with their mending. William dared to reach for Aurora's hand. He leaned closer, not caring if Josefa heard.

"I would very much like to court you. If you feel the same, I'll ask your father's permission today."

Aurora's heart pounded and the room swayed. *How can I feel what I thought was lost forever?* When the whirling room settled, Aurora's smile turned to dust.

"I don't know how my family will feel about this." *Why*, she wondered, *did life have to be so tangled?*

"Let me talk to your father. At least let me try. I want to be able to talk with you alone, to really get to know you." He squeezed Aurora's hand.

Aurora wrapped her fingers around his. "Maybe I should talk to my father first. This will be so sudden for him. I'll send word, and you can come back next week."

William let out a slow breath. "Maybe you're right."

William again thanked the family and started to reach for Aurora's hand as she followed him to the door. A quick glance at Josefa's frown changed his mind. Instead, Rita took Aurora's hand as they waved goodbye.

✳✳✳

Aurora asked Rita to help her take the basket of clothes to her room. She bundled up the boys. They were grateful, for once, to stay inside their room. Rita put another piece of wood in the little fireplace and Aurora rubbed four little hands until they stopped shivering. The warmth of the fire filled the boy's room. They sat on the bed with their wooden horses and little wagon.

Rita sat close to Aurora. "Did I see what I think I saw?" Rita chuckled.

Aurora fell back on the bed and put her hands on her cheeks. "What am I going to do?"

She lay staring at the ceiling, her thoughts swirling like golden leaves caught in the wind. *No one was too happy about me and Flavio because we were cousins, but we loved each other so much that our parents knew it would do no good to try and stop us. But we were family, Hispanos. I know a gringo killed my Flavio, but should we hate them all?*

"I tried not to think about William. I didn't even talk to you about him. I tried to look at the other men in Lemitar. I even imagined being their wife, but I felt nothing." Aurora put a shaky hand to her lips. "When I saw William for the first time, I felt like I was floating. It was

154

just like the first time Flavio kissed me. I was so scared; I didn't sleep for fear that Flavio would haunt my dreams."

"I wondered why you were so quiet for a while." Rita answered. She put her arm around Aurora. "Would Flavio want you to dress in black and keep your eyes on the ground for the rest of your life? You're only twenty years old." She pointed to herself. "Some women haven't even married at your age." Rita bent and mimicked an old woman walking with a cane.

Aurora laughed and slapped Rita's shoulder. "I know," she sighed, "but there's a lot to think about. It isn't as easy as marrying one of the men I've known forever."

Rita shook her head, "You mean he's not a *Hispano*."

Aurora drew a deep breath. "I just want the chance to know him better, to see what his world is like. Is he as kind as I think he is? He even talks different than us."

Rita put her nose in the air. "I bid you adieu." She bent with laughter at her own joke, but Aurora stood and crossed her arms.

"I'm serious. If Papá would just give me a chance to see for myself, maybe I won't like him when I get to know him."

Rita got up, grabbed the hem of her skirt and twirled around. "And maybe you will," she winked.

The color rose in Aurora's cheeks. She covered her face with her hands and twirled around the room too. "I feel like a silly girl when I'm around him."

The sisters sank back onto the bed and begin to make a plan. "You already know what to tell Papá," said Rita. "You just want a chance to get to know William. You may find out that you don't even like him. That's when you stop. If Papá doesn't think you'll stay with him, he'll probably let you keep seeing him."

Aurora shook her finger. "Yes, that's exactly what I'll say." She hugged Rita and headed for the door. "Come with me," Aurora said. "This will take more courage than when I told Papá that I wanted to marry my cousin."

They bundled up the boys and hurried across the *plazita*. Esquipula was smoking his pipe by the fireplace. Josefa sat close to the window, mending her grandchildren's pants. When the boys were settled at the table, Aurora scooted the extra chair next to her father. Rita sat on the edge of the bench. Aurora took a deep breath and glanced at Rita, who raised her chin and smiled.

"Papá, Mamá," Aurora began. "I think you know that William likes me, and I feel the same way about him." She stopped herself before blurting that she knew how the family felt about *gringos*. "I, uh, just want a chance to get to know him. Maybe after a while I'll like him more, and maybe I won't, but I need some time to find out."

Josefa put down her mending. "What else do you need to know? He's a Baptist, not a Catholic. He comes from Iowa not Spain. He doesn't know anything about our ways, and you don't know anything about his." She leaned forward and stared at her husband.

Esquipula tapped his pipe tobacco into a little bowl. He put his rough hand over his daughter's. "We know that you want your own home, and you're young enough to have another family, but there are so many good *Hispanos*. I've seen them looking at you after Mass."

Aurora dropped her head. "I know, but I don't feel the same way about any of them. You're more like *Tio* Manuel than José. You know how things are changing. People have come to New Mexico from all over. They're changing everything. William seems to be a good man. He wants to be part of the life that we have. He's not like the men I see sitting in front of the saloons. He has a business and is well respected. Look what he's doing for Socorro when nobody else would do it."

"And what about the boys? Will they be raised in the Baptist Church?" Josefa asked. "Will they be *gringo* or *Hispano*? Will they forget who their father is?"

Josefa's raised voice startled the children. Manuelito ran to his mother and Flavito clung to Rita's hand. Josefa closed her eyes and took a deep breath. "Will we lose them?"

Aurora stood. She took Flavito and swayed back and forth to comfort him. Esquipula reached for Manuelito. The four-year-old folded easily into his arms.

"We shouldn't talk about this in front of the children," Esquipula stated firmly.

He took Manuelito to the cupboard and handed him a *bizcochito*. When he put the plate on the table all the children swooped down on the cookies.

"Let's go to your room," Esquipula suggested.

Stepping into the wind, Aurora was grateful for a few minutes to breathe and think. She thought she would have to plead with her father. She didn't count on her mother blocking her way. As they huddled against the wind, Aurora admitted that she hadn't thought of the questions her mother asked.

Esquipula sat in the rocker and Josefa settled at the edge of the bed with Aurora. *Another turn,* Aurora thought. *My life is taking another turn and I don't know where this is taking me.* She stared at the dust dancing in the shaft of light coming through the window.

"You have a lot to think about, *Mija.*" Josefa patted Aurora's hand. "You're not a girl anymore. You have two sons that you're responsible for."

"I know," Aurora rose and started pacing, "and you're right, Mamá. I haven't thought about the things you asked about." Aurora pressed her lips into a thin line. "But don't you see? I'll never have a chance to find out if I can't even talk to William alone." Aurora's voice quivered. "You'll never lose the boys. You'll never lose me. But I can't marry the first *Hispano* that offers me a house so I can stop living under my father's roof."

She drew in a ragged breath and her voice got stronger. "I like what William is doing, and I like that he's doing it for us. He says he wants to be part of New Mexico. Maybe that means he'll be willing to become a Catholic. And the boys, he's always so happy to see them. I'm not asking for you to get the church ready. I'm just asking for a chance to find out who he is and what I'm really feeling."

Esquipula raised his eyes to his wife. "And if I say no?"

Aurora stopped pacing and crossed her arms. Her voice rose to a high pitch. "Papá, how can you say no to just letting me talk to him without the whole town listening?"

Esquipula rolled his eyes. "If you're going to start acting like a child, I'll treat you like one."

He walked to the door and lifted his chin. Josefa reacted to his signal and rose. "We have a lot to think about. We can talk some more in a few days."

When Rita finished folding the boy's clothes, she loaded her basket and ran to Aurora's room.

"What did they say?" she asked breathlessly.

Aurora sat with her elbow propped on the arm of the rocker, her head in her hand.

"Mamá is stuck on him not being a Catholic. They're worried about the boys. Maybe he'll convert. Maybe he'll be a good father to the boys."

Rita put the last little shirt on the shelf. "Maybe you won't even like him once you get to know him." She hunched her shoulders and looked back at Aurora.

"You're right, but I'll never know if I can't even talk to him alone." Aurora rose, sending the rocker banging against the wall. "And why do I need my parent's permission? I'm a widow with two children. I asked them out of respect, but I can do as I please." She drew herself up and lifted her chin.

"Be careful," warned Rita, her voice wavering. "You're living under your father's roof. Your little family depends on him for everything."

The moment her words slipped out of her mouth she knew she had gone in the wrong direction.

Aurora began to rant about how she didn't want to live in her father's house anymore. "Why did Flavio have to die?" She wailed. "We were ready to move to our new home. We were so happy about the new baby."

Aurora crumpled onto the bed and beat the pillow with her fists. When her sobs turned into soft whimpers, she reached for Rita with a shaky hand.

"Sometimes my heart aches for him, but I know he'll never come back. I just want the chance to fill my heart again."

Rita nodded and wiped a strand of hair from Aurora's forehead. "Just be careful how you speak to your father. You know he'll give in to you. He always does. Keep telling him that you just want to talk to William. Really, that's all you want to do."

Aurora sucked in a ragged breath and turned to Rita. "This morning I was thinking about how different it is this time, and how hard it all may be. It was hard enough talking Papá and *Tio* Manuel into letting me and Flavio marry. This is so much more. Then I think, why should it be? New Mexico is full of people from all over. We should all be moving ahead." She looked hopefully at Rita.

35

The next Sunday, Aurora and her boys rode with her brother, Andres, to Socorro. Andres and Barbara were baptizing her cousin Clara's son.

The family followed Clara home for the baptismal feast. After they finished eating, Aurora and her brother, Santa Cruz, slipped quietly from the house. William sat on the edge of the park bench, unable to control his tapping foot. Several buggies and a few wagons circled the park. People were strolling beneath the trees. When he saw Aurora's buggy, William stopped himself from leaping toward it. Instead, he tipped his hat at Santa Cruz and offered Aurora his arm.

She glanced at her brother, straightened, then slipped her arm into William's. She jerked when she heard her name being called. Gloria and Alberto were crossing the little oval park. The women hugged, their words tumbling over each other. Alberto took a step backwards when he noticed William. Gloria joined her husband when she realized that William was with Aurora.

"You remember William De Baun," Aurora said. "He and *Tio* Manuel are making Socorro into a legal town and I'm helping."

"I was at the meeting." Alberto stepped forward and shook William's hand. "I've been wondering how it's going. When will Socorro be a legal town?"

The couples started strolling. Aurora tucked her arm around Glorias as they walked behind the men. While William explained where they were in the process, Gloria drew Aurora close.

"So?" Gloria whispered. Seeing the flush of Aurora's face, she kept going. "How brave you are, walking with William in the park. I just saw Rufina. What do you think she'll say?"

"She's here in the park?" Aurora looked from side to side. "I didn't think they came to the park after Mass."

Gloria spotted Aurora's sister-in-law climbing onto her buggy. She tugged on Aurora's arm. "Let's go see them now. They'll think William is just talking to Alberto."

Aurora's lips tightened. She's started to let Gloria know that she didn't care who saw them. Then she remembered that she hadn't told *Tio* Manuel about her interest in William. She said a silent prayer for strength, because tomorrow she would talk to Flavio's father.

Gloria started moving toward Rufina's buggy when she was stopped by a tug from Aurora. "I can't just leave William with Alberto." Aurora waved her handkerchief and smiled at Rufina and Antonio.

Rufina caught a glimpse of the handkerchief, recognized the young women and waved back. She nudged her husband. "It's good that Aurora is getting out with her friend."

Aurora sagged into Gloria. Both women covered a giggle with their hands. Then they turned back to the men, who by now had laid claim to a park bench.

Gloria gave Aurora a glancing kiss on the cheek and reminded Alberto that she had to help her cousin with the Sunday meal.

William didn't wait for the couple to turn down the path before reaching for Aurora's arm. He covered her hand with his own. They strolled along the brick pathways. Santa Cruz walked slowly behind them.

William steered the conversation away from Socorro politics and toward Aurora. As their walk unfolded, so did her story, but she left out the most painful parts. Then she asked about his life.

William's boyhood memories warmed Aurora. His stories about growing up on an Iowa farm were like her own childhood. She smiled to herself as he described, with awe, the beauty of the land that she took for granted. She chuckled when he spoke of the noble people who inhabited this land—the land he thought was only an empty spot on the map. Aurora clutched his arm a little tighter when William began to talk about making Socorro a solid part of his future.

Aurora wrapped her shawl tightly around herself, then William took off his coat and draped it over her shoulders. It swallowed her up. The smell of wool and *piñon* smoke enveloped her. She breathed in deeply and caught a hint of peppermint soap. It reminded her of when she had leaned close to him in her kitchen.

By the time the chilly air forced them to end their walk, William knew something of Aurora's sorrows and dreams. Standing in front of her buggy, words toppled over words. "When can we meet again?" whispered Aurora.

"Can you stay in Socorro for another day . . .or maybe I can go to Lemitar."

"Santa Cruz has to get back to the farm, but my *mamá* is sending me to town next week for winter supplies. It's always a two-day trip.

I'll stay with Rufina. Perhaps I can take my evening meal with you." Aurora paused. A sparkle flashed across her eyes. "The Grand Central, maybe?"

William cut her off. "What about the restaurant at the Windsor? It's practically empty until the stagecoach comes in."

Instead of the embrace and kiss he wanted to give her, William leaned in close and took his coat. Aurora glanced around and found that the park was empty except for Santa Cruz, huddled on a bench. She put out both hands. William enfolded them with his. They held each other with their eyes for a moment, then he helped her onto the buggy.

36

The back door of the store creaked open. Severo was at his usual spot, bent over the ledgers.

"Is *Tio* Manuel here yet?"

Severo blinked and looked up. Then he tilted his head toward the front of the store. Aurora couldn't read his expression, so she just brushed past him. The November chill had kept customers away. The old men who held court around the stove hadn't arrived yet. Aurora said hello to José then pulled *Tio* Manuel to the back corner of the store.

"I have to speak to you, *Tio*. Can we go in the back room?" When they passed Severo, he and Manuel exchanged shrugs.

"We need some more coffee back here," Manuel said.

Severo swiped the blue enamel cups from the shelf and hurried out of the room. Aurora sat on one of the crates and stuffed her shaky hands into her pockets. She slowly looked up at her uncle who was sitting, arms crossed, on the only chair in the room.

"*Tio*," she stammered. "Has Papá said anything to you about William De Baun, I mean about me and William?" Aurora was surprised at the tears that threatened to overflow. She put her hand to her mouth.

Manuel blew out a deep breath and stuffed his pipe with a pinch of tobacco. "We've talked about it. You know that no one expected you to stay alone forever, but. . ."

Aurora broke in, ". . . but everyone expected me to find someone from Lemitar, someone I've known all my life."

Manuel uncrossed his legs. "Well, yes *Mija*. Then I remembered that my niece doesn't always do what everyone expects."

Aurora let loose a rush of nervous laughter mixed with the trickle of tears. "I didn't go looking for anyone *Tio*. I barely know him. I just want a chance to find out who he is."

Manuel waved her words away and drew Aurora to him. "Flavio wouldn't want you to be alone. He would want you to be happy." Now they were both weeping, for all that they had lost, and for what might lie ahead.

❋ ❋ ❋

Aurora traveled with Andres to Socorro. He was charged with

bringing back the last of the flour from Manuel's grist mill. Aurora picked up supplies that couldn't be bought in Lemitar. Insisting that it would be too cold to take the boys, Aurora left them in Rita's care.

After loading the wagon, Aurora and Andres settled in at Rufina's. Her chatter bounced past Aurora. It was getting dark outside, but the clock on the mantle had only struck five o'clock.

Rufina and Antonio sat stiffly as Aurora's words tumbled out.

"William is taking me to dinner. We're going to talk about the incorporation. Um, it's going well but there's more to do."

Soft little grunts escaped from Rufina. Antonio lit his pipe and stared out the window.

It was past six o'clock when Aurora jumped at the sound of William's buggy pulling into the yard. She held onto the arms of the chair to keep from running to the front door.

When Aurora turned to say good-by to her cousin, Rufina had already joined her husband on the back porch.

Aurora slipped outside. She took William's arm as he helped her into the buggy. He moved close and Aurora's doubts fluttered into the wind.

William was right. The Windsor only held two other guests. He guided her to a table in the far corner of the dim restaurant. William ordered quickly for both of them, then slid his chair next to Aurora's. They held hands underneath the table. At first, they spoke in hushed tones, but when the two cowhands left, William waved his arm around the room. "Alone, at last!" he proclaimed.

Aurora put her hand over her mouth and giggled. She felt like a schoolgirl escaping the eagle eyes of the nuns. She cleared her throat. "This isn't going to go on." Aurora straightened. "What reason is there for us to hide?"

William leaned in and kissed her softly. "No more hiding," he smiled. The rest of the evening was spent wrapped in loud voices and soft laughter.

After supper Aurora invited William to meet Rufina and her family. After sipping coffee, Antonio stretched and announced that he had to get up early in the morning. Rufina shuffled toward the kitchen and the couple was finally left alone. Aurora and William sat on the settee near the fireplace. They chatted about the progress of the incorporation, the new brick factory, and the gold foundry. Every time Aurora looked over her shoulder, she saw Rufina puttering around the kitchen.

At first, they sat at each end of the little couch. But as the evening crept along, they moved closer, their hands woven together, their voices softening.

Rufina settled in her chair with her knitting. Her gentle snoring finally signaled an opportunity for William and Aurora to wrap each other in guarded passion.

❊ ❊ ❊

Aurora had volunteered to take her father's signed approval of the petition to Socorro. She and Rita were supposed to stay with Gloria and come back the next day. The early snow held off. Aurora and Rita had only to endure the pelting of blowing dust. Aurora didn't dare let Rita in on her plan until they were well on their way to Socorro.

She uncurled her fingers and touched Rita's arm. "I hope you don't think badly of me. I'm never alone with William. All we talk about is Socorro, and we can barely touch. I can't stand it any longer, and William. . ." Aurora lifted her arms to the heavens.

Rita's momentary silence made Aurora grimace. Rita cleared her throat and looked down at her hands. "I know what you mean. Remember Ricardo Sandoval. He works for Papá."

Rita flushed crimson. Aurora turned and stared at Rita, her mouth wide open.

"The only time we can meet is after I've cleaned the kitchen," said Rita. "Then I can make an excuse to feed the chickens or gather eggs. I'm tired of meeting behind the chicken coop, but if I tell Papá, we'll never be rid of Santa Cruz trailing behind us." Rita giggled. "Ricardo will be in Socorro this afternoon."

The young women shared a tight hug. Their laughter floated toward the river. Aurora put her finger to her lips and Rita nodded in agreement.

❊ ❊ ❊

The two women went into William's office. Aurora carried a large envelope that William had purposely forgotten at Lemitar. He glanced between Rita and Aurora, then caught Aurora's wink. Jonathan had gone to Magdalena for a few days to tie up the sale of a mine.

Rita said a quick goodbye and steered the buggy out of town. She covered her head with her *mantilla* as the buggy left Socorro. Rita turned toward Ricardo's uncle's old house. The sickly old man had

164

moved in with his daughter last summer. In the empty house Rita and Ricardo were finally alone.

❋❋❋

William's room was quiet, the curtains drawn. He put a finger to his lips and shushed Aurora. "Listen, there's no one around." Pointing to the window, he whispered, "and no one is watching."

Aurora hugged William fiercely for the first time. She pulled away and danced around the room. William caught her, and kissed her with a passion that made the world disappear.

It was the next morning when they heard Rita returning with the buggy. Aurora and William froze. Each rolled out of the bed. Aurora scrambled for her clothes. William pulled on his trousers and tucked in his shirt. Thankfully, Rita had driven the buggy behind the building. She sat on the bench in the *plazita*, a dreamy smile plastered across her face.

Aurora tried to wrap her hair into a presentable bun. She smoothed her dress and buttoned her shoes. At the first sight of William struggling with his clothes, they both erupted into uncontrollable laughter. With their passion spent, they kissed gently and hugged as if this were their last farewell.

❋❋❋

The family was huddled around the table, grateful for the warmth of the fireplace. After supper Aurora's eyes darted around the table, then she cleared her throat.

"I'm tired of making excuses to go into Lemitar when William is meeting with *Tio*," she blurted. "You know why I'm going. I feel like a thief in the night, and I don't like it."

She surveyed her family. All eyes were on her. Even the children had put down their spoons. She sat up straight and put her hands on the table. "Papá, you said I could visit with William. When he comes to Lemitar we'll meet at *Tia* Juanita's house."

Aurora gave her mother a sideways glance. "You know that *Tia* will be close at hand. She'll make sure that no improprieties are taking place." She rolled her eyes and turned toward Josefa. "And I will make it known to her that our visits are not for the town gossip."

Aurora leaned back and waited for the stunned response. Everyone looked at one another. Some shrugged, and some raised eyebrows. Silverware began to clatter again. Esquipula raised his hand and conversations resumed. Rita hunched her shoulders and gave her sister a sly smile.

✳✳✳

Often Aurora would take the boys with her. They would play with *Tia* Juanita's two little girls in the kitchen. *Tia* Juanita hummed while she cooked and mended. She stayed far enough away to give Aurora and William their privacy, but close enough to hear snippets of their conversation.

When William first started visiting, Flavito would hide behind Aurora's skirt. William would always bring the children a little candy treat. The first time William presented his gift, he snatched it away from Flavito when he reached for it. William was sharing a game he had played with his father as a boy. Instead of the giggles he had expected, Flavito exploded into red faced wailing. Aurora had to carry him into the kitchen and hold him until he stopped crying.

"I'm so sorry," stammered William, "I didn't mean to make him cry. I was only playing with him."

Aurora's face was almost as flushed as Flavito's. She was both embarrassed by her son's behavior and miffed at William for playing such a cruel trick. Her little boy had only known generosity and the love of her family.

37

A month after Christmas, it was announced at Mass that William Tell De Baun would soon be eligible to receive the sacrament of reconciliation. William began taking his instruction at Lemitar. While Father Martinez waited for William's baptismal certificate to arrive from Iowa, William rode to Lemitar once a week. The first few times, he stayed in one of the rooms above Manuel's saloon. Taking his evening meals with Aurora's family gave him a chance to ask Josefa and Esquipula endless questions about what he was learning.

Father Lopez in Socorro had assured William that if he had already been baptized, the process of becoming a Catholic would be simpler. But no one seemed to have told old Father Martinez about this. William sat for hours at Lemitar learning the history of the Catholic Church.

Often, he would have to stand and pace as the old priest droned on about saints and rituals. William took note. He promised himself that he would shorten his speeches in court, so he wouldn't put the jurors to sleep.

When he agreed to join Aurora's church, William thought there would be a few visits with the priest. He would make the sign of the cross, and be sprinkled with water. Now Father Martinez was talking about becoming a Catholic during Lent, with fifty more days of instruction. William rode home thinking of how to shorten the process. Next time he met with Father Martinez, William would explain that he didn't have time for this. The Tylor Watkin shooting case was coming up and William had been called to be the judge.

When William went back the next week, and explained how busy he was, Father Martinez put his hands behind his back. "I understand," he quipped. "Perhaps Aurora could become a Baptist." The old priest shook with laughter. "Pardon me, *Señor*," the priest smiled. "I've known the Vigil family for many years and trust me, if you don't become a Catholic, you might as well send for a wife from St. Louis."

Father Martinez walked to the corner of his office. He cleared his throat. "My son, if the only reason you want to convert, is to win the hand of Aurora, you're wasting both of our time. God calls us to be faithful followers of his church. Your reasons have to be right with. . ." He pointed skyward. "Go home and decide if this is really what you want to do."

All the way home, William thought about the quiet dignity of the Mass. He remembered watching eyes lifted to the heavens and hands folded in prayer. His law partner, Jonathan, had told him about these hearty *Hispanos*. He didn't have to tell William how proud they were or how much their faith and families meant to them.

When he got to Socorro, William turned his buggy toward the San Miguel church. The heavy, hand carved door creaked open. William slid into the last pew. The smell of frankincense clung to the thick adobe walls. Heavy *vigas* spanned the ceiling, holding up the heavens. Along the walls, the Stations of the Cross depicted the journey of Christ to his resurrection.

William closed his eyes and envisioned the small clapboard church he attended as a child. He started to hum one of the hymns his mother had taught him. How different this church was. Now that he was alone, William had a chance to look at the wooden carvings of the saints and the Virgin Mary. He had gone West thinking he would settle in a town much like the one he'd grown up in. He thought he would easily fit in with the people who lived there. But this wasn't an empty western land. It belonged to people who still clung to the traditions of their forefathers.

Even in his strict Baptist community, he could have courted a woman without the whole family watching. Aurora was a widow with two children, yet she was being treated like a young girl in need of protection. William put his head in his hands and wondered if it was worth it. Fading light stretched the image of a stained-glass window across his pew. He stared at the colored light and slowly his thoughts began to settle.

He could stay close to the other Easterners and create an enclave among the people who founded Socorro. He tried that when he first arrived. Then he began to see cracks in his idyllic view of the great Americans who came to move the natives forward. There was a widening gap between the rowdy drifters and the people who were trying to bring Eastern refinement to the West.

Caught in the current of change were the proud *Hispanos*. They held tightly to their Spanish traditions and resentments of the *Americanos* who attempted to take their land and change their culture.

William soon found himself drawn to the solid values of Socorro's original people. When he first became interested in Aurora, William took comfort in her family. They cared enough to protect her from suspicious outsiders. William laughed at the memory of wanting to tear Aurora's clothes off while her shy little sister sat cleaning beans at the table. *Perhaps,* he thought, *the family went a little overboard.* William stole a look at the altar, half expecting Saint Michael to come alive and bash him for his unholy thoughts.

William stood to leave but, instead, he walked toward the altar. In the fading light within San Miguel, William realized that the solid walls surrounding him were like the family that held Aurora and her sons. He heard their strength in Aurora's voice when she talked about making Socorro the center of the state.

William could talk to Aurora about anything. Her comments and questions reflected an intelligence that he hadn't seen in other women. He shook his head at the memories of puffed-up aunties pushing their silly nieces toward him, hoping they would catch a lawyer. He let out a snort of laughter that echoed around the church. *I guess sitting through these instructions is better than squirming through another tea party.*

So what if he had to spend endless hours, once a week, learning about the Catholic Church? Father Lopez had assured him that as soon as his baptismal certificate arrived, he would be much closer to receiving the sacrament of reconciliation. If he kept pinching himself to stay awake, he might begin to understand why these devout people surrounded themselves with this religion—Aurora's religion.

The week before Easter, William took his First Holy Communion. A celebratory dinner was held at Esquipula's after Mass. Few people attended. Bitter April winds kept spring at bay and gave the towns-people a good excuse to stay away. José and Telesfora had no excuses. They sat, stiff jowled, in the corner. Every time the boys passed by, Telesfora reached out and hugged them. When she put them down, she glared at William and made the sign of the cross.

Everyone made an effort to ignore José's dire comments. Esquipula raised his wine glass, "*Salud,*" he toasted. "To the newest child of God. May he grow in his faith with the help of our Holy Mother Mary."

Everyone joined the toast, some with glasses held higher than others. Aurora stood next to William. She looked up at him, her face glowing, as if she were looking directly at the sun.

38

Their wedding was held in Socorro at the San Miguel Church. William's law partner, Jonathan, was his best man. Rita was the matron of honor. The reception was held at the Garcia Opera House. Aurora's family filled it to capacity. Scattered among the guests were Judge Eaton and his wife. Lucy Allaire, president of the Ladies of Culture Society, sat next to him. Two other lawyers and some business owners were clustered at the same table.

William had written to his parents, telling them the good news, and offering to pay for their train trip to come to his wedding. His mother wrote back, saying that there was much to do around the farm in the spring. She also feared that his father couldn't travel because his coughing had returned.

William and Aurora stood behind the wedding cake from the French bakery and lifted their glasses as toasts and blessings were recited. William didn't understand most of them, for they were in Spanish. When everyone cheered, "*Salud!*" William repeated and took the opportunity to give his bride another kiss.

Jonathan cleared his throat and began to speak. William noticed, for the first time, that his guests were few, and not that familiar. Then he looked around the overcrowded room filled with Aurora's family, his family now.

Tables were piled with platters of steaming food. Aurora's relatives had cooked for days. They all brought their special dishes to the feast. There were piles of *chili relleno*s—little balls of ground pork stuffed with green *chili*. Tamales were stacked on other platters. Deep pots of beans with chicos sat next to them. Bowls of red *chili* were scattered among the dishes. Plates of *suspidos* looked like clouds of meringue. The little dollops melted in the mouth.

On another table were the delicate sweets that William had ordered from the French bakery. Chocolates were displayed on a three-tiered dessert plate. Pink bonbons were stacked on a china platter. Fluffy macaroons filled crystal bowls.

Before the dancing began, people filled their plates and sat at long tables. William's friends placed a smattering of pastries on their plates while Aurora's relatives stacked their plates with all the foods that they didn't usually get until Christmas.

William's guests huddled at one table with their napkins on their laps. Once in a while a brave soul went to the big table and sampled a *relleno* or *suspido* and declared it delicious.

The first dance was a waltz. Esquipula's eyes were brimming with tears as he held his daughter. With Aurora smiling up at her father's weathered face, he said a silent prayer. He was sending her off with a man from another world. He asked God to walk with her on this unfamiliar path.

William tapped Esquipula on the shoulder and claimed his bride. As they twirled around the dance floor, the voices in the room faded, then the walls disappeared. It was only the two of them, together at last. When the music stopped, they stood for a moment with Aurora's hand folded close to William's heart.

The first dance ended and a *rancherdita* churned the crowd to life. As couples spilled onto the dance floor, Aurora glanced at her *Tio* Manuel who was sitting with his head resting in his hand.

She fanned herself with her hand and pulled William toward the bridal table. "Let's sit," she whispered. "I want to watch my friends celebrating our wedding." William was only too glad to sit this one out. All the food, topped with Esquipula's homemade wine, didn't go well with galloping around the room.

Instead of sitting, Aurora slipped behind her uncle. She wrapped her arms around his shoulders. "Oh, *Tio*, I know this is hard for you. I have to keep pushing some sadness away too. What can I say? My life wasn't supposed to be like this, but here I am."

Manuel gave her hands a squeeze, "I know *Mija*. I'm old enough to know that life doesn't stand still. You should live in happiness instead of sadness. Now go. Go back to your husband." He clenched his hands together to keep them from shaking. ".. . and be happy."

Aurora turned to Isabel, gave her a kiss on the cheek and placed her head against Isabel's for a long moment. When she heard Isabel sniffle, Aurora patted her shoulder. "*Lo siento Tia.*"

Isabel waved her words away. "Flavio is at peace. He's not with us, but he's at peace, and you have to go on with your life." Isabel put a gloved hand on Aurora's. They both sighed deeply, then Aurora moved back to William.

When the celebration finally exhausted itself and the guests trickled home, William and Aurora slipped away to the Windsor Hotel. They spent the next two days away from the world, exploring every inch of each other. Aurora found out more about William in those two days than she had in the year before. Aurora didn't want this time to end, but William had to get back to his work.

✳✳✳

William was building Aurora a spacious brick house, but she had given little thought to where they would live until it was finished. For now, they wedged their belongings into the rooms behind his office. There were only two rooms besides the cramped kitchen. Aurora had to climb over her trunk to get to the bed.

In the morning Aurora balanced on one of her little trunks. Looking in William's cracked mirror, she twisted her hair into a bun. Then she climbed over the bed and into the kitchen. She expected to see William sitting at the table with a mug of coffee, but the kitchen was empty and the stove was cold.

Aurora climbed back over the bed and squeezed into William's office. He noticed her movement out of the corner of his eye. He slowly put down his pen. When he looked up, Aurora was planted in front of his desk.

"We can't stay here long," she groaned. "Where will the boys sleep? I can't leave them with *Tia* Telesfora for more than a few days."

William finished signing the deed he was working on. "Uh, I know, but the house won't be finished for months. I thought you would want to be here in Socorro to oversee the finishes on the interior."

Aurora put her hand on her forehead. "What about the boys? Why can't we stay at my father's house? There are two rooms already fixed up and we can make you an office in the saddle room. Andres could move the saddles into *Tio* Bernardo's old house."

William picked up his pen again. His eyes moved from his paperwork to Aurora. "You want me to move to La Parida and ride to Socorro every day on these roads?"

Aurora shrugged and raised her hand. "Would you have to go every day? Aren't there many days that you do paperwork in your office?" Aurora's arms were crossed.

William stood and walked around his desk. "Let me think about this."

Aurora put her arms around him and snuggled against his chest.

"I'm beginning to see why you always get your way with your father," William sighed.

Aurora laughed and motioned toward the kitchen. "I'll make you

172

some breakfast."

William was right behind her. He shuffled her into the next room and breakfast was forgotten.

The next week Aurora escaped the confinement of William's rooms. When she entered Rufina's parlor, she breathed in the smell of freshly baked *molletes*. Before Rufina set a mug of coffee in front of her, Aurora began her tale of woe. She rolled her eyes. "I knew William was building me a house. He said the building was well on its way. Then I remembered *Señor* Eaton saying that the last load of bricks wouldn't be ready until next month. I didn't think I would have to wait months to move in."

Aurora brushed some crumbs off the table and took the coffee and sweet roll that were offered. "I don't see why we can't stay with my family until it's finished."

Rufina drew in a deep breath. She busied herself with slipping *molletes* into a basket so her words wouldn't escape. *Oh Mija, of course you didn't think.* She made the sign of the cross on her chest. *You have no idea what is in front of you and your children.*

William's partner, Jonathan, knocked on the office door loudly. When there was no answer, he crept inside. Papers on the desk had piled up so high that they slipped onto the floor.

"Hello, is anyone here?" He was grateful that William's bride wasn't there. He looked around the cluttered office and shook his head. *What was he thinking bringing her here? Now I'll never get any work out of him.*

William shoved the bedroom door open and slipped into his office.

"Is Aurora still here?" asked Jonathan.

William shrugged, "I think she's visiting her cousin this morning."

Jonathan glared at William's desk. "Looks like you're getting behind. I know the trial is taking up a lot of your time. I hope that's all it is.

William shook his head. "We have to figure out something different. This isn't working." He grabbed his jacket. "I'm hungry. Let's get a bite to eat. I'll catch you up on the trial."

William and Jonathan took their noon meal at the little French restaurant across from the park. They sat at the table next to the back door and spoke in low voices. Discussion of the saloon shooting was no one's business but their own. With William's report given, the conversation shifted.

"Looks like I'll need to spend a lot more time helping you with the paperwork," grumbled Jonathan. He whisked the crumbs off of his thick mustache. "I assume the little lady will stay in the living quarters during office hours."

William breathed deeply. "She's wants us to move back with her family until the house is finished."

Jonathan slapped his knee. "Are you crazy? How do you expect to be in court and meet with your clients living out in hell-in-gone? What happens if a flash flood washes out the road?" Jonathan stood and slammed his chair into the table. He shook his head. "Oh, and what if I need a document and you have it at La Parida?"

William wiped his lips and put his napkin on the table. "I'm not moving tomorrow. I'll take my time and we'll plan what can go and what can stay; besides it won't be for long. We can move into the house in a couple of months even if it isn't quite finished. Look, it's important for the boys to be with their mother."

Jonathan put his hands up. "So, why can't you find a place in town?"

"I thought about that, but it doesn't make sense to move all of our things, only to move again in a couple of months. I can make this work. Trust me."

Jonathan pointed a finger at William. "You damned well better!" He shoved on his hat and marched toward the courthouse.

William spent the rest of the afternoon going through stacks of trial briefs. The light was fading when he gave up on trying to decide what to take to La Parida. *I need it all.*

He leaned back in his chair and lit a cigar. Then William bolted upright through a cloud of smoke. *What if someone comes in and Jonathan isn't in the office, a defendant or a land sale. I pick up most of my clients when he's out. I can't be out of the office most of the time. I'll just have to explain things to Aurora.*

✳✳✳

Aurora sat on the edge of the bed listening as William explained. "I just can't be away from my office all week. Maybe we can find a furnished place to rent here in Socorro."

"Rent!" echoed Aurora. "What are you thinking? I have family and friends in Socorro. They would be insulted if we paid for a house to stay in. There's my cousin Rufina; oh, and Gloria has a *casita* behind her house."

William waved his hands. "Stop! Stop! We can't all pile in on your cousins, and I don't know how Gloria's husband feels about me. Look, just for now, why don't you go back to your father's house. I may have to stay in town during the week. When I'm in court, I'll have to be here until the case is over, but at least you and the boys will be with your family."

Aurora's brows knitted. "Let me talk to Gloria," she muttered.

William wrapped his arm around Aurora's shoulder. "I've thought about this. I don't want to be beholding to anyone; besides it will only be for a couple of months. You and the boys can come and stay for a day or two while you're checking on the house. I can go to La Parida every Friday evening."

Aurora crossed her arms. She moved toward the window. A wave of dejection washed over her. She forced the feeling out of the pit of her stomach. "Maybe when I come and see you, I can leave the boys with Telesfora so I won't have to take them out in the wind." Aurora didn't turn away from the rippled windowpanes for a long time.

❋❋❋

The last month had gone by faster than Aurora expected. Every time she dropped the boys off at Telesfora's she choked back tears and gave them so many kisses that they wiped their cheeks on their sleeves.

While William worked, Aurora watched the staircase go into her new house. She strolled through every room as the walls went up. Gloria squinted and nodded as Aurora described the progress on her house. With every description of Aurora's grand house, Gloria seemed to slip a little further away from her friend.

At the end of the month Aurora crept through the back door of William's rooms. She put her ear to the office door. When she didn't hear voices, Aurora pushed open the door with her elbow. She was carrying a heavy wallpaper sample book. On top of the book were piled drapery samples. "Look what came into *Tio*'s store," she squealed.

William started and looked up, then he turned back to signing papers. "Uh, Aurora, just a minute."

Aurora set the samples on the floor and grabbed an armful of Williams paperwork. She turned from side to side, looking for a place to put it them.

"Put those back where you found them!" William was on his feet. He plucked the papers from Aurora's hands. "I had them all in order." He started to say, "Don't you understand, this is my law office?"

But, when he looked up, he saw Aurora's wide eyes and open mouth. William caught up to Aurora as she marched toward the buggy.

"Please forgive me," he pleaded. "It's just that I've gotten so far behind since the trial began." He put his hands on his hips and took a deep breath.

Aurora crossed her arms. "Maybe I should just go back to La Parida until you have time for your family." She twisted away from him. "Whenever that will be."

William looked at his bride's quivering lip and lowered his head. "Oh, my dear, I have been ignoring you." He reached for Aurora, but she took a step backwards.

176

Aurora tried to push past William. Her voice was sharp as steel. "I've hardly seen you since we married."

His long arm blocked her path. "Please don't go. You're right. I haven't spent enough time with you." He looked back toward his office searching for the right words.

"The Watkin trial will be over this week. I have to do my paperwork in the evening to keep up but, after this week, I'll be much freer." His voice rose an octave. "Besides, the house is almost finished; then this crazy staying here and there will be over." He reached for Aurora. This time she stepped forward.

William gave Aurora a gentle kiss on the forehead "We'll all be together soon and, you'll see, things will be better."

❅❅❅

As the days got warmer, Aurora went to the new house more often. When the leaves started budding, she took the boys with her to Socorro. While William met with a client, Auora took the boys out for some fresh air. They walked past the park and down McCutcheon Avenue. The boys stopped often to inspect a trail of tiny ants or click their sticks along wrought iron fences. When they came to the two-story brick house, they huddled together just inside the gate.

"This is your new home," Aurora smiled.

Flavito stared, brows furrowed, at the big house. He shook his head and pulled at his mother. "No!" he protested. "I live with my *abuela*."

Manuelito took up the protest. "I don't want to live in this house! I want to go back to *Tia* Telesfora's."

Aurora squeezed Manuelito's hand. He yelped and his mother pulled her hand away. "What's the matter with you?" she screeched. "Your new father has built us this fine house and you're crying about it." She turned on her heel and started up the road. The boys scrambled after her, wide-eyed and crying.

❅❅❅

Rufina brewed another pot of coffee and sent the boys out to play. She sat with her cousin at the kitchen table. "What happened *Mija*?"

Aurora pounded the table. "I can't believe those two! We've been living in two rooms with a dirt floor and they wouldn't even go inside the new house. All they did was cry for their *abuela* and *Tia* Telesfora."

177

Rufina leaned back, then dared to speak. "You have to understand; they're just children. A big house means nothing to them. Living with their grandmother and *tia* is all they've ever known. You want the big house. They just want their family." Rufina sank back in her chair and waited.

Aurora's fury didn't take long to flare. "But I'm their family! I'm their mother! Shouldn't they be happy to be in the new house with me?" She let out a tight breath.

Rufina put her hand over Aurora's. "This is going to be a big change for them. Help them get used to it. Now that it's warmer take them for a walk every day and go past the house. Tell them about their rooms and the stairs, and the big kitchen. Don't try to force them to go in. I think that before long, they'll go without you even asking."

Aurora got up and put her hands on the counter. "Maybe you're right. To tell you the truth, it's been a little hard for me to get used to the changes. All I've ever known is La Parida and my family."

❋❋❋

That evening they ate at the little restaurant at the Park Hotel. William had finished filing the papers for a land sale to the Union Pacific Railroad and he wanted to celebrate. Aurora told him about the boys, and the house, and what Rufina had said.

"Good idea." He ruffled Manuelito's hair. "Manuelito, I bet you're big enough to climb the stairs in your new house."

Manuelito cocked his head. "What are stairs?"

William roared with laughter. "Oh, my Lord, I forgot that adobe huts don't have stairs."

Manuelito turned to his mother who was sitting bolt upright. She slowly eased herself out of her chair, gathered her little boys, and took a step toward the door. "We don't live in huts."

When the food was served, William was sitting alone, his face as pale as the tablecloth. He paid the waiter for the food and told him to give it to the miners who had just come in.

William walked around the park then back down Camino Royal to his office. He needed the time to sort out another of his blunders and think of how to make up for the hurt he had caused Aurora.

William opened the door slowly in hopes that it wouldn't creak, but the old wood gave up a warning. The boys were nestled in a cot in the corner of his office. William looked into the bedroom and found it empty. When he stepped into the *plazita*, Aurora turned her back to him. He reached for her, but she jerked away.

"So that's what you really think of us, a bunch of animals living in mud huts. . ." She didn't get all the words out before her lips started to quiver.

William perched on the bench and cradled his head in his hands. "Aurora, you're dearer to me than anyone else in the world. I'm so sorry for offending you. Of course, I didn't mean to say that you lived in a hut."

Aurora spun around. "That's what you said. *Tio* José says that lawyers start lying as soon as they open their mouths. Why should I believe you?"

William stomped across the yard and stood against the sagging fence. He had to clamp his jaw shut to keep from skinning José alive with his words. Now he chose his words carefully. This was a case he didn't want to lose.

"You know that *Tio* José doesn't have anything good to say about anyone. You have to believe me. I admire your family so much—your uncle Manuel with all his enterprises and your father with his farm. I admire the way your mother wants to protect you and your children. You're the finest people I've ever known. When I use the word hut, it is what we call the sod houses on the prairie. They're made of mud and grass. The people living in them are strong, enduring people, just like your family."

Aurora let his words soften her a little, then her eyes narrowed. "You were laughing at Manuelito because he didn't know what stairs were. You were insulting us just because we don't live in big brick houses. You think you're better than us."

"If I thought I was better than you, I wouldn't have given you a second look but, since the first time I saw you, I couldn't stop thinking about you. You're so different from other women around here. You're intelligent and curious. You understand what it's going to take to move Socorro forward. How can you think that I don't respect you?" William reached for her hand and this time Aurora didn't pull away.

"Please forgive my ignorant blunders."

She walked around the little yard shaking her head. Then she stood in front of William with her hands on her hips. He put both of his hands out and Aurora reached for them.

40

As May melted into June, the outside of the house was finished. Aurora spent the summer in a flurry of decorating and decision-making. The high ceilings unnerved her. *What a waste of space*, she thought. When she spoke, her words echoed around the room. She did love the wallpaper though, soft greens with little colorful birds balancing on branches. The furniture finally arrived from St. Louis. *Tio* Manuel had sent a special freight wagon for it.

Aurora had planned to fill her new house with the furniture she had bought for Mesilla. When she slid the dust covers off, the room filled with almost three years of dust. It engulfed the air and stirred her memories. In the end, she couldn't bring herself to live with the things that had been hers and Flavio's.

Rita had married Ricardo in the spring with the family celebrating in Esquipula's *plazita*. Aurora had Ricardo load her furniture into the wagon and rode with them over the hill to Rita's adobe. The bed filled the back room and the chairs towered above the worn kitchen table. Rita and Ricardo looked from the furniture to each other.

Rita blinked and said, "I guess the house in Mesilla was bigger than this one."

Ricardo just shrugged.

Aurora giggled. "You'll find a place for all of it." She elbowed Ricardo. "Maybe you can build your bride a big bedroom behind this one. Then you'll have a room for your babies."

Ricardo slapped his forehead and turned toward Rita. "Now I know where you learned how to act like a banty rooster."

As Aurora climbed back onto the wagon, she turned to Ricardo. "Please let her come with you the next time you ride to Socorro." She turned to Rita. "Wait 'till you see my parlor and the kitchen." She clapped her hands like a child waiting for a candy stick.

"Well, tomorrow I have to open *Tio* Manuel's grist mill," Ricardo answered. He winked at Rita who was squeezing her hands together and smiling hopefully. Ricardo hunched up his shoulders and smiled, "I want to see it too."

❇❇❇

The couple stood fixed to the floor in the entry hall of Aurora's new house. Their lips parted as their eyes moved up and up the oak staircase. Rita ambled around the parlor as if in a dream. She touched the heavy satin drapes and grinned at Aurora.

"Wait until you see the kitchen." Aurora tried to pull Rita through the dining room, but she latched onto one of the chairs. "My whole house could fit in here. What are you going to do with so much room?"

"I'm going to have parties, baptisms, maybe even weddings. And the cooking will be done in the kitchen, away from everyone. The food will be brought into the dining room. It will be set on the buffet just like the restaurant at the Grand Central Hotel."

Rita put her hands to her mouth to hide the little girl giggles that erupted.

When she stepped into the kitchen Rita froze. "No, this," she waved her hand across the room, "is bigger than my whole house." She looked up and up at the cabinets that went to the ceiling. The soapstone sink was cool to her touch and there was a pump. . . inside the house.

Rita danced to the pump on her tip toes. She looked at Aurora, pointing to the pump. Aurora nodded. Rita lifted the pump handle as if it were a scepter, and slowly pushed it down. Then she gave it two more pumps and watched in awe as water gushed from the gleaming black pump.

When she got to the stove, Rita touched the satiny iron with reverence. The cast iron scroll work gleamed in the sunlight streaming from the big window above the sink."

"I've never seen a new stove before. Aren't you afraid to get it dirty?"

Aurora had been leaning against the bead-board wall soaking in her sister's reaction.

With all of Rita's questions answered, the young women twirled each other around the room. They laughed as if the years had not passed since they were children.

Ricardo slapped his thigh and joined their laughter. He waged a finger at his wife. "Don't go getting any ideas," he teased. "We can barely afford the wood to put in the stove."

Aurora stuck out her tongue at Ricardo. Her childhood friend chased her around the kitchen in mock anger.

"You've been hiding your pennies since you were a little boy," laughed Aurora. "When are you going to let loose for my poor sister?" They continued their banter up the stairs.

To the right were two rooms for the boys, papered in brown stripes. The shelves were almost empty, but Aurora planned to fill them with toys and books. Across the hall there were two empty bedrooms.

To the left of the stairs was Aurora and William's bedroom. The tall bed was elaborately carved. In the corner was a short dressing table with drawers on each side of a long mirror. On the other side of the room was a tall chest of drawers. All three pieces were fashioned of oak with burl wood inserts.

"Oh!" sighed Rita. She reached for Ricardo's hand. They explored the room as if they had been transported to a fairy land. Rita carefully opened a door that led to a nursery. Flavito's cradle stood near the window, but the rest of the room was empty. Aurora and Rita shared a mischievous smirk.

"Not yet," admitted Aurora, "but hopefully soon."

Ricardo waved the women away and stuffed on his hat. "I've had enough of this hen-cackling," he laughed. "I'm going to do something important."

His boots clattered down the steps. Before Ricardo opened the heavy oak door, he took one more look around. He let out a long, low whistle as he went out the front door.

"Let's sit in the parlor," invited Aurora. "I'll have Anita, uh my maid, make us some coffee."

Aurora hooked her arm in Rita's and they pranced down the stairs. They settled into the maroon upholstered chairs. Sipping coffee from bone china cups, the women fell into a comfortable silence. Then Aurora leaned forward.

"Oh Rita, I wish you could come live with us. There's plenty of room. You and Ricardo could stay in the room across the hall from the boys until the *casita* is finished."

Rita looked down and started wringing her hands. "You know we can't. Ricardo works for Papá and we can't live so far from the farm."

"I don't know what I'm going to do without you. Anita will be alright for a while, but she lets the boys do whatever they want. Does she know how to take care of the rugs and all this oak furniture? William wants me to learn how to cook some American dishes and Anita won't be much help."

"Can't you find someone from Socorro, an *Americana* who knows how to cook?" Rita tapped her chin. "Maybe you can find someone who can help the boys learn English while she's here."

"I'm teaching the boys a little. William only lets them talk to him in English, so they're learning." She squirmed and lowered her voice. "Besides, I'm learning too, about all of it. In Socorro there are women's clubs and societies. They have ideas to improve the community. It's so exciting."

Aurora sank back into her chair. "But I don't know many *Americanos*." Her eyes darted from side to side. "Wait, there are a few who go to San Miguel."

"Ask Father Lopez or the sisters," suggested Rita. "Maybe one of the girls from Mount Carmel School can help."

"You may have a good idea. I would make sure that the sisters find someone I can trust. I don't want anyone wagging their tongue if they see me make a mistake. I want William to be proud of me, especially around the *Americanos*."

They nibbled on another raspberry scone. Aurora's thoughts drifted to the convent school, then back to the parlor.

She reached for Rita and their fingers touched. "But it won't be the same without you."

Rita lowered her head. "I've missed you since the day of your wedding. I thought we would all live at La Parida forever."

Aurora shrugged, then smiled a little. "Socorro isn't that far away. The boys always want to see *Tia* and Mamá and I'm still bringing things back for the house."

Rita breathed in a gulp of air. "And you'll come and see me every time you're in La Parida?"

"Always, and when you have your babies, I'll be there to help."

The sisters held each other in a long embrace. "Come on," smiled Aurora, "I want to show you the wedding dishes *Señora* Dougherty gave me."

❋ ❋ ❋

It was Sister Mary Agnes who found a girl for Aurora. Sophie O'Neil came from Magdalena. Her father had died two years ago in the Graphic Mine cave-in. Since then, Sophie had helped her mother with the cooking at the Mountain Queen Saloon.

"She's a good girl," Sister Mary Agnes said. "Her mother sent her to us because Magdalena is getting too rough. She'll be safe with us. She's earning her tuition by helping the sisters prepare meals at the boarding school."

183

When William interviewed Sophie, she kept her hands folded on her lap and her eyes on the floor. He kept asking her questions because he wanted to hear her speak. With a name like O'Neil, William didn't want the boys learning English with an Irish brogue. To his relief, Sophie explained that her mother was from New England and hadn't wanted to go out West. Her husband had convinced her that he could strike it rich in Magdalena. Sophie looked up for the first time, her voice raised, "And now look at the fix we're in. Mother is trying to save enough money to get us back to her family." She dropped her eyes again. "This job will help."

41

"I suppose I must have a tea for her," Mrs. Dougherty sighed. With raised eyebrows, she looked at the women in the Ladies League. "I would like to see her house; they say it's grand."

Julia Dougherty held her cake in midair and continued. "I've lived in Socorro longer than all of you and I've gotten to know the locals. Aurora comes from a fine family. The Vigils and the Pinos do a lot for the community. It would serve us well to take Aurora into our circle."

She took another sip of tea. "I suppose it's time for the East to come together with the West. It would serve us all."

Jonathan's wife passed the little tea cakes to Mrs. Taylor.

❋ ❋ ❋

Aurora sat on the edge of her chair with an embroidered napkin on her lap. She breathed a sigh of relief that the cakes and pastries were familiar to her. Instead of coffee, Mrs. Dougherty served pale tea. Aurora watched the other women carefully, then poured cream and sugar into her cup. At the first taste, she squeezed her eyes shut and puckered her lips. She hoped the other women hadn't noticed.

Aurora had met most of the women at her wedding, although she couldn't put names with faces yet. Three of the women were much older than herself. When they told her where they lived, Aurora realized that they were neighbors. "You must invite us over for tea," Priscilla gushed.

Evelyn jumped in, "Everyone's been wanting to see your beautiful house. They say your furniture was brought from St. Louis on a special freight wagon."

Aurora sat up a little straighter. "Yes, it was my *Tio*, uh, uncle's freight wagon. He goes to St. Louis to purchase goods for his store." To her surprise, bragging about *Tio* Manuel made her feel uneasy.

The older women spoke in high pitched voices. Everything they said seemed to be rehearsed. Aurora felt like she was in a school play. She began to see which women sat the stiffest and bragged the most. This was nothing like the gathering of women she was used to. Her friends circled the kitchen table and did their share of the cooking. The room was always filled with laughter and talking about each other's business.

Aurora couldn't wait to leave and tell Rita about these strange females. A lump formed in her throat when she remembered that Rita wouldn't be there when she got home. *Gloria*, she thought, *I'll tell Gloria about this and we'll have a good laugh.*

Aurora's thoughts snapped back to Julia's parlor. At precisely two o'clock the tea was over and the ladies hurried out the door. Discovering that Evelyn lived only two blocks away, Aurora offered to take her home. Evelyn accepted, and on the way, Aurora let Evelyn do most of the talking.

It turned out that Evelyn's husband was a professor at the new School of Mines. "I don't understand most of what he talks about," Evelyn admitted. "That's why I want to make friends with the women in town. It's been kind of lonely since we moved from Missouri."

If Aurora closed her eyes, she could imagine Gloria chattering away. Evelyn seemed to know all the latest gossip. Laughter came easy for her. Evelyn's youngest child was Manuelito's age and she only lived two blocks away. They made plans to meet the next week. It would be an easy walk for Aurora and the boys.

William was waiting on the porch. "So how did it go?"

He wrapped his arms around Aurora. For the first time since she entered Mrs. Dougherty's house, Aurora let her shoulders drop.

"I was so nervous at first, but Mrs. Dougherty made me feel at home. There were four other women at the tea. I remember meeting them at the wedding, but I didn't remember their names. It turns out that Evelyn Taylor lives not far from here. I'm going to visit her next week. She reminds me of Gloria. I'm sure I'll find out all about the other women from her."

She took William's hand. "Meeting all these new people is so exciting. Estella and Gloria and the rest of my friends have been with me since I was a little girl. Meeting these women almost feels like I've gone back East. They're so different."

William chuckled and kissed Aurora on the cheek. Aurora's fingers flew to her lips. "Evelyn said her husband was a professor at the School of Mines. I hope you're with me when I meet him. I wouldn't know what to say."

William lit his cigar and patted Aurora on the shoulder. "You've made a good choice. I've known the Taylors for a while and she'll make a good friend. She's a lot like you, but her family is from St. Louis. Her husband said that when she first came out here, it was like a different world for her. I know just how she felt." William took Aurora's hand. "You can help each other. Maybe you can introduce her to some of your friends."

Aurora agreed, but the knot in her stomach warned otherwise.

By the next day Aurora had changed her mind about going to Gloria's. *I'll give them a chance,* she thought. *I'll go see Gloria after I visit with Evelyn. Then I'll have more to tell her. Oh, and maybe I'll invite Gloria and Evelyn over so they can meet.*

42

Aurora had Juan drive her to Lemitar to pick up the furniture for William's study. She was grateful that William had hired Juan. He did all the heavy lifting and took care of the horses.

Telesfora's wagon was parked in front of Manuel's store. Aurora looked to the heavens. Her little boy's shouts drowned out her groan.

"*Tia* is here!" shouted Manuelito.

The boys bolted into the store. Telesfora knelt down and embraced both of them. Three-year-old Flavito started singing *Las Mañanitas* to her. Everyone in the store roared and clapped.

"Come and give your *abuelo* a hug." Manuel knelt and opened his arms wide. His two little grandsons rushed to embrace him. Telesfora was right behind them.

"Let me take them to the house while you're telling the men what to load," Telesfora said. "You can pick them up on your way back to Socorro. I'll have something for you to eat when you get there."

Aurora's jaws tightened. She looked from Telesfora to José. "The boys will be fine here at the store. I'm sure they want to spend some time with their *abuelo* ."

Telesfora studied the floor. "I suppose that would be alright. I'll be in the store for a while too. Then perhaps I can take them to see Isabel."

Aurora's jaw relaxed. *How long had it been since Isabel had seen her grandsons?* On the way home she planned to visit Isabel then go see Rita as promised.

Aurora rolled her eyes, then nodded. Telesfora started showing the boys all the new things in the store. Manuel sent Severo to the saloon to get each boy a bottle of sarsaparilla.

Aurora went out to the storehouse leaving Manuel to enjoy his grandsons. On the way out, her stomach began to tighten. When Aurora went back inside, she put her hand on Telesfora's shoulder.

"*Lo siento Tia*, but I don't have time for all this visiting. I have so many things to do at home. I'll come back on Sunday and spend the afternoon with all of you." Aurora glanced at Manuel. His smile had drained away and the light in his eyes dimmed.

"Of course, I'll stop and visit Isabel on my way home today, but I can't stay long. She'll understand."

Flavito hid behind the counter. Manuelito stomped his feet, his fists tightened into little balls. "I won't go!" he screeched.

Aurora stood in front of her five-year-old son, and stomped one foot. "Yes, you will go! Besides, we're not going home right now. We're going to see your *Abuela* Isabel. We have a present for her."

Flavito peeked out from around the counter. "What is it, cookies?"

"You'll have to come with me. You can see what I brought her when we get to her house. She's waiting for us. Let's go."

Telesfora followed them to the edge of the porch waving and dabbing her eyes. She stepped into the road and watched the buggy until it was out of sight.

Isabel was waiting at the gate when they arrived. "I heard the buggy. I was hoping it was you."

She held Flavito's face in her hands and sucked in her breath. His green eyes pierced her grief and made it come alive again. She stood and worked at trying to swallow back tears. "He looks so much like Flavio."

Aurora reached for her hand. She wanted to tell her how many times her first husband had haunted her dreams. In most of them, the faces of her little boys replaced Flavio's. When she dreamed, she always woke with a start, but she told no one about them.

Aurora didn't have time to tell Flavio's mother how much she treasured the resemblance. Flavito was jumping up and down with the package in his hand.

"Open it, open it!"

"What is it, *Mijito*?

"It's for you *Abuela*. We brought it from the store."

Isabel took Flavito's hand. "Well, let's go inside and see what it is."

The boys crawled onto the kitchen benches while their grandmother carefully opened the brown paper package. The box was from a jewelry store in St. Louis. She opened it carefully and found a filigree brooch with an emerald in the center.

"*Tio* Manuel had this sent back with my furniture." Aurora touched the brooch softly with her fingertips.

"That Manuel, he spoils me." Isabel smiled.

"What is it?" Manuelito shouted.

Isabel showed them how the brooch worked. Against her better judgment she let each boy wear it for a while, as long as they were sitting at the table.

"Let me fix the boys some *atole*," Isabel offered. "It's been so long since I've seen them. I know you've been busy with your new house, but it's finished now. I hope we'll see more of you and the boys."

"I will come more often now that it's summer, but I want you to come and see my new house. You're not going to believe how beautiful it is, and you know you're welcome any time.

Isabel busied herself heating milk for the *atole*, ignoring Aurora's invitation. Isabel's children clustered around the table. Some climbed onto benches. Others tugged at Manuelito.

"Can the boys go out and play?" begged Francisco.

Isabel poured each of them a cup of *atole* and sent them to the porch. When Manuelito and Flavito followed she put her arms out.

"Stay inside with me for a while." She looked at Aurora with the same despondent eyes that Aurora had seen at the store.

"I want to be with them as long as I can." She followed Manuelito with her eyes. "Telesfora brought the boys the other day when the men were moving your furniture to Rita's. She was worried that they would be in your way."

Aurora bit her lip and thought for a moment before she spoke. "I'm grateful for Telesfora's help. I'm glad she brought the boys to see you, but now that the house is finished, I won't need her help anymore. I've hired a girl from the convent school. She's going to teach the boys English too. Telesfora doesn't have to worry. You know she can come into town with you or José and she's always welcome in my home."

When Aurora drove away from Isabel's, she felt the silence of her mother-in-law. As she drove up the hill toward Socorro, she shivered. Aurora had the haunting feeling that a cord had been broken that bound her to her family.

❋ ❋ ❋

The next Sunday Aurora made the dusty trip to La Parida. She was comforted by the thought that she would be taking her last load of furniture back to Socorro. She had hoped that William would come along to help Ricardo load the wagon. When Aurora asked him, William held up two hands full of documents and shook his head. Aurora set her jaw and slipped silently out the back door.

Aurora was glad to see Rita's wagon in front of her mother's house. *Good,* she thought, *one less place to stop.* She scrambled out of the buggy and lifted her sons down before they had a chance to jump.

Aurora helped her mother put the food on the table. Rita had told everyone in La Parida about Aurora's beautiful house; about the crystal and the china, about the wallpaper and the soft furniture. She told them about the big bedrooms that were up the stairs. Most of all, she told the women about Aurora's kitchen.

"Mamá, please come to Socorro and see my house. I know Papá is busy in the fields, but you can come with Telesfora or Isabel. I want all of you to see it."

Josefa's eyebrows rose. She glanced at the galvanized tub. "Well, not this week," she laughed softly. "I have to wash all the blankets. You know how they get in the winter."

Aurora took her mother's rough red hands. "I'll send you some lilac salve from the mercantile."

Josefa chuckled. "Don't worry *Mija;* I have some *azafrán* from La Señora. You should take some."

Aurora shook her head. "Next Sunday, after Mass, you will be the first guests at my dinner party."

Josefa snorted. Her brows knitted. "You know how much there is to do after the winter." She glanced at Aurora's pleading hands pressed against her heart. "Oh, I suppose we can go to the late Mass at San Miguel, then to your house."

Aurora swished toward the door. "I'll go talk to Papá." Aurora turned and hugged her mother after gently scolding her for not making Barbara do the heavy washing.

Josefa shook her head stiffly. "She has enough to do for her own family." She rolled her eyes. *Aurora has no idea what I'm talking about.*

Aurora put her finger to her temple. "I'll find you someone. Mamá, you are the *dona* of this farm. You shouldn't have to do all his hard work." Aurora kissed her mother on the cheek, gathered up her boys, and walked down to the fields.

Josefa groaned. She pulled herself up and pranced to the wash-tub. "*Dona* Josefa!" she laughed.

43

William came home to a flurry of activity in the kitchen. Aurora was following Sophie around, learning how to make shepherd's pie. She wanted her mamá to taste the food she was now making for William. A pot of beans was also on the stove, steaming up the windows. The boys were standing on chairs at the counter. Each one was twisting a wad of sticky dough. Manuelito patiently attempted to show Flavito how to roll out a circle.

William put his hands on his hips. "What have we here?"

Everyone jerked to a stop. "Oh, William, I'm so glad you're home. I want to know what you think."

"I think," answered William, "that you're turning your boys into little kitchen helpers when they should be roughhousing outside."

He started to reach for Manuelito, but Aurora put her arm out. "We always let the little ones play with some dough so we can cook without worrying about them. Now that you're here, you can take them outside." Aurora winked at William. He gave her a peck on the cheek.

"I'll be back in a while. I have some briefs to look over. I can take them out for a little while, but I'd plan to do a lot of work at home this afternoon."

Aurora stood in silence for a moment thinking of how her father and brothers would take the boys to the farm or the corrals. Her sons never seemed to be a burden to them.

She shook off the memories and chased after William. He was already sitting at his desk with a pile of papers in front of him. "I thought you could help me make up my mind about the meal for tomorrow."

William dropped his pen and squinted at Aurora. The light coming through the window made the loose curls around her face glow. With her lower lip pushed into a pout, she looked like a child in the schoolmaster's office. William stood and embraced his little wife. He sat her on his lap and held her tight.

"What did you want to talk about?" He forced himself to listen, then finally interrupted. William assured Aurora that she should serve both the shepherd's pie and all of the food her family usually ate. "Make plenty. You know how much I like your cooking."

Aurora skipped back into the kitchen. The afternoon was spent making *carne de olla*, and puffy biscuits. Aurora didn't notice that William hadn't returned.

✳✳✳

"We have a new house! We have a new house!" Manuelito and Flavito announced in unison. They hopped up and down and tugged at their *abuela*. "You have to come see our room." Manuelito's eyes widened. He pointed toward the banister. "It's up the stairs," he said in a reverent tone.

Before they sat down to their meal, Aurora guided her family around her beautiful new home. Josefa touched everything: the oak banisters, the marble buffet top, the fine bone china, and the upholstery on the overstuffed chairs. She kept her thoughts to herself. *It is all very grand, but the walls are cold. There is no smell of piñon wood in the kitchen. The kitchen is big yes, but there is no table for the children to gather and learn to cook from their mother. There is no place for the tías to sit and visit while their meal is being prepared.*

Esquipula shook William's hand. "This is a fine house you have provided for my daughter. I'm sure she'll be happy here." With his brows knitted, he gave Josefa a quick glance.

"And you'll come to see us often I hope," invited William. "Now you'll have a place to stay when the family comes to Socorro. We have plenty of room." William took Esquipula to the backyard to show him the unfinished stable.

Aurora led her mother into the dining room. Sophie gathered up the children, washed their hands and faces, and sat them in their places at the table. Josefa smothered her grandchildren with kisses, then put a soft hand on Aurora's face. She started into the kitchen to help serve. Aurora put her hand over her mouth to suppress a giggle. "No, Mamá, Sophie will bring the food in."

After her family left, Aurora sauntered toward the porch to talk about the day with her husband. She looked across the street and the joy of the day faded a little. When Aurora looked out, she didn't see rose colored mountains in the distance. She couldn't smell the wheat and the corn. She couldn't hear the rustling of cottonwood leaves.

She saw a house across the street. She heard the clatter of wagons and buggies. She sat, put her elbow on the arm of the chair, and tilted her head. Her mother's words came back to her. *How can you hear the crickets with all this noise?*

193

44

While the summer heat came alive, Aurora invited her friends and the rest of her family to see her new house.

"This looks like the houses in St. Louis," *Tio* Manuel observed. He lingered in every room. At the end of the tour, he slapped William on the back. "It looks like the East has come to our little Socorro."

Isabel dug her fingers into the palms of her hands to remind herself that the past could not be erased. She admired the furniture and sipped coffee in the parlor. She forced a smile toward Aurora, but couldn't manage to lift her eyes to William.

Manuel wiped his mustache and pushed himself up from his chair. "I'm sorry we can't stay longer. I have to meet with *Señor* Bursum at the bank." He gave Isabel a sideways glance. "Oh, and Isabel has some lace work for Rufina. I bought in St. Louis." Manuel took his wife's elbow and helped her up.

Aurora looked from her aunt to her uncle. She drew in a deep breath. "Oh, I'm sorry you can't stay longer. Perhaps next time you can have supper with us." Her voice trailed off as she followed Flavio's parents to the door.

Isabel managed to hold in a shuddering breath until they reached the buggy. As they drove out of the yard, Manuel put his big hand over hers. "Don't worry, *mi amor*, we did our duty to the family, but we don't have to go back."

Isabel put her hand over her mouth and looked away.

Aurora waved goodbye, but she was unnoticed. She hurried inside and brushed past William. She took the stairs two at a time. Aurora leaned against the closed bedroom door and let her hands uncoil. When her heart stopped racing, Aurora crept downstairs. With each step, she braced herself for her talk with William. She thought it was important to explain why her aunt and uncle had left so suddenly.

She found William in his study propped behind one of his law books. She was well into her hurried explanation when William looked up with a scowl. "I understand, your uncle had business to attend to. Men have more on their minds than tea parties."

Aurora's mouth dropped open, but no words escaped. The tightness in her chest threatened to stop her breathing. She was standing in the hall, not knowing how she got there. Aurora went outside to check on the boys. Then she wandered through the downstairs rooms.

When she stepped back into William's study, her voice had returned. Aurora's eyes flared as she rushed towards William's desk. She cleared her throat, pulling him away from his law book.

"What is it now?" He asked dryly.

Aurora slammed his book shut. "Listen to me!" she screamed. "I need to talk to you, but you never listen to me!" She clenched her jaw, and willed her eyes not to fill with tears, but her tears had a mind of their own.

William stood and reached for Aurora. She pulled away. "What are you talking about? Why are you so upset?" questioned William. "I thought the visit went well. Manuel is a busy man."

"Didn't you see the sadness in *Tia's* eyes? Couldn't you see that they were anxious to leave? Maybe you didn't, because you've forgotten who their son was." She pounded her fist on the desk and slapped the air. "Oh, go back to your precious law books. What happens in my family is no concern of yours."

Aurora flew out of the study, leaving William stunned into silence. No amount of coaxing would make Aurora bring up her uncle's visit again, so William slipped back to his desk and finished the brief he was preparing.

❋ ❋ ❋

Aurora lifted her spirits by inviting Gloria to come over in the middle of the afternoon. When Aurora opened the door, the front porch was crowded with all their friends. Gloria smiled at Aurora, "They all wanted to see your house."

Her friends wanted to go into the kitchen, for that was the place for visiting while making meals. Instead, Aurora led them into the parlor. They sat stiffly on the edge of the furniture. Sophie brought in little pastries and a silver teapot that was filled, not with tea, but with coffee. Aurora didn't think her friends were ready for tea yet.

Gloria put her nose in the air and held her cup with her little finger sticking out. "So, this is how the *Americanas* visit. I guess we'll have to get used to this when we come to your house. But don't think you'll be treated like a dona when you come to my house." The clattering of china halted.

Aurora stared at her friend, mouth agape. She sucked in her breath. "I just wanted to treat you to a tea," she stammered. "I know

195

you're not used to this. I'm not either, but I'm trying, because this is the world I'm living in now. This is what William's friends do."

Aurora put the teapot down with a shaky hand. She rushed into the kitchen with the excuse that the scones had been forgotten. She pressed both hands on the counter to steady herself. *Do they think I'm looking down my nose at them? I bet they're laughing at me right now. What was I thinking, having a tea?*

Aurora called to her friends, "Come into the kitchen. It's cooler in here." The gaggle of women clutched their teacups to their chests and joined Aurora in their nesting place. Settled into chairs brought from the dining room, their gossip began in earnest.

45

The summer heat began to drain Aurora. Every time she went to Rufina's, she felt the relief of the thick adobe walls. They sat in the little back room. The small windows were shaded by the cottonwoods that grew at the corner of her house. Aurora sipped mint water and listened to Rufina talk about who she saw and what they said. Rufina lifted her head a little when she repeated the advice she had given to her young friends.

Aurora had very little to add, just what was going on in Gloria's life. She thought about her new sewing circle and how much she enjoyed Evelyn. But her life didn't seem to fit into the rhythm of Rufina's.

Aurora was grateful, though, that she had Evelyn for her friend because, with her, she could practice being in William's world without having to be so stiff and formal. Evelyn, like Gloria, knew all the gossip of the *Americanos* in Socorro and loved telling stories. They visited back and forth often. Aurora finally trusted her enough to admit that she needed practice with the teas and committee meetings.

"I had to get used to them too," admitted Evelyn. She told Aurora that her family had lived on the edge of town. Her grandfather farmed the land along the river. Evelyn had spent most of her days in her grandmother's kitchen. "I don't know who makes the rules for the teas and committees, but they're not my favorite thing to do."

Aurora squeezed Evelyn's hand and breathed a long sigh of relief. She made up her mind that she would be part of the women's circles when she needed to, but the rest of the time she would be Aurora from La Parida.

Aurora planned to go to the farm to visit her family, but the days slipped by. Her busy weeks were filled with Ladies League meetings to discuss laws and rules for their newly incorporated town. Then there were planning committees to decide what food and entertainment would be offered at the election rallies.

Once in a while, Gloria would drop by when she came to town. When Gloria knocked, Aurora would put away her planning diary and invite her old friend into the kitchen where Aurora had installed a sturdy wooden table and four chairs.

"I want you to meet Evelyn," said Aurora, her eyebrows hopefully raised. "She's a lot like us. Can you come over next week when you're in Socorro? I'll have to set a time to make sure she can be here when you come."

Gloria raised her voice to a high pitch and started to say, "Oh yes, I'll have to check my social diary to see when I'm free." But one glance at Aurora's tight lips convinced Gloria that her lifelong friend wouldn't think this was funny. "I won't be coming back until next Friday. So, what is Evelyn like?"

Aurora tried to make her new friend seem like any other young housewife and mother. "She has three children, just like you, and they're about the same age. Her husband works at the School of Mines so he knows a lot about what's going on in Socorro."

Gloria nodded, but didn't voice, *everything that's going on with the Americanos, who cares?* Riding home, Gloria began to wonder if she really wanted to meet this Evelyn. She wasn't even sure about going back to Aurora's big house if she had to act like a prissy *Americana*. As she bumped along the rutted road, Gloria twisted her lips. By the time she got home, a sadness had settled where the knot in her chest had been.

❋❋❋

Aurora ran to the door at the sound of Gloria's wagon. Evelyn was perched on the edge of Aurora's parlor chair. Polite nods were exchanged when Aurora made introductions. After the children finished eating apple pie in the kitchen, they were all sent outside to play.

As Evelyn set a bon-bon on her dessert plate, Gloria began talking about her friends. Aurora giggled nervously and tried to change the subject. Her head turned back and forth trying to explain to Evelyn who Gloria was talking about.

It was hard for Gloria to remember to speak English when her native tongue was more comfortable. When Gloria and Aurora were talking about their friends, Evelyn stared, with her face scrunched up.

Every chance she got, Evelyn broke in and talked about her friends and the building going on in Socorro. Of course, Aurora knew all the people she was talking about. Sometimes their conversation got so long that Gloria faded into the wallpaper.

By the time the visit was over, Aurora was exhausted. She wished she could talk to Gloria alone before she left, but Gloria gathered her children and rushed to the wagon. As her wagon clattered into the street, Gloria didn't turn and wave like she usually did.

198

Aurora didn't offer Evelyn a second cup of coffee. As she began to pick up the teacups, Evelyn said a quick goodbye. She hurried down the street with her children running to catch up with her.

After Aurora waved goodbye to Evelyn, she went upstairs and sank into an armchair. She folded her hands and looked toward the heavens. *How do I do this?* She bowed her head, and in her silence her question was answered. She would keep her old friends separate from her new friends. This seemed simple enough.

Aurora planned to see Gloria the next day. She had so much to explain. But the next day, the heat wave that was suffocating Socorro held tight. Aurora's queasy stomach and headache were blamed on the heat.

She certainly didn't want to drive all the way out to Gloria's in the middle of the day. *I'll see her after Mass on Sunday,* thought Aurora. *In fact, I think I'll invite them over. I don't know how Alberto feels about William, but maybe this will be a chance for them to get to know each other. After all, Alberto seems interested in seeing Socorro prosper and William always says he wants to be a part of the Hispano community.*

On Sunday, Aurora followed Gloria out of San Miguel. "Please, all of you, come to my house. Sophie has made a light lunch for us."

Alberto grunted softly, "Maybe, just for a while. I have to get the water to the cattle. With this heat, I have to go to the ranch every day."

The women sat in the parlor with the drapes closed against the heat. "I have to tell you how hard it's been trying to fit in with the *Americanos.* I thought we could all be friends, but they know people you don't." Aurora reached forward and touched Gloria's arm. "But you know, we all have the same stories."

Gloria muttered, "Well, maybe I should try another visit." But, the flat tone of her voice let both women know that this probably wouldn't happen.

❋ ❋ ❋

William and Aurora weren't able to sit on the porch that evening. Even though the sun had gone down behind the big Socorro Mountain, the heat was still too much to bear. Aurora put the boys to bed and joined William in their bedroom.

"I can see why you like Alberto and Gloria," said William as he lowered himself onto the rocker. "He knows a lot about ranching. His uncle leads one of the crews of the Graphic Mine. He's heard talk about the railroad building a spur to Magdalena." William lit his pipe and waited for Aurora to respond. He had cleared the afternoon for the visit, determined not to make any more blunders.

"I'm so glad you got along with Alberto today. I want Gloria and her family to feel comfortable in our home. The visit with Evelyn didn't go so well. The wives of your friends live in a different Socorro than Gloria does." Aurora puffed out a quick laugh, ". . . and I used to."

William looked at Aurora with his head cocked. "Are they really so different?"

Aurora wrung her hands, then peered out the window. "I think Evelyn is a lot like me. *Señora* Dougherty wants me to join her entertainment committee for the Young Republicans. Evelyn said she would tell me about it so I would know what was going on before the meeting."

"Well then, there you go. Rely on Evelyn to help you through these first few months. I'm sure that by Christmas you'll feel as comfortable with the Americans as you do with your closest friends."

46

The next day Aurora rose with the sun, put her boys in the buggy and headed toward La Parida. She was so glad that Rita hadn't had her baby yet. She needed so badly to talk to her. The boys giggled as the buggy rolled up and down the hills. When they passed Escondida, Aurora drove the buggy off the road. She stopped underneath the cottonwoods until her stomach stopped lurching and her vision cleared.

When she got to Rita's, Aurora took the water Rita offered and sank into the chair. "I didn't know what I was getting into," Aurora admitted. "I thought everything would be about the same. Maybe it's the big house, or maybe it's that I haven't been around the *Americanas* much. Yes, a few of them come to *Tio's* store. A few go to Mass and we say hello to each other, but Rita I thought they were like us."

Aurora gulped down her peppermint water and refilled her tin cup. "They're nothing like us. Their houses are different. Their food is different." A quick smile flashed across her face. "Oh, Evelyn isn't so different. We get along, but I don't know many of her friends, not the way I know all of you. When she talks about her friends, I feel like a stranger standing outside her window. It's so different when I visit with Estella or Gloria, or especially you. We know all about each other." Aurora rolled her eyes. "Of course, we do; we've known each other since we were children."

Rita slapped her knee. "That's it. We've known each other since we were children. You're just getting to know these other women. It's like going to school. You couldn't learn to read until you learned the letters. Give yourself some time. Learn the letters before you try to read them."

Aurora embraced her sister. "I knew you would help me through this. I only wish you could be there with me. If we lived closer, we could talk every day and you could help me learn the letters."

Rita began to stand up, but Aurora shook her head. "What do you need? I'll get it for you."

"I was going to get some more water."

Aurora poured Rita a cup from the enamel bucket. She crushed a mint leaf at the bottom of the cup before filling it with cool spring water. La Señora had taught them that mint settles the stomach. For women who were expecting, it was a welcome relief.

Aurora fanned Rita with her ivory fan. "Here, Rita, you keep this."

Rita would have usually rejected the idea of taking something so fine from Aurora. She groaned. Rita could hardly stand the heat pushing down on her heavy body. She rubbed her neck and took the fan from Aurora.

"La Señora said that most babies were born beneath the full moon," Rita sighed. She pointed to the sky. "It's almost full. I'll be so glad to carry this child in my arms instead of under my heart." Rita reached for Aurora with a shaky hand. "I have to tell you, I'm a little scared. It hurts so much, doesn't it? I remember when you had Flavito. It hurts so much."

Aurora sat beside her sister and let Rita lean on her. They were silent for a moment. Then Aurora said, "I'm sorry *Mija*. Yes, it does hurt, but only for a while. You're strong. You'll get through this like we all have."

Riding back to Socorro that evening, Aurora thought about what she had said to Rita. *We are strong*. Aurora had never been afraid of anything. She laughed out loud. Her laughter was carried on the breeze blowing down from Santa Fe. *My family has been on this land since before there was a country. I'm just as good as they are, maybe even better. It's for them to learn about my ways as much as it is for me to learn about theirs.*

✳✳✳

At first the Ladies League reminded Aurora of the little cluster of women that helped raise money for the convent. These were the same women who met in the sanctuary to organize the fiestas. Aurora sat quietly while the League women cackled and argued. "We need to make Socorro a safer place, especially for our women," stated Mrs. Eaton." Aurora's hopes faded. These women weren't the same.

Evelyn rose cautiously and cleared her throat. "How are we going to do that without the help of our husbands? When I told my husband about the men sitting outside the saloon jeering at me, he just laughed and said that I should have walked to the other side of the street."

"Well then, it's up to us to keep ourselves safe," answered Mrs. Dougherty. Her fat jowls quivered. She took out a lacy handkerchief and patted her forehead. She turned to Aurora and tapped her finger on her chin. "Your husband recently became a judge." Her pale blue eyes lit up. "And in a few months, he'll be the mayor. Of course, we'll start with him. Certainly, he wants to clean up this town as much as we do."

Aurora's breath caught in her throat. She hoped that the redness of her face didn't reveal the panic she felt."Well, yes, but he has so much to do. He's still doing his law work and finishing up the incorporation. There are rules to be set up, laws to make, business to take care of." Aurora looked around the room. Teacups had stopped clinking and side conversations paused. Aurora's cheeks heated even more when she realized that all eyes were on her.

"This is the perfect time to us for to press him to make Socorro safe." Mrs. Eaton's shrill voice pierced the air. "You spoke of laws and rules. Let's make sure there are laws in place to secure the safety of Socorro's citizens."

Aurora put her hand to her breast, hoping to stop the shaking in her chest. She held onto the chair and closed her eyes

"Are you alright?" asked Evelyn. "You've gone pale."

Aurora took a deep breath and opened her eyes. As she had feared, the room was still spinning. Little beads of perspiration popped across her forehead. "It's the heat. It's so hot in here that it's making me sick."

Evelyn looked at her friend Priscilla then back to Aurora. "Let's go outside and get you some air."

They sat on the back porch. The fountain in the middle of the *plazita* cooled the breeze slightly.

"I'm sorry. I just haven't been feeling well lately. I'm sure it's because I've had so much to do, and now with the heat."

"Are you sure it's the heat?" Evelyn patted her own tummy.

Aurora sat up straight. "I've been so busy. There's been so much to learn. I didn't even think about. . ." She looked up at Evelyn. A smile crept across her face.

47

Josefa sent word with Santa Cruz. Rita had a fine baby girl by the light of the full moon. Aurora packed her bags and persuaded William to go to Mass in Lemitar on Sunday.

This journey reminded William of when his mother traveled across the barren fields when a new life was brought into the world. He put his arm around Aurora. "You know, I never paid much attention to the goings-on of women back in Iowa. I guess I didn't realize how much it meant when my mother was gone to help a neighbor with her birthing."

Aurora elbowed William's ribs. "If men had babies, there would be fewer of them in the world. Giving birth isn't for the weak. I'm only glad that I'm here to help Rita. Remember when I stayed with Gloria? It was even harder because she had other children to care for." Aurora bit her lip and fanned herself. She didn't want to tell William about her suspicions until she saw the *curandera*. "We're lucky to have La Señora to take such good care of us and our new babies," Aurora smiled.

"I'm sure she does very well," William huffed, "but, now that there's a doctor in Socorro my children will be delivered by him." He gave Aurora's hand a squeeze. "No weeds and potions for you. You'll be cared for by all that modern medicine has to offer."

Aurora pulled away. "La Señora knows more about curing, and birthing, and saving lives than all the doctors put together. She delivered me, and my children."

Aurora's rounded eyes stopped William from his planned speech about the importance of sterile environments and patented medicine. Instead, he flicked the reins, shrugged his shoulders and mumbled, "We'll see."

✳✳✳

Aurora and William baptized Rita's first baby after Mass. To celebrate the birth of Maria de la Luz, a table was set in Esquipula's *plazita*. The family gathered underneath the mulberry tree, where its shade and a little breeze offered respite from the heat.

Instead of bowls of hot *chili* and steaming pots of beans, there was cold pork and chicken. Squash had been plucked from the garden. Big ripe tomatoes were sliced thick. Tortillas had been replaced by corn cakes baked in the outside *horno*.

Manuelito and Flavito drooped at the table, quietly waiting to be served. Their curly hair stuck to their foreheads. Bare feet dangled underneath the table. Their cousins huddled in the shade of the front wall, but Aurora's boys didn't have the energy to join their games.

Josefa piled food onto a plate and started to take it to Rita.

"Let me take it," offered Aurora. Since she had arrived at her parents' house, Aurora had been busy helping her mother. She had barely gotten a peek at Rita's soft baby girl. She balanced Rita's plate on one arm and her own in the other. Andres ran ahead and opened the door.

The shutters of Rita's dimly lit room were closed to keep the blistering sun from seeping in. Aurora knocked, then slipped inside. She offered to prop Rita up on the pillows, but Rita waved her away.

"My back hurts," Rita moaned. "I always thought it would be wonderful to stay in bed all day. Now I can hardly wait to walk around or sit on a chair."

Rita reached for the cradle. "Every time I look at little Maria de la Luz, I can't believe she's mine. When I hold her the pain goes away. You know, I think it's a miracle."

Aurora laughed and nodded. She remembered the joy she felt the first time she held Manuelito. But try as she might, she couldn't remember Flavito's birth.

She swallowed her sadness. This was her sister's day. She pulled the covers down to the foot of the bed and fanned Rita with the cotton sheet.

When Aurora had finished eating, she scooped Rita's baby into her arms. She pulled the blanket away from her face and rubbed the soft down on top of her head. "Of course, we'll call her Luzita." Aurora smiled as little Luzita wrapped her hand around Aurora's finger. The baby stretched, and scrunched up her face then settled back into a peaceful sleep.

"She's beautiful," Aurora whispered. "I'm so glad everything went well for you. Has La Señora been back to see you?"

"She came yesterday," answered Rita. "She brought some salve of *yerba de mansa* and *punche* to help me with the soreness. Besides that, everything is going well. She said that Luzita is perfect and healthy."

"I was hoping to see her while I'm here," said Aurora. "I think she'll be able to tell me if baby Luzita will soon have a little cousin." Aurora blushed then clapped her hands like a child at Christmas.

Rita's open mouth stretched into a grin. She reached out and embraced her sister. "I hope so," she laughed. "They can grow up together like we did."

❄❄❄

The sun finally fell behind the mesa. Ricardo helped Rita into the buggy. Then Aurora handed Luzita to her mother. Their house was just over the knoll. Ricardo put the little cradle in the wagon. It had once held Manuelito. Now it welcomed Maria de la Luz.

Ricardo had made up a bed for Aurora in the little room behind the kitchen. Aurora warmed up the food she had brought from her mother's. Rita nibbled on a little of it. As soon as Ricardo left to fetch water, Rita pushed away from the table. She stretched and bent. Aurora rubbed her back.

"I've laid in that bed for so long that I'm beginning to feel like an old sack of potatoes. I don't feel any pain from the birthing, and I don't see why I should stay in bed for two weeks." She circled the table with her hands on her hips. Ricardo rushed back into the room and plopped the bucket down on the table.

"Shush, quiet!" Aurora and Rita both warned.

Ricardo hunched up and put his finger to his lips. He grabbed the last of the cold pork and made a big show of tiptoeing out of the house. Rita rested her hand on Aurora's shoulder. "He'll be gone to the fields tomorrow and we can do whatever we want."

By the end of the week, Aurora's hands were reddened by the constant washing of diapers and baby clothes. She had forgotten how important it was to wake up early and do the washing before the sun blistered the day. She wouldn't let Rita carry water buckets into the house. She made sure that Rita took a nap in the afternoon.

Aurora picked up little Luzita every chance she got. She loved rocking her in the big rocking chair that Flavio had brought to Snake Ranch. The baby wouldn't stand being rocked for very long. She opened her almond-shaped eyes and squirmed to be rid of the tight swaddling.

"Alright little one; I'll put you back in your cradle. I know it's too hot to be held so closely, but I won't get to see you for a while. I want to hold you close to my heart as long as I can." Aurora's eyes glowed. "I've forgotten how it feels to hold a baby," she cooed. "I've been so

206

busy with the house and my new friends, but maybe it's time to slow down and take care of my little boys. Who knows, maybe I'll have a baby girl to take care of soon."

❋ ❋ ❋

William left Aurora to take care of Rita. As he drove the buggy back to Socorro, and for the first time in months, had time to think. How quiet the house would be without the racket of two little boys. He took a deep breath and let it out slowly. *I'll be able to come home and go directly to my study. I can read the notes from the trial without being interrupted.* He thought about how Aurora rushed to him as soon as he came through the door. She always wanted know what was going on at the courthouse. The cold peppermint tea was always welcome, but he would have to push his papers aside and tell his wife about his day. That always put him further behind.

By the end of the week William's desk was cleared off and the silent house began to unnerve him. The rooms seemed dim without Aurora's light. When Aurora got home, William was waiting at the door. He lifted each boy into the air, then tickled their tummies. Eruptions of giggles rewarded him for his effort. "I'm so glad to have you back. The house was so quiet without all of you." They strolled into the house with William tightly embracing his wife. Sitting on the porch after supper, Aurora snuggled against William.

"I saw La Señora while I was at La Parida. I thought it was the heat that was making me tired and sick."

William scooted forward and held Aurora at arm's length. "Are you alright?"

Aurora dropped her eyes. A smile twitched at her lips. "La Señora said that I was healthy and that our baby would be too." She let her words fall over her husband. William's eyes widened.

"I don't know why you're surprised," Aurora teased.

William gave Aurora a hug that lifted her off the bench. Then he sat her down like a china doll. "How are you feeling? Did La Señora say you're doing alright?"

"I'm tired all the time and sometimes I feel dizzy, but that's normal. La Señora gave me tea of *alhucma* and *yerba buena* to keep me from getting sick in the morning."

William pulled away and tightened his jaw, but stopped short of telling Aurora to throw those damned weeds away. Instead, he advised her to go see Dr. Wilson. He put his hand up to stop her protest.

"I would feel better knowing that you're in a doctor's care right here in Socorro. Oh, and take that tea. I want to know what the doctor thinks of it."

Aurora gasped. "These are the same herbs that I took when I was carrying my sons. They really helped."

William threw his hands up in surrender. "Fine, just promise me you'll see the doctor too."

This time it was Aurora's turn to surrender. She nodded and patted William's hand. *I guess it wouldn't hurt to go once just to keep William happy.*

48

William wanted to slow down and spend more time with his family, but now that he was a judge, he had to sit on the bench for the Joel Fowler trial. The escape and recapture of Fowler kept the town on edge. The victims of his cattle rustling demanded a hanging. It took all of William's wit to keep the courtroom from erupting into violence.

While the jury was deliberating, he dragged himself to his office where he faced a mounting pile of legal work. By the time he stepped into his house, the boys were asleep. Aurora turned her back on him, and marched up the stairs.

Aurora was in the kitchen when William came down for breakfast. She held her head in her hands and barely nibbled on the toasted bread Sophie made for her. She closed her eyes and breathed deeply until her stomach stopped lurching.

"I don't remember feeling this sick when I was expecting the boys."

"That's it, this is enough!" stated William loudly. "I'll have the doctor come over this afternoon." He took a deep breath, then kissed Aurora on the cheek. "Maybe it's the heat and you have been too busy." He looked over at the little pouch on the counter. "Maybe you shouldn't drink anymore tea made from those weeds."

William grabbed the cloth bag and took a sniff of La Señora's herbs. To his surprise, lavender and mint filled his senses. He arched his eyebrows.

"You see," said Aurora. "They're calming herbs for my digestion." She wanted to tell him how the *curandera* had learned from her Zuni mother, who had learned from her mother. Her people had relied on these ancient cures since the first Spaniards came to New Mexico.

But before she could say anything, William tilted his head. Looking down at her like a father, he commanded, "Promise me you'll see the doctor and slow down until the baby arrives."

"But the Ladies League is counting on me. They want me to work with you. When you become mayor, you can make laws that protect us from the men shooting up the streets after they've been in the gambling halls all night. We need to make Socorro a safe place for women and children." Aurora was standing with her hands on her hips.

"I agree, but right now I can't do anything to help you. As soon as this cattle rustler is put away, I can turn my attention to other things. The Fowler case should be over by the end of the week." William put out his arm to stop Aurora from pacing. He reminded Aurora that her health was more important than the League.

"I'll tell Jonathan's wife that the laws to protect Socorro will have to wait until I become mayor. Oh, and I'll stop by Dr. Wilson's and have him come over and take a look at you."

Aurora stiffened, but she knew better than to try to dissuade William. "Fine, I'll see your doctor," she said as she gazed out the window. *Next week I'll plan a trip to visit Rita and her baby. La Señora should be there.*

As soon as William stepped out the door, Aurora unwrapped a tiny gown. She held up the gossamer dress she had bought for Luzita. Aurora counted the piles of diapers, and inspected the other little dresses trimmed with lace and embroidery. She brushed her fingers across the soft delicate fabric then looked skyward. "You have given me two fine boys. If it is your will, I pray you will give me a little girl."

✳✳✳

"Are we almost there?" Manuelito shaded his eyes with his hands. He stretched his neck to look over the knoll.

The journey to La Parida took longer this time. Aurora had to stop and rest beneath the shade of almost every tree that hugged the road. The boys seemed to know that they should stay close to the buggy. Aurora climbed back into the buggy and Flavito snuggled beside his mother. He reminded her of her promise again and again.

"I want to hold the baby," whispered Flavito.

Aurora laughed. "Alright my little man. If you're very careful, you'll get to hold Luzita. . . and you know what? Pretty soon were going to have a baby of our own!"

Manuelito's eyes grew wide. "I'll teach him how to walk so he can play with us."

Flavito sat up. "Yeah, and I'll teach him how to make mud balls to throw at the cousins. Oh, and I better teach him how to run. He can stay in our fort. Manuelito, you can climb up the tree and watch for Vicente and his brothers." Flavito rubbed his mother's arm. "We'll take good care of him."

Aurora gave her son a squeeze. "What if it's a girl?"

Manuelito twisted his mouth and shook his head. "I don't think it will be a girl because she can't go outside and play with us. Girls have to stay inside and help their mamá."

"Not all the girls," argued Flavito. "Sometimes Maria plays with us, and so does Dolores and Agnes."

Manuelito tapped his chin. "Maybe she could pretend to be Vicente's friend. Then she can come and tell us what the older boys are planning."

By the time they crested over the last hill, Aurora's boys had planned out their baby's life. They started bouncing up and down when they spotted their *abuela*'s house. The horse had barely stopped when they climbed out of the buggy. Manuelito stumbled over Flavito to get to the door.

"*Abuelá*!" shouted Manuelito. "Were going to have a baby brother!"

Flavito elbowed him. "Or maybe a baby sister! We're going to teach her how to walk and run and spy on the big cousins!"

Josefa knelt down and folded her two grandsons into a warm embrace. "I'm so glad you're happy about your new baby. The whole family will love her just like they love little Luzita."

"So, La Señora told you," Aurora smiled.

Josefa grinned. "Nothing is a secret for very long in La Parida."

"Can you come with me to see Rita and the baby? I brought her some new clothes. Besides, I know La Señora is going to be there today. I need to see her."

Josefa's brow wrinkled and she put her hand on Aurora's arm. "Is there something wrong, *Mija*?"

Aurora said that she didn't feel the same as she did when she was carrying the boys. She felt sick almost all day and there was a tightness in her stomach.

"I don't remember having that when I was carrying the boys. I just wonder if it's going to be a girl. Maybe that's the difference. What do you think?"

Josefa shrugged. "They say there is a difference between carrying boys and girls, but I've never been able to tell. I do know that each baby is different. Maybe living in that big house, going up and down the stairs, and trying to keep up with the *Americana*s, has been too much." Josefa reminded Aurora about the heat. She fanned herself with her apron, then guided Aurora to the rocking chair. "Maybe La Señora can give you something to help you rest."

Josefa served her daughter a glass of cool water laced with peppermint from the garden. Aurora took a drink and breathed slowly in and out. She licked her lips and smiled."

"Oh, I love mint water in the summer. The Americans brew green tea and let it cool. That's what they drink. I think it's bitter and it doesn't agree with my stomach. This is much better." She leaned her head against her mother.

Josefa packed a basket of food so Rita wouldn't have to cook. It was tied onto the back of the buggy. The boys jostled with their cousins for room in the back seat. Josefa gave all the children a stern warning that the baby might be sleeping.

"Rita doesn't need a lot of racket around the baby. You can go play by the ditch behind her house. You can take off your shoes and walk in the water, but don't make me have to wash your clothes." The warning was given with a shake of Josefa's finger.

Flavito pulled on his mother's sleeve. "You said. . ."

Aurora tussled his hair and gave her three-year-old a wink. When the other children ran behind the house, Manuelito and Flavito stood like two little wooden soldiers. "You said we could see the baby," ventured Manuelito.

"We'll be very quiet," Flavito cupped his chubby hands, "and I promise I'll be so careful when I hold her."

Aurora put her finger to her lips as they tiptoed into the house. After Luzita was held for a while, each boy examined her little fingers and toes. With the black fuzz on her head smoothed down with kisses, the boys were ready to splash in the water.

La Señora knocked on the door then stepped inside. She fanned herself with a big paper fan. "Will this heat ever end? The *chili* is beginning to wilt in the fields. The women, their feet are swelling and their backs are beginning to ache. Even the ones who have just started their journeys are suffering."

Aurora put her hand on the old woman's gnarled fingers. "That must be it; I've been feeling so sick. It wasn't this way when I carried the boys. It must be the heat.

The *curandera* gave Aurora another bag of *yerba buena* and *alhucema*. She added three pinches of *yerba de mansa* to keep down the heat in Aurora's body. She told her to rest and put her feet up as often as she could. She had Aurora lay down and pressed her hands against her stomach.

"When did you say your last visit came?"

Aurora shook her head. "I think it was three months ago; yes, at the beginning of the summer."

Aurora looked at the healer, trying to find something in her eyes that would tell her not to worry. La Señora laid a hand on Aurora's arm. "You seem a little bigger than you should be for three months, but maybe it's the heat. Maybe you're just swollen. I'll stop by next week when I go to Socorro. The herbs will let your stomach rest. Just remember what I said. Now is not the time to save Socorro. This is a time for you to take care of yourself and the life within you."

49

William met Aurora at the door. He took her elbow and led her into the parlor. "I saw Dr. Wilson today. He said to stop by his office in the morning. I'm worried about you, Honey. Maybe your cousin Rufina can take care of the boys for a couple of days so you can rest. It's cooler in my office. I can have Juan put a cot down there so you don't have to climb the stairs."

Aurora laid her head against her husband's chest and wrapped her arms around him. "It would be nice to be able to rest, but the boys will be fine here." She assured William that Sophia was taking good care of them.

"I asked Jonathan to tell his wife that you're not feeling well and you won't be attending her meetings for a while. I'm sure she'll understand."

❋❋❋

The next morning Aurora sat on the edge of a chair in Dr. Wilson's waiting room. She had never been examined by anyone but La Señora. Letting a man even see her without her clothes was unthinkable. Her foot began to tap uncontrollably. *I don't care what William wants; La Señora has been taking care of me since I was born and she'll be the one to take care of this baby.* Just as Aurora stood to leave, the doctor appeared at his door.

Dr. Wilson was as thin as a rail with a generous white mustache. He extended a welcoming hand and a soft smile as he guided Aurora into the examining room. "Please, sit down Mrs. De Baun. I know you're bound to be nervous. I understand that this isn't your first child. I assume that your others were delivered by a midwife. I can assure you that I have delivered many babies and you and your child will be more than safe in my hands."

Aurora looked around the white room. A low table sat in the center of it. Glass cases with instruments and bottles lined the walls. She pressed her back against the door.

"Is this where you intend for me to have my baby?" Aurora asked, wide eyed.

"Oh no, no, this is my examining room. You'll have your child at home, but I will be there to assist in the birthing. Please come and sit down. I was told that you haven't been feeling well."

Aurora didn't sit. She reached behind her for the doorknob. "I mean no disrespect Dr. Wilson, but you see, the midwife who delivered me will deliver my baby." Aurora explained how La Señora had taken care of her and her children all of their lives. "I trust her. Perhaps if one of us gets sick we'll come to see you, if La Señora can't be reached. But my family has depended on her as long as I can remember. She's never failed us." She opened the door, then turned back to the doctor. "This was my husband's idea."

Aurora took three long strides across the waiting room. She didn't bother glancing back at the doctor who stood with his hands in the air. He shook his head and muttered, "These people with their weeds and witches."

As Aurora walked across the park and up McCutcheon Street, she thought about what she would say to William. Of course, he would be disappointed, and maybe a little angry, but he would just have to understand that not everything new was better.

The more she thought about William referring to La Señora's cures as weeds, the faster she walked. *Her weeds and potions saved little Flavito's life when he was born too soon. Her powders broke Andrés' fever when he fell off the water wheel at the gristmill. La Señora wrapped his legs with yerba de mansa and it began to heal in three days. What did the doctor have that would be better?*

Aurora was panting by the time she got home. She called for Sophie and dropped onto the settee. "I need water!" she shouted in a hoarse voice.

Sophie came running from the kitchen. Aurora took the water in her shaking hand. She gulped down half a glass, put her hand on her chest, and worked at slowing her breathing. "I'm alright," she said. "I just walked too fast from the doctor's office. Sophie, get me some paper from William's office."

Aurora scribbled a note. She handed it to Sophie. "Tell Juan to deliver it to La Señora. I need to see her as soon as she comes to Socorro."

Because the jury had reached a verdict, William had been able, for the first time in weeks, to come home for his noon meal. When he heard raised voices, he rushed out of his study. He stopped short at the sight of Aurora. Her eyes were closed. Her chest rose and fell quickly. He looked from Sophie to Aurora, then knelt in front of Aurora. He took her hands. "Aurora, what's happened? Are you alright?"

Aurora opened her eyes and tried to stop the room from spinning. "I'm alright. I just walked too fast from the doctor's office."

William shot Sophie a look and she scurried into the kitchen. He sat beside Aurora and pulled her toward him. "I'm really worried about you."

Aurora buried her head in William's chest. Her tears came as a surprise to both of them. "This time is so different. The tea that La Señora gave me has helped, and yesterday she added *yerba de mansa*. That will cure anything. I think I just need to stay in the house until this heat has passed. It should only be two or three more weeks."

William nodded in agreement. "I feel better knowing Dr. Wilson is only a few blocks away. He can be here at a moment's notice."

Aurora pulled away and studied her folded hands. "About Dr. Wilson," she started.

"What happened? Did he give you bad news? Is that why you rushed home?"

Aurora shook her head. "No, he didn't say anything."

William cocked his head and Aurora pulled herself up to her full height. "Dr. Wilson will not be taking care of me. He's a man. How can I let him examine me and deliver my baby? La Señora will deliver my baby."

William rose and began to pace. He kept his clinched fists at his side. "I thought we had settled this. You're not feeling well. This pregnancy is different. La Señora is, who knows where. What's going to happen if something goes wrong and she can't be found?"

Aurora's lips began to quiver. William sat beside her and calmed his voice. "I know you're a little worried. I am too. I don't mean to scare you, but it makes no sense. We have a doctor right here. Dr. Wilson is well-qualified and . . ." He looked at Aurora. Her back was stiff and her lips were drawn into a tight line.

"I won't allow a man to examine me. Besides, what does a man know about taking care of a woman after she's given birth? Does he know how to teach a new mother how to feed her baby? Does he have the medicine to stop the cramping after the baby's birth and the soothing salve to mend her torn body?"

Williams eyes shifted from side to side. *There has to be a closing argument that will win this case.* "Alright, it doesn't have to be one or the other. Dr. Wilson doesn't have to examine you the way you're thinking, but you can talk to him about how you're feeling. I tell you;

he knows about pregnancies and he'll make sure that everything is alright. La Señora can examine you too. Go ahead and take her medicine. If you feel safer in her hands, by all means, she can attend you at the birth. But Dr. Wilson is nearby. If there's a problem he can be here in a few minutes. If you visit him every week, he'll know what's going on, and he'll be able to help you if La Señora can't be found."

Aurora's mind cleared as the dizziness passed. She stood and took a few shaky steps toward the window. "Maybe you're right." She was trying so hard to embrace William's ideas, and going to the doctor was one of them. She turned and forced a smile.

Sophie brought the boys down for dinner and the family ate together for the first time in weeks. "We've wrapped up the Fowler trial so I'll be able to spend more time with you." William winked at Manuelito and brushed the crumbs away from Flavito's lips. He looked up at Aurora. "The evening has cooled down a little. If you feel up to it, let's walk to the park."

The boys chased each other around the grassy oval as William and Aurora walked arm-in-arm beneath the shade trees that circled the park. Aurora leaned against William's shoulder. "I didn't know if you would be mad at me because I wanted La Señora to be my midwife. I was even planning on keeping her a secret. She squeezed William's arm. "I don't want to hide anything from you. Tomorrow I'll go see Dr. Wilson again."

50

The summer heat finally lost its grip on New Mexico. *Chili* was picked and *ristras* were hung. The cottonwoods shimmered golden in the autumn sun. La Señora rested her hand on Aurora's swollen middle. "I know you're tired all the time, but the baby's heartbeat is strong. This will be a big baby. Perhaps it is good that you have a doctor nearby. This may be a hard birth for you."

Aurora squeezed the old woman's hand. "You have to stay near Socorro."

La Señora leaned Aurora back onto her pillow. "Don't worry. It will only make you feel worse. The journey of three women in Socorro is getting close to the end. I will be near if you need me."

By the time the wheat was harvested, Aurora's back began to ache. She tried to remember how big she was with Manuelito in her sixth month. It seemed that she was about this big when he was born. She sent for La Señora to bring her more tea to settle her stomach. "Why hasn't my sickness disappeared? I can't remember being sick for this long with the other two."

Lying on the cot, Aurora allowed La Señora to rub and press and listen. She had Aurora turn on her side. She cupped her hands over the little lumps that moved from time to time. When the examination was over, La Señora rubbed her hand across Aurora's forehead. "*Mija*, I think there are two of them."

Aurora sat up straight. She covered her face with her hands, then grabbed La Señora's shoulders. "Two. . . two babies? No wonder I'm getting so big!"

"You have three more months to go, so you need to take very good care of yourself. You need to rest and put your feet up. Never mind the latest fashions. Wear loose gowns so nothing will keep the babies from moving. I'll come by every week to check on you. Don't worry, I have delivered two babies before. With God's help, all of you will be healthy."

Aurora felt foolish sitting in Dr. Wilson's waiting room. Of course, La Señora was right. She was always right, but William would want to know what the doctor had to say. Aurora marched into the office as she usually did, but this time instead of sitting on the chair, she climbed onto the examining table.

"I told you that my midwife is going to take care of me when I give birth. She's been examining me too. She has told me that I'm going to have two babies and I believe her. I'm as big as a horse and everything is different this time. My back hurts. My ribs hurt sometimes, and my legs feel shaky. I can hardly stand to eat anything." Aurora crossed her arms. "Now I want to know what you think."

Aurora held on to the doctor's crooked arm as she eased back on the examining table. As he reached for his horn, he allowed himself a little smirk. He put his horn on the front of Aurora's stomach, then lowered it and raised it and moved it from side to side. "By golly, La Señora is right! I hear two heartbeats." The doctor gave her the same instructions that La Señora had.

Doctor Wilson handed Aurora a bottle of milky liquid, with the promise that it would help settle her stomach. Not wanting to insult him, Aurora took the bottle. She planned on throwing it in the dust-bin as soon as she got home.

Aurora had felt silly asking the handyman, Juan, to hitch up the buggy just to take her a few blocks to the doctor's office. She had intended to go to the bakery and buy some macaroons to celebrate her news. She would tell William about the two babies after supper.

It wasn't far to the bakery, just around the park and down California Street, but the bouncing of the buggy and the smell of horse manure in the street changed Aurora's mind. She tapped Juan on the shoulder. "Just take me home. I don't feel too good."

By the time the buggy turned up McCutcheon Street, Aurora was sweating. When they got to the house, Juan took her arm but, before they got to the back door, Aurora was heaving the contents of her breakfast onto the ground.

"Sophie!" Juan yelled. The girl came running. She held Aurora up while Juan ran into the house and grabbed a kitchen chair.

"Sit *Señora* De Baun." Aurora dropped onto the chair and held her forehead. She wanted to take a deep breath, but the taste of bile made her stomach gallop again. Sophie ran from the kitchen with a glass of water. Aurora rinsed her mouth and took a much-needed deep breath.

She sat back in the chair with their eyes closed. Her hands shook, but she did feel better with Sophie fanning her. Juan ran to the kitchen and got a wet cloth to lay across Aurora's brow.

"Shall we get *Señor* De Baun? Juan asked.

Aurora waved him away. "No, I think I'll be fine. I just needed to sit on solid ground for a while." Sophie and Juan each took one of Aurora's elbows and helped her into the parlor. When Sophie went into the kitchen, Manuelito was pressed against the cupboard, eyes wide. "Sophie, what happened to Mamá? Is she sick again?"

She was just a little sick to her stomach. "She'll be fine."

Flavito skirted around the table and ran down the hall. "Mamá!" he squealed. "What's wrong with my mamá?"

Sophie grabbed Flavito by the hand and pulled him back into the kitchen. He ran to his brother and hung on tight. Both boys started to whimper. They crept to the parlor door and leaned in.

Aurora took several deep breaths and drank the rest of the water. She reached for Sophie. "Just help me to the cot. I need to lie down." When Aurora walked past the parlor door, both boys clung to her skirt.

"Not now," Sophie said., Your mamá is sick."

Flavito began to wail. Sophie marched the boys back into the kitchen. Juan knelt and took the boys in his arms. Sophie took down the cookie jar and the boys sniffled back their tears. Juan sat them at the table and poured each a glass of water. Sophie ripped off her apron and stuffed on her bonnet.

"Stay here," Sophie commanded. "I don't care what she says; I'm going to get Dr. Wilson."

"Shouldn't we get *Señor* De Baun?" Juan asked, shifting between Sophie and the door.

"I think he's in court today. Let's see what Dr. Wilson says."

Sophie took the boys upstairs and set them on the bed. With one boy on either side, she put her arms around them and rocked them gently. "This baby is making your mother sick, but she'll be alright. I'm going to get the doctor. I'm sure he has something that will make her feel better."

Sophie sat on the floor and began to stack their little metal soldiers into the wagons. "Stay here and play. I'll be back in a jiffy." By the time Sophie slammed out the door, the boys were driving their wagons across the floor.

✳✳✳

Dr. Wilson untied Aurora's high-top shoes and looked at her swollen ankles. "I'm going to confine you to bed rest. I'll give some powders that will help the swelling in your feet and ankles. Later in the week, if the swelling goes down, you can walk around the house, but no more going into town."

Aurora sat up and put her hands on the cot to steady herself. "I feel better now. I can't stay in bed. I have too much to do. Now, with two babies coming, I have to get more clothes and blankets. And what about another cradle? The nursery isn't ready yet."

Dr. Wilson folded his spectacles and put them in his case. "Your ward, Sophie, can do all that. Right now, the only thing you have to do is take care of yourself and those babies."

"What about the boys? Who's going to take care of them? They're so frightened. Who's going to take care of them?

51

A note was slipped to William during the noon recess. He ran home to find his wife upstairs in a summer nightgown, her feet propped on pillows. He leaned over and gave her a gentle kiss on the cheek. William pulled a chair beside the bed. He pushed a curl from Aurora's brow, then wrapped his hand around hers. "Something's not right. You didn't have this much trouble when you were expecting the boys did you?"

Aurora squeezed William's hand. "No, but when I was expecting them, I was only carrying one baby at a time." She grinned at William who stared back, eyes wide. Aurora raised her eyebrows and smiled shyly. "Yes, there are two of them. That's what's giving me all the trouble."

"When did you find this out?" William's voice rose.

"Just today," Aurora lied. "Dr. Wilson listened to the heartbeat to make sure the baby was alright and he heard two heartbeats."

"Oh my God! Wait, you're carrying two babies?" As much as William wanted to keep hold of his wife's hand, his thumping heart propelled him upward. "Two babies! We'll get help. Dr. Wilson will come and see you every day." William started pacing "What about the birth? What did he say about the birth? He'll have to be here. We'll have to tell him to be available any time, day or night." He stopped in the middle of the room. The color drained from his face. "You're so small. How can you carry two babies?"

Aurora sat up and put her hands out. "Sit with me, *mi amor*. We have to think about this. She shook her head. "I tried going to the bakery this morning, but I got very sick. Now the doctor says that I need to stay in bed for a while. Maybe Rufina can send one of her daughters to help out."

William sat on the edge of the bed. Silence stretched between them. Each was wrapped in their own worries.

"If Rufina sends her daughter, the boys will still be underfoot." William stood and looked out the window, his hands on his hips. "They love staying at their *Tia* Telesfora's. Maybe she can take them until you're feeling better." Aurora didn't answer. William turned to see his wife studying her swollen ankles.

Aurora looked up slowly. "Perhaps you're right, but just until I'm feeling better."

William raised the window and called for Juan to hitch up the buggy again. Aurora shook her head. "Before he takes the boys, he'll have to go to Mamá's. I'll write her a note. If the boys are going to stay with Telesfora, Mamá will need to let her know so *Tia* will be ready for them."

William took the stairs two at a time. He tore a page from his notebook and ran back upstairs. Aurora scribbled as fast as she could, telling her mother about the two babies and that she needed help from Telesfora. She also told her mother to send for La Señora.

"Sophie, get up here!" William yelled down the stairs.

When he tromped into the boy's room, they were huddled in the corner. Flavito clung to his big brother, his lips quivering. "Is my mamá going to die?" Manuelito stuttered. Then the dam broke. Both boys sobbed until their faces turned crimson.

Sophie stepped into the room and turned toward William. "The poor little waifs are scared to death. They don't know what's happening." She scooped them up and rocked them gently. "There, there, your mum is going to be just fine. She got a little sick, that's all. She needs to rest." She wiped Flavito's face with her apron and whisked the hair out of Manuelito's eyes. "Let's go see her, shall we?"

The boys gulped and sputtered. Holding hands, they tiptoed into their mother's room. Aurora patted the bed. She scooted to the middle of the bed, then opened her arms.

"Be careful," Sophie warned as she lifted each boy onto their mother's side. They cuddled beside her. Manuelito touched his mother with one soft finger. He sat up and wiped his wet cheeks on his sleeve. "We thought you were going to die, like our chicken when she couldn't lay an egg."

Aurora pulled her son to her. "I'm sorry our loud voices scared you. I'm just a little sick, but the doctor said that I'll get well if I stay in bed for a while." Aurora patted her middle and assured her boys that the babies needed a little rest too. "The doctor gave me some medicine to make me feel better."

Flavito sat up. "Is it La Señora's medicine?"

Aurora glanced at Sophie and decided that a little lie wouldn't hurt. "Yes, and she's coming to see me this afternoon."

Flavito nestled into his mother's arms. Aurora let out a long breath and waited for another wave of nausea to pass. Then she whispered.

"Papá has a good idea. While I'm getting better, why don't you go visit *Tia* Telesfora?"

The boys squealed and Sophie lurched forward making sure they didn't bump their mother. Manuelito hunched his shoulders and Flavito put his finger to his lips. Before they crawled off the bed Manuelito turned to his mother. "Mamá are you really going to be alright?"

"I'm fine, I'm fine. But, instead of having one baby brother or sister, I'm going to have two."

Manuelito arched his back and gawked with eyebrows raised. Flavito looked from his mother to his brother. "Two babies! Does that mean we each get one?"

Aurora laughed. "Yes, I suppose it does."

"But you're not a cat mamá. You're only supposed to have one baby." Manuelito's frown reminded her of her beloved Flavio when he was worried. She wanted so much to tell him that he looked just like his father but, for the last year, she had tried hard to make the boys think of William as their father.

"Sometimes a woman will have two babies. I'm alright. I just get tired a lot, so I think it would be best if you went to visit *Tia* Telesfora while I rest. It won't be long until we're all back together."

"When we come back will you have the two babies? What will the babies be? Will they be boys or girls? Will I be able to hold them?" Flavito babbled.

Manuelito swatted at his little brother. "You ask too many questions." Flavito stuck out his lower lip.

"It's alright, *Mijito*. I'm full of questions too."

Manuelito hopped off the bed. "But what about my school? If I stay with *Tia*, I won't be able to go to school."

William had been listening at the door. He stepped into the room with a cool glass of mint water for Aurora. She looked up at him and shrugged her shoulders. Her eyebrows were drawn together. *Everything is happening so fast. The doctor just said I had to rest in bed for a while.* She looked at Manuelito and cupped his little face with her hand. "Just for a few days so I can get some rest."

William rubbed his chin. "If the boys stay with Telesfora more than a few days, Manuelito could go to school with one of his cousins in Lemitar. Wouldn't that be fun?"

Manuelito was silent. He put his hand behind his back, then started pacing like William often did when he was thinking. "I guess it would be alright. I could go to school with Juanito." He turned to his brother. "Flavito, you can stay at home and play with all our other cousins."

52

The next morning Josefa's buggy turned into Aurora's yard. Telesfora sat beside her. The women didn't bother to knock. They just walked in like everyone did in La Parida. "Yoo-hoo, Aurora?" Josefa called.

Sophie ran to the door. She was holding a cast-iron frying pan. "Oh, it's you. I didn't hear you knock."

The two women looked at each other, eyebrows raised. "Where's Aurora?" they asked in unison. Telesfora started toward the kitchen.

"She's upstairs. Let me go check. She may be asleep."

Aurora's mother and cousin were only a step behind Sophie. Aurora was curled up in the bed. Her chest gently rose and fell. Sophie put a finger to her lips and they backed out of the room.

The boys were building a fort in the backyard. When they saw their *abuela*'s buggy, they ran into the house without dusting off their clothes or washing their dirty hands. When Telesfora heard the back door slam she took Josefa's arm. The women scurried to the kitchen.

The boys were smothered with kisses while Sophie tried in vain to shush them. Both boys fought for a chance to tell their mother's story. They were excited about each getting a new baby. Then their faces turned to worried frowns when they talked about how sick their mother was.

"This is why we're here," *Tia* Telesfora said. "We're going to take you back with us and give your mother some time to rest."

"Where's Mamá?" Manuelito looked around the kitchen. Telesfora led him to the table and sat him down. "Your mamá is taking a little nap. We'll see her pretty soon. Have you had anything to eat today?" As Sophie looked on, both women scoured the kitchen and, before long, a hearty meal was set on the table.

The smell of roast beef woke Aurora. She got up and started down the stairs then remembered what Dr. Wilson had said. She thought she heard voices so she took two cautious steps and leaned over the banister. "Mamá, is that you?"

Both women bolted from the table and rushed toward the stairs. By the time they got to the top, Aurora had gone back to bed. Josefa leaned down and smothered her in her embrace. "Oh *Mijita*, the family will be blessed with two babies!" Josefa wiped her eyes with her handkerchief.

Aurora covered her mouth and, for the first time, allowed her tears to flow. "I've been feeling so bad lately. I have to tell you, Mamá, I'm worried."

Josefa sat at the edge of the bed with her hand on her daughter's back. "I know you're worried, but we're here to help. Telesfora will take the boys and I'll send Yrinea to take care of you. I won't let you remain in the hands of that girl, Sophie."

Telesfora patted Aurora's hand and hurried off to help the boys pack their clothes. Manuelito puffed out his chest and announced loudly, "We already have everything we need." He showed them the carpet bag that William had packed for them. Beside it sat a small wooden crate filled with their favorite toys.

"Oh, my boys, we're going to have so much fun! And don't you worry about your mamá. We're sending your cousin Yrinea to take care of her."

Flavito scrunched up his face and tried to pronounce the strange name. Telesfora threw back her head and laughed. She winked at Flavito. "We can call her Ne- ah."

"Nea," Flavito repeated slowly, "that's lots better."

Telesfora settled the boys onto the back seat of Esquipula's buggy. She planned on leaving the boys with Isabel and coming back in the morning with Nea. When she told Josefa about her plan, Josefa put her fingertip to her lips.

"Will that be alright with José? You know how he is when you're gone too long."

Telesfora just huffed and swatted at the air. She drove out of the yard with the boys at her side and a wide smile across her lips. The last thing on her mind was what José thought about the situation.

✳✳✳

William opened the door and stuck his head inside. "I'm home!" he announced. Instead of being met with two little boys shouting, "*Bienvenidos* Papá!" he was met with silence. It was only then that he reprimanded himself for shouting. He had forgotten that Aurora might be sleeping, so he tiptoed upstairs. He strained to identify the low voices coming from her room.

"Josefa, I'm so glad you're here. Aurora must have told you the news."

Josefa stood and extended a hand to her son-in-law. William folded her hands in both of his and pulled her close. "Were going to have two babies. Wouldn't it be wonderful if we had a boy and a girl?" He moved to the bed and kissed Aurora gently.

Josefa patted William's arm. "As long as they are healthy and Aurora goes through the birth without any trouble, that's all that matters."

William nodded and took a step away from the bed. Aurora was propped up on pillows. The curtains were drawn. A pitcher of water sat on the little table next to her bed.

"Is it alright for you to be sitting up? The doctor said that you're supposed to keep your feet up."

Aurora reached for her husband. "I was just drinking some of Mamá's tea. As soon as I'm finished, I'll lie back down."

Josefa told William that Telesfora had taken the boys and would bring Nea back in the morning. She explained that Aurora was worried about buying extra clothes for the second baby. "Sophie can do that while Nea is here." Josefa didn't tell William that Nea would be bringing back La Señora's herbs to take down the swelling in Aurora's ankles. She only mentioned that Nea had been learning from La Señora, so Aurora would be in good hands. William just sucked in a breath.

Josefa went to the kitchen to help Sophie. She had given birth to five children and her ankles had swollen during her summer pregnancies. She knew that the first thing La Señora would say was drink plenty of water. She also knew that Aurora's swollen ankles were of serious concern. Nea had begun to help La Señora with the care and birthing of the mothers in Lemitar. She said a little prayer thanking God that Nea would be by Aurora's side.

53

Pushed by autumn winds, brown withered leaves rustled across the sand. Aurora was still confined to her room. Gloria and Rufina stopped by from time to time and Aurora was grateful for the news of the outside world.

Aurora had put aside the bottle of medicine that Dr. Wilson had sent her. Instead, she drank the bitter tea that Nea brought from La Señora. The swelling of her ankles retreated, but just going up and down the stairs tired her.

The day that Estella came from Lemitar with a *ristra* of bright red *chili*, Aurora demanded to be helped down the stairs. They celebrated by heating up the beans and tortillas that Estella brought. Aurora only added three drops of *chili* to her beans. The doctor had told her not to eat spicy foods, but she couldn't resist.

Estella told her that news of her twins was all over Lemitar. Women were busy stitching two little matching gowns and knitting two soft blankets. Telesfora would bring a basket of baby clothes the next Sunday. Aurora could hardly wait for Sunday because Telesfora was also bringing back her boys.

Telesfora and José arrived late in the afternoon. The boys scrambled up the stairs. Aurora was sitting in the rocking chair waiting for them. She embraced each one as if she would never let them go. "You're home!" she cried as she cupped each of their faces in her hands. "I've missed you so much."

"Where are the babies?" Flavito asked.

Manuelito pointed to his mother's tummy and explained that the babies weren't here yet. The boys played with toys in Aurora's bedroom while she and Telesfora visited. Aurora's eyes never left her sons.

"We can't stay long," said Telesfora. "José has to get back so he can help Manuel load the wheat. The boys have done so well. Of course, they miss you, but Manuelito has been going to school with Juanito, and I've taken Flavito to see Josefa and Isabel almost every day. They love seeing them. Isabel tries to hide her tears, but I know that her wound is opened a little at the sight of Flavio's children.

Aurora swallowed down the lump in her throat. She pulled the curtain back and gazed out the window. Telesfora's voice drifted past her. "Being in Socorro has been exciting," she interrupted, "but more and more I miss La Parida and Lemitar."

Just as her words fell, José walked into the room. "I hear you talking, and I'm glad you think it's good for the boys to be with their family. We think so too. Why don't you let them stay a little longer, at least until the babies arrive?"

Aurora shook her head. They had been gone for more than a month. She told José how much she missed her sons. She waved at her boys and they waved back with big smiles. "I think they should stay."

Telesfora and José exchanged a glance. She put her hands together as if in prayer. Her voice softened. "You still need your rest. La Señora tells us that you're doing better, but you know how much it takes to run after two little boys."

"I'm doing a lot better." Aurora shuffled to the bed and lay down, "and I have Nea and Sophie to help me. I need the boys with me."

Telesfora frowned at her husband and shrugged. José let out a long sigh, then his jaws locked. He went into the hall and began pacing back and forth. He wanted so much to tell Aurora that he thought the boys belonged with their family, the Vigils, not with the *Americanos*. He just didn't know if this was the right time to argue.

Finally, he walked back to the doorway. "You know that the boys will stay with us when the babies arrive, and during your confinement. If you need us to come and get them at any time, just send the word." He tilted his head toward Telesfora. She caught his signal and stood to leave.

"We are your family," said José. "No one can take better care of you and your children than your family."

Telesfora knelt and opened her arms wide. She squeezed each boy goodbye. Then she gave Aurora a hug and rushed José out of the room.

As soon as they left the room, Flavito threw down his toy and ran after them. "Mamà Telesfora! Where are you going?"

"We have to go home. *Tio* José has to help your *abuelo* ."

Flavito scrambled to the bottom of the stairs and grabbed his aunt's skirt. "No, you can't go! You have to stay here with us! My mamá needs you!"

"Your cousin Nea will be here to help your mamá. She needs your help too. Who's going to bring her water? Who's going to sing to her and make her laugh? She needs you to stay and help."

Flavito looked up the stairs. "Are you coming back?" he asked. His face twisted into the threat of a sob.

"As often as I can, and you're going to stay with us after the babies come. When they're two weeks old we'll all come back to see them."

Flavito gave one decisive nod and climbed up the stairs. José chuckled to himself. "He looks like his *Abuelo* Manuel when he's ordering people around," José said. Telesfora laughed with him, remembering all the times she had seen her father make a decision with one big nod.

✳✳✳

José and Telesfora spent the night with Rufina. Telesfora told her that Aurora's swelling had gone down, but if she didn't stay off her feet, it would come back. She lamented about leaving the boys with her.

Rufina grunted. "You know this isn't a good sign." She recounted how *Señora* Martinez had the same problem. "The baby came early and the *señora* almost lost her life."

Telesfora's hand flew to her mouth. "I think it's best not to tell Aurora about *Señora* Martinez," she whispered. She made the sign of the cross above her heart.

Rufina promised she would stop by Aurora's every few days and let the family know immediately if anything happened to Aurora. Satisfied that they were doing everything they could, Rufina took Telesfora into the bedroom to show her the tiny clothes she was sewing for the babies.

Rufina's husband, Antonio guided José outside. The men soaked in the cool of the evening. Antonio braced himself for whatever rant José was about to deliver. When José began to wiggle in his chair, Antonio took a quick gulp of whiskey.

"You know that the house in Socorro is in Aurora's name but, if something should happen to her, the boys would be put out on the street. Everything would go to the husband. Aurora has land that was Flavio's. Part of everything Manuel owns will someday go to Aurora. If something should happen, it would all go to the *gringo*. We can't let that happen."

Antonio sat up straight. "I never thought of that." He shrugged, ". . . but what can we do?"

José started rocking back and forth. "I've been thinking. What if Aurora gave her property and house to the boys?"

Antonio put down his pipe. "The boys! What rights would they have? They're just children."

José's shook his finger in acknowledgment. "You're right'" He stood and rubbed his hands together. "I'll have to talk to Manuel about this."

Antonio rolled his eyes. "José, you're forgetting one big thing, *Señor* De Baun. He's becoming a powerful man in Socorro."

José snarled. "The Vigils and the Pinos were powerful long before that wet-nosed *gringo* was born." José's voice rose. "We Pinos got our land in the Socorro land-grant!"

"I'll get us some coffee." Antonio escaped to the kitchen. He knew he was in for a long evening. Once José started in on the land grants there was no reprieve. Time, with all its changes, seemed to have passed over José without notice. *Maybe if I move my chair back from the lantern light, I can take a little nap,* thought Antonio.

✳✳✳

José and Telesfora waited until the noonday sun warmed the air before starting back to La Parida. Bundled in an old blanket, Telesfora steeled herself for the long journey home. They hadn't even left Socorro before José started talking about his plans for taking the boys out of William's clutches.

With no way to escape, Telesfora finally burst into an argument she knew she couldn't win. "I don't understand why you think William is after Aurora's property. The boys are always talking about their daddy, how he plays with them and takes them to town. You've seen how he is with Aurora. He's just as worried as we are. Since the Fowler trial ended, he's been working at home so he can help take care of her."

José spat a long brown stream of tobacco over the side of the wagon. He wiped a thin strand of saliva on his sleeve. "Yeah, but now with the babies coming—his babies—you just watch how things will change." He bit off a chunk of tobacco from a twist, and slapped the reins.

Telesfora looked out at the distant mesas dusted with snow. Her throat tightened and tears welled up in her eyes. She retreated to the furthest side of the seat and dared to speak again. "Where do you get these ideas? No one else is thinking what you're thinking. I haven't heard Manuel or Isabel say anything about William except that he's trying hard to be one of the family."

José tightened his grip on the reins as the wagon skidded around a corner. "Be quiet. I have to watch the road!" No words passed between them for the rest of the journey.

Esquipula had sent Santa Cruz to build a fire at José's house. When Telesfora saw the smoke coming from the chimney she breathed a sigh of relief. But tears filled her eyes again as the silence of the empty house enveloped her. She busied herself with taking food from the cold back room and putting it on the stove. The last thing she wanted to listen to was José's rant about the evils of William De Baun.

Telesfora sat at the kitchen table with her head in her hands, letting José go on and on. She hummed a lullaby to herself, trying in vain not to listen. José snapped his mouth shut and glared at Telesfora.

Spying the dreamy look on her face, he barked, "You haven't heard a word, have you? Don't you care what happens to Aurora's sons?"

Telesfora blinked. Her head jerked up. José slapped the air, stuffed on his hat and stomped out the door. "I'm the only one who gives a shit," he spat.

❄❄❄

December's icy winds locked everything in place. January would bring the snow. February's frigid sunshine would begin the thaw, but would offer little reprieve. The roads would be rutted and impassable. Aurora's babies were due in early March. Telesfora put her elbows on the table. She drew her hands into fists and rested her head on them. *More than three months,* she thought, *without being able to see the boys. If Aurora should give birth early, how would I get to Socorro and bring the boys back?*

Aurora hadn't thought about Telesfora and her worries. She looked out the window at the gray sky, then down at the floor. She noticed that she couldn't see her feet. She jerked the drapes closed and waddled to the softest chair in the parlor.

Aurora always hated this time of the year. The festivities of Christmas were over and there was nothing to look forward to except the long gray days of winter. She had come down to dinner on Christmas day, and had to admit that Sophie and Nea had done a wonderful job of cooking the big ham that William bought. Wrapped in a blanket and stretched out on the settee, Aurora had watched her sons open the gifts from their *abuelos* and their papá. Then it was back upstairs to spend the rest of the dreary day in bed.

William brushed his hand across Aurora's cheek. She flashed a quick smile, then burrowed under the covers. By the time William reached the bottom step, he was determined to cheer Aurora up.

He had tapped Manuelito on the shoulder and put his finger to his lips. "Let's go upstairs and keep Mamá company. She shouldn't be alone on Christmas day.

Aurora slipped into the rocking chair. She spent the afternoon watching Flavito and Manuelito scurry from one new toy to the other. Manuelito lined up his toy soldiers and Flavito rocked fearlessly on his wooden horse. William brought up coffee and *bizcochitos*. A gentle smile drifted across his face as he looked from his wife to his little family.

✳✳✳

Aurora was grateful when Evelyn stopped by to share the news of the committees. Linda, Judge Pino's wife, was drawing up all the concerns she planned to present to the City Council. The friction between the Socorro natives and the newcomers was getting worse. The frozen earth had stopped the mining in Kelly and Magdalena. The miners, with time on their hands, spent their days in the gambling halls and saloons.

Evelyn's voice rose to a high pitch. "We've all started sleeping in the same room because the gunfire frightens the children. Mrs. Pino took her list of concerns to William. Now that he's mayor she's sure that laws will be passed to end this madness."

"I'll talk to him about it too," Aurora promised.

That afternoon with the help of Sophie and Nea, Aurora crept downstairs again. Nea wanted her to go straight to the cot that had been set up in William's study, but Aurora was tired of lying down. She hadn't seen the first floor in almost a month. She walked through the rooms touching the furniture, admiring the mahogany sideboard filled with her wedding china.

William helped Aurora into his leather chair. Aurora lifted her skirt past her ankles. "See, the swelling's gone down," she smiled up at William. "I think I can stay downstairs for a while. After all, I need to talk to you about the committee and its concerns."

William dropped his head and groaned. "The only concern you should have, is taking care of yourself."

Aurora twisted her hands. "That's what I'm trying to do." She put her hand on William's arm. "I can't stand being up there by myself. I

234

miss you and I miss being with my boys. I want to talk to you about everything that's going on in Socorro, but you don't come to bed until after I'm asleep."

"Promise you'll lie down when you're feeling tired," William put his hands on his hips, "and for heaven's sake, don't lift a finger. That's what Sophie and Nea are here for. I've put a blanket on the cot, so it'll be more comfortable. If you need to take a nap, Sophie will know to keep the boys quiet."

✳✳✳

As soon as William left for the office, La Señora slipped through the kitchen door. She breathed a sigh of satisfaction when she found Aurora at the dining room table. Her eyes dropped to Aurora's ankles. Then she lifted Aurora's eyelid. "Good, good, your eyes are clear and the swelling is going down. Get up and walk, keep the blood moving," ordered La Señora. She ground up some more birch bark. She took a pinch of it and showed it to Nea. "This is how much you give her every morning, no more."

"And this is for?" Nea questioned.

"For the blood, to keep it from thickening."

Nea nodded, glad to have another remedy to use when La Señora grew too feeble to take care of her people.

La Señora sat beside Aurora, put her hand on her chest, then signaled Nea to do the same. "Feel her heart beat. It's steady and strong. If it starts galloping or quivering, get Aurora to bed right away. Send for me. It doesn't matter what time of night. I'm staying at Ana's. Her baby will come before the week has passed. I'll stay in Socorro at my sisters until the snow melts."

She cupped Nea's face in her hands, then turned to Aurora. "You heard what I said to Nea. Pay close attention to your heart. You can walk around, but walk slowly. Raise your arms, slowly. Your ankles look better. I'll give Nea a paste of powdered *linasa*. She turned to her assistant. "Boil this in water with a little cornmeal. Mix it with a tiny bit of lard and rub it on Aurora's ankles. Rub gently, up toward her heart. And not for very long. Do this at least three times a day."

By the end of the week the swelling in Aurora's ankles had almost disappeared. The pain in her back didn't burn anymore. Aurora was convinced that getting out of bed and walking was the best thing she could do to help the medicine work.

Aurora instructed Sophie to bring the children down after William

235

had gone to work. She sat by the fire and helped them dress. They brought some of their toys downstairs so their mamá could watch them play. As Aurora watched Juan drive Manuelito to school, she realized that she wouldn't have much company, except for Flavito, so she turned to Nea for conversation.

Nea told her about the different plants and what they would cure. "I don't know who she learned from, but La Señora knows about what's inside the body. She's teaching me about the heart, and the kidneys, and the lungs. It seems that the reason your ankles are swelling is because your kidneys aren't working so good." Nea sat back. She put her hand over her mouth when she saw Aurora's eyes widen.

Aurora looked down at her ankles and gasped. "Is it serious?"

Nea shrugged. "I just know that La Señora shook her finger at me and made me swear that I would make you do exactly as she said."

Aurora wrapped her arms around her middle. She looked up at Nea. A little gasp escaped as she raised her hand and swore to follow La Señora's instructions. Then she got up and slowly walked around the parlor, holding onto the furniture.

That evening William hugged Aurora and helped her to the dining room table. The color in her cheeks had come back and she didn't complain about being sick anymore. She gave William a peck on the cheek and told him what the doctor had said.

"Dr. Wilson said that it would be alright for me to walk around the house and even do a few things." This wasn't a lie. When the doctor saw how much Aurora had improved, he did feel that a little exercise and being with her family would do her good.

By the end of January Aurora was helping the women cook. Sophie would do all the lifting, but Aurora sat at the table, chopping and stirring. Nea taught Sophie how to make tortillas. Aurora sat close by, reminding her to twist her wrist every time she flipped the tortilla.

She welcomed Manuelito home every day. He would tell her what he learned at school. He told her about Sister Mary Elizabeth with a loud voice. "I don't like that one," he said with a scowl, "but my teacher, Sister Angelina, is nice." Aurora whispered that Gloria's daughter, Martina, felt the same way and they shared a giggle.

Aurora got one of William's folders and Manuelito carefully put all his schoolwork in it. She waddled into the study and placed the folder on William's desk, then she rested on the narrow bed that had replaced the cot.

54

Aurora's eyes lit up when she saw the buggy with Telesfora sitting next to her mother and sister. They covered their heads with their shawls and ran into the house. The women chattered like schoolgirls, anxious to see Aurora.

"I'm sorry we didn't send you notice," Telesfora said. "The man who brought the freight to Manuel's store said the roads were good. The frost is still in the ground. We had to come before it warms up and the roads turn to mud."

Aurora only heard bits of Telesfora's words. She had folded herself into her mother's arms, with Rita wrapped around both of them.

"I've been so worried about you," Josefa sniffed as she wiped her eyes, "but Nea sent word with José, so I knew you were better."

Aurora put her hands on her back and waddled into the parlor, signaling for her family to follow. "I am better, but my back is beginning to hurt again. I think I'll sleep downstairs tonight."

Josefa glanced at Telesfora, her brows raised. "I'll send Nea to get La Señora."

Aurora waved the idea away. "I'll be alright. I just need to start resting more."

Sophie and Nea rushed from the kitchen when they heard familiar voices. After giving tight hugs and soft kisses, Sophie led Rita into the kitchen. "We'll make some coffee. I made an Irish cake. It's really good."

Aurora started to sit, but her mother lifted her by the arm. "Let's go into the kitchen. We need to warm up."

Of course, Aurora thought, a smile creeping across her face. *The kitchen is where women gather.* The afternoon was spent with laughter spilling over gossip. When shadows drifted across the kitchen floor, Josefa tapped Telesfora's arms. "It will be dark soon. We better start back home."

Aurora felt a pang in her chest and reached for her mother. "Can't you stay Mamá? Barbara can cook for Papá and the family." Tears welled up in Aurora's eyes. She hadn't realized until now how much she missed her family.

Josefa gulped the last of her coffee and slowly put down the cup. "How will I get back home? Not many people are traveling yet. The

February winds are melting the snow. Soon the roads will be soft clay." She squeezed Aurora's hand. "I'll talk to Manuel. He knows who's coming and going. I'll come with whoever is traveling to Socorro. Maybe I'll be back in a few days and I can stay with you until the next day. You have almost a month before the babies arrive. The roads will be better by then and I'll come often."

Telesfora embraced Manuelito and kissed the top of Flavito's head. She wiped her eyes and gave Aurora a pitiful glance. "Why don't you let me take the boys so you can get the rest you need?"

Aurora rolled her eyes. "They're fine with me. I don't feel that bad, and I have a lot of help."

Telesfora shrank back in her chair. Josefa busied herself with putting the dishes into the sink. Looking out the window so Aurora wouldn't see her tears, she said, "I wish we could take you back with us, but I'm afraid the trip would be too hard for you." She swallowed her tears and straightened. "I'm going to send word to Rufina telling her that she needs to stop by every day."

Aurora wrapped her shawl around her shoulders. Arm-in-arm she walked her mother to the porch. She waved goodbye and rushed into the house before her tears spilled down her cheeks.

The boys escaped Sophie's clutches. "I want to go with *Tia*!" Flavito stomped both feet.

"Me too!" shouted Manuelito. "I like going to school in Lemitar."

The protest of her little sons was too much for Aurora. She couldn't bear the memory of Telesfora's face and the sadness in her mother's eyes. "You have to stay with me!" she shouted. Aurora shook her finger at Sophie. "Keep them in the kitchen!" The rest of the afternoon was spent in William's study. Wave after wave of hot tears washed over her.

❋❋❋

As winter lost its grip, the pain in Aurora's back increased. Sometimes her left leg tingled and she was afraid of falling. Dr. Wilson was called. He said that one of the babies was pressing against her back, pinching a nerve in her spine.

La Señora visited almost every day. The herbs she gave Aurora helped ease the swelling in her ankles but when La Señora saw the yellowish tint of Aurora's skin she mixed up different powders. With Nea at her elbow, the *curandera* crushed *canutillo del campo* and mixed it with three pinches of *flor de San Juan*.

"Boil the tea and let it cool overnight. Aurora is to drink a glass every morning." La Señora wrapped watercress seeds in a damp cloth and set it on the shelf above the stove. "In three days, the seeds will sprout and be ready to eat. Put some of this *berro* in every meal she eats."

La Señora didn't want to frighten Aurora, but she knew the babies were lower now. Before she left, La Señora ordered Sophie to hurry to Dr. Wilson and give him a message.

"Tell him that Aurora's ankles are swelling again and her skin is yellow. This can't go on much longer. The babies are ready to be born."

Sophie looked at her with her mouth agape. "I thought the babies weren't supposed to arrive 'til March."

"This is why you must go to Dr. Wilson right away. The color of Aurora's skin has me worried. I'm afraid that no matter what I do, she's going to get worse." La Señora put her hand on Sophie's arm and shook her head.

Sophie put her fingers to her mouth. "You need to stay with her. I wouldn't know what to do if the babies come too soon." She glanced at Nea and the lines across her forehead began to soften.

Sophie turned to La Señora. "Why don't you stay here? You can sleep in the back room with me and Nea."

La Señora nodded in agreement and struggled into her coat. "I'm going to talk to El Gringo. The doctor can't be here day and night. Even if De Baun insists that the doctor delivers the babies, I need to be here from the beginning of her labor."

Sophie's eyes widened and La Señora put her finger to her lips. "We don't want to worry Aurora. It will only make things worse."

La Señora waited for Sophie to come back from Dr. Wilson's then she marched to the courthouse. She sat on the hard bench for an hour. She couldn't keep her knees from bouncing up and down. *I could be with Aurora instead of sitting here waiting for Don De Baun,* she thought. By the time she was escorted into his office, the old woman's voice was crackling.

William stood and offered La Señora a chair. "To what do I owe this pleasure?"

William's greeting made La Señora grimace. "I've been visiting Aurora from time to time," she announced. "I know you prefer Dr. Wilson, but I have been delivering babies and taking care of mothers since before you were born."

William nodded. "Of course, of course; you're well respected in this community and I know that you're much more than a midwife. It's just that Dr. Wilson knows all the new medical practices. I felt that Aurora would be in good hands with him, no disrespect to you."

The shoulders of La Señora raised and she tightened her grip on the arms of the chair. "I'm not here to win the contest between me and the good doctor. I've been taking care of your wife and I came to tell you that she will soon be delivering the babies. Her blood isn't right. The water in her body is making her sick. I don't know why this happens but, if she doesn't give birth soon, both she and the babies will be in danger. If you don't believe me, ask Dr. Wilson," she huffed.

William staggered backwards. His pointed finger was raised, questions tumbling in his head. He stuttered out, "What, um. . .why?"

La Señora interrupted. "I didn't mean to scare you. I only came to ask your permission to stay with your wife. She needs someone with her who knows what to do if anything goes wrong. Send for Dr. Wilson the minute she goes into labor but if she should start getting sick before that she may need someone right away."

William's face lost all its color. He fell back into his chair. His eyes moved from side to side before he spoke. "Dr. Wilson hasn't said any-thing about this."

"She only started getting sicker a couple of days ago. You see, I've been visiting her all this time because I knew the situation might change quickly. I sent Sophie for Dr. Wilson. He should be at your house by now."

William grabbed his coat and rushed into the hall, then stopped. He stuck his head back into the office. "Well, let's go!" He waved his arm as he ran down the hall.

La Señora lagged behind as William trotted up McCutcheon Street. He stopped once, swaying from one foot to the other. The ancient woman waved him on.

"I'll be right there. You go on ahead."

William yanked the door open, rattling the stained-glass window. He stopped short when he stepped into the study and found it empty. Nea poked her head out of the kitchen and pointed upward. William took the steps two at a time. He found Aurora in bed with Dr. Wilson listening to the babies' heartbeats. Aurora reached for William.

He looked from her to the doctor. "Is everything alright?"

"I'm glad La Señora sent for me. "The babies have dropped. They will come soon even though it's too early." He started to say more, but Aurora's nervous whimpers stopped him.

"Isn't there anything you can do to delay the birth?" William asked.

"Usually I try, but Aurora isn't doing well. I think it's best that the babies are born as soon as possible."

Aurora's hands began to tremble. When William turned to his wife her quivering hand was over her mouth. La Señora walked to her bedside and laid her hand softly on Aurora's foot.

"I'll be with you day and night. I've taken babies as early as yours and they're still living. What you have to do now is stay in bed and let us take care of you."

William gave Dr. Wilson a sideways glance. He nodded in agreement.

55

Three nights after the doctor's visit, Aurora was awakened with a sharp pain that started in her back and gripped her entire middle. La Señora hurried upstairs when she heard Aurora scream.

"When did the pain start?" she asked.

Aurora arched her back and breathed deeply. The pain had eased a little. She moved her head from side to side. "I don't know. I guess this is the first one, but it hurts so bad." In between panting breaths, she recalled that the labor with her two sons had started with small cramps that grew harder over the hours. This was nothing like before.

At daybreak Juan drove the buggy to La Parida. Josefa bundled herself against the early spring winds and sat close to her nephew, Juan. He hoped to get Josefa to Aurora's before the babies were born, but when they arrived two tiny baby girls were cradled in Aurora's arms. Dr. Wilson had delivered the babies with La Señora's help.

The second baby girl was smaller than the first. It was La Señora who finally got her to breathe. After she was delivered, the doctor had taken La Señora's hand. "I'm glad you were here," he said gently.

William moved away from the bed to let Josefa be with her daughter. Josefa pushed Aurora's hair back and kissed her forehead. She peeked at the tiny bundles that Aurora had nested in her arms. Her eyes widened. She had never seen babies so small. Their skin was transparent and their eyes seem to be locked shut. Josefa looked up at William. His face was a mask of fear.

"Oh *Mijita*, they're so tiny, but so beautiful." She reached for the smallest girl, but Aurora drew her infant tightly to her chest. "I can't let them go. If I do, God will take them."

La Señora gently took the smallest baby from Aurora's arms and rubbed her teeny feet and hands. She turned her over and laid her across her arm. Then she patted her back gently. She nodded at Aurora. "We have to keep reminding her that she is in this world. She's weak, but if we can get her through these first few days, her chances are good." She put the baby back in Aurora's arms. Aurora's eyes didn't open when her baby was placed against her chest.

Father Lopez was called to the house that afternoon. He baptized one of the babies Maria Josefa and one Maria Isabel. There was no clinking of glasses or a house full of relatives to celebrate the births.

The priest patted William's shoulder and slipped quietly out the door.

La Señora and Josefa kept each other awake for two days. They took turns holding little Isabel, whispering to her and trying to get her to suckle. They told her the names of her *abuelos*, her brothers, her mamá and papá. Then came the list of all her aunts and uncles, and all of their children.

"You belong to us," Josefa murmured. "We will never let you go."

But, despite all of their efforts, on the third day of her life, the angels came and took Maria Isabel home. William sat staring at the wall. He kept thinking that he would awaken from this nightmare. He couldn't believe how much he hurt for this precious baby who had brightened his life for only three days.

Esquipula went with William to pick out a tiny box. Aurora didn't attend the small funeral at San Miguel. Esquipula asked Father Lopez to keep the Mass as short as possible. The women were anxious to get back to Aurora and little Maria Josefa.

Aurora had slipped into a familiar silence. She nestled Josefita in the crook of her arm, only noticing the baby when she squeaked.

La Señora made Aurora sit up. She made her look at little Josefita. "You have a daughter, and she needs you. She's almost as small as Isabel was. If you don't want to lose them both, you need to talk to her and move her. Remind her that she belongs here with you."

Aurora looked down at her baby as if seeing her for the first time. She nodded slowly at La Señora. Then she opened her mouth and let out a cry of anguish.

"I don't know why God is punishing me! He took my Flavio and now my baby." Her eyes grew wide. "I won't let God take this one!"

Aurora's mother shuddered. She wrapped her arms around her daughter. "No one knows why God takes some and leaves others, but La Señora is right. Aurora, you have a daughter and it's up to you, no, it's up to us to make sure that she lives."

Aurora cupped the baby's head in her hand. She wiped away the tear that had fallen on her Josefita's nose. "God can't have this one," she muttered.

William had been standing against the door. He closed his eyes and stopped breathing. Then he pushed himself away from the door and crept down the stairs. He began working from home. He turned over most of the mundane paperwork to the new lawyer that Jonathan had brought into the firm. William kept taking out his watch and checking the time. He crept up the stairs every hour. If Aurora was sitting up, he would slip into the room. As soon as little Josefita finished feeding, he took the baby in his big hands and pressed her to his chest.

When Esquipula returned to La Parida, he took the boys with him. Two weeks later Telesfora brought the boys back to see their sister. William met them at the back door. Their hands were scrubbed and faces shined. He inspected their clothing and deemed them clean enough to visit the baby. Before he took them upstairs, William knelt down and wrapped them in his arms.

"I don't know if your *Tia* told you, but one of the babies only lived for a few days. She was too little." He intended to give them a quick lecture about how careful they would have to be around the baby, but Manuelito stopped him short.

He grabbed his brother's hand and nodded. "*Tia* told us that the angels took her to be with our first papá, so he wouldn't be lonely. Then she started crying."

Flavito made a rosebud of his lips. "I don't know why she was sad. We have one baby and our first papá has one."

The breath went out of William, and his throat tightened. All he could do was squeeze the boys tighter and hope they didn't see the tears rolling down his cheeks. He took each one by the hand and tip-toed up the stairs.

The boys sat at the foot of the bed. They made a nest out of their crossed legs. When William was satisfied that Josefita would be safe in their arms, he let each boy hold their sister for a few minutes.

Manuelito put his hand on the soft bundle. His head jerked toward his mother. "She looks like a doll."

Flavito unwrapped Josefita's teeny hand, and his mouth popped open. With big eyes, he looked from Manuelito to Aurora. "I didn't know babies could be this little. *Tia* Rita's baby was this big." He opened his arms wide. A chuckle ran through the family and lifted their sadness for a moment."

Josefita squirmed and opened her eyes. "Look, her eyes are open and she's looking at me," Aurora grinned. "I swear, when she heard my voice, she looked up at me." Aurora took Josefita from Flavito and handed William his daughter. He didn't know how deeply he could love until he looked into Josefita's blue-gray eyes.

William made sure he was home when Dr. Wilson stopped by for his daily visits. After two weeks Dr. Wilson examined Josefita and declared that she had grown. Her breathing was stronger, and all her limbs were working. Aurora just nodded as the doctor gave his verdict. She had heard it all from La Señora a few days before.

56

William carried the little cradle downstairs so Josefita would be close to Aurora as she started running her household again. Aurora had gained back some of her strength but, when William ventured into the parlor, he found her slumped in the rocker. When he spoke to her, Aurora jerked, as if awakened from a dream.

She looked up, struggling to focus. "Where's Isabelita? I can't find her."

"You mean Josefita? She's in the cradle. Do you want to hold her?"

Aurora wrinkled her brow. She turned slowly and stared into the cradle, then swallowed a silent cry. "No, Isabelita. I can't find her!" She stood and began to circle the room, her eyes wild.

"Nea!" William yelled. "Take the baby. Send Sophie for the doctor." William cornered Aurora. He opened his arms, inviting her to let him comfort her.

"Did you find her?" Aurora drummed William's arms as he guided her to the settee. He rocked her and kissed her gently. *Should I say something about Isabel's passing? No, that may set her off again. It's best to wait for the doctor.*

Aurora took a ragged breath and pushed to free herself from William. "I better check on the baby. La Señora said to move her a lot. Do you want to hold her?"

"You mean Josefita?" he whispered. William's stomach tightened. He looked toward the door. *Where's that damn doctor?*

"Of course, Josefita. God took Isabelita, but He can't have Josefita."

William's eyes followed her to the window. She pulled the drapes aside, then started swaying, her eyes fixed on the ones she'd had lost. Aurora didn't look away from the window. The boys were playing outside. They waved to Aurora. She didn't wave back.

William turned toward the kitchen when he heard the doctor's voice. "Stay here with her," he ordered Nea.

William met the doctor in the kitchen. He told Dr. Wilson how Aurora had acted. The doctor glanced around the corner and saw Aurora smiling and reaching for the baby that Nea held. He turned and looked at William with his eyebrows raised.

"I know she looks fine now, but when I came in, she was looking for Isabel. She sits and stares out the window most of the time. That's why I brought the baby downstairs. I figured it would help Aurora get back into her daily life."

"Has this happened before?" questioned the doctor.

William turned to Sophie. She looked from William to the doctor, then her eyes darted toward Aurora. "Mr. De Baun, I'm glad you brought Aurora and the baby downstairs. The missus cries a lot and I have to remind her to hold little Josefita. The other day I heard her saying, 'She's gone! She's gone!' She started talking about Flavio. 'I'll never see them again.' That's what she kept saying. I have to keep reminding her that she has a baby to take care of. One day she got really mad at me and said, 'Don't you think I know I have a baby? So, what if Josefita was born, it didn't bring her father back.' It was like her thinking was all mixed up."

"It scared me, Mr. De Baun, but I didn't know if I should say anything because she was talking about her first husband."

"What's she talking about?" Dr. Wilson asked.

William motioned toward the table and poured two cups of coffee. He told him about the death of Aurora's first husband. He hadn't thought about Aurora having baby Flavito a month after her husband died.

"I've seen women get the blues after their baby is born, but they seem to come out of it while caring for their baby." Dr. Wilson tapped William's arm. "Sometimes they have other children to take care of too. It doesn't usually last long. I'll give her some powder to help her anxiety. In the meantime, I think it would help for her mother to be here. You might want to talk to her and find out what state of mind Aurora was in when she had her second child."

Sophie made Aurora a cup of atole and William reluctantly stirred a pinch of powder into it. *I can't believe I'm thinking this, but I wonder if something* La Señora *has would be better for Aurora. After all, she was there when Flavio died and when Aurora had Flavito.*

As soon as the doctor left, William wrote notes to Josefa and La Señora. He needed to talk to both of them. He started to hand the notes to Sophie then crumbled them up and threw them in the stove. "Watch her very closely," he said to Nea. "I think I'll ride out and talk to Josefa."

When Josefa saw William's horse galloping down the road her

heart thumped into her throat. She put a trembling hand to her mouth. *Oh no, not the other baby! She can't lose them both.* Josefa swung the heavy wooden gate open and ran to meet William. *"Dios mio!"* she cried, "Not Josefita too."

William shook his head as he climbed down from the horse. "No, no, it's not the baby, It's Aurora." He gestured toward the house. Santa Cruz took the horse and William followed Josefa into the house.

"She seemed to be alright when the babies were born, but now she's getting things all mixed up. This morning she was looking for Isabelita. Sophie says she talks a lot about Flavio. We have to keep reminding her that she has to take care of Josefita."

Josefa put her hand to her chest. William's words made her heart leap into her throat again. She put her hands in her lap so William wouldn't see them trembling.

"I don't know what to do." William put his hand on his mother-in-law's arm. "I don't know much about what happened when her first husband died. I guess I didn't think much about her having a baby so soon afterwards. We didn't talk about it. Now that she's lost another loved one, it all seems to be too much for her."

Josefa had put the memory of Flavio's death away in a dark room so she wouldn't feel it every day. She knew that Aurora had done the same. The family thought that if no one talked about it, the pain would be bearable enough to go on with their lives.

Josefa poured William a cup of coffee, then piled cookies on a plate and brought them to the table. She needed time to push the pain down again.

She tried to tell William about the darkness that had settled over Aurora for months after Flavio died, but the memories overwhelmed her. She held her head in her hands and cried.

Finally, Josefa wiped her eyes and took a deep breath. She talked quickly, leaving out a lot of the details. Josefa sniffled and ended with, "It took a long time for Aurora to come back to us. We all helped take care of Flavito until Aurora was able to care for him."

William put his hand on Josefa's shoulder. "I'm so sorry this happened to Aurora . . . to all of you." He shook his head. "This can't happen again. I know you have Esquipula and the children to take care of, but you have to come and talk to her. Maybe you can stay for a few days. Nea is there, but I'm not sure she understands what's going on."

William gathered up his hat and jacket. "I have to get back to her, but I thought I should talk to you at your house so Aurora wouldn't hear."

Josefa's eyes darted around the room. She was already making plans to put some clothes in a basket, give her daughter-in-law instructions, and call for Santa Cruz to hitch up the buggy.

William hugged Josefa and began his long ride back home.

✳✳✳

As the sun began to fade, Josefa arrived with Rita and her little girl. Telesfora was right behind them. When Aurora looked out the window and saw her family, she flung the door open and ran to meet them. She practically dragged Rita from the wagon and hugged her so fiercely that Rita could hardly breathe. Then Aurora held her sister away from her. "You know about my baby?"

Rita cradled Aurora in her arms. "I heard about the birth of your baby girls. I'm so sorry that little Isabelita was too small to stay with us. But everyone is saying that Josefita will be alright."

Aurora shoulders dropped. She whispered to Rita, "She's so little. I'm afraid she will leave me too."

"We won't let her go," Rita assured her.

"I'm going to stay with you for a while." Rita promised. "We're going to dress Josefita in the little gowns that I made for her. If they're too big I'll make some smaller ones. Let's go in. I can hardly wait to see her."

The clutch of women hurried into the house. Aurora was surrounded by the women who had helped her survive in the past. Manuelito and Flavito had already rushed in the back door. When the women stepped through the door, the boys were standing on each side of the cradle watching their baby sister.

Manuelito waved to Telesfora. "She looks like a doll," he whispered.

With the boys sitting stiffly on the settee, Aurora carefully placed Josefita in the arms of each of the boys. Josefita squirmed and gave Flavito a treat by opening her eyes. They marveled at her tiny fingers and wanted to see her toes again. William carefully unwrapped his daughter's feet. The boys looked from their sister to each other, whispering oohs and ahhs.

57

Surrounded by her family, Aurora's grief began to ease its grip. It was only sleep that kept her tied to her pain. She took naps in the afternoon. When she woke, she talked about confusing dreams. She clutched her mother's arm. "Flavio had baby Isabelita and he didn't know what to do with her."

One afternoon Aurora awoke with an agonizing scream. She clawed at the air. Her mother rushed to her bedside, but Aurora looked past her. "He was right here. Flavio was right here, and he was trying to give Isabelita back to me. He kept saying, 'She's not mine'." Aurora began to tremble. "I tried to tell him that I knew she wasn't his, but he needed to take care of her. He couldn't lose her because someday I would be with both of them."

Aurora's eyes darted around the room. When they came to rest on Josefita she cried, "Where are my boys? I want Flavio to see them too. He has to know that I'm taking good care of them!"

"They're downstairs with Rita. Calm down. I'll tell Nea to bring them up."

Aurora reached for her mother with a shaky hand. Nea and Rita had been hugging the door frame. Nea started to fetch the boys, but Josefa's head shaking stopped her. She called Nea close and whispered. "The boys can't see her like this. Send Sophie for La Señora."

Rita sat with Aurora while Josefa talked with La Señora in the kitchen. "What do you have that will settle her mind?"

"Aurora's sickness is in her heart," La Señora explained as Josefa wiped her eyes. "Maybe we could convince her that Flavio will take Isabelita to an angel. I could talk to her. I'll tell her that my people believe that babies are kept by the angels in a special place. When it comes time, Flavio will guide her and she will know where to find Isabelita."

✳✳✳

After the women left, Aurora sank back into silence. She fed the baby and changed her, but it was William who talked to Josefita. The paperwork on his desk piled up. He was either yelling at the boys to be quiet or checking on Aurora and the baby.

After La Señora talked to Aurora about the angels taking care of Isabelita, she seemed to relax a little. When Manuelito came home from school, Sophie washed his hands and made both boys change their clothes. With a stern warning to walk and speak quietly, they were allowed to sit in the parlor. Aurora looked into the distance and told them about their other sister who was with the angels now.

William kept talking about the baby who was with them. He kept showing Aurora how she'd grown, how pink she was, and how round her face was getting. William sent Sophie to invite Evelyn over. He sent a note to Gloria asking her to come and visit. He sent Josefa another note telling her that it may do Aurora good to visit with her family from Lemitar.

❄❄❄

Evelyn crept through the back door. Sophie bundled up the boys and sent them out to play with Evelyn's little ones.

"Where is she?" she whispered to Sophie. "Is she awake?"

Evelyn tiptoed through the dining room. She glanced into the parlor, looking puzzled. She turned to Sophie. "Didn't she hear the boys thundering to go outside?" The sight of Aurora, still in her dressing gown, sent a shiver through Evelyn.

Sophie whispered, "It's best to act as if nothing's wrong. Visitors seem to perk her up. I'm so glad you came."

Evelyn fluffed her hair, straightened her skirt, and put on a smile. "Aurora dear, I came to see the baby, and you, of course."

Aurora blinked and looked up. Evelyn gave her a peck on the cheek. She gently pulled the blanket away from Josefita's face. "Oh, she's beautiful, "sighed Evelyn, "and she's grown!"

Josefita opened her mouth. She squirmed from side to side until she found the little fist that she had been searching for. When it was securely in her mouth, she began to suck on it.

Evelyn laughed. "My babies used to do the same thing. They're like little birds, aren't they? Can I hold her?"

Aurora squeezed her baby and began to turn away. Sophie put a gentle hand on her shoulder and nodded. Aurora looked at Evelyn's smiling face and slowly handed her the baby without saying a word. Evelyn loosened the blanket and inspected Josefita. She had indeed grown, but after a month, the baby wasn't as big as her own children when they were born.

Evelyn glanced at the basket sitting next to Aurora's chair. She drew out a soft pink gown. "Look at this beautiful little gown. Did you make it?"

251

Aurora peered at the gown as if she had never seen it. She frowned. "No, I think Rita made it. She was here the other day and she made some little clothes for Josefita."

Aurora touched the gown, "Oh, I think I was going to embroider some little flowers along the hem." She tucked the gown underneath Josefita's chin and smiled. "Maybe I'll wait until she grows a little more."

Evelyn took her first normal breath. She kissed the soft golden fuzz on the top of Josefita's head. "I think she has her father's eyes. Look how bright they are."

Aurora drew herself into a small corner of the chair. "Flavito has his father's green eyes. You know his father is gone and so is Isabelita."

Evelyn looked to Sophie for a response, but Sophie just put her hands up.

"But you have Josefita and she's beautiful." Evelyn put her hand on Aurora's knee. "You have a daughter. Remember how you used to tell me that I was lucky that I had a daughter. When we would go to the store you would look at all the cloth you could make little dresses out of. Now you can."

Aurora's body unfolded. She cocked her head and looked down at her baby. "But she's so little. All she can wear are the little gowns that Rita made."

"Oh, but she's grown so much since the last time I saw her. It won't be long before she can fit into the gowns you made her."

Seeing that the light had come back into Aurora's eyes, Sophie hoped that Aurora would get out of her chair. "What did you bring for us to eat Evelyn? It sure smells good."

"Oh, it's my flan. Maria, from next door, taught me how to make it, and I want you to taste it and see how I did." Evelyn walked toward the kitchen and signaled for Aurora to follow.

With Josefita in her arms, Aurora sat at the table and tasted the caramel dessert. The women sipped weak coffee from Aurora's bone china cups and Evelyn shared all the gossip from the committee meetings.

"I've told everybody how beautiful Josefita is and they all want to see her. I told them that maybe at next month's meeting the baby will be big enough for you to bring her."

Aurora scrunched up her shoulders. "Oh, I don't know about that.

What if someone is coughing or they haven't washed their hands. No, I better wait until this summer."

Sophie patted Evelyn on the back. Her wink said, "Keep talking".

"I'm just about finished crocheting Josefita's blanket. It's almost as soft as she is. When I'm finished, I'll start on Belinda's blanket. You know she's expecting her fourth by the end of the summer. Come with me to the store next week and help me pick out the yarn."

"The store? What about the baby? I can't leave her." The idea of going out of the house had become foreign to Aurora.

"It should take less than an hour," said Evelyn. "As soon as you feed her, you can leave her with Nea and Sophie. Come over, then we can walk to town. Getting out in the sunshine will do you good."

Aurora glared at Sophie. "We'll see," she muttered.

58

The next day Gloria came with her three children. Manuelito and Flavito acted like it was Christmas. For the past week they had been banished to their rooms. Although they had plenty of toys to play with, they had to keep their voices low. They couldn't chase each other around like they did at Mamá Telesfora's. When Gloria arrived the boys quickly escaped outside.

Gloria put both hands over her mouth. "Look how big she's getting! Her little arms are filling out." Her smile faded when she studied Aurora's pale complexion and distant stare.

Aurora told her about Evelyn wanting to go to the store. "I guess I wouldn't mind going," she said, "but I'm afraid to leave Josefita."

"I have to go to the store today," said Gloria. "Why don't you ride with me? We can take the baby. We'll leave the rest of the children here. We can bring them back a treat from the bakery."

Aurora's eyes grew wide. Her breath caught in her throat. "I can't take the baby! She's too small and what if someone is sick and they touch her. I can't lose her too."

Aurora looked from the kitchen to the parlor then wandered into the spacious room. She stopped short when she spotted William.

William had pulled the drapes back. He nodded at Aurora and patted the cushion beside him. "I can understand why you don't want to take the baby to town. I think she's too small too. Maybe when I finish this paperwork, we can go for a walk. Gloria's right; this sunshine will do you good. I'll carry Josefita and we'll only walk as far as you want to."

Aurora twisted her hands. "Maybe in a few days."

William let out a deep breath and retreated back to his study.

Gloria poured Aurora another cup of coffee and tried to find more to talk about. She told Aurora that her brother was living with her now. He was working at the brick factory in Socorro. Her eyes lit up. "Oh, and I was thinking about going to Lemitar in a few days to see my cousin Florinda. Come with me. You can spend some time with your mamá. Maybe Rita can come over." Gloria started to suggest that they could stop by Isabel's but, when Aurora's shoulders tightened, Gloria abandoned her complicated plans.

Gloria wasn't sure if Aurora was even listening anymore, so once in a while she reached for Aurora's hand. She asked Aurora if she'd seen any of their friends lately.

"I haven't seen hardly anyone. I didn't even go to Isabelita's funeral, and afterward no one came to the house."

Gloria hesitated, then leaned toward Aurora. "I came over. Rita and your mother were here. Don't you remember?"

Aurora stood and begin to move about the room, speaking to no one in particular. "At least when I lost my Flavio everyone came." She stared into the distance. "Then they left me alone."

"Even after you had Flavito?" asked Gloria.

Aurora's mind twisted backwards. She remembered lying in a dark room with her baby beside her, then sitting in her father's leather chair by the fire. She remembered the smell of *piñon* wood burning in the cook stove, and her mother bringing her a plate of food. She thought she remembered Rita humming a childhood song.

Aurora glanced from the parlor to the stairs. "I stayed in the back room and Mamá took care of me. This house is too big. There's no little room to hide in."

Gloria touched Aurora's hand than tiptoed into William's study. She told him what Aurora had said. "Maybe she needs to be home for a while."

William began shaking his head. "This is her home. Nea and Sophie have been taking good care of her and the baby. I'm afraid if she hides away, she won't ever come out of this."

Aurora stood on the porch while William helped Gloria settle her children into the wagon. He patted her on the shoulder then looked at the ground. "She seemed to be better for a while."

Gloria nodded. A hopeful smile flashed across her face. "She asked about our friends. She even scolded me for letting my brother stay too long at my house." Gloria shrugged than whispered, "It doesn't sound like she'll go to Lemitar with me. I tried."

William handed her the reins. "That's all you can do, and I think your visit helped." He rolled his eyes to the heavens and sent a little thank you. *Maybe Aurora will start getting better now.*

Gloria promised to stop by every time she was in town. She knew from the way Aurora acted that she wasn't ready to face the world outside of her house. *Little by little,* thought Gloria. *I'll bring the world to her and she'll come back to us.*

William returned to Aurora's side. When she talked about the invitation to Lemitar her voice rose. She jumped up and circled the room. "Do you think it will be alright to take the baby so far?" She walked to the front door and shook her head. "Oh no, no, I better not."

William led her back to the settee. He sat and took Aurora's hand. "I don't know. Maybe in a few weeks I'll take you to see your folks. I don't have much on the docket. We can go on a Friday and come back on a Monday. I think it would be good if Nea went with us. It's been a long time since she's seen her mother. Spending a few days with family would be good for all of us. It would be great for the *abuelos* to see Josefita. Don't worry, I'll be with you." William folded his arms around his wife and for the first time in weeks she let him kiss her.

59

The boys started pointing when they spotted La Parida. It didn't take long before they were begging to go to Mamá Telesfora's. Instead of sending them over, Aurora sent Rita to tell Telesfora she was home. "She can come here and visit them. Every time they go over there, I can hardly get them to come home with me."

When Telesfora heard that the boys were at Josefa's she almost knocked José over getting out the door. As she came through the gate, she and the boys ran to each other. Flavito tugged her toward the house. "Come and see our little sister. She's grown a little, but she still looks like a doll."

Aurora's vacant stare was no longer visible. She savored having her mother's freshly made tortillas smothered with butter. She smiled at the little gowns that the neighbors presented. Aurora pressed them to her chest and thanked the women she had grown up with.

Josefa turned to Aurora. "I talked to William. We think it would be good if you stayed a little longer. That way everyone can come and visit with you and Josefita."

A little smile crept across her lips as Rita told her how worried everyone had been about her.

When Telesfora came in, Aurora's smile faded. As she watched her carefully holding the baby, Aurora thought, *this one is mine, all mine.*

❋ ❋ ❋

Estella broke the tense silence when she rushed through the door and threw her arms around Aurora. She kissed her cheek. "Where have you been? Why haven't you come to see me?" she laughed.

Aurora left Josefita bundled safely in Josefa's care and the two friends walked, arm-in-arm, to Rita's house. The three young women sat behind her house under a cottonwood and looked across the fields sprouting with pale leaves

Every time Estella told her about one of their friends, Aurora had to think for a minute. It didn't take long to remember who Estella was talking about, but it seemed like she had been gone for years. When Estella went back into the house to get more water, she closed her eyes and smiled. She had been so excited about her big house in Socorro, so proud of all her new friends on the committees, but she had never felt as warm and comfortable as she did today.

✳✳✳

After Estella ran out of stories the friends strolled back to Josefa's. As soon as Josefita was back in Aurora's arms, Telesfora turned to her. "Manuel hasn't been feeling so good. Why don't you take the boys to see him? They'll make him feel better." Telesfora looked from Aurora to Josefa.

Aurora waved her hands frantically. "If he's sick, the boys may get sick too and bring the sickness to Josefita."

Josefa had thought about that too, and agreed with Aurora.

Telesfora raised her hands in surrender, but she knew that she would find a way to take the boys to see their grandfather. After all, he had helped raise them when his precious son had passed from this world.

✳✳✳

José had scurried after Telesfora to Josefa's. After taking a quick peek at Josefita, he ran to the fields to find Esquipula. "You know Manuel isn't doing too good," he said. When he saw the worried look on Esquipula's face he changed his mind about going into a tirade. He had planned to remind Esquipula that Manuel was talking about changing his will. Instead, he examined ears of corn while he formed another plan.

"Telesfora wants to take the boys to see Manuel. You know, part of everything that Manuel has, will someday go to the boys." José paused. He shot a look at Esquipula, trying to read what effect this had on Manuel's brother.

When Esquipula didn't stop shoveling, José trudged forward. "We have to protect what the boys will someday inherit, and even what they have now. Telesfora told me that Aurora is still having a hard time. *Santa Maria*, I'm glad that she's still with us." He wagged his finger. "Yes, but if something had happened to her, William, not the boys, would have gotten everything that should be theirs."

As usual, when José started talking, a knot formed in Esquipula's stomach. He tried to busy himself with opening the gates to the canals. The more José talked the less Esquipula could corral his temper. "You're talking about my brother dying and wondering what would happen if my daughter had died. You're worse than a buzzard. Besides, what business is it of yours who gets Manuel's inheritance?"

José tucked his chin into his chest and tromped up the hill toward the house. All the way back he berated himself for saying too much. He mumbled to himself, "I'll talk this over with Telesfora. She has a softer way of saying things. "She can make Aurora understand that the family has to take care of the boys." By the time José reached the house, he was able to quietly ask how Aurora was doing.

He put his hand on Aurora's shoulder. "It's good to be home, yes? You don't know how much your family loves you." One glance at Telesfora's pursed lips warned him not to say more.

On the way back to their house, José dropped his voice. "The boys would be better off with us." He leaned close to Telesfora and whispered. "I heard Manuel talking to Severo about his will. He said he had talked to De Baun about the will. The *gringo* told him that if Isabel remarried, then she died, everything would go to her new husband. Her children would get nothing."

"You see how sick Aurora is." José poked his temple with his finger than shook his fist. "That *gringo* son-of-a bitch will get everything if Aurora dies. I'm going to talk to Manuel tomorrow and see what we can do to protect the boys. . . without De Baun knowing anything about it."

Telesfora's jaw tightened. "How can you talk about Aurora dying?" She turned her head away so José wouldn't see the tears welling up in her eyes. The rest of José's words flew past her. When they got home, José sat at the table sipping coffee. He tried to choose his words carefully but, as usual, he couldn't make Telesfora see things the way he did.

She did agree that the boys needed to be taken care of. Her hand went to her heart. She knew too that no one loved them more than she did, but the idea of planning for Aurora's death was unthinkable.

José started to remind her of Flavio's sudden death, but remembered, in the nick of time, that he was talking about her beloved little brother. He finally gave up and went outside to spit off the *porche*. *Manuel will understand,* he thought. *I'll talk to him in the morning.*

60

When William went back to La Parida at the end of the week, he was greeted with Aurora's wide smile. On their way home, she talked all the way to Socorro. She repeated Estella's gossip and how everyone thought Josefita was beautiful.

Maybe it's over, William thought. Her endless talking was a sign that he was right. William breathed a sigh of relief and hugged Aurora.

Aurora hadn't told him everything. She had missed being surrounded by strong adobe walls and gentle friendships. She was careful to keep this to herself. She didn't think William would understand. After all, he worked so hard to provide this rich, good life for her and her sons.

❄ ❄ ❄

The evening after Aurora came home, William left his paperwork on his desk. Instead, he sat with Aurora on the front porch and talked as they watched the boys playing underneath the big chinese elm tree. Sometimes Aurora told William the same stories over and over again, until there was nothing left but a distant smile. William nodded and tried to listen.

By the end of the week Aurora began to talk less, but William was determined not to let her slip back. One evening, after supper, he settled Aurora into the wicker chair on the front porch and handed her the baby. Then he went back into the house. "

"Where are you going?" asked Aurora.

"You'll see." He waved for the boys to follow him. "Come on, I need your help." When they came back, Manuelito had a coil of rope over his shoulder. Flavito carried a board, and William dragged a step ladder. All three were soon busy with the task of putting up a swing. William kept asking Aurora which branch they should put it on, and how high they should make the swing.

When they finished, the boys took turns on the swing with William pushing them higher and higher. He grinned at the sight of Aurora watching them, instead of staring into space.

"Can Mamá have a turn?" Manuelito jumped up and down. Flavito grabbed his mother's hand and pulled her toward the swing.

Aurora and Josefita sat on the squeaky contraption. William

pulled it back a few inches. The gentle motion gave Aurora a start. The boys clapped and whooped every time she went up in the air.

The next day, when William came home for his noon meal, Aurora was nowhere to be found.

Sophie folded her hands and slowly began to speak. "She wouldn't come downstairs. I think she's still in her dressing gown."

William closed his eyes and dropped his head. He crept up the stairs to find Aurora curled up in bed. He crossed the room in three long steps and scooped up Josefita. The baby squirmed and William took a deep breath. He shook Aurora gently. She blinked up at him and rubbed her eyes.

"I didn't feel like getting out of bed today." She propped herself up against the headboard and reached for the bundle in William's arms. "Come here my Isabelita. I dreamed that you were with the angels, but here you are."

William turned away. "This is Josefita," he announced. When he turned back, Aurora had slipped back under the covers."Josefita?" she whispered.

William ordered Sophie to gather up clothing for the boys. While Sophie tiptoed around gathering up all of the clothes she could find, William slipped back into his bedroom. He was relieved to find Aurora sitting in the rocker smiling down at the baby. Her hair fell in tangles over her shoulders. Her bare feet poked out from beneath her wrinkled gown.

She smiled up at William. "Isn't Josefita beautiful? Everyone in La Parida loves her."

William closed his eyes and leaned against the wall. "Yes, they do," he sighed. "I bet they would like to see more of her. Why don't we go for another visit after the sun goes down?"

"Back to La Parida? Oh, but I'm not dressed." She touched her matted hair. "My hair. . . what time is it? I don't hear the boys. Are they outside?" Aurora stood and took a wobbly step toward the bed.

William lurched forward and grabbed her arm. He gently took her elbow as she sank to the edge of the bed. He sat down beside her and kissed her on the temple. "It's alright, you don't have to hurry. We won't leave until this evening. I'll get Sophie to help you." He took Josefita and handed her to Nea who was lingering at the door.

❋❋❋

By the time they passed Escondida, Aurora was leaning forward

261

and smiling. She clapped her hands when they spotted the adobe walls of her father's house. William assured her that he would be back the next Sunday. Aurora nodded absently.

Juan had been sent ahead, so when the gates were swung open, Josefa met Aurora with open arms and a cautious smile. One look at William's troubled eyes confirmed Josefa's worry.

William took the carpetbags into the little room on the other side of the *plazita*. The window had been opened to air out the room. Fresh sheets were turned down, ready for Aurora's stay. Josefa slipped into the room and touched William's shoulder.

He turned with a start. With Josefa sitting on the edge of the bed, William told her how Aurora seemed to be getting better, then worsened. "I've thought a lot about this," William said, "It seems that if Aurora is left alone too long, she starts getting confused." He buried his face in his hands, his shoulders heaving.

Josefa waited for him to take a breath. He wiped his eyes on Josefa's handkerchief and muttered. "It almost broke my heart when Aurora thought Josefita was Isabelita."

William leaned forward and took Josefa's hand. "I don't know what to do. I can't just leave her here forever, but being with family seems to help." William looked down at Josefa sitting with her hand clutched to her chest. He clamped his hand over his mouth, then dropped into the rocker.

William stood and fanned himself with his hat. "I can't stay. I have to be in court tomorrow. Maybe if we keep talking about Josefita. . ." He started wagging his finger. "Oh, and you can take her to Manuel's store. That always cheers her up. And her friend, um, Estella can come over. Maybe, when we go back, Rita can come with us for a few days."

"I'm sorry; I was just thinking out loud," he chuckled. "My partner, Jonathan, says my rattling drives him up a wall. It's just that I'm so worried about Aurora."

Josefa nodded and moved her hand to pat William on the knee. She changed her mind and let her hand rest on his arm.

"We'll do everything we can," assured Josefa."Aurora's mind slipped when we lost our Flavio. It took some time, but she finally came back to us." Josefa looked up at William. A glint flashed across her eyes. "It was the children. Yes, we'll keep reminding her that she has a beautiful little daughter to take care of. Josefita will bring her back." Josefa made the sign of the cross and stepped to the door. She lifted her face to the sun, closed her eyes, and took a deep breath.

When William and Josefa went back into the *plazita*, they found Aurora helping Barbara. They were setting the table underneath the mulberry tree. Aurora carried out a basket full of dishes.

"It's too hot to eat in the kitchen," announced Aurora. She fanned herself with the apron she had retrieved from beside the stove. She gave William a peck on the cheek. "Go tell Papá that the food is almost ready."

William left the women to finish setting the table. As he walked down the path toward Esquipula's fields he was weighted down with confusion. *I can't just leave her here. What's going to become of my child? How can she go from staying in bed all day to organizing the evening meal? She acts as if everything is fine.*

William froze. *Was she acting at home?* He dropped his head. *Maybe she would rather be with her family.* He groaned, then willed his feet to move forward.

William spotted Esquipula and hastened his pace. He stepped into a rut and stumbled forward. The near fall jolted him out of his worries.

Esquipula was trudging up the path with his head bent. It wasn't until William shouted, "Hello, *Señor* Vigil!" that he lifted his head.

Esquipula's eyes grew wide. "Aurora?" he panted, searching Williams eyes. "Oh no, don't tell me it's the baby!"

William shook his head as his words tumbled out. "No, no, *Señor* Vigil. I'm sorry if I frightened you. Of course, you would assume that something was wrong. William flashed a quick smile. "Josefita is fine, but I'm concerned about Aurora. She was confused at home, but she seems better this evening. What do you think?"

Esquipula told William that Aurora had been getting better during her first visit but, there were still days that she curled up in bed and didn't speak to anyone. "Sometimes the boys would go see her. Josefa would hear them laughing and Aurora would come out of her room. Then, sometimes she got mad and told them to get out. The other day she scared Flavito because she grabbed him and started crying, 'My Flavio, my Flavio."

William looked at the sky and clenched his jaw. *Is she ever going to be alright? What about Josefita? What's going to happen to her if Aurora doesn't come out of it?*

"But she will come out of it," Esquipula promised. "La Señora said that she's seen this before. When babies are born, sometimes the mother's thinking gets all tangled up. She's watching Aurora very closely, giving her *rude* to smoke. It calms her. We'll keep reminding her that she has a beautiful baby daughter and two fine boys. You'll see; every time you come to see her she'll be better."

William shook his head and kicked a dirt clod. "I guess no one can tell me how long it will take, but as long as I know she'll eventually get better, I can wait."

"Esquipula wiped his brow with a red bandanna. "Ay, *Mijita*." He sighed and looked toward his *hacienda*. ". . .and now with Manuel so sick."

61

La Señora pointed a gnarled finger at Manuel and ordered him to stay in bed. His cough had worsened over the past three days. He was sure that if he just stayed away from the dusty grist mill his cough would go away. When he wasn't able to come to the breakfast table, La Señora was sent for.

Telesfora ran to Esquipula's to give him the latest news about his brother. She twisted the hem of her apron and looked around to make sure the children were playing outside. Before she could open her mouth, Josefa jerked her head toward Aurora. She pursed her lips and nodded.

When Josefa set a glass of water in front of Telesfora, she whispered. "Aurora got here yesterday. We're losing her again."

By the end of the day Josefa couldn't keep the news of Manuel's illness from Aurora. Neighbors stopped by to ask about him, saying they had lit a candle at the church for him. They all agreed that he was in good hands with La Señora.

Aurora peered out of her room when she heard horses. She listened at the door before entering her mother's kitchen. Bits of conversation seeped through the old wood. Someone was sick. She tiptoed off the porch and retreated back to her room. She didn't creep back into the cooking room until she heard wagon wheels fading away.

Aurora wasn't surprised to find that Telesfora was sitting at the table. She and the boys were busy cleaning a pile of beans. When Telesfora noticed Aurora, her words hung in midair.

Aurora leaned against the door. She met her mother's gaze. "What are you trying to hide from me?"

When Josefa told her how sick Manuel was, Aurora's eyes widened. "I can't lose him too!" she wailed.

She buried her face in her apron. Josefa rushed to embrace her. Rocking her gently, Josefa made little shushing noises.

Telesfora guided the women to the bench. "I saw him yesterday. His color is better, and he's sitting up. He's starting to order Severo around and wants to go back to the store. It's only La Señora's threats that are keeping him in bed."

Josefa nodded. "He's drinking her *ponil* tea morning and night."

Telesfora waved her hand in front of her nose. The whole house smells of *plumajillo*. La Señora boils the flowers in the morning and the smell seems to soak into the walls."

Aurora sat up. "I always liked that smell. Mamá would put honey in my tea. It would stop my coughing. I always knew that when I was given te *de plumajillo* I would start feeling better."

"There, you see," smiled Telesfora. "Your *Tio* will be well in no time." She shot a wary glance toward Aurora. "Perhaps you can go see him in a day or two. I know seeing the boys would really be good for him."

Both women held their breath. Telesfora patted Aurora on the back. Aurora scrunched up her shoulders.

"I can't take Josefita. What if she gets sick? Whatever is making *Tio* sick is in the house. If I get sick, then the baby will too."

Telesfora sighed and nodded. "I'll let you know how Manuel is doing. If he's well enough to sit in the *plazita*, maybe you can pay him a short visit. You can leave Josefita with your mother. You don't have to stay long."

✳✳✳

Isabel found Aurora in the *plazita* when she came to see Josefita. She took Aurora's hand and smiled. "Manuel is so much better." She slipped her arm around Aurora's thin waist. "Stop by tomorrow. You know how much he loves seeing the boys."

The next day Aurora held each boy by the hand and stood at the far end of the porch. It hurt Aurora to see her uncle so pale and weak. His strength seemed to return when he saw the boys. Manuel started to reach for them, but pulled back when he saw Aurora leaning backwards.

"It's so good to see all of you. It's been too long." He looked at the boys and his lips began to quiver. "When I get better, I'll take you out on the horses." He managed a weak smile. Manuelito tried to wiggle free from his mother, but her grip tightened.

"When can we go *Abuelo* ?"

Manuel chuckled, then coughed. "Pretty soon, *Mijito*. I'm feeling better. When it gets a little warmer, your mamá will bring you back." He looked at Aurora. She raised a shaky hand and nodded.

✳✳✳

Aurora was surprised to see José waiting for her at the gate. As they walked back to Josefa's he let out a slow breath and took Auro-

266

ra's hand. "He's getting old. Manuel isn't as strong as he used to be."

"He's going to be alright." Aurora's words stuck in the lump that had seized her throat. She looked hopefully into José's eyes. "He can't leave me now, not now."

José's lips tightened. *Will there ever be a good time to talk to Aurora about protecting her boys?* He squeezed Aurora's shoulder. "Don't worry *Mija*, you know how stubborn Manuel is. I'm just glad you and the boys went to see him. I knew it would make him happy."

José guided Aurora to an ancient cottonwood. "Let's rest a minute." He fanned himself with his hat. The boys ran after a little striped lizard and José tried again. He crossed his leg, lit his pipe, and mustered his courage.

"You know how important you and your sons are to the family. When Manuel got sick, I started thinking about how sick you were with the babies." He blew out a puff of smoke.

"I was worried. If something happened to you, what would become of your sons? Oh yes, the family would take care of them, but what about their inheritance?"

Aurora twisted and glared at José. "What are you talking about? Sometimes I think the devil possesses your tongue!" Aurora jumped up. She called the boys and started toward the house.

José ran after her. "Aurora, stop! I know I don't say things right sometimes, but I'm always worrying. *Graciasa a Dios*, thank God that you're getting better. I was just saying that I was worried for a while, and I thought about how we could protect the boys." He grabbed her arm.

Aurora pulled out of his grip and started opening the gate. Without turning she said "You don't have to worry; William will protect them."

José balled up his fist. He marched toward the fields, kicking up dust as he went. *Maybe I should talk to Esquipula again. He could get Aurora to understand.* He topped over the knoll and looked for Esquipula, then remembered he was at the house. José shuffled back to the cottonwood tree and dropped onto an old stump. *I was right. This is not the time. Aurora is still confused. She thinks William loves them and that he wouldn't think of taking their land.*

62

The next Sunday William pulled himself away from his trial notes. On top of everything else, he was judging another case. A miner had killed his partner for his silver. He shook his head. *There were a lot of witnesses. It should be an open and shut case.*

The sunlight was beginning to fade. If he was going to get to La Parida before dark, he would have to put down his pen and go see his family. He didn't mind the ride. The silence cleared his thoughts. As he rode toward Esquipula's, the words he would write to the railroad started forming.

Then his thoughts turned to Aurora and the children. How quiet the house had been for the past week, and how far away the troubles of his family had been.

✻✻✻

Manuelito and Flavito ran to meet William and his silence was broken. He took each boy by the hand. Aurora was waiting for him at the door. She seemed to have blossomed during the past week. He hugged his little wife and hoped that all of her agony was behind her.

"Wait 'till you see the baby." Aurora beamed." She's starting to get big."

"You mean Josefita, our daughter?"

Aurora stopped in the middle of the room. Her eyes darted back and forth and her brows knitted. She let go of William's hand and walked to the cradle. She picked up Josefita and turned to William. "Yes," she stammered. "Look how big Josefita is getting. I told God he couldn't have this one. He heard me. See how beautiful she is!"

Aurora showed William the two new gowns that her mother had made for Josefita. "These will cover her feet. The ones she's wearing were too short."

William unwrapped the blanket and kissed the little pink toes that were sticking out of her gown. "I swear, she's grown three inches since I saw her last." Sitting on the bench, both were transfixed by Josefita. Her eyes were wide open. She wrapped her hand around her father's finger and made little purring noises.

"Look," William said, "She's talking to me. Do you think she's saying, I want to go home?"

As William took his daughter in his arms, he was aware of the silence in the room. Even the children stopped and looked from Aurora to William.

Josefa crossed the room in three steps. "Soon," she smiled, "I think they should stay a little longer." The worried look in Josefa's eyes told William that his wife was not yet ready to leave her family.

All the way home William thought about Aurora. *Is this where she belongs? This is where the boys want to be. What was I thinking—that she would thrive in a big house, sipping tea, and going to committee meetings?*

63

William dragged himself out of bed as the first beams of daylight reached his eyes. As he drove his buggy past miles of mesquite and sagebrush, his busy week fell away. He began to think of Aurora. *I can't make this trip every week. I have so much to do. Yes, I want her home, but only if her unsettled confusion has left her for good.* His buggy bumped over hills and dipped into arroyos.

Then he thought about the railroad agent. The letter from the railroad to Aurora was one of many that lay piled on his desk. Lately he felt like a treed cat with a pack of dogs barking at him from every side.

As mayor of a newly incorporated town, he had to preside over meetings. New laws and regulations were presented. Committees were set up to review them. Everyone had their own idea about how Socorro should be governed.

Now the railroad agent was hounding him. He was anxious to tie up the land for the railroad spur to Magdalena. Part of it would go through Snake Ranch. William tried to explain that his wife was too ill to attend to the matter. The agent only raised his eyebrows and said there was another chunk of land further to the east that would do. William had to act faster than he wanted to.

❋❋❋

When Aurora saw the dust cloud on the road, she pulled the heavy gate open. Manuelito grabbed Flavito's hand and they jumped off the *porche*. When they reached William, he was in Aurora's embrace. He ruffled their hair and led his little family into the house. Aurora put the baby into William's arms.

He drew a breath. "I think she's grown since last week."

Aurora leaned against his arm. "I think she starting to look like you. I hope her hair doesn't turn dark." She reached up as if to kiss William, but whispered instead. "You know her sister Isabelita is with the angels. La Señora told me about a special place where all the babies are taken care of. She knows about these things." Aurora looked skyward and made the sign of the cross over her heart. "They have Isabelita, but they can't have Josefita."

William leaned down and kissed the top of Aurora's head. "You can be sure of that. We'll keep her safe." He shot Josefa a hopeful glance, then squeezed Aurora's arm.

Aurora placed Josefita in her basket and helped Josefa set glasses of water on a tray. While the women scurried around the kitchen, William joined Esquipula in the shade of the mulberry tree. Gazing straight ahead, William asked, "How is she doing?"

Esquipula took off his straw hat. "I can't tell you as much as Josefa can. All I know is that her mamá goes to Aurora's room every morning and makes sure she comes into the house. Aurora and the boys have been helping Josefa plant her garden. They like being in the sunshine. The color is coming back to Aurora's cheeks."

William's jaw tightened. "What about the baby? She knows it's Josefita? Does she talk about Isabelita?"

"She knows Isabelita is no longer with us." Esquipula turned to William. "She wanted to go visit Flavio's grave. She wanted to tell him to help take care of Isabelita."

Esquipula gulped. He walked toward the chicken coop. When there was no longer a threat of tears, Esquipula came back to the bench "Josefa wouldn't let her go. She told Aurora that Isabelita was with the angels. Josefa even told her that Isabelita was with her own baby; the brother that Aurora didn't know about." Esquipula scanned the distance, then fell silent. William patted his father-in-law on the shoulder and lit his cigar.

✳✳✳

After dinner, William took Aurora's elbow, moving her toward the *porche*. "I think I'll go see Manuel while I'm here," he told her. "They say he's feeling better." He was relieved that Aurora didn't want to go with him. He kissed her cheek and started walking up the hill.

Esquipula whistled and waved his hat at William. "He's at the store today!" He slapped the air. "When is that man going to slow down?"

William spotted Manuel's buggy in front of his mercantile. He had recovered enough to go to the store, but Severo had taken over the running of the business. Manuel was usually with his family on Sunday, but he wanted to make sure Severo and José were familiar with the new merchandise.

José unlocked the front door. As usual, he greeted William with a scowl.

"Is Manuel here?" William asked with an exaggerated smile.

José answered with a jerk of his chin toward the back room. As soon as the office door closed, José tiptoed across the store and pressed his ear against the door. *Is Aurora getting worse? Has something happened to the baby?*

Manuel pushed himself up from his chair and offered his hand to William. "And Aurora, is she getting better?"

William nodded at Severo then sat on the stiff wooden chair. He told Manuel that she seemed to be accepting the loss of Isabelita. "I'd like her to stay another week, just to make sure she's still going in the right direction. There's, um, some business I have to take care of for Aurora, but I don't want to burden her with it."

"The sale of the property to the railroad," blurted Manuel. "The agent has been pestering me for weeks."

Manuel explained that the agent had asked him about selling a parcel of the Vigil property. Manuel had finally sent him to William with a letter stating that the land belonged to his grandsons Manuelito and Flavito. He had bequeathed them all of the land that would have gone to his son Flavio. Aurora was their legal guardian. It would be her decision.

William took a deep breath. He had wondered how Manuel would feel about the sale. Would the old man be glad that his grandsons were going to start a nest egg, or would he want to hold onto his son's land for them?

"Me and Severo have talked about this." Manuel said. "Now that Flavio is no longer with us, the property of Snake Ranch is of no use to me. What the railroad wants to buy is only a small part of the ranch. The boys are so small. It will be years before they know if they want to go into ranching."

Severo closed the ledger book. "I say, sell to the railroad and put the money into the bank in Aurora's name." He stood and stared at William.

"Of course, I can put it in a trust for them," agreed William, "but what about Aurora? She's their guardian and would have to sign for them. Would she understand what's going on? Besides, I hate to bother her with this right now."

Manuel drew a breath that caught in his throat. When his racking cough subsided, he whispered. "I hope she's doing better." He shook his head and looked away. "She had such a hard time when our Flavio died. When Flavito was born I don't even think she knew what was going on. Now it's happening all over again." He shook his head again.

I'm glad you brought her home. The family brought her back once and we'll do it again.

"So, what shall we do about the railroad sale? They're pushing me to make a decision soon."

"I'll talk to Esquipula and then to Aurora. Even if she doesn't quite understand what's going on, I'll try to make her see that I approve and that we're doing what's best for the boys."

When William returned to Esquipula's, Aurora was sitting in the rocker with little Josefita at her breast. When she looked up at William her cheeks were pink, her hair had been combed, and she was smiling. William shuddered. *Is this where she belongs?* The next evening, William rode home alone.

64

All week-long José nipped at Severo and Manuel. Manuel waved him away, but José said, "I know what's going on. "You know I'm always listening." José eyes narrowed. "The *gringo* can't wait to get his hands on the Vigil land. Now that Aurora isn't right in the head, De Baun will steal everything."

Manuel rose quickly, his chair slamming against the wall. "This is none of your business!" Manuel grabbed his son-in-law by the arm and ushered him out the back door. "Do you want everyone in Lemitar to know our business?" Manuel hissed. "You better not try to make trouble about this. Hell, you can't even feed a burro on that land, and the railroad will pay top dollar for it. William is going to put the money into a trust for Flavio's sons."

"A trust, what's a trust—and whose name will be on it? I suppose El *Gringo* said this has to be done right away. Aurora doesn't even know what day it is. He's going to slip this right past her, and you're going to let him?"

Manuel pounded his fist on the stair rail. "Do you really think I would do anything to bring harm to Flavio's sons?

Jose's lips tightened. He walked backward, up the stairs. As he pushed back through the door, he whispered, "We just have to keep an eye on that *gringo*. He's a sharp one."

It doesn't matter if they won't tell me anything, thought José. *I know what's going on.* He finished unpacking two crates, then dropped into a chair. Complaining of a headache, José said that he needed to go home. "You should go too." He shook his finger at Manuel as he stepped through the office door. "Rest this afternoon. We can finish this tomorrow."

Manuel just shook his head and stomped to the back door of his saloon. He slipped behind the bar and took a rare shot of whiskey.

The bartender grinned, "José?"

Manuel walked toward the door shaking his head. "José," he answered.

❋❋❋

José tumbled off his horse and ran into the house. He eyed the boys playing under the kitchen table. Telesfora started, piercing her finger with her needle. "I brought the boys home. . ."

274

José lifted her out of her chair and half dragged her into the back room. "I knew it! I knew it!

Didn't I tell you something like this was going to happen?" He started pacing.

Anger boiled up Telesfora's throat. "What are you talking about, you crazy old man?"

"Crazy am I! That *gringo* is starting to sell off the land that belongs to the boys. Aurora won't even have a say in it. He's convinced Manuel to agree to it, but I won't let it happen!"

Telesfora threw her hands up, but by the time her questions had fully formed, José was out the door.

"Where are you going? Wait! You're not going to upset Aurora."

As José hopped off the porch, he yelled back, "I'm going back to talk to Manuel!"

Telesfora yelped, "Oh no!" *José is getting worse. What kind of trouble is he going to stir up now?* She wanted to run to Josefa's and warn her, but José hadn't really explained what was going on. Besides, she didn't want the boys to hear about this craziness. Telesfora ran outside. She walked toward the road, then back into the house. *Papá won't let José upset Aurora.*

Telesfora turned and called to the boys, "We're going to see your *Abuelo* Esquipula." She shaded her eyes and searched for Esquipula. When she saw him riding his horse toward the canal, she hurried toward him. He tied his horse to a mesquite bush and ran to meet his niece.

"Telesfora, what's happened?"

Telesfora shook her head. "I just came to tell you that José is stirring up trouble again and I don't want Aurora to be upset by it."

The boys tunneled under a big mesquite while Esquipula and Telesfora crouched in the shade of another. Telesfora told him what José had said. She wasn't able to answer most of his questions because she didn't understand what José was raging about.

Esquipula rolled his eyes. "This is about the sale of the land to the railroad. Manuel talked to me about it. He thinks it would be a good idea. How did José find out?"

Telesfora just shook her head. "What about Aurora?"

"Don't worry about it, Telesfora, you just take care of the boys. Manuel won't let José get out of hand. Besides, this will probably blow over the way most of José's crazy ideas do."

Esquipula climbed back on his horse. Telesfora watched the boys play hide and seek for a while. When she felt her shoulders dropping and her breath slowing, she walked back to the house with the boys. She pointed out all the new buds on the trees. "Pretty soon," she said, "the seeds you planted will come up in your garden."

65

Estella visited Aurora often and brought news of all her friends. "I've told everyone how beautiful Joséfita is. They all want to see her." Estella glanced at Josefa. "Why don't you bring her to Mass on Sunday?"

Josefa assured Estella that Aurora would be at the church on Sunday.

On their way to church Josefa and Aurora cuddled in the back seat of the buggy. Josefa wrapped her shawl around Aurora. "Everyone wants to see Joséfita. You don't have to let anyone hold her if you don't want to."

The women poured out of the church and encircled Aurora. Their pitiful looks had been put away. They were in awe of Josefita's blue eyes and soft yellow hair. Aurora put her hand on her forehead. She sighed deeply as she told her friends about all the gowns she had made to replace the ones Josefita had grown out of.

When Margarita held out her arms, Aurora drew Josefita closer. Estella stood behind Aurora with her hands on her shoulders. She gave her a quick squeeze and reminded her that Josefita was almost two months old. "I think it would be alright for your friends to hold her." Aurora shot a worried look at Estella. Her friend nodded. Slowly Aurora handed her baby to Margarita.

✸ ✸ ✸

After the noon meal, Aurora decided to walk to Telesfora's. She wasn't tired of talking about how much everybody loved Josefita. The sun was shining and La Señora had told her that the fresh air would be good for the baby. While she walked down the road, she had a strange feeling that she had done this all before. *I'm living in my mother's house,* she thought. *My boys were sent away for someone else to take care of.* By the time she got to Telesfora's she had made up her mind that she was going to gather up her children and go home. Before she knocked on the door, she sat for a while on the chair outside the wall. She put her face to the sun and smiled. *At least now I have a home to go to.*

She marched into the house and announced that she and the boys were going back to Socorro the next day. Telesfora's mouth flew open and she shook her head. When she regained her voice, she cupped Aurora's face. "Are you sure you're ready to do this?"

Aurora assured her that she no longer felt like she belonged at La Parida. She knew it was time to go home.

Telesfora's face twisted into a mask of sadness. She sniffled, then straightened. "Well why don't you go to Socorro and see how things go? Leave the boys with me until you're settled in. I can take them home next week." Aurora lifted her chin, a sign that Telesfora was very familiar with.

"No, I think we should all go home. Poor William has been without his family long enough."

Aurora stood to leave, but Manuelito ran out the back door and hid behind the water trough. Flavito started wailing, "*Tio* José promised that I could ride the horse when he came home."

"You see," Telesfora raised her voice. "This is too sudden. You go on ahead and give me time to get the boys used to the idea of going back to Socorro. It will only be a few days."

Aurora wanted to grab Flavito by the arm and shake him so he would stop screaming, but Josefita started crying. Her little gown was wet and Aurora knew she had to get back to her mother's house.

Aurora glared at Flavito and he hid behind Telesfora's skirt. She looked down at her own wet skirt. "I have to get back and change her."

When Aurora revealed that she would be leaving the next day, Josefa took the baby and led Aurora to the bench on the front porch. Josefa started to send Santa Cruz for La Señora, but Aurora put her hand on her mother's arm.

"I'm alright, Mamá. I can tell I'm getting better every day. I feel like I don't belong in my mother's house anymore."

Josefa embraced her. "But this seems so sudden. Why don't you wait until next Sunday? That will give you time to get everything packed and send a message to William. Let him know that you're coming home. I'll tell Telesfora."

"She knows. I was just over there. The boys made me so mad. They didn't want to come back with me. Telesfora spoils them."

"Don't be so hard on them. Nobody knew about your plans to go back to Socorro. Remember *Mija*, they're just little boys and maybe they don't know where they belong."

Aurora stood and leaned against the porch post. "Maybe you're right. I'll have Telesfora bring the boys over here. They'll stay with me until we leave for Socorro." Aurora breathed deeply. "This will be better."

Aurora took the baby into the bedroom to change her clothes. Josefa let loose of a deep sigh. *Was this another turn of Aurora's mind? Would she be ready to go home next Sunday? Should the boys go with her or stay in La Parida where there were so many to care for them?*

The rest of the afternoon was spent gathering clothes and putting them in her carpetbag. When the day cooled, Aurora washed out little gowns and diapers and put them on the line to dry. She sent a note with Santa Cruz. "Tell Telesfora that I want the boys back for the evening meal. They'll be staying with me until next Sunday."

When William got the note from Aurora, he could hardly wait for Sunday. The sun had barely peaked over Strawberry Hill when William drove out of Socorro.

While Aurora gathered her belongings, Esquipula took William to see his newly planted fields.

"She's almost back to her old self," Esquipula smiled. His eyes widened. "She even started talking back to Josefa, letting her know that she didn't need to be told what to do." Esquipula grunted. "Yesterday Aurora snapped at her mother. She said, 'Why am I helping you when I have my own house to run?' "

A cautious smile crept across William's lips.

When Aurora got home, she went from room to room. She touched her fine china, and ran her hand over the thick upholstery. She drifted upstairs and stared at the huge oak bed. She knew this was her home, but she felt like she had stepped into a foreign land.

With the baby asleep, Aurora watched the boys play in their room. They seemed glad to be back, but they too were touching their toys and looking out the window, rediscovering their yard.

Aurora kept herself busy in the kitchen, helping Sophie prepare a roasting chicken for the evening meal. She kept glancing out the window, looking for William's buggy.

Before William reached the back door, Aurora was in his arms. She smothered him with kisses. The past three weeks seemed far away. William basked in the laughter and chatter of his family. He didn't even care that they ate at the kitchen table, instead of the dining room.

When Aurora started to help Sophie clear the table, William pulled his wife close. "Why don't we go for a little walk. The weather is perfect this time of year."

As they strolled toward the park, Aurora kept reminding herself that Socorro was her home now. She held her head high, remembering that she was the wife of the mayor. But her mind kept drifting back to the small adobe rooms with thick walls that had kept her safe.

By the end of the week the high ceilings and large windows began to engulf Aurora. She had Juan hitch up the buggy. The boys jumped and clapped when they found out they were going to Gloria's.

The minute Aurora saw the high adobe walls, she felt lighter. The friends talked and laughed all afternoon. Aurora helped Gloria make corn tortillas for enchiladas. The boys picked peppermint from Gloria's garden. Manuelito crushed it in a small *metate*. Flavito's job was to put it in glasses that were filled by Gloria's daughter.

When it was time to leave, tears welled up in Aurora's eyes. "Come and see me every time you come to town. That house is too big for me. Maybe if I fill it with my friends, I can start to feel like I belong there again.

❋❋❋

Sophie slipped into William's study as soon as she heard the front door open. She told him how happy Aurora seemed when she went to Gloria's. He put his hand on his chin. "Well, she has a lot of friends and family in Socorro. I'll just have to make sure she visits them often so she won't get homesick."

After Mass, William took his family to Rufina's for a visit. When the boys saw Telesfora's buggy they ran into the house and started looking for their Mamá Telesfora. Aurora frowned as she turned to William. "No one told me she was going to be here."

When they left, the boys begged to go home with Telesfora. Aurora knelt and held their hands. "We have to stay in Socorro. You're papá misses us. Now that the cold air is gone, we'll go to see your *abuelos* and your *tia* more often. Aurora was surprised that she wasn't angry with them. She understood what it felt like to want to go home. She looked up at William holding his little daughter. *I have to try to make my home in Socorro.*

William loaded the family into the buggy. He convinced the boys to go with the promise of peppermint sticks from the Torres Mercantile. When William swung them onto the buggy, he did so with a little more force than intended. "This is not going to happen again," he hissed. "You belong at home with us."

❃ ❃ ❃

When William left for work, Aurora looked around the house for a place to build a little chapel like the one in her mother's house. Every room had a function, so she took the corner knickknack shelf from the parlor and put it in the bedroom. On the top shelf she placed a statue of the Blessed Mother. On the next shelf she put a gown that Isabelita had worn. She wished she had a picture of her tiny angel, but perhaps when she looked at Josefita, she would know what Isabelita looked like.

Every morning Aurora went outside and gathered flowers from her garden. If there were none blooming, she brought in leaves that reminded her of angel wings. She put them on the shelves of her makeshift altar. She knelt on a pillow in front of the shelf. With folded hands she prayed to the Blessed Mother and all of the angels to take care of her little one.

Nea and Sophie didn't know whether this was a good thing or not. At least Aurora knew that one of her babies was with God.

"We shouldn't let her spend too much time praying at the altar," said Nea. "She may go back and stay there like she did before. Let's give her fifteen minutes, then I'll make up some excuse for her to take care of her children or the house."

Sophie agreed and the two young women set up a plan to distract Aurora every day. Most of the time it was Josefita who brought Aurora away from her prayers. When she was hungry, she had no problem letting the whole household know it.

One morning Aurora saw the boys standing at her bedroom door and waved for them to come in. They clung to each other, inching their way into the room. She made them kneel and pray for their father and their little sister. The boys were willing to say a short prayer, but when Aurora went on and on, Flavito stood to leave. Aurora grabbed him by the shoulder and pushed him back down.

Manuelito scrambled downstairs and told Sophie what had happened. She glanced at Nea. "We have to keep the boys away from her when she's at the altar." Sophie put Flavito on her lap while Nea made breakfast. She tried to explain that his mother was praying for the sister that God had taken. "Maybe it would be best if you just came down for breakfast and give her some time alone."

William intended to get home early now that the Abram Baca trial was over but, soon after the Baca brothers were jailed, relatives helped them escape. Judge Pino forced the sheriff to deputize half the men in town. At first most of the *Hispanos* refused.

Judge Pino stomped into the courtroom with William trailing behind him. The judge pounded his gavel. "Don't you people understand? This is not about the *Americano's* laws. A man has been murdered." He looked around the room. The men stood; their heads bent. When the silence stretched on, eyes raised and hats were twisted.

"What if you had tried to defend the women in that church? Do you really think that Abram Baca would've spared your life because you are a *Hispano*? Judge Pino went on. "These are evil men, a danger to all of us. The law is here to protect you and your families. We can't let these men get away."

The men shuffled toward the judge's bench and put their marks on the deputies list. Each signature was rewarded with the presentation of a little star. The men glanced at each other; eyebrows raised. When William pinned a star on one man's shirt, the others smiled and nodded. Soon all the stars were pinned in place.

"The Bacas have family down toward El Paso del Norte," Judge Pino announced. "That's probably where they're headed." His jaw locked as he nodded toward the sheriff. "Get going!" He ordered.

❄ ❄ ❄

When William got home, he was anxious to tell Aurora about the escape. He knew Aurora's family was related to the Bacas and wanted to know if she knew them. He expected to see her in the kitchen visiting with Sophie and Nea; but he found her curled up in the corner of her big bed, rocking the baby. He quietly closed the door and crept downstairs.

Sophie jumped when she heard William step into the kitchen. "Why is Aurora still upstairs in bed? I thought she was getting better. How long has she been like this?"

Sophie and Naya glanced at each other. Sophie stammered, "We thought she was taking a nap with the baby."

Nea put her hand on William's arm. "Let me go up and talk to her."

At first Nea began to tiptoe up the stairs, then she stomped so Aurora wouldn't be startled. She poked her head through the doorway, smiled and said, "Your husband's home in time for supper tonight."

Aurora lifted her head slowly. She was silent for a few moments as if untangling Nea's message. Aurora handed Josefita to Nea and scooted off the bed. She tried to press the wrinkles out of her dress, then walked to the bureau. Nea put the sleeping baby in her cradle and helped Aurora fix her hair.

"How are you feeling?" Nea asked.

Aurora looked in the mirror and pinched her cheeks. She held onto Nea's hand. "I am getting better, you know. I just woke up and wanted to hold Josefita a little longer."

Nea nodded. Aurora rolled her shoulders and took a deep breath. She took the baby from the cradle and stepped slowly downstairs.

William kissed Aurora on the forehead and took Josefita. He rocked her back and forth. "I've never seen anything more beautiful. I think she's going to look just like you."

Aurora dug her fingers into the top of the chair. She fought to keep her mind on what William had said instead of letting it float back to the day when Flavio gazed at his little son and said, "He's beautiful. I think he's going to look just like you." She gripped the arm of the chair and smiled. She looked around the room to make sure she was in her Socorro home.

The boys ran into the parlor. They started to rush at William, but when they saw him holding the baby, they froze. Manuelito grabbed his brother by the arm. Eying their parents, they waited to see what kind of mood their mother was in.

William slowly unfolded the story about the Baca brothers. As Sophie helped the boys wash up, Aurora squeezed her eyes shut, then opened them wide. "What were you saying about the trial?"

"It's the Baca brothers, Antonio and Onofre, and their cousin Abram. How are they related to your family?"

Aurora tapped her chin and turned to Nea who reminded Aurora that her grandmother was a Baca.

"I don't know any of them very well. They live in Socorro and San Antonio. What happened to them?"

William's put down his fork softly. *Aurora hasn't heard about the murder of Anthony Conklin. She probably doesn't know that he died defending the woman the Bacas were harassing.* William glanced toward the kitchen. A thin smile crept across his face. *I'll have to thank Sophie and Nea for keeping all this from Aurora.*

William watched Aurora smashing potatoes and spooning tiny bits into Josefita's rosebud mouth. *What was I thinking, bringing this mess into my home? Aurora can't handle this.* Aurora didn't mention the Baca brothers again and neither did William.

"You don't have to help with the dishes. That's what Sophie's for." William touched Aurora's elbow and pointed toward the back door. He pushed the swing gently back and forth. With his little daughter in his arms, William began to talk to Aurora. He told her about the new laws that were in place and the growing tension between the *Americanos* and the *Hispanos*. He hoped she would join the conversation like she used to. Instead, she just nodded occasionally. She stared at the yard, hoping that William would think she was watching her boys.

68

Evelyn stopped by after the Ladies League meeting to talk about the fundraising dance. "The money will go to hire more deputies. It's more important than ever now that the Baca brothers have escaped." She took a sip of coffee and glanced up to see Sophie shaking her head. Her eyes were wide. They darted toward Aurora. Evelyn's hands flew to her mouth. She nodded her understanding and changed the subject. "I was hoping that we could count on you to be on the decorating committee."

Aurora stiffened. She leaned forward for the first time since Evelyn arrived. "Oh no, I couldn't possibly be away from Josefita!" Aurora's hands balled into a fist. "Besides, I could care less about putting flowers on tables and watching everyone stride around with their noses in the air."

Evelyn's jaw dropped. "I didn't know you felt that way about us. I just thought that getting back into the community would help. I know you've been down lately." Evelyn scrambled to the back door and called for her children. As she dashed home, Evelyn wondered what she had said to upset her friend so much.

Aurora watched them from the window then hurried back to her room and knelt to finish her prayers. It wasn't until Manuelito came home from school that Aurora emerged.

They sat on the back porch. Aurora listened to him read. His words slipped past her and swirled around Flavito. He waved as he galloped around the yard on his stick horse. Aurora raised her hand and forced a thin smile.

Nea brought her the wailing baby. Aurora unbuttoned her blouse and fed Josefita without looking down at her. "Aren't those clouds beautiful?" she said to no one in particular. Aurora handed the baby back to Nea and followed her into the house. Nea held out Josefita, but Aurora moved past her and drifted back upstairs.

Nea waited at the front door for William's return. He looked from her folded hands, to the staircase. "What's wrong now?" he groaned.

"*Señor*, I didn't know if I should say anything, but I'm getting worried about Aurora. She spends most of the day upstairs." Nea pursed her lips and took a sideways glance toward the stairs. "This morning she kind of chased *Señora* Taylor away."

"Sometimes when the baby cries, I take care of her. We try to get her to come downstairs. Sophie tries to keep the boys quiet. One day Aurora threw a pillow at Sophie and told her to stay out. I told Sophie not to run upstairs every time Josefita whimpers. I don't think it's helping Aurora for us to take care of the baby. We need to let Aurora do it." Nea hung her head. "I think she's slipping back."

William stood, holding onto the railing, one hand on his forehead. When he realized that Nea was still standing beside him, he patted her on the shoulder. "I'm glad you told me."

William dropped into the chair behind his desk. Numbness enfolded him. He looked at the ceiling and slowly closed his eyes. Then he slammed one fist into the other as he thought about what to do. *Would Dr. Wilson know, or maybe I should talk to* La Señora? *She got better when she was with her family. Maybe I should just leave her there.*

William had Nea write a letter to Josefa. She wrote about Aurora's mornings at the altar and long afternoons in bed. Nea even told her that the boys seemed frightened of their mother. They never knew if she was going to hug them, or chase them out of the room.

"You have to come and see her," she wrote. "Aurora told me that she was trying hard. For a while she was doing better. Now I don't know."

✳ ✳ ✳

"What are you doing creeping around, watching me?" Aurora screamed at Nea. Nea put her hands in front of her. She tiptoed to the bed and gently put her hand over Aurora's.

"I'm worried about you, so is *Señor.*"

Aurora jerked her hand away. "Has he said something? What did you tell him?"

Nea stood and drew herself up. "We can all see that you're going away from us again. You got better at La Parida. We all want to help you come back to us."

Aurora walked to the window. She touched the altar as she passed. "I'll try harder," she spat.

Nea took a step toward her, then changed her mind. "We'll help you," she whispered as she left the room.

That evening Aurora made sure she was dressed and her hair combed before William got home. She put a new gown on the baby and wrapped her in her finest blankets. Before she came downstairs, she knelt at her little altar and prayed for her mind to be in this place and not with Flavio and Isabelita.

When she came downstairs, William was in the kitchen with Sophie. He gave Aurora a kiss on the cheek. "We were just talking about how warm the weather is getting. Sophie thought you'd like a ride out to Gloria's tomorrow."

✳✳✳

The next morning Sophie filled a basket with pasties and her Irish cake. She added a jug of lemonade that she had worked on for an hour. Nea crept up the stairs. Aurora was kneeling in front of the altar. When she saw Nea, she made the sign of the cross and rose.

"What is it?" Aurora asked flatly.

"Well, the sun is shining and it's not too hot yet. Sophie made the cake Gloria likes so much. Remember, we talked about driving out to see Gloria." She smiled hopefully.

Aurora stood in front of the mirror brushing her hair. She shrugged. "Alright."

As they drove past the springs that supplied Socorro's water, Aurora broke her silence. "I didn't understand what William was talking about, did you?" She turned to Nea. "I don't know the Bacas very well. Most of them are good people, but I've heard the ones that live near San Antonio aren't so nice. I don't quite understand why everyone is in such a state. Maybe Gloria can tell me."

When they got to Gloria's, everyone settled in the *plazita* where the children could play under the cottonwood tree. The late spring breeze was a welcome relief from Gloria's kitchen. They chatted about how much the children had grown. Gloria was glad she had time to think. What would she tell Aurora about the Baca brothers?

"It all happened in a church. The Spanish Methodist Episcopal Church." Gloria pointed as she said each name. "Abran Baca and his brothers started picking on one of the women right in the middle of the service. They should be ashamed of themselves." Gloria made the sign of the cross on her chest. " They wouldn't stop." Gloria glanced at Nea and took a deep breath.

"Finally, an *Americano*, Conklin, tried to make them stop." She shot a pleading look at Nea. "One of the brothers shot Conklin. They were arrested, but they escaped."

"A man was shot?" Aurora's eyes widened.

"I'm afraid so." Gloria didn't go on to say that Conklin had died.

288

She only rushed through the escape. Gloria patted Aurora on the hand. "This is the men's business. They're taking care of it." Gloria thought about telling Aurora that her husband had been deputized along with most of the men in town, but Nea's shaking head prompted her to change the subject.

With a nod, Gloria pulled out a little gown that she had made. She put it in Aurora's lap and asked her to inspect the stitches. "I don't think it's as good as yours, but I think the stitches will hold."

Aurora tugged at the seams and smiled. Gloria didn't know how much Aurora had understood. Since the subject had been changed, Gloria decided she had said enough for now.

69

A week passed before Gloria went to town again. At the mercantile, she traded eggs for coffee and red cornmeal to make *atole*. She stopped at the church and dropped off the altar cloth she had mended, then drove to Aurora's.

Sophie heard the wagon rattling into the yard and ran upstairs. She tapped on the door that was now kept closed.

"Ma'am, I think Gloria is here. Do you want me to have her come in?" Sophie put her ear to the door and listened for sounds of movement.

"I'm just finishing with my prayers. Josefita is sleeping so don't bring her down. Make the children stay outside. I'll be down in a minute." *What does she want now?* Aurora thought. *Why can't everyone just leave me alone?* She twisted her braid into a knot at the nape of her neck.

Aurora didn't tell Sophie to bring them peppermint water. She sat on the edge of her chair and nodded absentmindedly as Gloria begin to chatter.

Gloria hadn't intended to bring up the Bacas again, but everyone in the store was talking about their escape. "You know how big the family is. No matter what, they'll all stick together, especially when they think they're going against the *gringo's* laws." Gloria's mouth snapped shut. She shot a quick glance at Aurora. "Oh, I'm sorry."

Aurora sat back. Her shoulders drooped. She shook her head and patted Gloria's hand.

"It's alright. I'm used to listening to my *Tio* José." The women leaned toward each other and giggled. Sophie and Nea were listening at the kitchen door. They smiled at each other and both gave a sigh of relief.

With the subject of the Baca brothers having been untangled and put in its place, Gloria began telling Aurora about the railroad spur that was being built to Magdalena. Everyone in Magdalena was looking forward to it because their cattle and sheep could be shipped on the railroad.

"My brother and father both got a job working to build the spur. My father asked me if the tracks were going through Snake Ranch. Are they?"

"I don't think so. William hasn't said anything about it." Aurora changed her mind about rushing her visit with Gloria. She stepped toward the kitchen and asked Sophie to bring them peppermint water. "Oh, and do you have any of those ginger cookies left?"

Aurora gave Gloria a glass of water, then passed the cookies.

"Well, my father said that the tracks would just about have to go through the ranch," Gloria continued. "It's the best and the flattest way to get from Socorro to Magdalena."

Aurora shrugged. "I'll ask William tonight, if he comes home at a decent hour."

Gloria noticed Aurora's confused look and that she had begun to twist her hands.

Gloria sat back and crossed her legs. She talked about her sister who recently had another baby. Now that her brother was working on the railroad spur, he and his family could move out of their father's house.

Aurora had stopped listening.

❋ ❋ ❋

When William got home, he went to his study with Sophie following close behind. She stopped just shy of the threshold. William dropped his satchel on the desk and studied Sophie. She mouthed, "It was a good day."

The boys scooted past Sophie. They stood like little soldiers in front of the big mahogany desk. William patted the boys on the head. "Let's go see what we can find in the kitchen."

They ran down the hall. When they reached the kitchen, Sophie handed each boy a muffin. Josefita lay kicking in a basket that sat on the kitchen table.

William took Josefita and bounced her on his knee. Her giggles made him erupt with laughter. "She gets more beautiful every day."

"Where's your mother?" William asked.

Manuelito murmured. "She's upstairs."

With Josefita in his arms, William started up the stairs.

"I thought I heard you come in." Aurora turned and smiled I was just putting some things away."

William leaned over and kissed Aurora on the cheek. Aurora glanced toward the hall, but William put his arm around her. "Come sit a while. The girls can put supper on. Tell me about your visit with Gloria."

Aurora perched on the edge of her chair. "Gloria told me that there is a railroad spur going to Magdalena. She wondered if the tracks were going through Snake Ranch. I told her you hadn't said anything about it, so I guess not." Aurora had drawn herself up, her arms across her chest.

William walked across the room, and pulled the curtains back. He ambled back, trying to figure out what to say.

"Well, sweetheart, the track is going through a small part of the ranch."

Aurora straightened and stuck out her chin. William put his hand out as if to stop what she was about to say. "Manuel said this small piece of land wasn't good for grazing. The price the railroad paid was more than fair." William started to tell Aurora about the trust that he had set up for the boys, but she stood and stomped her foot.

"You and Manuel decided!"

Josefita started whimpering and Aurora shouted for Sophie to take care of her.

"You decided what to do with the land that belongs to my sons, and you didn't say anything to me!" Aurora began pacing.

"I, um, you were. . ., and the railroad needed an answer right away." William stammered. "You haven't been yourself since the baby was born and I didn't want to bother you with this. You see, I did talk to Manuel about it. I wouldn't have sold the land if he didn't want me to. I sold it for the boys."

Aurora whirled around. "And what did you do with the money, my sons' money?" She poked herself in the chest.

William put his hands out. "Calm down; I put the money in a trust for them. You know I wouldn't take anything from them."

Aurora ran out of the room and down the stairs. When she got to the parlor, she screamed. "And whose name is on the trust?"

70

With Nea holding the baby, Aurora steered the buggy toward Lemitar. As she sped along the rutted road, the boys huddled in the back seat. When they reached the store, Aurora hopped down and burst through the back door. Nea took the boys around the front. Manuel opened his arms, but Aurora just stood in the doorway with her hands on her hips.

"Come in *Mijita*. What's wrong?"

"Why did you let William sell part of Snake Ranch?"

Manuel pulled out a chair and motioned for Aurora to sit. "So, you talked to William about the sale. Did he tell you that it's a very small strip of land, not good for anything but growing cactus? I thought it would be better for the boys to have the money than that tiny piece of land."

"But I'm their mother. It should have been my decision. The boy's land is my land!"

Manuel leaned back. He shook his head and shrugged, trying to find an answer for his niece. This was more like the Aurora he used to know. *Was this a good sign? Had she come back, or was she going somewhere else?*

"Did William explain that he put the money in a trust for the boys. This will help them in the future."

Aurora nodded. "He told me about the trust. Whose name is on it?"

Manuel held his hand in front of him. "He put it in his name. He's the guardian for now. He didn't think you were able to handle this right now."

Aurora stood and walked to the door. "I know I haven't been the same since the babies were born, but I'm getting better. He could have told me about this, but he didn't. He went behind my back." She whirled and pointed at her uncle. "And you helped him!"

Manuel shook his head. "The railroad agent said the sale had to be done right away so they could get started. I told you that the little strip of land that William sold was nothing compared to the rest of the ranch. I did what I thought was best for my grandsons."

Aurora sagged against the door frame. *We own the land, the Pinos and the Vigils. Flavio's land belongs to my sons. My land will someday belong to them.* Aurora fumed. *Even the house in Socorro is in my name.* She sat on the back step and put her head in her hands.

Manuel thought about sending for Telesfora, but the thought of José coming with her changed his mind. *Maybe Aurora just needs some time to think about this.* He left her sitting there and went into the store to visit with his grandchildren. He was surprised and pleased to see how chubby Josefita had become. After a while, the back door creaked open and Aurora slipped through. "Can I talk to you, *Tio?*"

Manuel handed each of the boys a licorice stick and followed Aurora to the back room.

"I've been thinking. What can we do to make sure that what belongs to the boys stays in the family?"

"Why don't you talk to William? He knows about property and the laws."

Aurora's lips tightened. She leaned closer to her uncle and whispered. "The family needs to figure this out."

Manuel took Aurora's hand. He sat next to her on the cot and assured her again that the land that was sold was worthless to the ranch.

"My sons own what would have gone to Flavio." Aurora said. "I guess someday they'll have part of everything you own. They have to be protected."

Manuel reminded her that the money from the sale was in a trust for them.

"Yes, but it's in William's name. Shouldn't it be in my father's name or yours?"

Manuel rubbed his chin. He started to tell Aurora that, by law, she and her children's property were under the control of her husband but he just grunted and kept silent. He knew that was exactly what Aurora was trying to prevent. He put his arm around his niece's shoulders.

"You know I think highly of William and I suppose you do too, since you married him. Do you think he's an honorable man?"

Aurora frowned. She told her uncle about what was happening in Socorro. "The *Hispanos* are tired of the *gringos* making new laws and telling them what to do. William is busy all the time, trying to keep the peace. We barely see him anymore."

"What does this have to do with the protection of the boys and their land?"

"Well," said Aurora, "It looks like the *Americanos* are trying to swallow everything up that belongs to us."

Manuel rolled his eyes. He was struck with the thought that Aurora sounded just like José. Surely, she had more sense than he did.

"I think you're worrying about nothing. William had to make a decision and he made the right one for the boys."

"Everything is all mixed up, *Tio*. I just want to protect my sons. If William is the man that you think he is, he'll agree to let someone in our family be in charge of my son's property." Her arms were folded across her rigid body.

Manuel patted her on the back. "I'll talk to Esquipula. For now, let me assure you that the money from the sale is safe. Why don't you take the boys to see Isabel? She would love to see them." Manuel opened the door to the store and invited her to pick out something for the house. Aurora clicked her tongue. She rose slowly. *This isn't over,* she thought.

On the way to La Parida, Aurora wondered when she had started thinking of William as the enemy. She turned her buggy away from Isabel's and headed toward Rita's. *She'll let me sit and think.*

She walked along the little ditch that ran behind Rita's house, trying to clear her thoughts. When the air cooled, the smell of red *chili* reached her nose. Aurora sauntered back into the house.

Aurora was talking as she passed through the door. "Manuel is right. William is an honorable man. He loves me. He wouldn't do anything against me or my children. I just want to make sure that nothing is taken from my sons."

Aurora moved to the window. She let her thoughts spill out. "Oh, but he's hardly ever home and he only has eyes for Josefita."

Rita looked up from the stove. "Papá and *Tio* Manuel won't let anything happen." She set the spoon across the frying pan. Then Rita smiled and shoved her sister. "Aurora's back," she laughed.

Aurora shook her head and rolled her eyes. "I hope so. You wouldn't want to go where I've been."

"Then come and eat with us. I'll feed your beautiful daughter, but I'm sure she would rather have you."

Aurora looked at the mesa turning from rust to gold. "I better get back to the house. Mamá will be wondering where I am." She took a few steps, then turned back to Rita with a smirk. "Now that everybody thinks I'm crazy, they're all worried." Rita stretched her lips with her fingers and crossed her eyes. Aurora shook her head and rolled her eyes.

❋ ❋ ❋

Aurora had dropped Nea and the boys at Josefa's. Nea sent the boys outside to play, then sat with her head propped in her hand. "I don't know what to do," said Nea. "Did you know that William had sold some land to the railroad? Aurora is really mad about it."

"What? William can't sell Aurora's land!" Josefa set the pan on the side of the stove where it was cooler.

Nea put her hands together as if to say, forgive me. "I wasn't trying to listen, but Aurora was yelling. William sold a piece of land from Snake Ranch, land that belongs to the boys. He said that he talked to Manuel and *Tio* said it was alright."

Nea reached across the table and clung to Josefa's hands. "I don't know what's going on with the land, but when Aurora was yelling, the boys hid underneath the table. Aurora wouldn't listen to anything William had to say. She had Juan hitch up the buggy and here we are. It was like she woke up out of her trance and turned into the old Aurora, only madder. I was thinking that the boys should stay with Telesfora until Aurora settles down." Nea looked up at Josefa. "They looked so scared, and that wasn't the first time."

Josefa grabbed a cloth and wiped some crumbs from the table. "You know how she is about Telesfora. We need to tell La Señora what's going on. If Aurora wasn't suffering with the loss of her baby, I would say that she is just fighting to get her own way." Josefa filled two glasses with water and brought them to the table. "Maybe she's coming back."

Nea leaned back and shrugged. *Josefa doesn't need to be burdened with what I've seen in that big house.*

❋ ❋ ❋

José saw Aurora's buggy in front of Esquipula's. He prodded Telesfora to go see what was going on. "This morning at the store I couldn't hear what Manuel and Aurora were saying. They were sitting in the back room, but Aurora didn't look as mad when she left. This has got to be about the land sale." He handed Telesfora her shawl and grabbed her elbow, but she put her hand against the door frame.

"I don't want to go over there and stir up trouble." Her voice began to tremble. "Aurora doesn't want me around her boys."

José closed his eyes and dropped his hand from Telesfora's arm.

296

"I know this breaks your heart, especially because the boys want to be with you, too." José led Telesfora to the table.

"I heard Aurora yelling at Manuel. I don't think the boys should be around her until she's better." José reached across the table and wrapped his hand around Telesfora's. His voice became softer. "You know, my Telesfora, where the boys belong, and so do I."

Telesfora looked around the room. Suddenly the heat of the kitchen became suffocating. She squeezed her eyes tight to hold back the tears. "I don't know why God hasn't given us children."

José sat beside her and rocked her back and forth. "God willing, he will give us two little boys."

Telesfora slapped her hand on the table. "Aurora should have stayed with us and married one of the men from around here. Now look at her. She doesn't know where she belongs, or where her children belong. She's like a tumbleweed blowing across the desert."

✳ ✳ ✳

Aurora slipped into the office chair so quietly that William didn't notice. When he saw her, he started. He peered at her as if inspecting a trapped animal. She raised her head slowly, then dropped her eyes.

"I'm sorry. I shouldn't have gotten so mad at you." She smiled and shrugged. "I'm getting better, really I am, but sometimes I feel like I don't know what's going on. When I found out you had sold the land that belonged to my sons, I thought you were trying to get away with something. I thought you were taking advantage of me because I was having trouble."

William knelt at her side and wrapped his hands over hers. "I've been so worried about you, but I can tell you're getting better. Losing our baby was hard for both of us. Then little Josefita was so tiny. He looked up at her, trying to read how his words affected her. He was relieved to see her nodding in agreement.

"But look how well our baby is doing. We're going to be alright. And the boys—you know I wouldn't do anything to hurt them. I just didn't want to bother you with this land deal. I promise, from now on, I'll tell you everything, especially when it comes to the boys."

The lump in Aurora's throat kept her voice tight. She didn't trust what she was about to say. *What if William took it the wrong way?* She took a deep breath and spoke quickly.

"At home, with my family I realized we are so much a part of this land. Yes, I know things are changing. I know what you're doing for

Socorro, but our land is part of the family. Keeping it means there will always be a family, there will always be a place where Manuelito and Flavito belong. I know there will be changes, but some things mustn't change."

William pulled his wife up and embraced her. "I'll talk to Manuel and Esquipula. You don't have anything to worry about." That was all he managed to say.

✳✳✳

After the last freight wagon was unloaded, José and Manuel sat underneath the cottonwood.

"I hope Aurora is alright." José brushed the toe of his boot across the dust. "She seemed really troubled when she was here last week." José eyed Manuel.

Manuel took the pipe out of his mouth. *I might as well tell him what's going on. He always finds out anyway.* He told José about the land sale and how he approved of it, then how upset Aurora had been.

"I think it was a blessing in disguise. She seemed to have gotten over the sadness of losing the baby." Manuel smiled a bit and leaned back against the tree. "God willing, she's come back to us."

José was silent for a while. He knew he had to pick his words carefully. "You know she's right though; the boys will inherit a lot of land and it should be in the hands of the family. . ." He stopped short of saying, ". . . not the *gringos.*"

Manuel blew out a stream of smoke. "On Sunday I'll talk to Esquipula, I don't know what we can do, and William will have to agree to anything we decide."

José drew circles in the dusty soil with a branch. *I'm their godfather and Telesfora is their godmother; who better to manage their property?* "You know we love the boys like our own." He made the sign of the cross on his forehead. "We don't know why God hasn't given us children, but to Telesfora those boys are just like her own."

Manuel's memory snapped back to the day Flavio was born. Isabel had been so sick. La Señora said she had lost a lot of blood and needed to stay in bed. Telesfora was fifteen years old, and she just took over. She took care of the younger children and cared for baby Flavio like he was her own. When Isabel came out of her confinement, Telesfora kept taking care of Flavio. Isabel was so grateful. She had six other children to care for.

A distant smile crept across Manuel's lips. "Yes, from the time Flavio was born, Telesfora took care of him. I'm not surprised she feels the same way about his children."

✳✳✳

José sat at the table sipping coffee while Telesfora fixed his supper. He sighed deeply. "The house is so empty without the boys. Manuel was telling me how you helped raise Flavio. What would be better than for us to raise his sons?"

Telesfora spun around, her stirring spoon waving in the air. "Why do you say things like that, to torture me?"

José jumped up and patted the air with his hands. "No, no, *mi amore* Aurora has been unable to care for them since the baby was born, and now she's thinking about having someone in the family take over their rights and property. We're their godparents. Nobody in the world is closer to them than us."

A deep line marked Telesfora's brow. "Are you saying that we should raise Manuelito and Flavito? We can't. They have a mother and now a new father. I think Aurora's getting better. I'll take care of the boys as much as she needs me to, but they're her children." Telesfora slammed the frying pan onto the stove. Chopped potatoes flew into the air.

"And what makes you think Aurora would give her children to me?"

José's eyes lit up. "You see how she is with them. Didn't Nea tell you that the boys were scared when Aurora and William had that big fight about the land? Haven't the boys told you that they have to be quiet in the house? They play outside most of the time.

"Remember? Nea was telling you about the hours that Aurora spends on her knees in front of the altar, and how she yells at the boys when they need her for something."

Telesfora flipped the potatoes. Lard spattered across the surface of the wood stove. "She's grieving, again, this time for the loss of her baby girl. Men don't understand what that feels like, and she is getting better."

José lit his pipe. "Is she?"

71

After Mass, Manuel and Esquipula sat on the shaded side of the house. Manuel asked Esquipula what he thought about putting the boys' land into the hands of someone in the family. Esquipula shrugged and said he didn't know anything about how the law works. He took a puff from his pipe and crossed his legs. "I don't suppose it would hurt to make sure the boys' property and rights are protected." He tapped his pipe on the edge of the bench. *What do we really know about this De Baun?*

Manuel waved his hands as he told Esquipula about the changes in Socorro. Now that it was an official town, there were new laws and rules. All the new ideas from back East had come to New Mexico. Manuel leaned forward. "You know, the husband has control of everything."

Esquipula sat looking at his fields for a while, then said, "But the boys are not William's children. Does he still have the right to control their property?"

"He must. He sold that Snake Ranch property to the railroad. He asked me what I thought, but I didn't have to sign for the sale." The brothers looked at each other.

Esquipula shook his head. *Surely there would be more children for Aurora. What if she lost another one or what if she stayed the same?* He took his hat off and wiped his brow. "With Aurora the way she is, something has to be done."

❈ ❈ ❈

José studied Manuel as he drove away from the grist mill. *Something is going on. Manuel never takes grain to Socorro. That's my job.*

After his grain was unloaded, Manuel drove his wagon to Rufina's.

"Papa, what a surprise. Is everything alright?"

Manuel shuffled from one foot to the other. "I uh, have some business to do in town. I didn't want to make the long trip back in one day. Besides, I haven't seen you since I was in my sickbed. I'm better, but I get so tired."

Rufina put a gentle hand on her father's face. "We thought we were going to lose you. I'm so glad you're feeling better. *Graciasa Dios* that you're strong enough to come visit me."

Manuel took his daughter's hand and kissed her fingers. "I'll spend the night. I want to talk to Josefa's cousin, you know, Judge Pino." Manuel waved her away when he saw the worried look on Rufina's face.

"It's just about some property. I'll talk to him after supper." Manuel refused Rufina's offer of coffee. "I think I'll just rest a while."

Rufina smiled as she led her father to the back room, knowing that he would be asleep before she reached the kitchen. She gently draped a quilt over him and slipped back to her cooking.

After the evening meal, Manuel walked across the plaza to Salomón's. Manuel took the small glass of bourbon Judge Pino offered. Sitting on the *porche*, Salomón waited for Manuel to tell him why he was visiting. Manuel leaned toward the judge and asked him if he had heard about Aurora's troubles.

"*Seguro*," answered Salomón. "Of course, I see William at the courthouse every day. He's running himself ragged trying to keep up with everything. One day he tells me that Aurora's getting better. The next time I see him, he hangs his head and says she's not doing so good."

Manuel shook his head. "Josefa tells me that Aurora is trying hard to get better, but something is troubling her. We want to help her if we can." Manuel explained about the land sale and how Aurora wanted to protect the boys' property rights. He took a sip of bourbon.

"I wouldn't even consider talking about this, but with Aurora the way she is. . ." Manuel wiped a drop of bourbon from his mustache and looked at the ground. He whispered, "You never know what's going to happen in this *pinche* of a life."

Salomón patted him on the arm. He stood and stretched. "So, you're asking me how to go about shifting the control of the boys' property to someone in the Vigil family."

Salomón rubbed his chin and took another sip. "Well, Aurora's husband can make decisions about their land since the boys are minors."

Manuel's foot started twitching. He hoped Josefa's long-winded cousin wouldn't go into every detail of the law.

"Aurora is worried that William will take advantage of the boys," Manuel explained. "I don't think he's that kind of a man, but since the loss of her baby, Aurora hasn't been herself. Maybe with some kind of legal document in place she would have peace of mind."

"I talked to Esquipula about this and I started thinking. With the way everything is changing, maybe it would be a good idea to protect their rights. Who knows what the new laws will bring?"

Judge Pino tapped his forehead. "Well, let me see, the legal father of the children would have the right to make decisions about their property. Right now, William is their legal father because he's married to Aurora." Salomón shrugged and opened his hands in surrender.

Manuel sagged back into his chair. Both men were silent as the seriousness of the matter sunk in. Manuel stood and leaned against the porch post. "I'll have to talk to Esquipula again."

❄❄❄

As the sun rose from behind the lavender hills, Manuel sat with Esquipula. "I couldn't sleep last night," Manuel groaned. "This business about Aurora's children, I thought there would just be some paperwork. I thought it would be easy for you or me to be able to make the decisions, you know, about the boys' property."

Esquipula poured his brother a cup of black coffee. He and Josefa sat, waiting for Manuel to tell them more. Manuel took a quick sip. "You know, I talked to Salomón. He said that whoever had the legal custody of the children would be their guardians."

Josefa reached for Esquipula's hand. "What does this mean?"

"If these papers are signed, they would give the legal guardians all rights as their parents. This would also ensure that the boys would live with someone from the family if anything were to happen to Aurora."

Josefa and Esquipula stared at each other with furrowed brows.

"So, the family would be in control, not the *gringo*?" questioned Esquipula.

Josefa gave her husband a hard nudge with her elbow. "But what about now? I think Aurora is getting better." She gave Esquipula a hopeful smile.

"They can stay with her as long as she is able to care for them," nodded Manuel. "If she doesn't come back to us, everything will be arranged and legal."

Esquipula straightened. "But, if she can't care for them, of course we would take them."

Manuel shrugged. "Salomón said the family would have a better chance of getting this done if they were placed where it was best for the boys."

Esquipula and Josefa both raised their hands. "What better place than with their *abuelos*?" smiled Josefa.

"This is what kept me up all night. I was thinking about how Telesfora took care of Flavio when he was born. She was always more like a mother to him then a sister. It doesn't look like God will bless her with children. She loves Flavio's sons as much as she loved him." Manuel took a handkerchief from his pocket and wiped his eyes.

Josefa and Esquipula looked at each other. She put a trembling hand to her chest. A long moment of silence stretched between them.

Josefa sniffled. "The boys are so happy with her. She's been looking after Flavito almost from the time he was born."

Esquipula put down his cup. "They even call her Mamá Telesfora."

The three sat in a circle of thoughts and worries. Josefa twisted the corner of her apron. Esquipula offered his brother another cup of coffee, but Manuel waved him away. Josefa looked from one brother to the other.

"What about José?" she murmured.

Manuel raised his hands. "As crazy as he is, we all know he loves the boys. I've always been able to keep him from making a complete fool of himself. If we write up the papers so that Esquipula and I have to agree to anything concerning Flavio's sons, he won't be able to make any decisions without us."

Josefa straightened out her apron, then frowned. She drew out one word at a time. "So, if someone from the family becomes their guardian, they can make decisions for the boys even if Aurora is still. . ." She paused and made the sign of the cross over her heart. ". . . is still with us?"

Manuel nodded. "That's what I understand from Salomón. If Aurora is unable to make decisions, the family can."

Esquipula leaned forward. "Not the *gringo*?" He grunted and rubbed his chin. "What about Aurora? Does she know about all of this?"

Manuel shook his head. "I'll talk to William. If he agrees, it should be him who talks to Aurora. He'll have to be careful how he says things, but it was her idea to put the boys' property into the hands of the family."

Josefa quit chewing her fingernail. "But this, giving the boys away, none of us expected this."

"Salomón said this will only be on paper. The boys will stay with

Aurora unless she can't care for them, but their property and rights will be transferred to us." He glanced at Josefa over the rim of his cup. "This business of wanting to protect the boys and getting mad at William for selling the land, tells me that she is coming back to us."

Josefa nodded. "She seemed better when she came back from Rita's." She tapped the table with her knuckles as she thought about the things Nea had told her. *Perhaps it would be a good idea to have everything arranged for the boys if Aurora is not quite herself again.*

72

Aurora was waiting for William at the front door. "Did you talk to Papá about putting the boys' property into the hands of the family?"

William hung his hat and coat on the hall tree. "I talked to Manuel and your father at the courthouse this morning."

He led Aurora into his study and put his satchel on his desk. He waved toward a chair, but Aurora leaned against the door, her arms crossed. William took a deep breath and walked toward Aurora. He put his arm around her. She stiffened.

"Sweetheart, you know I love you and I'll always do what's best for you and the boys. Please come and sit down." He cleared his throat and went into the kitchen for a glass of water. He crooked his finger, inviting Nea to come closer. Then he whispered to her, "Be prepared. I don't know how Aurora is going to react to what I have to tell her." Then he walked slowly back to his study.

"Manuel talked to Judge Pino. The boys' rights and property can be transferred to someone in your family, if this is what you really want."

Aurora's face softened. Her shoulders lowered a bit. William drummed his fingers on the desk and made his voice as soft as he could. "But, Aurora, the thing of it is, if we do this you will be giving up your parental rights to the boys."

William cocked his head and stared at Aurora. Her mouth opened and closed, as she struggled to form the right questions.

"What do you mean, I will no longer be their mother?"

"Only on paper. It's the only way this can be done. But, as far as everyone is concerned, you will always be their mother." He put his arms around Aurora. "And I will always be their new father. We all agreed that when you start feeling better, if you want to reverse this decision, it will be reversed, legally reversed."

The color faded from Aurora's face. She walked to the desk and bent her head. She thought about the day she had sent Sophie and Nea to town and she couldn't find the boys. She had run halfway down McCutcheon Street. Flavito was sitting on the curb crying. Manuelito had climbed onto a stone wall. He was looking up and down the street, hoping to find where home was. Aurora didn't realize she had left Josefita alone in the house until she got back with the boys in tow.

Aurora had spanked the boys so hard that their cries woke their sister. She had pulled them upstairs, put them in their room and slammed the door. When she flew downstairs with Josefita she stumbled and almost fell. She had sat on the bottom step crying out for Sophie to help her. With the boys wailing and Josefita crying, Aurora frantically looked in every room for Nea and Sophie.

When Sophie and Nea returned, they found Aurora sitting on the bottom step, her hair hanging over her shoulders. Her blouse gaped open as Josefita fed. As soon as Nea stepped inside, Aurora rushed to her and grabbed her arm. "Don't ever leave me alone again!" Aurora didn't tell the women exactly what had happened, but she made them swear not to tell William.

Aurora's mind drifted back to what William was saying. She caught the name Telesfora, then started stitching his message together. Yes, it would be Telesfora taking care of her sons if she couldn't. Who else could she trust with them? Isabel had a pack of children underfoot, and her mother was caring for Andres' children while he and his wife help Manuel at the store. Aurora lifted her head. "Perhaps this would be the best thing for right now."

The next Sunday, Judge Pino brought the papers to Aurora's house. William and Aurora sat with the judge at the dining room table. The judge looked at Aurora after reading each paragraph to make sure she understood what he said. When Judge Pino explained that the boys would be in the custody of Telesfora and José, Aurora shook her head violently.

"José?" She hadn't thought about José having custody.

William saw a familiar panic in her eyes. He stood and wrapped his arms around her. "We don't have to do this," he whispered.

Aurora struggled to stand. "You told me this would only be on paper, but if I give my children to the care of Telesfora and José. . . " Aurora twisted away from him. Her eyes grew wide and wild. "You know him. I will never see them again!"

Both the judge and William shook their heads and waved their hands. It was the judge's deep resolute voice that finally put her panic to rest.

"Listen, *Mija*." He read the sentence stating that, although parental rights were being transferred, the boys could remain living with Aurora." Any decision made on their behalf would have to be approved by Esquipula, Manuel, and you of course." Judge Pino took off his spectacles and laid them on the table. "José would only have the authority to help care for them."

William folded his hands around hers. "No one in your family, including me, would ever take the boys away from you. Telesfora only wants to help, and neither Manuel, Esquipula or I will let José make any decisions without our approval. It's written in the decree."

Aurora took in a slow breath. Her stomach tumbled one more time. She walked up the hall, through the kitchen, and back across the dining room. *Telesfora has always been there to help.* Her mind drifted back to the foggy time when Telesfora cared for her newborn after her husband had died. She stood in front of the window and dragged her hands across her face. William's words seeped through her memories.

"It's only on paper, to protect the rights of your sons, like you wanted." William took a few cautious steps toward the dining room. "I'll tear this paper up if this isn't what you want."

Aurora stood frozen in the sunlight. "Can you tear it up anytime I want?"

William moved closer and hung onto the back of the chair. "Any time, I swear to you."

With a shaky hand Aurora signed the papers.

She started back up the stairs, but William chased after her. "I think we need some air. Let's go for a ride." Aurora sagged against the railing. After a long silence she lifted her head. "I'll get Josefita ready," she mumbled.

William shook Judge Pino's hand. "I hope we're doing the right thing. I would have never approved of this if Aurora was herself. But the more I thought about it, the more I believed that some safeguard should be put in place, especially if it makes Aurora feel more secure."

Judge Pino slapped William on the back and nodded. "I'll see you in court tomorrow."

✳ ✳ ✳

William loaded up the family and drove to the new brick factory. It was on the way to Magdalena, and Aurora asked William if he remembered her cousins who lived there. "Maybe next Sunday we can go see them."

"Sure." William agreed. "Maybe we can stop at Water Canyon for a picnic."

307

Aurora put her hands together. "I don't think the boys have ever been there." She turned around and smiled at her sons.

Both boys were standing to get a better look at the huge building. William told them that this was where the bricks for their house were made. He drove the buggy to a pile of discarded bricks and let the boys pick out a few to make a little building of their own.

When William looked back at Aurora, she was wearing a smile that he hadn't seen in months. He took little Josefita from her and stood so they were shoulder to shoulder. "I built you a house out of these bricks, a house to keep you safe."

William wrapped his arms around Aurora's waist. "We can tear the papers up anytime you want to. As soon as you feel better, we'll do just that."

73

With school out for the summer, Manuelito was home all day. The constant banging of the back door and the boys running through the house set Aurora's nerves on fire. Sophie put their toy box on the back porch so they wouldn't tromp upstairs and wake Josefita. When Aurora stepped down the stairs, the boys froze.

"How many times do I have to tell you that the baby might be sleeping? Come in quietly," she hissed.

In the weeks that followed, Aurora still prayed at her altar. She prayed for patience. She prayed that her mind wouldn't float away again. She forced herself to get up from her altar and go downstairs with the baby. She ate breakfast and the noon meal with the boys. Aurora pretended to listen to them, but she was always relieved when they went back outside. Now that summer was upon them, the boys only played outside in the early morning and the cool of the evenings.

When they came inside, they talked about what they'd done at Mamá Telesfora's. When Flavito pulled Aurora to the door to see the brick house he had made, Aurora realized that she hadn't talked to Telesfora about giving the boys' rights to her. *Perhaps*, thought Aurora, *they would enjoy a visit with their auntie.*

"Yes, yes, it's very nice." Aurora patted Flavito on the head.

Aurora stepped back into the kitchen. She stood on a chair and reached for a big square basket on the top shelf.

"Let me help you," offered Sophie.

"Pack it with food for a picnic. We're going to La Parida first thing in the morning. We can stop at the river to eat our morning meal."

Sophie stood with her mouth open. "Is Mr. De Baun going too?"

"No, it's just us," Aurora answered. "I have something to talk to *Tia* about."

Sophie started chewing on her fingernail. *I'll tell mister about this as soon as he gets home.* She tapped her chin and puffed out a breath. *What's going on now?*

✳✳✳

William stood stock-still when he saw Aurora brushing her hair at the mirror. "You're up early. What's the occasion?"

She turned and smiled. "I thought I would take the boys to see Telesfora. I haven't talked to her about the papers I signed." She twisted her hair into a braid, turned and looked intently at William. "I want to make it clear to Telesfora that the boys are still very much mine."

William started to assure her that Telesfora had the best interest of the boys at heart, but Aurora brushed past him. She scooped the sleeping Josefita up and crept across the hall.

Manuelito rubbed his eyes and stretched. He nudged his grumbling little brother. "Come on were going to see Mamá Telesfora." They scrambled into their clothes and ran downstairs.

Sophie had prepared a carpetbag with clothes just in case they wanted to stay a few days. They all climbed into the buggy and headed to La Parida.

On the way, Sophie sang an Irish song and Nea followed with a childhood song she had learned from her mother.

When Sophie sang, the boys listened and watched her intently. When Nea sang, they giggled and repeated words spoken in the tongue they had grown up with. Aurora sang about a mother hen and her little chicks. The boys began to clap and sing along with her.

"That's the song that Mamá Telesfora sings to us when we go to her house," Manuelito laughed.

Even little Josefita was bouncing up and down with the rhythm of the songs. Aurora turned to Sophie. "I'm going to start speaking some Spanish to Josefita. She needs to learn the language of our family."

Sophie touched Nea's arm. *Perhaps the worst is over.*

As Sophie helped the boys out of the buggy, they grumbled. "I thought we were going to see Mamá Telesfora."

"First you have to visit your *Abuela* Josefa, and look, all your cousins want to play with you."

"Come on, we're building a fort behind the corrals," Francisco announced.

Flavito tumbled over Manuelito and their *Tia's* visit was quickly forgotten.

As Aurora and Sophie walked to the house, she took Sophie's arm. "I need to talk to Telesfora alone. You can bring the boys over after their noon meal."

Aurora gave her mother a peck on the cheek. She told her she wanted to make sure Telesfora understood that she was not giving up her boys to her. She started out the door with Josefa close behind.

Josefa caught up with Aurora. "We've talked, me and Telesfora." Josefa took her daughter's hand. "Most of it was about José. Everyone knows how he is. Telesfora told me that Manuel sat him down. He let him know that the rights of the children were not in his hands. Manuel said that José left with his hat in his hand." Josefa chuckled. "You can be sure José won't go against the family's wishes."

Aurora squeezed Josefa's hand. "But does Telesfora understand?"

"Aurora, you're as close to her as a daughter, and Flavio. . ." Josefa's eyes rolled to the heavens. "She would never do anything to hurt you or your children." Josefa hugged Aurora and turned toward the corrals. "I have to check on the children. I think they went to look at the horses."

✳✳✳

Telesfora set a plate of freshly baked bread on the table. She took a jar of quince jam from the cupboard. As she poured two cups of coffee, Aurora closed her eyes and breathed deeply. Instead of the demanding speech that Aurora had planned to impart, the conversation was gentle.

"Of course, I will help with the boys, but I will never take them from you." Telesfora's eyes overflowed. She put her hands over her face. "God hasn't given me children. Sometimes the pain is too much. Why would I cause any mother the pain of losing her children?"

Aurora got Telesfora a glass of water and offered her a handkerchief. The visit ended with embraces and kind words of understanding.

✳✳✳

Josefa talked Aurora into spending the night and going to Mass with the family. Word was sent to William to join them.

After Mass, a long table was set under the mulberry tree. Telesfora and Isabel brought food that filled the air with the aroma of home and family. Rita and the rest of the women bustled around the kitchen heaping platters and carrying them outside.

William rode his horse to La Parida at daybreak. He joined the knot of men sitting on the porch. José huffed through his nose when he saw William. He excused himself to go to the outhouse. As soon as he left, William spoke to Esquipula and Manuel.

"I'm not sure I'm comfortable with José being in charge of the boy's property. Aurora isn't either, but I assured her that we wouldn't let him do anything without her consent. This seems to have eased her mind."

Manuel tapped his pipe on the bench and nodded at Esquipula.

311

"José knows he is to do nothing without our consent."

Aurora had agreed to let Nea stay home for a week. The winter had separated her from her family for too long.

"Remember," Aurora warned, "not a word to anyone about what goes on in my house. I better not hear tongues wagging when I come back to get you."

"Oh no, no, *Señora!*" Nea made the sign of the cross on her chest and put her finger to her lips. Then she broke into a broad smile. She almost hugged Aurora but, at the last minute, she remembered her place.

Flavito pushed Manuelito forward. His eyes darted from Josefa to Aurora. "Mamá, mi *abuela* thought that since Nea was staying, we could stay too. Mamá Telesfora said she would help look after us." The boys leaned on each other with their chins tucked into their chest. When Manuelito peeked up, he was surprised to see his mother nodding and smiling.

Manuelito grabbed his little brother. "Come on, Flavito! Let's go tell the boys we can stay!"

"Don't slam the. . . " yelled Aurora, but the boys were already out the door and jumping off the wooden porch.

Sophie waved goodbye to her friend. She turned and watched Nea get smaller as they rode away. The buggy ride back to Socorro was quiet. All the way home, Sophie was hoping that, indeed, Aurora was getting better. *I don't know what I'll do if she starts acting crazy again.* She thought about who she would go to for help. *William was busy all the time in court. Gloria lived too far out of town. Evelyn wouldn't know what to do any more than I would.*

It seemed that Sophie didn't have to worry. With the boys gone, the house was quiet. Aurora didn't spend much time in her room. She either carried the baby or talked to her most of the morning. Sophie couldn't tell if Aurora knew what was going on in the household or if her mind was someplace else. If she was someplace else, at least she seemed happy to be there.

74

When Aurora returned to La Parida she turned into Telesfora's yard first. She wasn't surprised to see the boys playing underneath the mesquite bushes. Telesfora stepped outside lugging a wooden crate. She heaved it onto her wagon and wiped her face on her sleeve. "Come in, come in," she waved to Aurora. "I need a little rest."

Aurora glanced at the crates and baskets piled on the porch. The windows were steamy from pots boiling on the stove. "What is all this?" Aurora asked.

Telesfora handed Aurora a glass of water and motioned toward the porch. She dropped onto the bench and breathed deeply, then put her hand on Aurora's arm. "It's the time of the year when me and José take supplies to the ranch. I go to cook for the men. The vaqueros are bringing the cattle down from the hills.

Snake Ranch, thought Aurora. *Ay, mi Flavio.* She stepped off the porch. "It's a good thing I came for the boys. They're not going to that terrible place."

Aurora marched toward the mesquite bushes and ordered the boys to get into the buggy.

"*Tio* José said we could go to the ranch!" wailed Manuelito.

The boys rode back to Socorro, kicking and crying all the way.

By the time Aurora got home she was shaking. She stomped to her room and slammed the door, leaving Sophie to care for the boys.

Aurora nursed Josefita, put the sleeping baby in her cradle, then crawled to the corner of her bed. *Is Telesfora trying to torment me? I never want to hear about that place again.* Aurora remembered Telesfora's promise. She said she would never take my boys away. Then Aurora thought about José and how he was always yelping in her ear. *Do they think that now that I've signed a paper, they can do whatever they want with my sons?*

❄❄❄

Aurora heard the front door open and flew down the stairs. William pressed himself against the wall when Aurora screamed, "I will never let the boys stay with Telesfora again!"

She told him about José wanting to take the boys to the ranch. He put his arms around her and tried to reason with her. She pushed him away.

He threw his hands up and walked toward his study. "We'll talk later about never letting the boys see Telesfora."

Aurora retreated to the kitchen. By the time dinner was over, her anger toward Telesfora was fading. She smiled at the boys. "You'll be glad you came home with me because your papá has a big surprise for you.

That evening the family walked to the park. William had heard that a magician was putting on a show. Manuelito and Flavito sat on the edge of their seats. They laughed and cheered at each new trick. William held Josefita. He kept looking at Aurora to gauge her reaction to the show and was relieved to see her smiling.

On the walk home, William wanted to tell Aurora about the committee meeting he and Manuel had attended. There was a time when Aurora would have been interested in the new laws that were being put in place. Instead, he walked in silence, holding Aurora's hand and listening to the boys relive the magic show. He was sure there would be an ongoing show in his backyard for the rest of the summer.

Now that Manuelito had finished his second year at school, Flavito was anxious to join him in the fall. Flavito chattered about showing his friends his magic tricks on the first day of school.

❋ ❋ ❋

After Aurora put Josefita to sleep, she came back down to find William sitting on the back porch. The boys were setting up a sheet tent and discussing who would perform each trick. Aurora sat beside William and put her head on his shoulder.

"Do you want to know what the committee was voting on?" William asked cautiously.

"Well, I guess so," Aurora answered. She sat up and listened for a few minutes, then started asking questions about the new laws.

❋ ❋ ❋

Manuel had spent the night with his daughter, Rufina. He decided to pay Aurora a visit before he went back to Lemitar. He tossed each boy into the air, then squatted so they could search his pockets for hard candy.

When Aurora heard him coming into the yard, she hurried downstairs, tucking stray curls back into her bun. She let herself be folded into his big bear hug. As she led him into the kitchen, Aurora told him about her visit with Telesfora. She knew he would understand why she didn't want the boys to go to Snake Ranch.

314

Manuel agreed with her. "This is not the time. They're still so small and there will be other summers."

Then Aurora told him about her decision that Telesfora was not to take care of the boys anymore. "I haven't been able to sleep since I decided that. I wish I didn't get so mad, but it's confusing. *Tio*, I'm trying, and I think I'm getting better, but sometimes I just need someplace quiet to put my thoughts back together."

She slipped her hand into her *tio*'s and lowered her voice. "I didn't tell Telesfora that she couldn't take care of the boys. William is the only one who knows what I was thinking. Don't tell her. I do still need her to help sometimes."

Manuel squeezed Aurora's hand. "Of course, *Mija*, and you know we'll always be here too. I'm sorry talking about Snake Ranch brought up the pain of losing Flavio but, that sorrow is in the past. Yes, and you lost your little Isabelita but, you have three fine children. William is making a good life for all of you. Look at what you have now and let the past stay in the past."

She looked up at her uncle. "I'll try harder."

Her uncle sat back. "For you *Mijita*, try harder for you."

❋ ❋ ❋

The next day Aurora helped Sophie pack a basket with food. Sophie held the baby as they rode toward Gloria's house. The boys were anxious to show Gloria's children the magic tricks they had learned. Aurora convinced Gloria to leave the rug beating for another day and join them for a picnic at the springs.

Gloria didn't live far from the springs that came out of the side of the mountain. Someone had built a dam in the little creek that ran from the spring. Cottonwoods grew in abundance, fed by the year-round water.

Beneath the trees, Aurora spread a blanket and put out the food she had brought. Josefita lay in the shade, cooing, and trying to catch her elusive toes. The women talked quietly as they watched their children splash in the shallow pool.

"I just came back from Lemitar yesterday," Gloria said. "Oh, and I went to Estella's. She may have some news about a fourth baby, but she's not sure yet." Gloria's eyes lit up. "The best news is that my brother has found a house in Socorro and he sent for his family last week. That's why I was really cleaning. The dust he brought from the brick factory got into everything."

Aurora leaned back against an old cottonwood and took in all of Gloria's news. She thought about the parade of people who took advantage of Gloria's kindness. It seemed that every time she visited, another of Gloria's relatives was living with her. Then she recalled her own family, always there to care for each other.

Aurora told her friend that José and Telesfora were going to Snake Ranch. Then she recalled her conversation with her *Tio* Manuel.

Gloria sat up straight. "Oh, Aurora, I've known Telesfora as long as you have. You know she only wants to help." She nudged Aurora. "Who knows what José wants."

The young women chuckled and turned back to their children. Their conversation was shattered when Flavito screamed. By the time Aurora looked to see what had happened, Flavito was retaliating by splashing Manuelito back. Aurora started to get up and stop the water fight, but Gloria pulled her back down.

"They're alright. Look, they're laughing."

Gloria's chatter started up again and Aurora forced herself to listen. Before she knew it, she started asking questions about Gloria's sister-in-law. She told Gloria she would stop by her brother's house and drop off some clothes that the boys had outgrown.

On the way home the exhausted boys slumped against Sophie. Every time Sophie's head bobbed, she woke with a start and looked to see if Josefita was still in her arms. Aurora was grateful for the silence.

Her *tio*'s words filled her thoughts. Aurora tugged on the sadness that had surrounded her for so long, but she couldn't bring it back. She glanced at her little family. *Perhaps it is time to let the sadness go.*

75

When Evelyn invited Aurora to join her at Julia Dougherty's on Sunday afternoon, Aurora started to shake her head. William's law partner's wife always made her nervous. Aurora feared that she would be cornered into some kind of voluntary service for the Ladies League. Then she remembered the promise she had made to her uncle. She mumbled, "I guess I can go. I can't remember the last time I saw her."

Evelyn reminded her that Julia had brought Josefita a lace gown and soft silk blanket. Aurora pretended to remember the visit.

As Aurora waved good-by to Evelyn, she promised to see her at the next meeting.

At the Ladies League, Aurora returned the women's hugs stiffly and said that Josefita was growing and healthy. Aurora had decided to leave Josefita at home so she would have an excuse to leave early. She took her place next to Evelyn and leaned back in her chair. By the time she had sipped one cup of weak, bitter tea, Aurora's foot was tapping and she was eying the door.

Salomón Pino's wife, Linda, tried to talk her into being on the decorating committee for the Fall Festival.

"Oh, I couldn't. This is the busiest time on the farm. I have to help my mother make *chili ristras*."

The women stopped talking and eyed Aurora.

"Oh, I've seen those bunches of *chili*s hanging on the *porches*," said Evelyn. "I thought they were just for decoration."

Aurora sat up a little straighter. "No, that's the way we dry *chili* to store it for the winter. We dry a lot of other food too—squash, corn, apples. Everyone in the family helps pick the *chili* because there's only a short time between when it turns red and the frost comes. Then there are the grapes to harvest. We all help with that too."

The tea cup in Julia's hand froze in midair. "But surely, my dear, now that you're married to William you don't have to help on the farm."

Aurora looked at the circle of women. They were all staring at her as if inspecting a dog tracking mud across the carpet. Aurora tensed her jaw and got up to leave. Her china cup rattled against the saucer as she put it on the dining room table.

She clutched the edge of the table for a minute, then strode back into the parlor and sat on the edge of her chair. With her head held high and her voice as steady is she could make it, she said, "You women haven't been in New Mexico very long, so I don't expect you to know what life is like for the families who have lived here for hundreds of years. Yes, I'm the wife of the mayor, but I'm also the daughter of Esquipula Vigil, a farmer."

She wanted to say more. She wanted to tell them how her father and his brother came all the way down from Truchas when the Mexican government gave out a land grant near Socorro. She wanted to explain that their houses had walls around them to protect them from the Apaches. She wished she could tell them about the disappointment in her father's eyes when his vineyards were washed away by the flood, and how he had replanted the next year. But, when she looked around, she saw confusion, or was it pity, on the women's faces. So, she just thanked her hostess and said that she had to get back to her children.

Aurora drove her buggy down Church Street toward the park. She was grateful for this time alone so she could get the high-pitched, squawky voices out of her head. She had planned to get some pastries from the French bakery for dessert, but the errand was forgotten.

In her silence, she ranted and raged against the newcomers, with their noses in the air when she told them about her family's farm. By the time she turned her buggy onto McCutcheon Street, confusion had set in. Wasn't she supposed to be one of them? After all, she was the mayor's wife. It seemed like years ago that she had married William and was so excited to be a part of this circle of women. She had looked forward to taking part in building Socorro's new social circles. *How long has it been since I was serving tea and showing off my new home to all the women that I thought were my friends?*

She was glad that Josefita was awake when she got home. She went upstairs and fed her hungry baby, then fought the urge to crawl into bed and sleep. Instead, she held the baby in one arm and glided her hand along the stair rail. As she descended, her eyes swept across the wallpaper and high ceilings. She stood in the middle of her dining room, staring at her delicate tea set. She pulled the heavy satin drapes across the stained-glass window that her uncle had brought from St. Louis.

Aurora walked into the parlor and ran her hand across the soft maroon velvet that covered her armchair. Then she ambled through the doorway of William's study. Aurora felt like a child, sitting in his big leather chair, her feet dangling.

William, she thought, *I'm married to William De Baun, the mayor of Socorro.*

Aurora's hands started shaking as she pulled herself out of the chair. She spread a blanket on the floor and set Josefita down, then slumped down beside her. Josefita reached for the rattle that her mother shook. Aurora drew her knees to her chest and thought she would rather be in her mother's kitchen helping her make tortillas.

Voices from the kitchen snapped her out of her daydream. Sophie and Nea were chopping and stirring. Manuelito slammed through the back door with an armful of wood for the stove. Trailing behind him, Flavito headed for the water bucket.

Sophie invited the boys to sit. She gave them each a square of cornbread slathered with butter. "Dinner will be ready soon." She kissed each of the boys on the cheek. "This will tide you over."

Aurora scooped Josefita up and strolled to the kitchen. *I can't let them find me curled up on the floor.* She gave Flavito a kiss on the forehead and took a sip of water.

Sophie watched her curiously. Nea's eyes darted to Sophie, then she cleared her throat and asked how the afternoon went.

"It wasn't so easy. I'll tell you, but don't tell anyone else. I didn't feel like I belonged there." Aurora shrugged. "I don't know most of those women very well."

She handed Josefita to Sophie and dropped into a chair. Then her gaze fell on her little boys, baked brown by the New Mexico sun. They were happily chatting with Sophie and Nea, mixing English and Spanish as they described their magic tricks.

Aurora frowned at the memory of her first meeting with Julia. The woman had put her arm in front of Aurora's children and taken a step back. Julia's children had skirted around Manuelito and Flavito as if they were diseased.

Aurora rubbed her forehead and let out a long sigh. "Where do I belong?" she mumbled.

William's meeting kept him at the courthouse well past dinner-time. Judge Pino broke out his private stock of whiskey after the nominees were named. More than one toast was raised to the prospective delegates.

William picked his way home by the light of the full moon. He circled the rooms downstairs, then plodded up to the bedroom. He pulled Aurora out of her rocking chair. She put her finger to her lips and shushed him.

"Let's go downstairs. I have some exciting news," William smiled.

Sitting at the kitchen table, William attempted to pour himself a cup of coffee out of the empty pot. "Never mind the coffee. This calls for a celebration," he said over his shoulder, as he wobbled into the dining room. He came back with a glass of wine in each hand.

"What is it?" Aurora asked, both hands on her chest.

"I've been nominated as one of the delegates to the Territorial Convention. If I get elected, we'll all have a trip to Santa Fe."

Aurora covered her open mouth with both hands. "Santa Fe? All of us? I've always wanted to go to Santa Fe. When will you know? How long will we get to stay?"

William waved her questions away. "Whoa, whoa! I've just been nominated. I won't know until next week if I've been selected."

They escaped to the coolness of the back porch with William telling Aurora how important it was to represent Socorro at the Territorial Convention. His words tumbled past Aurora, but she couldn't quit smiling. She slipped her arm through his and rested her head on his shoulder.

As he talked, Aurora remembered her afternoon. She was glad that nothing was mentioned about Julia's tea party. She had planned to tell him how out of place she felt and how those women looked down their noses at her. If William became one of the delegates, she would want to be by his side, not on the farm string *chili*.

❄❄❄

The next morning Aurora was surprised to see Salomón Pino's wife at her door. Aurora invited Linda inside and ordered Sophie to bring them refreshments. Aurora asked Linda if she would like some tea. She wrinkled her nose and asked if Aurora had any coffee.

Aurora laughed. "I don't like it either. Rufina told me that a little lemon will help, but it's still not coffee."

Sophie returned with steaming cups of coffee and a plate of her ginger cookies.

Linda took Josefita and stood her on her lap. The baby giggled, and bounced, and waved her arms. To Aurora, Linda had seemed like another stranger. Her husband, Salomón, was a cousin of her mother's, but they had only seen each other at occasional weddings or fiestas.

"I was so glad to see you at *Señora* Dougherty's yesterday afternoon. Your mother told me about the birth of your beautiful baby, but I've been so busy that I haven't gotten over to see her or you." She handed Aurora a gift for Josefita, a delicate pair of silk booties embroidered with little pink roses.

They chatted for a while about the family, then Linda broached the subject she had come to talk about. "I'm so glad you said what you did about the family and the farm. Don't worry if the *gringas* don't understand. It hasn't been easy to learn their ways, but with Salomón being the judge, I felt like I should get to know the wives of the business leaders. They're good women, but so different."

Aurora leaned forward and found herself listening, really listening to Linda. "How long have you been friends with them?"

"Oh, two or three years. Like I said, they're different, but I started enjoying being involved in all the things they were doing. Living in Socorro is a lot more exciting than living on the ranch. When you married William, I looked forward to getting to see you at all of our meetings. You were at one meeting writing down some ideas for Socorro, then you were expecting, and had the babies, and little Josefita was so tiny. Then I heard that you weren't well."

Aurora nodded. "Yes, I was just getting started. Now I have to get back into the circles again, especially since William is the mayor." She put her hand on Linda's knee. "This time I'm having trouble going from being Aurora Vigil to Mrs. De Baun."

Aurora looked deeply into Linda's eyes. They were soft and kind. The corners of them crinkled with a gentle smile.

"I know how you feel. Come over any time, and I'll come visit with you. We'll do this together."

❋❋❋

The next week Aurora visited Evelyn. "I'm so glad you came over,"

Evelyn sighed, "I've missed our visits."

When Evelyn finally ran out of things to say about the meeting, Aurora looked down at her hands. "I think I made a fool of myself at Julia's. I really didn't want to help with the Fall Festival and I couldn't think of any other excuses. The way the women were looking at me, I felt like a dirt clod in my father's field. What did they say about me after I left?"

Evelyn offered Aurora a glass of cool mint tea. "Oh, not much, Julia explained that you hadn't been well since the baby was born. She said that you had been resting a lot and hadn't been out socially. She said you'd been spending some time with your family. That seemed to satisfy the women who were curious about why you weren't more interested in the League."

Aurora told Evelyn the news about William being nominated. "We might be going to Santa Fe soon and I'll have to talk with the wives of the other delegates. I've been listening to William more carefully lately so I'll know what's going on.

"You know this is all new for me. I wasn't raised in a big city like Santa Fe. Socorro is the biggest place I've ever been to."

77

The afternoon heat was fading when William burst into the room. "I've been selected as the delegate! We're going to Santa Fe next month. The meetings will last all week."

Aurora clapped and bounced up and down. "I'm finally going to Santa Fe!"

As William washed up for supper, Aurora went to the back porch and fanned herself. *What am I going to do in Santa Fe? I don't know anyone.* Then she remembered Linda.

Aurora hurried into the kitchen. "Are Salomón and Linda going?"

William sat down to his cold ham and garden vegetables. "Yes, Salomón is going and we can travel with his family. You know we're going on the train."

Aurora's mouth dropped open. "Santa Fe, on the train? When did you say we were going, in a month?"

William had been to Santa Fe before and he told her about all the places she could visit. "I suppose there will be some evening events, maybe even a ball."

Standing in the middle of the room, Aurora's face went blank. William put his hand on her arm.

"Sweetheart, you only have to do as much as you want to. If you don't feel up to going somewhere we'll just say you're not feeling well."

Aurora patted his hand. "Oh, Josefita. . . I suppose I'll have to take her with me, but the boys can stay with Telesfora. They haven't seen her in quite a while."

William led Aurora to the front porch and looked at the chinese elm that shaded the yard. He hadn't thought about all of the family details. "The boys will be fine with Telesfora and we'll have Sophie go with us to help you with the baby."

For the first time in months, William saw a light in Aurora's eyes.

Aurora grinned. "I'll go talk to Linda first thing in the morning. She's been to Santa Fe. She'll know what everyone is wearing."

Aurora was glad she had a month to prepare for her journey. She had three seamstresses making new dresses. She packed and un-packed every time Linda talked about what the women wore in Santa Fe. Sophie was put in charge of packing for Josefita.

The boys were stuck in their rooms during the heat of the day. They often sneaked down to the third step and listened to their mother and Linda making plans.

Manuelito nudged his little brother. "Someday I'll take you to Santa Fe."

Flavito nodded. "Yeah, someday, but we get to stay with Mamá Telesfora. Papá Esquipula said we could play in the ditch when he's through watering the fields."

Manuelito's eyes widened. "Yeah, and *Tio* José is going to take us to the mill. Remember when he put some boards on those sacks of flour and we slid down?" The boys retreated back to their room to make their own plans for the week

✳✳✳

José caught Manuel at the door. "Did you hear that Aurora and William are going to Santa Fe?" José rolled his eyes and slapped the counter. "What did I tell you? The *gringos* are going to take over our government and everything else."

Manuel opened the back door and signaled for his men to bring in sacks of flour. He showed them where to pile them in the corner of the storeroom. When the heat in his cheeks had drained, he turned to José. "Open your eyes, man. How many times do I have to tell you that times have changed? I may even go to the convention if one of the delegates can't go."

José stuck his nose in the air, mocking his father-in-law. He pushed past him and marched toward the back door.

"Well, at least Aurora has sense enough to leave the boys with us. I'm going to the mill in Socorro next week. I'll take the boys to the mill with me. They like watching the gears go around and playing in the little ditch." I can bring them back to La Parida with me.

When José and Telesfora picked up the boys, he put on his best smile. "Don't worry about coming back for the boys right away. I know you'll be tired from the trip. Rest for a few days. Then maybe you can spend a day or two with the family. I'm sure Telesfora will want to know all about Santa Fe."

Telesfora glanced at her husband with eyebrows raised. After what she had heard from him in the past weeks, she couldn't believe how pleasant he was to Aurora.

Last week he had gone on and on, saying that he couldn't believe Aurora had taken up with that nest of vipers in Socorro. He had pounded his fist on the table and sworn he would do everything he could to raise the boys with the family. "I won't let my nephews follow in her footsteps!"

Telesfora had been so upset at his ranting that she threatened to go to Esquipula and tell him what he said. "I'll ask Josefa to take care of Aurora's sons. I don't want them getting any crazy ideas from you." She banged the door shut and stormed across the yard.

José caught up to her and tore off his hat. "Please come back inside."

Telesfora pulled her arm out of his grip. "It's like your hatred for the *gringos* has blinded you. Can't you see that those boys are not ours? They are Aurora's children."

José's jaw tightened. He ran his hand through his hair and begin to pace. "Oh, I know, I know. I'm trying to let go of the past, but when Aurora runs off with her fancy *gringo*, I want to tell her to leave the boys with us for good."

"You know she won't do that and if you keep acting like a mad man, Aurora won't leave them with us at all."

José batted the air and started back toward the house. "You're right. I'm trying not to get so mad anymore. It only makes my head hurt, and everyone yells at me."

Telesfora gritted her teeth and hissed, "You're like a dead branch. When a strong wind comes, it will break you. Manuel and the family are like willow saplings. The wind will only bend us and we will see another day."

Now, as Telesfora helped José load the boys into the wagon, José's kind words to Aurora rang in her ears. She shook her head, hoping that what she had said had softened Jose's heart a little.

78

It had always been easy for Aurora to move her friends around like dolls on a string, but these rooms were filled with strangers. In Santa Fe, she found herself fighting the urge to hang on to William's coat. Every time he introduced her, she stepped forward shyly, unable to look people in the eye.

As soon as she could, Linda took Aurora's elbow and led her into the hall. "*Levántate*, stand up straight. You're the daughter of Don Esquipula Vigil and the wife of Mayor De Baun."

Aurora pulled herself up to her full five feet-two and held her head high. The rest of the week was spent surrounding herself with the prominent women of New Mexico. She had listened carefully to William, Salomón, and Linda on the way to Santa Fe. When she spoke, she could now tell others about all the good changes they had brought to Socorro.

She raised her head a little higher when she told them of the new laws that her husband had put into place. Aurora made sure to mention that her uncle and father had taken part in the incorporation of Socorro.

✺✺✺

On the way home, Aurora and Linda went over every luncheon, the Governor's Ball, and all the women they had met. While William and Salomón talked about the laws they would put in place, the women gossiped about the dresses and manners of all the women.

The first two days back in Socorro were a blur. Aurora's head was pounding and she couldn't seem to get enough sleep. Now that Josefita was eating mashed food from the table, Sophie cared for the baby while Aurora slept. When she woke, Aurora slowly unpacked her dresses. She caressed her satin ball gown, then waltzed around the room with it. *Wait until I tell Gloria and Rita about the dinners and the Governor's Ball.*

By Friday, Aurora felt like visiting with Evelyn. As she walked around the corner, Aurora slowed her pace. *Evelyn will want to know all about my trip.* Aurora frowned. *I wonder if Rita and Gloria will be as excited.*

On the steps of Evelyn's house, Aurora put these thoughts away. By the end of the visit, the two young women were making plans to meet with the Ladies League so Aurora could tell them all about Santa Fe.

❋ ❋ ❋

William also spent the week basking in his Santa Fe trip. But Sheriff Garcia banging on the door jolted him back to Socorro's problems. They retreated to William's study.

It seemed as if the escape of the Bacas had emboldened the natives. Felipe Gallegos had beaten one of the Eaton's wranglers and the judge let him off scot-free. Three of Bursum's cattle went missing and no one knew where they were.

"It's like they're spitting at our laws." The sheriff snuffed out his cigar. "Something has to be done. We're going to have a meeting at Bursum's place tomorrow night."

"Jesus," grunted William throwing his pen across the desk. "I'll be there. You're right, something has to be done." He led the sheriff to the door and stomped back to his study.

Aurora's voice drifted in from the kitchen. Then Josefita started crying. William looked at the court files that had stacked up during his absence. He ran his fingers through his hair then slammed the door shut.

Aurora had tiptoed down the hall when she heard Sheriff Garcia's loud voice. She gleaned enough of the conversation to know why William slammed the door.

❋ ❋ ❋

"When are we going to get the boys?" Sophie asked.

"Oh, let's wait until tomorrow. I'll be rested by then."

They left before the morning dishes were washed. Aurora was glad to get away from the ugly side of Socorro. At the same time, she was anxious to tell her family about her fairytale trip to Santa Fe.

"Oh, and I'll ask Mamá what she knows about the Baca family. I know we're related."

When Aurora got to her mother's house, she held court like she used to before she married Flavio. The family sat under the old mulberry tree and listened as Aurora told them how she met the governor and his wife. She brought handmade lace *mantillas* for the women, sweets for the children, and imported pipe tobacco for the men.

The women gasped when Aurora described the governor's mansion. She held her hands to her chest and swayed as she told them about the reception hall with its candelabras and crystal. She spread out her arms.

"You should have seen the gowns, the lace, and the satins. Oh, and the colors . . . I could tell they were shipped from back East."

When Aurora finished telling them about her adventure, she yawned and declared that she was still tired. She retreated to her room for a nap.

Josefa helped Rita take the dishes into the cooking room. The crockery rattled as it settled onto the table. When Rita turned around, Josefa's hands were over her face. Her shoulders were heaving. Rita rushed to her.

"What's the matter Mamá?"

Josefa shook her head. "Nothing." She uncovered her face to reveal a huge smile. "Aurora, she seems to be herself again."

They both made the sign of the cross and offered up prayers of thanks.

✳✳✳

The boys ran and hid behind the mesquite bushes when they saw their mother coming.

"Don't you want to see the toys your father brought you from Santa Fe?" Aurora coaxed.

Flavito poked his head out, but Manuelito pulled him back. "Just one more week," he begged. "Papá Manuel said we could go with him to deliver the flour to the train. He knows the man who drives it, and he's going to let us get on the engine."

José broke in. "I'm going with Manuel, and I can take the boys home when we've finished unloading the wagons." He crossed his arms and waited for Aurora's objection.

"Well," she whispered. "I guess another week won't hurt."

José and Telesfora embraced each other with wide-eyed smiles.

Aurora knelt and opened her arms. As her sons ran toward her, Aurora was thinking about the meetings she had promised to go to. She gave each boy a peck on the cheek.

"When you get home, I'll tell you about my train ride. Your father has a meeting in Albuquerque next month and then we'll all go on the train."

The boys clasped hands and hopped around in a circle. Aurora gave her sons a little wave then turned around in the buggy seat. José and Telesfora waved, but Aurora looked toward Socorro.

On the way back to Socorro, Aurora raised her face to the sun.

She was relieved that the boys had stayed with José and their grand-father Manuel. Now that Nea had decided to stay and help La Señora, Sophie would have her hands full taking care of Josefita. She thought past her meetings, to her sons. *I spent so much time with my abuelos in the summer. Now it's the boys' turn.* A quick smile flashed across her face. *When school starts, I can teach them about Socorro's society. It will be good for them to know about both worlds.*

❋ ❋ ❋

On the train trip to Albuquerque, the boys couldn't sit still. Their faces were plastered against the windows. Every time they saw house or a cow, they tugged at Aurora and pointed at the new discovery whizzing past. Their chatter was filled with their adventure on another train, the one they had explored with Papá Manuel and *Tio* José.

"Wait until I tell Papá Manuel about this train!" shouted Manuelito.

Flavito turned to his mother. "Do you think we can see the engine?"

Aurora drew her son near to her. "We probably won't have time but your *Abuelo* Manuel can take you back to the train at Socorro."

Flavito pouted for a quick minute. Manuelito squealed and pointed to a longhorn cow and Flavito's disappointment was forgotten.

While William was at his delegate meetings, the boys begged to go back to the railroad station and watch the trains come in. Aurora sent them with Sophie while she meandered through the shops that encircled the plaza in front of the San Felipe church. The little adobe shops and narrow passages reminded her of the Socorro of her childhood.

Aurora's arms soon tired. Josefita wiggled and reached for everything Aurora wanted to see. *Why didn't I have Sophie take the baby with her?*

"Tomorrow you'll have to come with me," Aurora ordered. "You can watch the children in the plaza while I pick up the baskets I ordered."

Aurora woke the children early and rushed them through breakfast. She left all three children in the plaza with Sophie. Aurora promised she would only be a few minutes. She didn't realize that there was more to see in the *plazitas* behind the stores. The little hidden shops held ready-made clothes and hats. Aurora explored every one of them.

329

By the time she strolled back to the plaza, the boys were leaning against Sophie. Their faces were flushed. They pleaded for water. Sophie was bouncing Josefita to keep the hungry baby from crying.

Aurora took the children into the hotel restaurant and ordered sticky buns and water for all. As she fed little pieces to Josefita, Aurora kept looking out the window at the stores she hadn't gotten to.

Her idea to take the children to their room and put them down for a nap didn't go as planned. The open windows didn't do much to cool the heavy air. The boys raced around the room playing train conductor and Josefita was wide awake. Sophie sat in the corner looking like a wilted flower. Aurora stretched across the bed. Staring at the ceiling, she thought, *the next time I go to Albuquerque it will be without the children.*

✳✳✳

Aurora didn't have time to rest after her Albuquerque trip. She headed the committee to make tamales for the *fiesta* of San Miguel. Leaving Gloria and her friends to make mounds of tamales, Aurora ran off to oversee the decorating for the Fall Ball.

When she ran into Evelyn, Aurora talked her into helping rewrite the notes from the Ladies League meeting. In the middle of all of this, she had to get the boys ready for school. Flavito was about to start his first year.

Flavito's eyes widened when Manuelito told him he would be going to school with him. "Are we going today? Will Sister Angelina be my teacher too? Can I walk to school with you every day?"

Manuelito just kept nodding. "Today we're going to get new clothes for school. Come on!"

Aurora took her sons to the Torres Mercantile and bought two school uniforms for each boy. They would replace their outgrown summer clothes. Aurora wanted William to walk the boys to school with her on the first day, but he was on the bench to judge a trial.

She swallowed a little pang of disappointment, gathered her children, and took them to meet the Sisters of Loretto. The hallways were full of parents and fidgety children. Aurora began to push her way to the front of the line, expecting everyone to part the way for her. After all, she was the mayor's wife. Instead, many of the women that she knew just turned and glared.

79

Johathan stood and cleared his throat. "We can't let this go on or there will be total lawlessness in Socorro."

The men in Aurora's parlor all agreed with William's law partner. Aurora knew what they were talking about. Both Gloria and Evelyn had told her stories of *Hispano* juries letting their neighbors go free even though their crimes could be proven. Last week Adolfo Chavez was busted out of jail by his father. Apparently, Sheriff Garcia didn't realize he was gone until the next day, or so he said.

"I don't like the idea of taking the law into our own hands," William protested.

Aurora heard William's voice above the din. The roar of the other men got louder. Finally, one of them pounded his fist against the arm of the chair. "We have to take the law into our own hands because the locals are making a mockery of it. Now that they know they can get away with stealing and even killing, no one will be safe."

When they left, Aurora ran to William. Wide-eyed, she asked, "What's going on?"

"We're going to form a vigilante group. If the sheriff isn't willing to do his job, we'll have to do it for him."

Aurora shrank back. "I don't understand. What will this vigilante group do?" She reached for William's arm. "This sounds dangerous."

For the first time in Aurora's life, she locked all the doors and windows before she went to bed. William quit working in time to pick up the boys after school. Again, he struggled to do some of his work at home. He told Aurora that she should wait until afternoon to buy supplies for the house. By that time the men who had staggered out of the gambling halls the night before would be sleeping it off at home.

Soon their lives begin to shift. William started going out at night. The Socorro Committee for Public Safety had decided to form patrols to make sure the neighborhoods were safe.

William had usually gone to work before the family stirred. This morning Aurora slipped out of bed and let her snoring husband rest. She was helping Sophie get the boys ready for school when he plodded downstairs.

William sat at the dining room table and held his head in both hands. "We had to do it," he muttered to Aurora. "Juan Armijo shot

Ben Carter in front of everybody at the saloon. When we asked Sheriff Garcia to question the men who witnessed the shooting, he just shrugged and said, 'I know where they live. I'll talk to them in the morning after they sober up.'

"Juan had a reputation for being hot tempered and mean. Maybe everybody was afraid of him, but that's no excuse." He looked up at Aurora, his face pale and his hands raised. "I threw the rope over the tree branch, but I couldn't watch."

Aurora stumbled backwards and bumped against the wall. "They hung him? The men that were in my house killed a man?" She looked at William like a thief who had broken into her home.

William pressed his hands together as if in prayer. He pleaded, "The sheriff is doing nothing when the locals break the law."

"Well, get rid of him!" Aurora screeched. "There are plenty of good men who can do the job."

"We're working on that, but in the meantime, we have to keep our families safe."

✳✳✳

Aurora hired Sophie's friend, Alex, to walk the boys to school, then pick them up in the afternoon. When Aurora was at a meeting or social, she left early to make sure the boys had gotten home safely. The Committee for Safety continued their nightly patrols, and the women's groups were filled with talk of men hanging from the trees in Death Alley.

At the next visit to Gloria's, she told Aurora that the vigilante group was doing more harm than good. She looked down at her hands, then up at Aurora. She muttered that her husband didn't want Aurora in her house. He knew that William was one of the vigilantes that had hung his friend Juan.

"I told him there would never be a day when you weren't welcome in my house. We've all been friends since we were children and you had nothing to do with the hangings. We got in a big fight, but I meant what I said."

On the way home Aurora remembered how people had looked at her at the school. They didn't move out the way for the mayor's wife.

When she got home, Aurora found Manuelito sitting in the corner of the kitchen. His clothes were dirty and his face streaked with tears. Sophie pulled Aurora into the study and told her that Manuelito had been fighting. "I had to punish him for fighting, so I sat him in the corner." Sophie twisted her hands. "Please don't be hard on him. He said that some boys were acting like they were being hung and calling Mister DeBaun the hanging judge."

Aurora dropped into a chair and clapped her hand over her mouth. When William got home, she told him what Gloria had said.

"And today Manuelito got into a fight because the other boys were calling his daddy The Hanging Judge." Aurora started pacing around the room. "When is this going to end?"

William reached for Aurora's hand, but she pulled it away. She fled to the kitchen, circled the table, then went back into the study. She stood in the doorway with her arms crossed and announced. "The boys are not safe in Socorro. I'm going to put them in school at Lemitar."

William had to agree with her. He told her that it would just be for a little while. Things were beginning to calm down. The City Council had told the sheriff that either he upheld the law or he would be replaced.

✳✳✳

José rubbed his hands together when he saw Aurora's buggy sending up a dust cloud. *Those gringos, with all their big ideas and new laws, now look what's happening to Socorro. The boys are better off with us. Who better to raise them?*

Aurora assured Telesfora that it would probably only be until the Christmas holiday. But as the snow got deeper and the winds grew colder, the crime in Socorro was still being handled by the Committee for Safety.

Manuel bundled up the boys and made the long journey to Socorro so they could spend Christmas with their family. He returned them to their Mamá Telesfora after the new year. They gave their mother a glancing hug and rushed to the buggy. Huddled under their sheepskin blanket, the boys could hardly wait to show Mamá Telesfora their new toys.

It wasn't until the willows along the Rio Grande started budding that the people of Socorro began to feel safe again. Aurora broke away from her committee work and made the journey to La Parida. She drew each boy to her and squeezed them tight. Then she put her hand on top of each one's head. "How is it possible that you've grown so much in just a few months?"

They showed Aurora all the toys that José had carved for them.

Flavito twirled around to show off the wool coat that Telesfora had made. Telesfora gave them each a kiss and send them outside to play.

Aurora sat in Telesfora's kitchen; her hands wrapped around a mug of coffee. "Things are getting better. A new sheriff was hired." She pressed her knuckles to her lips. "I hope this means that the committee will be disbanded."

Aurora reached for Telesfora. "I was right to send the boys to you." She closed her eyes and shook her head at the memories. "Socorro was no place for children. But with the new sheriff and new laws, things are settling down."

Telesfora laced her fingers together. "Does this mean that you want to take the boys back with you?" Worry lined her brow. "School will be over soon. The boys have made friends. They love Sister Maria Antonia. By the time school is over things will really be settled in Socorro." Telesfora held her breath while Aurora sauntered to the window.

"I suppose it wouldn't hurt to let them stay until summer. It's just a couple of months."

❄❄❄

The winter months had rushed past Aurora in a swirl of meetings and teas. She was in charge of taking notes to be printed in the league's newsletter. No sooner did she hand off the task to one of the other members then another favor was asked of her. By the time the children were out of school, Aurora was grateful for an excuse to bow out of her social work. She handed the fundraiser list to Claire.

"I'm afraid I can't do this. I have to go get my boys from La Parida."

Early the next morning, Sophie sat in the back seat where the sides of the buggy offered some protection. She had to tie a scarf around Josefita's waist and wrap it around her own. Since the baby started walking, she hadn't stopped exploring, and Sophie was afraid that Josefita would leap out of the buggy.

Aurora couldn't remember the last time she saw her family. She looked forward to just sitting on the *porche* and listening to the crickets with her mother. Aurora was anxious to see the boys too, but with Josefita getting into everything, and two boys running through the house, Aurora wondered if she could keep up with it all.

When Manuelito and Flavito spotted their mother's buggy in front of Telesfora's they threw down their stick horses and ran to Aurora. She hugged them both, and stood each at arm's length. "It

334

seems like you've grown a foot since last week."

Sophie nudged her. "It's been months."

Aurora stood gazing past the lavender hills. She drew in a breath. "Oh, I guess so. I've been so busy." She gave Sophie an apologetic look, then started toward Telesfora's house.

Manuelito wanted to show her that he had learned to ride a horse. Flavito tugged at her skirt and pulled her toward a mud puddle where he was making tiny adobe bricks. He had constructed several little houses and told her that the village was called *La Villa de* Flavito. Both Sophie and Aurora listened carefully as he told them who lived in each tiny house.

The tour was cut short when Josefita squealed at the end of Sophie's tether.

The toddler's crying brought Telesfora out of the house. She hugged Aurora and ushered them into the house. Telesfora had busied herself with washing the winter's bedding and cleaning out storage trunks. She swept and dusted until her house gleamed. But keeping her hands busy couldn't keep this day from coming. She comforted herself by thinking that Aurora would soon tire of taking care of three children, and would return her precious boys to her.

Manuel's freight wagons were expected to come from St. Louis in a few days. He was glad that Aurora planned to stay with her mother until Sunday.

"The boys have been looking forward to watching the wagons come in and inspecting all the new goods." Telesfora squeezed Flavito. "I wouldn't want them to miss this."

Aurora smiled at the memory of gathering with all the children to cheer on the parade of covered wagons rolling through town. She and her cousins use to sit on the pole fence and watch as crate after crate was carried into the store.

José laughed and slapped his knee. He reached over and pinched Aurora's cheek. "You're grinning just like you did when you were a little girl."

Aurora blushed. "I forgot what it was like to grow up near Lemitar. Socorro is nice too, but it's no place for . . . "

She glanced at José and didn't finish her thoughts. *I don't want to give him fodder for a rant. Poor Tia has enough to listen to.*

Aurora hadn't planned to stay in Lemitar so long, but she got caught up in the excitement of being first to see the treasures from the East. When the last wagon was unloaded, Aurora tied a bandanna around her head. Her apron didn't keep the grime from staining the edges of her sleeves. She dusted the store shelves and ordered Manuel's hired man to put the crates along the back wall. The boys handed Aurora bags of sugar and tins of tea.

Manuel told the boys which crates they were allowed to look through. A pile of straw grew on the floor as Manuelito and Flavito gently revealed each brightly painted wooden horse and little cloth doll. With each new discovery they ran to their Papá Manuel and Mamá.

"Can we keep it? Can we keep it?"

Manuel lifted one eyebrow. "We'll see," he said again and again.

Manuel finally gave in and handed the boys a wooden box full of toy animals. He opened the back door and shooed them out to play. The boys scampered outside, clutching armfuls of little metal cows and horses. They built a little ranch, and herded cattle on the *porche* until the mosquitoes drove them inside.

Aurora was quiet on the way back to Socorro, wrapped in childhood memories of helping her *Tio* open crates from St. Louis and being the first to inspect the treasures within. The boys soon fell asleep clutching their tin soldiers and a little wooden wagon.

✳✳✳

"Oh look, your papá is home." The boys stirred as the buggy bumped into the yard. They rushed to William shouting over each other about how they helped their *abuelo* at his store. When William saw Aurora, he chuckled.

"What's happened to you? You look like a ragamuffin."

Aurora began to form a pout but, when she saw that William was holding out his arms, her pout turned into a crooked smile.

He led her into the study. "I have some news of my own." As the boys rattled on, William nodded and guided them toward the backyard. He turned to Aurora. "The Socorro Chieftain will be up and running by the end of the week. The printing machine has finally arrived." William was starting the newspaper, knowing this was a good way to promote Republican views.

"I thought you could help me organize the Chieftain, you know, the way you helped your uncle.

Aurora's eyes darted toward the kitchen. "Let me go get Josefita." She needed time to clear her mind. This always happened when she went from her world to William's. The thoughts of organizing a newspaper gave her a jolt.

To Sophie's surprise, Aurora changed the toddler and carried her out of the room. Josefita stretched out her arms when she saw her papá. William lifted her into the air, then giggles washed over both of them. He bounced her on his outstretched leg, then attempted to set her on the floor. When Josefita loudly demanded more, Aurora called for Sophie.

William pushed out one more bit of laughter. "I can't believe how big she's getting." He took a deep breath and tugged at his vest. "So, what do you think about helping me with the newspaper? It would only be for a while, until the editor puts out a few editions." When Aurora didn't answer, William tried again. "It wouldn't have to be every day."

Aurora's thoughts settled on Williams words. "Well, I suppose it would be interesting. I would know everything that's going on in Socorro." She leaned forward and smiled. "Oh, and I would know before anyone else."

Aurora sent word for José to take the boys back to La Parida the next time he came to Socorro to get flour from the mill.

"It'll only be for a couple of weeks, just until the newspaper is up and running." Aurora announced.

Her mornings were filled with feeding and playing with Josefita, giving Sophie time to do her upstairs house work. As soon as Josefita was put down for her afternoon nap, Aurora slipped out of the house and rushed to the Chieftain.

Sophie soon learned that she should prepare their evening meal later than usual. William often starting eating at an empty table. Aurora would rush through the door and join him, bubbling about everything that was going on in Socorro.

"I've been elected to be the official reporter for the Ladies League," Aurora declared with her head held high. "There has to be more than mining reports and political slants to print. We want to bring the news of Socorro's society to the community."

William wrapped his hand around his wife's and drew her close. He presented her with a soft kiss on the lips.

"I'm glad you're feeling up to doing this," he whispered.

Aurora took his hand and pressed it against her face. She nodded. "I'm alright. Oh, and today I was making sure that the Ladies League news was on the front page." Aurora threw her hands into the air. "Oh, and Sister Angelina came in with an announcement that school would start in two weeks. Where has the summer gone?"

❋❋❋

When Aurora arrived at Telesfora's, Flavito and Manuelito surrounded their mother. Sitting at the kitchen table, they showered her with stories about their friends and cousins. The boys exchanged hopeful glances with their Tia.

"Can't they stay? They've made so many friends here." Telesfora begged.

Aurora drew a deep breath. "Let me think about this."

She put her head down. Silence lay over the room like a sodden blanket. Finally, she rose, still frowning, and announced that she needed to take a walk.

As she wove between the sagebrush, Aurora's thoughts swirled. She took comfort in knowing that half the school children were family and were fiercely protective of her boys. *Is this where they belong?*

Had Telesfora won? Wouldn't they be better off in Socorro with their mother? She stopped at the top of a knoll. Her breath caught in her throat. *Hadn't the past few months been easier without two demanding boys underfoot?*

Aurora stood in the doorway. "They can stay, but only until school gets out for the celebration of our *Santo Niño*. By then I won't be so busy with the newspaper. Besides, the new sheriff is doing a good job. The Committee for the Safety of Socorro has disbanded. Socorro feels safer now."

The boys didn't protest when Aurora explained that they would have to go with her to be fitted for new school clothes. She promised that the first thing in the morning, she would take them to their *tío's* mercantile to get new clothes.

Telesfora squeezed Aurora fiercely. "Any time that anyone goes to Socorro we'll bring the boys to see you."

Aurora put a shaky hand to her lips. With her head down, she closed her eyes and nodded.

❄❄❄

Aurora settled into a routine of organizing fundraisers, and attending functions. Her visits with Gloria were rare. Rita had another baby. Aurora spent a week when Rita's second child arrived, but Nea was recruited to spend the rest of the month with her.

Since William had become a representative of the Republican legislature, Aurora hosted senators and businessmen in her home. She hired Linda Pino's girl to help. With Sophie's instructions, Luzita soon learned how to serve at these events.

Manuel brought the boys to Socorro to celebrate Christmas with their mother.

They stayed a week longer, than bundled against the January winds, Flavito and Manuelito traveled back to spend the rest of the winter with Mamá Telesfora.

81

Every year Manuelito and Flavito visited at Christmas and for a few weeks in the summer. As they grew, their summer visits became shorter. Their Papá Manuel needed them at the store.

As the years went by, William's involvement in the Republican Party grew. His newspaper was an outlet for his political views. Besides being a judge and a newspaper owner, he was now the superintendent of schools.

When thunderclouds rumbled above the Socorro mountains, Aurora began to see signs that William's nonstop activities were wearing him down. A cough that had started in early fall grew worse with each passing week.

Dr. Wilson led Aurora into the kitchen. He pulled off his wire-rimmed glasses and took a deep breath. "Aurora, I'm afraid it's consumption. I can give him powders to help ease his breathing, but there is no cure for this lung disease."

Aurora put her hands on the table to brace herself against the numbing constriction of her heart. The room grew dim.

Dr. Wilson fumbled in his bag and retrieved a bottle of smelling salts. The electric odor jolted Aurora out of a place that she didn't want to come back from. A sound escaped her that reminded the doctor of a wounded rabbit. He sat with his hand on her arm while he waited for Aurora to find her words.

They came slowly, reluctantly. "You said there wasn't a cure, but will he get better?" Aurora searched his downcast eyes. "Will he be like this for the rest of his life?"

Aurora stepped into the dining room, putting distance between herself and the doctor's answer.

When she didn't hear his voice, Aurora lowered her head and returned to the kitchen. She eased herself into a chair. The doctor's words streamed past the ringing in her ears.

"I'm afraid he's going to get worse. I can't tell you how long he's got. He's still a young man, and he's strong. We'll just have to see."

Aurora paid a visit to Julia Dougherty. This conversation was not for the League. She turned over her lists and notes. The Ladies League would have to go on without her. Aurora steadied her voice before explaining that from now on she would spend all her time caring for

William.

Julia nodded and reached for Aurora's hand. Aurora waved her away. She put a shaky hand to her lips. Julia moved closer and embraced her. With that act of kindness, Aurora's tears overtook her resolve to conduct herself with propriety.

William worked in his study when he managed, with Aurora's help, to climb down the stairs. When snow dusted the ground, Flavito's narrow bed was placed in the corner of his study.

Jason Woodward was assigned to William's position on the bench.

When he stopped by to pay his respects, Aurora met him at the door. She muttered a quick offer for him to come into William's study. As she handed him William's court records, William whispered, "It will only be for a few weeks."

But the look Aurora gave the young judge made him think that the job would be permanent.

As November's snow closed in, William was confined to his bed. Aurora had José bring the boys from La Parida before their Christmas vacation.

"They won't be going back," she said softly. She put an arm around their shoulders and led them into the house. José saw the weary look in her hollow eyes and didn't argue.

In late November, the whirlwind that was William De Baun whispered goodbye to his beloved Aurora.

Aurora retreated to her bedroom and didn't emerge for two days. When William's law partner came by, hat in hand, Aurora silently led him to William's study.

She stood in the doorway and wrapped her arms around herself. A shiver ran through her. She intended to see that Johnathan didn't remove anything that was dear to her, but the dim cavern of a room threatened to swallow her up.

"I'll have Sophie bring you some tea," Aurora offered flatly.

When Johnathan insisted that she needn't bother, Aurora didn't seem to hear. She drifted into the kitchen and didn't return.

William's oldest friend found Aurora sitting at the table, her hands wrapped around her cup. Johnathan put both arms out, inviting Aurora into his comforting embrace.

Instead of standing, Aurora raised her head slowly until their eyes met. The tears in Jonathan's eyes pulled her to her feet. Aurora patted him on the back as they embraced.

Aurora walked him to the front door with the promise of asking for help if she needed it. She leaned against the closed door, her head pounding at the thought of his wife coming tomorrow to help out.

❋❋❋

Manuelito tiptoed down the stairs. Aurora didn't notice him until she felt his soft embrace. At sixteen, her son felt he was old enough to be the man of the house. He tried his best to comfort his grieving family. His Papá William had always inspired him. He loved him, but not in the same way that he loved his Tio José and his *abuelos*.

Flavito took it upon himself to be his sister's caretaker. He was fourteen years old, and she was only ten. On the morning of William's funeral, Aurora and her three children huddled together on her big oak bed. Joséfita's tears seemed never ending, as her brother's arms wrapped around her.

"Don't worry Josefita," began Flavito, "We're not going back to La Parida."

Manuelito nodded. "Yeah, we're going to stay here and take care of you and Mamá."

Before going to William's funeral, Telesfora took charge of the kitchen while Josefa looked after her daughter. She followed Aurora's every move. Josefa watched for signs that she was again spiraling into endless grief. Although looking pale and drawn, Aurora seemed to have a strength that she hadn't possessed during her other two losses.

Manuelito was head and shoulders taller than his mother. When he put his arm around her, she leaned against him, then straightened.

"I have to be strong for all of you, especially Josefita."

"We'll be strong together," Manuelito answered.

Manuelito followed his mother into the San Miguel Chapel. Esquipula and Josefa moved forward and guided Aurora into the embrace of her family. The ringing in her ears didn't allow the priest's chanted prayers to reach her. Her father hurried her out of the side door after Father Lopez sprinkled holy water on William's coffin. He and Josefa waited with her in the buggy until everyone had gone to the cemetery.

November winds pushed the crowd into a huddle. Tumbleweeds clung to old wooden crosses. Dust whipped at coats and hats. With the thick black *mantilla* covering her head, Aurora leaned against her father as prayers flickered past her.

82

Aurora closed up her big brick house for the winter. She traveled, with her arms around Joséfita, to La Parida. As they rode into her father's yard, Aurora cupped her hands around her daughter's face. "We're going to stay with your *abuela* for a while, but it won't be for long."

Josefita pressed her face against her mother's shoulder. "Good," she sniffled, "because I really want to go home."

Aurora walked to her rooms in silence. *Back in my mother's house, but this time I have my own home to go back to.* She thought about how strange she felt when she first moved into the big two-story house with its high ceilings and wallpaper. Now she couldn't imagine herself living anywhere else.

Aurora and Joséfita made themselves comfortable in the rooms Aurora had lived in after Flavio's death. Josefita's little bed was placed across from her mother's. Esquipula brought over Aurora's heavy domed trunk packed with their clothes. A small chest with Josefita's dolls was placed in the corner. On the shelf, Josefa carefully placed Aurora's bone china tea service. Every morning Aurora and her daughter watched the sun color the mesas as they drank cocoa from the delicate cups.

❄ ❄ ❄

Josefita squeezed into Esquipula's wagon alongside her brothers and cousins. On their way to school Flavito sang a song in the language that Josefita didn't understand. Flavito expected a smile, but was met with a frown from his sister. Manuelito nudged him, "Don't you know any songs in English?"

The children stumbled through 'She'll be Comin' Round the Mountain'. They giggled at their own mangling of the words. Each in turn grinned at Josefita, but she didn't share their laughter.

Her brothers introduced Josefita to all their younger friends, but much of the time she didn't understand what they were saying. She stomped her foot and said, "Speak English!" She couldn't figure out the games they were playing. Josefita retreated against the adobe wall that surrounded the school yard. When Luzita offered Josefita her jump rope, Josefita burst into tears and screeched, "I want to go home!"

Her cousins descended upon her and tried to comfort her with gifts of marbles and sticky, lint covered candy. Flavito tried to explain that these children were her family. Josefita grabbed his arm and pulled him toward her. She bumped her head against his.

"I don't know any of them," she cried.

Flavito led her to the worn steps of the school house. He put his arm around his little sister. "Don't worry," he whispered. "We can just sit here until you get used to all of them."

Josefita wiggled away. "I don't want to get used to them. I want to go home!" She burst into a torrent of tears. "I miss my daddy!" she gulped.

After school Josefita and her brothers walked to their *abuelo's* store. For the first time, Flavito glimpsed a smile on his sister's face. She was busy choosing what she wanted her mother to buy for her. She picked out a peppermint stick and followed Manuelito into the storeroom. He lifted her onto a wooden table and let her direct the opening of crates and bins.

✳✳✳

When the day came that the wind finally stopped howling, Aurora and Josefita walked up the hill to visit Rita. Her little girl, Luzita, sat next to Josefita in school. After they drank *atole* to warm themselves up, Luzita took her dolls from underneath the bed. They weren't like the fine china dolls that Josefita owned. These were made from scraps that her mother had sewn together and embroidered faces on.

Josefita wrinkled her nose when she saw them. She started to laugh, but when Luzita took out a box of clothes she had made, Josefita saw the pride in her eyes. She remembered what her mother had said. "Not everyone lives like we do or has what we have, but they're just as proud of what they have."

Josefita thought of the times when they went to Gloria's house. The ceilings were low and all the walls were white. The windows were small, like little alcoves set into the thick adobe walls. The girls would set their toys in these, even turning one of them into a set for their play. Josefita had friends in Socorro who lived in houses like these. She was getting used to living in one herself.

While the girls played in Luzita's room, Aurora and Rita talked as if the last eleven years had not passed by. At first Aurora told Rita about her friends in Socorro. She reminisced about the gala ball she had last attended with William. When Aurora finally looked up at Rita, she noticed that her sister kept glancing toward her unwashed dishes.

Rita didn't know how to talk about such things. So, she asked Aurora how Gloria was doing, and had she seen Estella. Rita told her that she didn't go to Lemitar very often. Her children kept her busy and when winter faded, she would start helping her husband on the farm. Now it was Aurora's turn to silently take in what Rita was saying.

Aurora walked to the fireplace, took a deep breath, and sighed. She came back to the table and put her hand over Rita's. "I can't believe it's all happening again. How can I be back in my mother's house?" She shrugged her shoulders. "Where do I belong now?"

Rita sat quietly and listened as Aurora's worries poured out. Thoughts tumbled over each other like a landslide. "I have the newspaper, my house, and the building that William's office was in. I helped William set up the newspaper so I know quite a bit about it."

As she blurted out her options, Aurora's stomach tightened. She let out a slow breath, speaking to no one in particular. "Rufina's daughter, Agnes, is planning to attend the teacher's Normal School in Socorro. When Antonio died, Rufina and Agnes moved in with her oldest daughter in San Antonio. Rufina's afraid that Agnes won't be able to go to school now."

"Socorro is so far away from San Antonio. I was thinking that she could stay with me when I move back to Socorro. She would be better than the last girl Sophie sent me."

It had been two years since Sophie had married and moved away. Aurora made do with a series of Sophie's young friends to help her with the household.

"It would be good to have someone from the family stay with me."

By the time Aurora stopped mulling over her future, she seemed closer to knowing what she wanted to do. Aurora's words skipped past Rita. Her memory had spun back to the days when Aurora locked herself away in a darkened bedroom. She only emerged to look for her lost baby or Flavio. Rita patted her chest and rolled her eyes to the heavens. *Maybe it's because the years have made her stronger, or perhaps this time she isn't grieving for the loss of a child.*

As Aurora spoke, Rita realized that she had said very little about William. Rita started heating beans and *pozole* for the noon meal. This would give her time to decide whether or not to bring up William's death. Since Aurora hadn't said anything, Rita decided that her sister would tell her in her own time.

Rita opened the door and shouted to the children. The noisy clutch of children filled the room. They ate steaming bowls of beans and hominy laced with *chili*. Luzita licked at the butter that dripped from her tortilla.

Aurora savored every bite of the simple food. "We didn't have much of this at my house," she smiled. "William preferred American food because the heat of the *chili* disagreed with his stomach."

After the dishes were washed and set to dry, Aurora's eyes began to droop. "I think I need a nap." She yawned then shook her fatigue away. "I don't know what's the matter with me. I seem to be tired all the time."

Rita wrapped her arms around her sister and encouraged her to rest as much as she could. "After all you've been through, it's no wonder you're tired." Rita expected Aurora to fold into her and wail. Instead, she just let out a long sigh.

Aurora looked into Rita's brown eyes, then put her head on her shoulder. "It's so peaceful here and I don't have to do a thing."

When Aurora called for Josefita, her daughter begged to stay for a while.

"She can stay all night if she wants to. I'll bring her home in the morning." Rita offered.

Instead of going straight back to her mother's house, Aurora walked toward the fields. She wondered why she hadn't been able to cry since the night William died. She didn't know if this numbness would ever go away. Aurora thought about what she and Rita had talked about. How long had it been since she had felt this comfortable talking to a friend? She realized that in the past eleven years, almost every word she had spoken had been crafted to impress.

Aurora walked until the sun dipped behind the mesa. She pulled her coat tight and tucked her hands into the pockets. *What will life be like in Socorro without William,* she wondered? *My sons are securely nestled into the family, but what about Josefita? Wouldn't life be better for her in Socorro?*

Aurora's head began to throb. She picked up her pace a little, thinking that Josefita seemed to be getting used to being in La Parida. *Perhaps she could grow up with Luzita the way I grew up with Rita. Aurora shook her head. I don't have to decide right away.*

To get away from the sad looks and constant hovering of her mother, Aurora decided to go into Lemitar and pick up her children from school. They obediently went with her, but after a week, Manuelito told his mother that he usually worked in his *abuelo's* store after school. Flavito helped *Tio* José in the lumberyard. "We go home with *Tio* José," Manuelito explained.

When Manuelito told his mother about their afternoon jobs his shoulders tightened. He waited for her to cry and tell him how much she needed them. But instead of fiery words of how the boys belonged to her, not *Tio* José, Aurora just nodded.

"I see; I just wanted to get out of the house for a while. It feels strange not to have something to do all the time, and I'm not ready to go back to Socorro."

"Why don't you help Papá Manuel at the store?" Flavito suggested.

Aurora groaned a little under her breath. "I don't think I'm ready for that many people."

When the doors were closed at the school house for the summer, Manuelito and Flavito ran to their Papá Manuel's store. Manuelito's muscles were strong enough to carry two sacks of flour at a time. Flavito had learned to balance slabs of lumber on his shoulder. José had taught him how to slip them into the wagon without hurting his back.

The boys rode home with *Tio* José where Mamá Telesfora had the evening meal waiting for them. When they finished eating, they sauntered to their *abuela's* house. They sat with their mother on the *porche* until exhaustion made their eyes droop.

Aurora had been back to check on her house a few times during the summer but, she couldn't bring herself to enter William's study. Without him, the high ceilings and empty rooms echoed her hollow feelings. When she left for La Parida in the fall, Aurora didn't look back.

The wheat had been taken to the grist mills. The grapes were fermenting in huge wooden barrels. The corn was being shipped back east for cattle feed. Manuelito was as tall as his Papá Manuel. Flavito could kiss the top of Aurora's head with ease.

Aurora spent her days helping her mother string *ristras* of bright red *chili*. She looked forward to Sunday, a day of rest except for making a huge meal for the family.

She gladly accepted *Tio* Manuel's invitation for her family to spend the afternoon with them. He pulled Aurora away from the kitchen and led her to the *porche*. He lit his pipe and leaned against the wall. "I've been thinking about starting a store in San Antonio. It's growing, and Conrad Hilton could use some competition."

"San Antonio—who would be in charge of the store?" Aurora pursed her lips. "Surely not José."

Manuel laughed. "I haven't decided yet. It may be a while before I can get everything together. Don't tell anybody. I'm just thinking about it." He winked at Aurora. She crossed her heart and winked back.

✳✳✳

Manuel drove his wagon into Esquipula's yard. He took the coffee that Aurora offered. "I forgot how far away San Antonio is. I bought the building around the corner from Hilton but, I can't be going back and forth to manage that store too. The wagons will be back from St. Louis in a few weeks. I was thinking of having Manuelito manage the San Antonio store someday, but in the meantime. . ." He looked up at Aurora to see if she had caught his hint. She sat sipping coffee and gazing toward the mountains.

Manuel nudged Aurora's arm. "What if you ran the store?"

Aurora sat up straight. "Me? I wouldn't know the first thing about running a mercantile."

"I've thought about this. I would send Severo to teach you about the inventory and the sales." Manuel raised his hand. "Remember how you used to love working at the store. You would move things around so people could find them easier. When the wagons came in, it was like Christmas for you."

Aurora snorted out a quick laugh. It seemed like a hundred years ago that she went to her uncle's store after Flavio died. She shook her head at the memory of trying to keep her two little boys in tow while she unloaded crates.

"San Antonio," she sighed. "Let me think about it." That night Aurora could think of nothing else.

83

José helped Manuelito load Aurora's furniture into the wagon. She had sold her house in Socorro to Mr. Eaton. She also sold the furniture that wouldn't fit into her little house in San Antonio. José and Manuelito went ahead to start the unpacking.

As Aurora drove away from her mother's house, she pulled Josefita close. Josefita turned and waved to her *abuelos*, but Aurora looked straight ahead. She was grateful for her daughter's rambling. It covered the fear nipping at her heels.

As Aurora left La Parida she thought about what life would be like for her now. At first, she had her doubts about the sleepy little village of San Antonio. The farmer's wives, in their shabby dresses, only came to town when they ran out of beans to cook.

Then Aurora remembered her life with William in Socorro. When she thought about the Ladies League, Aurora wondered who was heading the committee for the musical refinement of Socorro? Who wrote the articles for the Chieftain? She remembered the news from the Republican delegates. This was news that she had brought from William to share with her friends.

William had only served as mayor for one year, but he had become an important part of the Republican Territorial Delegation. He was a well-respected judge and everyone tipped their hats to *Señora* De Baun. She didn't realize until that moment how much she had become a part of William's life.

Then her thoughts went back to Socorro's lawlessness and the vigilantes. Aurora seemed to be caught in the middle. People that she had known all her life took their resentment out on her. Confusion had set in. She was one of them, but she was trying so hard to be *Señora* De Baun.

As the distant mesa pulled Aurora toward her new life, she sighed. She wouldn't be *Señora* De Baun, wife of the judge, any more. Now she would only be Manuel Vigil's niece, the woman who ran the mercantile. She flicked the reins and gave Josefita a hug.

✳✳✳

Aurora took her dishes out of the barrel, then meandered outside. She leaned against the porch rail of her small adobe house. Yes, San Antonio was smaller than Socorro, but growing. Here, she would only have to run the store. A smile tickled the corner of her lips. After years of being chairwoman for the Ladies League, and the *fiesta* committee, and finding people willing to donate to the Sisters of Loretto, Aurora looked forward to just being the woman who ran the mercantile.

Aurora was surprised that Josefita liked the little house they were moving into. She didn't seem to mind the low ceilings and thick adobe walls.

"This looks like Luzita's house," Josefita chirped. Then her lips formed a pout. "I miss my best friend." She pressed her hands together as if in prayer and ran to her mother. "Maybe she can come and visit this summer."

Before Aurora could answer, Josefita skipped out the back door. "This will be where we plant our garden." When she had finished scratching out the plot with a stick, she skipped back into the house. "Maybe Manuelito can help us plant our garden. He'll be here all summer, won't he?"

"I hope so." answered Aurora, "Let's make up his bed in the back room. Papá Manuel is letting him stay until the grist mill opens. Oh, and he's bringing you a surprise."

Josefita took the sheets from her mother. Together they made the bed for her brother. When Papá Manuel's wagon came into the yard the bed-making was forgotten. Josefita jumped up and down at the open door.

"Luzita, Luzita!" Josefa squealed.

Rita's daughter, Luzita, clambered down from the wagon. The girls danced around each other, filling the air with giggles. Luzita stayed with Josefita for the first week in her new house.

Together the girls explored the town. They shyly watched the other children squirming in their pews as a priest droned on in Latin. They sneaked down alleys and peeked in backyards. By the end of the week, they knew where every child lived.

Every morning the girls skipped to the store with Aurora. Each opened crate was met with wide-eyed wonder. When Manuelito poured the hard candy into jars, he gave Josefita and Luzta a big handful.

Luzita giggled and whispered to Josefita. "I'm going to marry him someday."

Josefita beamed. "He'll be the finest husband in the land."

Every evening, the girls walked home, hand-in-hand with Manuelito. He often teased Josefita and chased her around the yard. When he caught her, Manuelito swung her around in circles.

"I wish you could stay here forever," Josefita cooed.

84

Aurora looked around the mercantile and smiled. With the shelves full of sparkling new merchandise, she put the open sign in the window. At noon she peered up and down the road. Then she turned back to her empty store. She waited days for the first woman to venture into the store. Most of the women were barely polite. They had known about the Socorro Committee for Safety. Some even had relatives who were punished at its hands. Aurora heard them whispering as they went out the door. She shook her head. *The vigilantes ended years ago.*

The first time she went to Mass, she and her little blonde daughter strode toward the front of the church expecting to find a place in the first pew. The families who had claimed these prestigious seats for generations turned in unison and refused to make room for them. From then on, Aurora and Josefita slipped quietly into the back pew.

✳✳✳

When Rufina stepped into the store, it felt like sunlight had broken through the clouds. Her daughter, Maria, reached across the counter and took Aurora's hand.

"Come and have a meal with us next Sunday."

Aurora squeezed Maria's hand, grateful for a meal prepared by somebody else. Even more, she was grateful for the family that would prepare it.

Aurora had sat in the last pew so she would be one of the first to leave the church. As the rest of the parishioners poured out, Aurora and Josefita were almost to Maria's house. Aurora didn't know Maria well. As she and her mother, Rufina, shared news about the family, the ice began to melt. Aurora told Maria how grateful she was to her uncle for giving her the chance to rebuild her life. She told Maria that she had sold her home and the newspaper.

After Aurora helped Maria wash the dishes, the women sat on the front porch. Words slipped from Aurora that she had held back for months. The tears that threatened surprised her.

"Here I am again." She dabbed her eyes. "First Flavio, then William, and now trying to find a place where I belong."

Maria cocked her head. She had always thought of her cousin as strong and full of spirit. She seemed small now, looking out at her children, one of them almost grown, and a little girl yet to raise.

Rufina broke in as she handed Aurora a glass of peppermint water. "And are you starting to feel like you belong here?"

Aurora shook her head as she told Rufina how disappointed she was that the women of San Antonio had been so cold toward her. Rufina twisted her handkerchief, trying to find the right words. "You know, a lot of people got hurt at the hands of the vigilantes and there are some like José who will never accept the changes that have come to the territory." She put her hand on Aurora's arm.

Aurora began to seethe, but Rufina's gentle touch dissolved her anger. She let her breath out slowly and listened to what Rufina had to say. "

"You've been through so much, *Mija*, and now you have to make these people understand that you just want to be Manuel Vigil's niece."

Rufina snickered. "You know how hardheaded we *Hispanos* can be, but little by little they will come to know you and understand that you just want to be one of them."

After her talk with Rufina, Aurora made sure to greet all her customers warmly and ask about their families. She put her tailored satin dresses away. She found a seamstress in San Antonio to make simple dresses and several aprons to wear at the store.

❈❈❈

Now that the store was running smoothly, Aurora decided that she could leave for a day or two. *Why not take Josefita to Socorro,* Aurora thought? *It would do us both good to get away.*

On Friday afternoon, Aurora left Maria's brother, Estevan, in charge of the store. He had helped her set up the store and assured Aurora that the mercantile was in good hands.

"We'll stay at the Park Hotel this time," suggested Aurora. "We can watch the stagecoach come in and I've heard that their little restaurant is excellent."

That evening, as they sat at their table, Aurora heard her name being called. Out of the corner of her eye she glimpsed a handkerchief waving over the heads of the other customers. Then Evelyn was rushing toward her. The evening was spent catching up on all of Socorro's news.

"There's going to be a League meeting tomorrow afternoon. Please come." Evelyn begged.

Aurora found herself nodding. "I could use some ideas for San Antonio."

On Saturday afternoon Aurora dropped Josefita off at Sophie's, then slowly drove to the Dougherty residence. She hoped to slip into the Ladies League meeting without being noticed. Instead, Evelyn clapped her hands and squealed, "Oh, here's Aurora. It's been way too long." The other women surrounded her with welcoming embraces.

"I didn't know if I should attend, since I'm not living in Socorro anymore, but we always had such good ideas for the town. She giggled nervously. "San Antonio could use some good ideas."

Linda Pino lifted her teacup to toast Aurora. "Excellent idea! Perhaps you can start a branch of the League in San Antonio."

The women discussed a fundraiser to buy a new piano for the Garcia Opera House. Evelyn gave a report on the building of a boardwalk over the muddy footpath leading to the plaza. One plan after another skipped past Aurora.

When the business meeting ended, the women talked about politics and their husband's involvement. Their lives revolved around whatever their husbands were interested in. Aurora left the meeting feeling like an orphan at a family reunion.

Evelyn walked her to the door. "Stay with me while you're in Socorro."

"Maybe next time. I've already paid for our room and Josefita is so excited about staying in a new place." Aurora almost told Evelyn that she would visit Saturday evening. Then she thought about filling the hours with conversation about people she was no longer interested in.

Aurora gave Evelyn a peck on the cheek and made the excuse that she wanted to see Gloria before she went back home. Josefita always enjoyed going to Gloria's because the children could swim in the shallow creek that ran from the springs.

Josefita squirmed when she spotted Gloria's house. "I haven't seen my friends all summer. Wait 'til I tell them about the Park Hotel."

Josefita's excitement went unnoticed as Aurora's thoughts swirled around her meeting in Socorro. The closer she got to Gloria's snug adobe, the more Aurora let her thoughts of the Ladies League fall away.

Aurora received the same welcoming embrace that she had received from the League, but Gloria's hugs seemed warmer. Gloria was in the middle of storing dried corn and apologized for the mess in her kitchen. She glanced at the gunnysacks on the table. "Let's go sit outside. I can finish this tomorrow."

Aurora put her hand on Gloria's arm. "With two of us, the work will go faster." She put on an apron and rolled up her sleeves. While they worked, Aurora listened to the news of Gloria's family and laughed about the antics of her children.

With the dried corn packed snugly into gunnysacks, they sat on the porch swing, swaying back and forth. When Gloria spoke of her husband, it was about how hard he worked, and that he was now the foreman of *Señor* Padilla's ranch.

As Gloria shared the news about all their friends, Aurora just nodded and h'mmed in agreement. *I haven't seen them in years,* she thought. A little lump of regret rose in her throat. On her way back to town, Aurora felt like a tumbleweed blowing across the sands.

❋❋❋

On the way to Socorro, Josefita snuggled next to Gloria's daughter. Aurora was glad she had invited a playmate along for Josefita. Martina had never spent the night at a hotel and never expected to have such a treat. They sat on the veranda of the little hotel and watched the people in the park. Aurora eased herself into a wicker chair and tried to untangle the uneasiness tugging at her. The memories of Evelyn and Gloria tumbled together. Her hands started shaking and she gripped the arm of the chair. She began to feel lightheaded.

As bits of the little girls' chatter seeped into her troubled thoughts, Aurora heard Martina talking about the sand dunes north of Socorro.

"Can we go Mamá, please? Josefita pleaded. "I've never been there."

"The sand dunes?" answered Aurora, "I used to go there when I was your age. Why not? We'll ride out tomorrow."

Aurora's thoughts drifted to the dunes that skirted Socorro. She hadn't thought about them in years. When she was a child, her family had picnicked there. She and her cousins would chase each other across the dunes. She could see them when she was on top of a dune. When she rolled down, her cousins slipped from sight. She had to climb up to see them again.

Aurora felt like she was standing at the bottom of a dune. It was hard to trudge through the deep sand looking for the people that she belonged to. They were in plain sight for an instant, then they were gone. She thought about her years in Socorro. They were good productive years, so busy, so full of excitement.

She was surprised that when she laid her William to rest, she had breathed a sigh of relief. She had told herself that she was just exhausted from William's long illness. Sitting at the kitchen table the day after William's funeral, Aurora realized that she had felt the same relief at the end of every meeting and dinner she had hosted.

When she had gone to the meeting today, she had intended to take ideas back to San Antonio. The little town sorely needed some social advancements. Then Aurora threw her head back and laughed. She couldn't imagine the women of San Antonio sitting in their Sunday finest, drinking tea while the weeds overtook their gardens.

Aurora went to bed thinking about all the women she'd met with today. She thought about Gloria and her old friends. A low wind blew a curtain of dust across the road. As Aurora closed her eyes, La Señora's voice faintly ruffled her dreams and tumbled over her memories.

The old woman emerged from the darkness and folded her gnarled hand over a younger Aurora's. Aurora turned with a start. "Oh, it's you. I thought you were my Flavio. I can't find him."

La Señora pulled Aurora to her. "He's gone *Mija*. He's with our Blessed Mother now."

"He can't be," sobbed Aurora, "I can't live without him."

"You will. You have to, for your children." La Señora took both of Aurora's hands. "Life is like the dunes," The old woman flashed a gaptooth grin. "Sometimes they even disappear, only to reappear against the mountain. Two years later the dunes are right back where they came from."

Aurora's jaw tightened. She began to rant at the old woman. Losing Flavio had been the worst thing to happen in her young life, and La Señora was talking about sand dunes.

The old woman put her hands up and patted the air. *Calma, calma Mija*, calm down. Perhaps you need to hear this in a simple way. The eighteen-year-old dropped her head onto the woman's shriveled chest. La Señora stroked her hair. She said simply, "Life is always changing. It never stays the same for long." She began rocking Aurora. "The only way to survive, is to change with it."

✸✸✸

Riding back to San Antonio, Aurora tried to make sense of her strange dream. *The dunes*, she thought. *My life is like the sand, always shifting. My friends, old and new, are all still here. I only have to search for the ones I want to share my life with. The rest can be found behind the dunes.*

When Aurora got back to San Antonio, she joined the women who took care of the church and planned activities for the school. Instead of volunteering to head committees, she sat quietly and waited to be asked to help. She went home thinking about the advice she could give to help them improve their service work. As Aurora stepped into her house, she shook these thoughts away. She wandered from one room to another. *This is not the time to take charge of anyone else's business.* She looked down the short, dusty street. *It's time to get my own life in order.*

85

When *Tio* Manuel brought a load of flour to San Antonio, he announced that he would be taking his wagons back to St. Louis in October. "Now that Manuelito has finished school, I want to take him with me—to see what the rest of the world is like." As Manuel began to talk about all the things Manuelito would experience, Aurora knew she couldn't deny her son the adventures that she had longed for.

A little knot tightened in her stomach. She had come to depend on Manuelito to help her with the store. After work, they always sat on the *porche* watching the sun slip behind the mesa. Aurora treasured these talks, but she still cringed every time he spoke of MamáTelesfora.

Manuel began shaking his head before Aurora finished asking if Flavito could come help her. "I'll need him at the store in Lemitar while I'm gone. I'm sending Melquides Luna to build a lumber yard behind your store. He's a good worker and he can help you."

Aurora hadn't thought about Melquides in years. He had been married to Flavio's younger sister, Margarita. He was left with a small son when Margarita died bearing her second child.

Aurora wondered if Melquides would move his family to San Antonio. Manuel told her that Melquides would be staying at his brother's ranch while he worked in San Antonio. His son, Rafael, would live at the ranch too.

Aurora cocked her head as Manuel explained Melquides' family ties. She had to ask him to repeat who was related to whom. One of Manuel's daughters was Melquides' stepmother. Unlike Aurora and Flavio, Melquides and Margarita were not truly cousins.

Aurora nodded. She only had a thin memory when it came to her cousin Margarita. During the time when her life had been torn apart by Flavio's death, then repaired by William, most of her cousins existed with little notice.

❋ ❋ ❋

When the sun rose the next day, Aurora found her *Tio* Manuel sitting on her back porch. He swiped a match stick across his rough trousers making the little red match head burst into flame. He crossed his leg and lit his pipe. Lifting his face to sun, Manuel exhaled a thick ribbon of smoke that drifted toward Aurora. When the sweet-smelling smoke reached her, Aurora coughed.

Manuel started. "Oh, I didn't see you standing there."

Aurora gently closed the screen door and joined her uncle. She linked her arm with his and laid her head on his shoulder, then sighed deeply.

Aurora smiled. "This is my favorite time of the day, before I have to think, and do for everyone else. This part of the day belongs only to me."

Manuel nodded. He let the lump in his throat dissolve. *Today, just think about today. Don't sit too long or all the memories will flood back.* He felt Aurora's hand on his gnarled fingers. Manuel took a puff from his pipe. *At least I have Flavio's sons.* He kissed the top of his niece's head. . . *and Aurora is back with the family.*

She patted her *tio* on the arm. "I'll make some coffee. We'll have time for a cup before the day pushes us out."

❋ ❋ ❋

The Sunday before Manuel's wagon left for St. Louis, Aurora made a big *fiesta* for Manuelito. Josefita hung little paper lanterns from the tree branches. Aurora put a pot of beans and *chicos* in the *horno* that sat in the corner of her backyard. She wrapped a pork roast in wet burlap and placed it near the coals nestled at the bottom of the adobe oven. The heat was shut in with a little dome-shaped wooden door.

Rufina and her family were invited to join the feast. Since Melquides was going to bring a load of lumber to San Antonio, Aurora invited him and his brother's family to join them too. She had seen his sister-in-law in the store, but hadn't visited with her.

Aurora got to know her while they made stacks of tortillas. As they ate beneath the ancient cottonwood, Francisca filled Aurora in on all the town gossip. She lowered her voice as she began sharing Melquides' story. His wife, Margarita, had always seemed to be in another place. When people caught her talking to no one, she would get mad and run away. She had gotten worse after the birth of Rafael. Sometimes Melquides would find her wandering down the road looking for her house. Near the end, she didn't even know who Melquides was.

After her second baby died, she slept for more than a week, then she was gone. Francisca made the sign of the cross over her heart. "I think Melquides blamed himself. He put his hand over his face and said that he should have never made another baby. That's all he would say, over and over."

Aurora forced herself to listen. The loss of a child and a wife brought back the pain she had worked so hard to forget. And now Manuelito was going clear across the country. She turned and faced Francisca and started asking questions about her children. Anything to keep from already missing Manuelito.

✹✹✹

Aurora got a telegram letting her know that Manuelito had arrived safely. The next Monday she tightly held a second telegram. Afraid of what it might contain, she ran to Maria's. Without saying a word, she pushed the telegram into Maria's hand. Her cousin looked from the telegram to her mother, Rufina.

"I got a telegram last week. I thought I could stop worrying." Aurora shook her head. "They got to St. Louis safely. I didn't expect to hear from them until they were on their way back. Something has happened. You read it."

Maria opened the telegram slowly and read silently. She looked up at Aurora and grinned. "Nothing bad has happened. It just sounds like Manuelito wants to stay and go to school in St. Louis."

Aurora tore the telegram from Maria's hand. She read it twice, then threw it on the table. "He wants to stay in St. Louis! What is he thinking? What is my uncle thinking? Surely *Tio* Manuel won't let him stay by himself. He's only a boy!" Aurora fled from the house without saying goodbye.

The man at the telegraph office looked at Aurora with raised eyebrows and pursed lips. She stammered, dictated a few words, then changed her mind. She tapped her fingers on the counter. Finally, the man on the other side of the counter handed her a piece of paper and a pencil. "Write down what you want to say."

Aurora used up four pieces of paper before she put her thoughts together. In the end, she simply asked *Tio* Manuel to explain why he would leave Manuelito in St. Louis. The boy who delivered the telegrams was kept busy that week, sending and receiving messages from and to Aurora. It turned out that Manuelito was so impressed with the industrial college that he had begged his uncle to let him stay.

Aurora ran to the lumberyard. "You have to watch the store for a while," she said to Melquides. She rubbed her forehead. "I don't feel very good."

Melquides took her arm and started to lead her inside. Aurora twisted away.

"I'll be alright. I just need to rest for a while."

She sat in her darkened bedroom turning over the idea of losing yet another child. She would lose this one to the world. Aurora looked at the corner knickknack shelf that had been an altar for her lost baby. She threw a pillow on the floor in front of it and cried out. Folding her hand into a fist she shook it at the God who kept taking her loved ones away. Then, as her tears turned into ragged breaths, she sat against the wall, exhausted.

As the shadows crept across the room, Aurora's thoughts wandered to another place and time. She remembered how much she had wanted to go to St. Louis and how often she thought of Lemitar as a prison. She sat up and drew in a deep breath. The tightness in her chest began to ebb. *He won't be gone forever,* she thought. *Manuelito will be back, and he will see all the things that I never got to.*

Aurora tromped to the telegraph office before she changed her mind. She sent this simple message. "He can stay for now, but he has to promise to come back." Aurora ran to the store. She lifted her chin toward Melquides, a signal that he could get back to the lumberyard.

Instead of leaving, he moved close to Aurora. "You looked so worried. Is everything alright?"

Aurora flinched, surprised to hear his voice.

Señora Armijo was picking through the basket of potatoes. Aurora moved closer to Melquides and told him about Manuelito's decision to stay in St. Louis. "I've endured so many changes in my life," she sighed, ". . . and now this." She touched Melquides' sleeve. "I suppose I will have to endure this too."

When *Señora* Armijo laid her basket on the counter, Melquides touched Aurora's arm.

"You're not alone," he whispered.

Señora Armijo raised her eyebrows because it was Aurora who offered to carry her supplies to the wagon. Aurora hurried back in and moved bolts of cloth so that the fall colors were on top of the pile. She started into the store-room, then turned back and rearranged the candy jars on the counter.

When she could no longer hold her thoughts together, Aurora called Melquides to watch the store again. She ran to the end of the street and pushed open the squeaky iron gate. Aurora knocked on

Maria's front door three times, then cupped her hands and shouted, "Where are you?"

Maria was in the back yard gathering laundry from the line. Rufina sat in the shade, hemming her granddaughter's dress. When the back gate slammed shut, both women jumped. Rufina rose as quickly as her old arthritic bones allowed.

"Aurora, what's happened? You ran out so fast the other day."

"I've been worried about you," Maria said. She led them inside and poured each a glass of water. The two relatives sat at the table, folded their hands and waited.

Aurora held her glass in both hands. Then she shook her head. "At first I didn't want Manuelito to stay in St. Louis. It's so far away. How could I lose him too?" She took a gulp of water that stuck in her throat. Aurora swallowed hard and went on to tell them that she finally realized he was getting the chance that she never had.

Rufina shook her head slowly. She glanced at Maria. "I know what you're saying. When I came to live with Maria, I missed all my other children. I visit them as much as I can, but these legs will hardly lift me into the wagon. It's hard being away from them, but I thank God that they're all well."

86

When Manuel returned from St. Louis, Aurora made the long journey to La Parida. She knew Flavito wanted to finish his last year of school at Lemitar, but she tried again to get him to help her with the store.

Aurora pushed past the crates stacked in the storeroom. *Perhaps I can make him see how much it would mean to have him near me.*

When Aurora rushed toward him with her arms out, Flavito put his hands up.

"I'm all dirty, Mamá." He surveyed the room. "Papá Manuel wants these crates unloaded by tomorrow."

Aurora took a step backwards. "Oh, I know how busy it is this time of year, but I thought this would be a good place to talk to you alone. *Tio* said that you wanted to finish school in Lemitar, but I could really use your help in San Antonio." She let her words fall, and leaned against the door. "So, whose idea is it for you to stay here?"

Flavito looked at the floor and took a deep breath. "Papá Manuel is getting old. He really does need my help." He lifted a small crate onto the battered wooden table. "I have all these crates to unpack," he snapped. Then he lifted his chin. "Papá Manuel said I could go with him to St. Louis next year."

"You too? You're going to leave me too?" Aurora's raised voice came out as a whine.

Flavito pushed back his hat. He could feel the heat rising from his throat. He clamped his jaw so the words he wanted to say wouldn't escape.

"It doesn't mean that I'm going to stay," he mumbled. "Why shouldn't I have a chance to see St. Louis too?"

Aurora frantically looked for a chair to drop into. Not seeing one, she brushed off a barrel and eased herself onto it. She closed her eyes and forced out her words.

"Of course, you should go and you will. I was just surprised that your brother stayed in St. Louis. I was hoping you would want to come live with Josefita and me and help me at the store."

Flavito shrugged and dug into another crate. "All my friends are here. I only have one more year to finish school." He neglected to say that he didn't want to leave his *abuelos* or Mamá Telesfora. "Maybe next year I can go help you in San Antonio."

Aurora stood and unclenched her fists. She nodded and reached up to tuck in the curls that had fallen across his forehead. She leaned in and gave her son a kiss on the cheek. He took what was offered, but returned nothing.

✳✳✳

The chilly autumn winds followed Aurora home. When she got to San Antonio, she had little time to dwell on the sting she had felt when Flavito turned away from her so quickly.

With both sons beyond her reach, Aurora's attention turned to Josefita. She asked Maria If her oldest daughter could prepare supper and keep Josefita company after school. Dolores was only four years older than Josefita, but she'd been at her mother's elbow since she could toddle.

Josefita had been going to the store after school, but now that the cold winds blew from the north, Aurora didn't want her walking to the store and then all the way home alone. Instead, Dolores walked home with Josefita. Most days Dolores' little sister, Patricia, walked with them.

While Dolores stoked the fires back to life and began making the evening meals, the two little girls set up displays in their pretend store. When they tired of playing and giggling about the boys in their class, they sat and listened to Dolores. They gazed up at her, dreamy-eyed, as she told them about the dances she went to.

With their faces cupped in their hands, Josefita and Patricia dreamed about the day they would dance too. After Dolores' stories, Josefita's dolls were dressed in gowns and waltzed around the room.

One afternoon Josefita put her finger to her lips and invited Patricia to follow her into the back room. The girls tiptoed past the kitchen while Dolores chopped potatoes. Patricia's mouth dropped open when Josefita opened a trunk and drew out her mother's gowns.

Josefita whispered. "Let's try them on." She slipped on her mother's green satin gown. It almost fit her. She was only twelve years old, but she was as tall as her mother.

"This is the gown she wore when she went to Santa Fe. Then she wore it to a ball in Socorro. I was just a little girl, but I remember how beautiful she looked."

The girls jumped when they heard the front door open. Patricia scrambled out of her dress. She was folding it when Aurora stepped

364

into the room. Josefita was struggling with the buttons on her gown, so when Aurora walked into the bedroom, she found her daughter dressed in her Santa Fe finest.

"I'm sorry Mamá. We were very careful with your things. I just wanted to show Patricia your beautiful dresses." Josefita began backing up, waiting for her mother's wrath.

Instead of a reprimand, Josefita heard her mother laughing. "Look at you. It almost fits you. I've been so busy that I didn't realize how much you've grown."

Aurora had put her memories of Santa Fe away in her trunk. Her gowns, hats, and fine kid gloves were useless in San Antonio. As Aurora helped Dolores set the table, she laughed at the thoughts of her satin and lace. *Where am I going to wear them. . . to the San Antonio fiesta? I had almost forgotten they were here.* She went out to the porch, tucked a strand of hair back into her bun, and listened for the crickets.

Melquides

Aurora closed up early, knowing that no one would come to the store in this storm. She was anxious to get home because *Señora* Trujillo said the school had closed early. Bundled against the snow, she almost didn't notice Melquides. Both of them were holding onto their hats. Their shoulders were hunched against the wind, so when they bumped into each other, it startled them. They both mumbled apologies as they hurried away.

Aurora took a few steps toward the house, then turned. "Melquides!" she called. "You're going to have to go all the way to your brother's ranch? I don't know if you'll even be able to see the road. Why don't you have supper with us, then you can stay in the back room of the store."

At first Melquides refused. He didn't want his family to worry, but his hands were so cold that he didn't know if he could hold onto the wagon's reins.

"Surely they know that you'll stay in town until the snow stops falling. You can ride one of *Tio*'s horses to the ranch as soon as the weather settles down."

Melquides threw his hands up in surrender. Arm-in-arm they pushed towards Aurora's. Josefita ran to her as she came through the door. She told her mother how the wind had blown the school doors open and the teacher couldn't keep enough wood in the stove to warm the school room.

"She sent us all home and took Selvia Gallegos home with her because Selvia lives so far away. The ones that live on ranches were sent to stay with relatives in town."

Aurora turned to Melquides. "See, I told you that your family would expect you to stay in town."

Melquides huddled next to the stove. Josefita tugged at her mother's sleeve and asked if Melquides was going to stay with them. Aurora assured her that this distant relative was only going to stay for supper.

"Be polite, Melquides was married to one of my cousins. He's family."

The wind rattled the windows and Aurora stuffed rags under the door to keep the snow from drifting into the room. Every time

Melquides thought about leaving, Aurora wiped the frost from the window and looked out. The snow was still blowing sideways.

"You can't go out in this. You can sleep in Josefita's room. She'll sleep with me."

After dinner Aurora poured Melquides another cup of coffee and they begin weaving memories together. He started with "Do you remember Juanito Vaiza?"

Aurora couldn't quite remember, but she thought he was one of the boys that used to throw rocks at the girls.

Melquides chided. "We used to hide from you because you could throw rocks better than the boys."

They laughed and told more stories about swimming in the canals and making forts underneath the mesquite bushes.

Aurora's laughter suddenly halted. She dropped her eyes to the floor. "William never understood my stories. Sometimes I would catch him looking at my family with the curiosity of a child poking at a horny toad."

Melquides nodded. He told Aurora that he had worked with men like that. "They all came from the South. For them, coming to New Mexico was like crossing an ocean. They didn't even understand our language."

Aurora looked down at the table. *An ocean,* she thought, *that's what it was like sometimes with William, tossing about in an ocean.*

Melquides took her silence for sadness. Their laughter faded as they began to remember the ones they had lost. The tightness in Aurora's shoulders unknotted. She sat back in her chair. Sharing with someone who felt the same depth of pain was like being wrapped in a favorite old blanket. As they talked, some of the sadness melted away from both of them. They knew, that with each other, their pain was understood.

❄❄❄

In the morning, the storm had blown itself out, but San Antonio was a white blanket. Melquides shoveled Aurora's walk, then trudged to the store. "I'll open up, but I doubt that you'll be busy today."

Aurora was grateful that she could spend the morning with Josefita in the warmth of their adobe. They put their chairs in front of the kitchen stove. Curled up like sleeping kittens, they sipped hot *atole,* and listened to the crackling fire.

After their noon meal, Aurora took Josefita to the store with her.

She stacked sugar tins and Josefita picked out fabric for another dress.

Melquides pushed the door open with his shoulder. The wood he brought in was used to bring the stove back to life. Then they sat in the chairs that were usually occupied by San Antonio's elders. While eating the lunch that Aurora had brought, Melquides explained that he had tried to get to his brother's ranch, but the snow drifts were higher than his horse.

"It looks like I'm going to spend another night in town. I'll open the door to the back room so it'll warm up."

Aurora softly laid her hand on his arm. "Of course, you'll eat with us tonight."

That evening they talked about all the people they knew, the things they did as children, and the way things had changed. Melquides raised his eyebrows, "Especially in Socorro, and you were part of all that."

Josefita rolled her eyes and retreated to her room. She sat cross legged on her bed, where she started the painstaking task of crocheting a scarf for Patricia. Once in a while she shouted, "Things haven't changed in San Antonio." She made sure her mother knew that she thought Socorro was so much more modern.

Melquides' green eyes danced in the firelight. Without a thought, he brushed his mustache with his fingertips. Then he looked at Aurora, drew her near, and gave her a whisper of a kiss. Aurora's eyes flared, then softened. Her small hand lifted, then settled over his.

The celebration of the *Santo Niño* was over and the Christmas decorations put away. With the coming of the new year, the weather still held its grip on the village.

Josefita had grown sullen as the dreary cloak of winter settled over her. Dolores no longer walked her home. The teenager had to help her mother with the new baby. Neither Maria nor Aurora thought it would be a good idea for Patricia and Josefita to be alone at Aurora's house.

Patricia found new playmates and Josefita shuffled home alone after school. Aurora had arranged for her neighbor, Salia, to stoke the fires and check on Josefita often.

One evening Aurora found Josefita sitting in front of the window.

"I hate this dark old house. I miss my big room and all my friends."

Aurora had to agree that the little adobe, with its whitewashed walls, was a drab substitute for her bright, roomy house on McCutcheon Street.

"But I thought you liked it here." Aurora questioned. "Where is all this coming from?"

Josefita crossed her arms and stuck out her lower lip. "Patricia doesn't like me anymore. What if I go to school in Socorro? I can stay at the Sisters' boarding school."

Aurora's heart leaped into her throat. She shook her head. "No, absolutely not! You're staying here with me."

Josefita ran to her room and slammed the door. Aurora pulled the curtain back and gazed at the brooding sky. *Perhaps a new room for Josefita would keep her by my side.*

Aurora tapped on Joséfita's door and walked in. "What about a big new room just for you?"

Josefita sat up. Sitting next to her on the bed, Aurora told Josefita that the new room could be built behind the kitchen.

"We would still have a little *plazita* and plenty of room left for your garden. You can help me plan it." Aurora saw the light come back into her Josefita's eyes.

❋❋❋

After the snow had melted away, Melquides and Aurora sat shoulder-to-shoulder drawing the plans for the new room. The twelve-year-old Josefita skipped to the backyard with Melquides. She held a measuring tape and had the final say about how big her room would be.

Construction began the next month. Josefita was disappointed when construction stopped until more adobe bricks were made. Aurora put her arm around Josefita and reminded her that it would give them time to order the wallpaper and fabric for the drapes.

Aurora kissed the top of Josefita's head. "Hopefully your room will be done by the time Manuelito returns this summer."

When the adobes were dry, the men began working again, putting up walls and windows. Every few days Melquides came to check on their progress. Over cups of coffee, he and Aurora discussed measurements, shelves, doors and windows.

When the builders left for the day, Melquides moved closer to Aurora. The conversation shifted to their families and laughter was woven into their stories.

As soon as word came that the roads were dry, Aurora and Josefita made the long journey to Lemitar. Josefita's eyes grew wide as she poured over the wallpaper books at her grandfather's store. She picked out a buttery yellow paper with splashes of pink flowers and bumblebees.

Aurora convinced Josefita that she didn't need new furniture. They would take Josefita's things out of storage and everything would look beautiful in her new room.

❋❋❋

The next week Josefita slipped into the kitchen. When she heard that Melquides was going to Socorro for lumber to make the rafters, she gave her mother a squeeze and smiled at Melquides.

"Can I go with him, please? I haven't been to Socorro in . . . ." Josefita rolled her eyes and tapped her chin. "I can't remember the last time I was in Socorro." She draped herself over Aurora.

Melquides shrugged. "Why not? Me and Rafael are spending the night with my sister. I can take Josefita to Gloria's."

Josefita shot up. "Gloria's? Well no. I was thinking of staying with Sophie. I haven't seen her baby since she was a newborn."

Aurora and Melquides exchanged glances. She reached for his hand underneath the table. As he squeezed it, Aurora nodded her approval. Aurora sent a note to Sophie asking if Josefita could stay with her until Monday.

✳✳✳

Sophie was feeding her baby when Josefita skipped through the kitchen door. She set her basket on the table, then told Sophie that she wanted to take a walk around Socorro.

Josefita walked past the park then stole away to the cemetery. She brushed the dust off her daddy's headstone. After biting back tears, Josefita put her little Santa Fe doll on his grave.

Still wanting to be alone, Josefita ran to McCutcheon Street. She thought seeing her house would make her happy. Instead, the memories that flooded over her brought only sorrow. She remembered how her father would toss her in the air when he got home. She thought about how they walked into church, arm-in-arm, with William leading his family procession. She always got the best seat at the end of the pew.

At night, when he wasn't too tired, her daddy read to her. Once, when he went to Santa Fe, he brought her back that doll with golden curls and a silk gown. He said it looked just like her. "My princess." That's what he used to call her.

Josefita sat at the edge of the sidewalk and let her tears drop on to the sandy road. Then she remembered how worried Sophie got when she couldn't find her. She pushed herself up, but instead of running back to Sophie's, Josefita dragged a stick along the dirt, as she trudged away from her home.

When Sophie saw Josefita's tear-stained face, she put away her reprimand. She drew Josefita close. "Did you go see your house?"

Josefita shrugged. In a muffled voice, she cried, "I'll never go back! My daddy isn't there anymore."

Sophie lifted Josefita onto her lap and rocked her like she did when she was a baby. She searched in vain for words that would take Josefita's pain away. Sophie wiped her tears away and kissed her cheek.

"I know something that will cheer you up. I heard that the train from St. Louis will be coming in next week. Guess who'll be on it?"

Josefita hopped off Sophie's lap and danced around the room. "Manuelito, my big brother is coming home! Does Mamá know? Wait till I tell her!"

The train rolled into Socorro on Saturday afternoon and Aurora was there to meet it. She wasn't surprised that Telesfora and José were there too. They waved the telegram that Manuelito had sent them.

Telesfora hugged Aurora. "Our boy is coming home!"

Aurora stiffened and glared at Telesfora, but her cousin didn't notice.

Manuel had sent word to Aurora with Melquides. The note contained the day and time of Manuelito's arrival. It announced that the whole family was getting together Sunday afternoon at Esquipula's house.

Aurora pulled Telesfora aside. "I thought he could spend the night with me in San Antonio. I'm sure he's tired from his trip. We'll go to La Parida in the morning."

Telesfora flinched as if she'd been hit with a branch. She looked at José.

"We have his room ready." José grumbled. "Telesfora even embroidered new pillow covers."

Aurora put her chin in the air. "We'll be there tomorrow. I haven't seen my son in over a year. Is it too much to ask to let me spend an evening with him?"

Telesfora's jaw tightened. *I'll see Manuelito this afternoon and I'll have him for the rest of the summer. I guess I can give him up for one evening.* She put her hand on José's arm. He must have been reading her thoughts, because he just shrugged. They sat on the train station porch craning to spot Manuelito.

When the slender young man stepped off the train, his relatives looked past him. It wasn't until he took off his hat and shouted Mamá, that everyone recognized him. They all rushed toward him, surrounded him with hugs and kisses.

When Manuelito saw Josefita, he opened his mouth wide and glanced at his mother.

"And who is this beautiful young lady?"

Josefita slapped at her big brother and giggled, "You know who I am."

He picked her up slowly, as if her weight was too much for him.

When she started squirming, he twirled her around.

The family drove their buggies up the street to the Grand Hotel. Over coffee and pastries, Manuelito was pelted with questions. He told them about the tall buildings and so many buggies in the street that it was dangerous to cross.

He told them about the university, and how he felt like a cactus in a mountain forest. When everyone fell silent and turned to him, he said, "You know, like I didn't belong."

Manuelito sighed and took another sip of coffee. *Sometimes I felt the same way when Papá William brought his friends to our house.*

Aurora told him about Joséfita's new room. "We'll have three bedrooms. You can stay with us while you're working at the store in San Antonio."

"But it isn't finished." Telesfora looked at Aurora as she placed her hand on Manuelito's.

Aurora hugged her son. "It's almost finished. Until it is, I can sleep with Josefita and give him my room."

Everyone looked at Manuelito. He raised his hands and shrugged. "We'll have to see what my *abuelo* has to say.

With that, Telesfora and José drove their empty buggy back to La Parida. Manuelito took the reins from Aurora and headed for San Antonio. On the way, he told Aurora of his plans to go back and finish school. He told her that in only two more years he could earn an engineering degree. "Maybe you and Josefita can come and see me while I'm there."

✹ ✹ ✹

After Mass, aunts, uncles, cousins, and friends all came to see Manuelito. The *fiesta* went on until the sun set behind the mesa. People were stuffed into every room, even spilling onto the porch. They slept on mattresses filled with straw. Two of the older boys slept in the bed of a wagon.

Monday's work was put aside and the prodigal son was celebrated until late that afternoon. With all his stories told and memories recounted, everyone reluctantly agreed that it was time to go back to their homes.

Aurora stayed the rest of the week and Manuelito went back and forth between Telesfora and his *Abuela* Josefa's house. Every time Aurora asked him if he was ready to go to San Antonio, he studied the floor.

"Papá Manuel has a lot for me to do in Lemitar. Besides, I want to spend some time with Flavito."

Finally, on Friday, Manuelito told his mother that he would take a load of lumber to San Antonio the following Monday. His grandfather told him he could stay and help Melquides in the lumberyard for a week. Manuel wanted Manuelito to get to know the business, then he needed him back at the store in Lemitar.

"It's only for two or three weeks, Mamá. Then I can spend more time with you."

Even though the sun followed her to San Antonio, Aurora shivered. *Telesfora has turned them all against me. Just because I live so far away, she thinks she can keep Manuelito to herself.*

Aurora was glad that the store was busy. It kept her from seething about the family keeping her son. She walked home with her head down. People on the street called out to her, but she didn't look out from under her umbrella. By the time she stepped through the front door, she was convinced that her family was plotting against her.

Aurora paced in the backyard and tried to sort out her thoughts. Surely *Tio* Manuel would understand how much she missed her son. As soon as she had rehearsed what she was going to say, Aurora reminded herself of what William used to tell her. "You make too much of everything." She remembered throwing a pillow at him when he dared to compare her to José.

Aurora jumped when the back gate creaked open. She threw her arms around Melquides and poured out her worries. He listened, then held her at arm's length.

"It's just for a few days," he said. "Manuel needs him to help José start up the grist mill. With all the new houses being built around here, surely Manuelito will spend the summer helping me at the lumberyard."

Aurora stuffed her hands into her pockets and stepped into the kitchen. As she poked slivers of wood into the cook stove she reminded herself that Manuelito would be with her most of the summer. The corners of her mouth finally turned up.

She rested her arm on Melquides, "Maybe me and Josefita can go back with him to St. Louis next fall."

The knock at the front door sent Josefita flying. Melquides stood grinning, with his hat in his hand. "I have a surprise for you." He disappeared for a moment and reappeared with a large wooden crate.

Josefita covered her mouth and started jumping up and down. "It's the wallpaper, Mamá. It's here, it's here!"

The paper was carefully rolled out and inspected. Then Melquides announced that he had another surprise. Josefita tore the string away from bundles of brown paper to reveal the beautiful rose-colored brocade for her curtains.

Aurora and Josefita made plans to go to Socorro the next day. "I'll have *Señora* Lopez start on the drapes. Oh, and I have to make arrangements with Mr. McFarlin." Aurora tugged on Josefita's braid. "He wallpapered our house in Socorro."

They hurried to the new room and took measurements for the curtains. "We can spend the night at Gloria's," Aurora sang to Josefita.

Gloria's? Why don't we stay at the Grand?" Josefita was bouncing on her tippy toes.

"Why not?" answered Aurora. "We have something to celebrate. The house will be finished before we know it."

It was a busy two days in Socorro. It took that long to arrange for Mr. McFarlin to work Aurora into his schedule. Then she had to find men to deliver the furniture. The next few weeks would be a flurry of finish work.

Aurora sent word that she needed Manuelito to help her at the store. She had to be at her house to make sure everything was done right.

It was Flavito who showed up with a wagon load of lumber. He said he would stay at Melquides' brother's ranch since there was so much going on in his mother's house. The furniture that Aurora brought back from Socorro was shoved into every nook and cranny.

"There are still two beds. You can sleep in Josefita's room. She can sleep with me."

When Flavito saw the hopeful look in his mother's eyes he decided to stay. *It will only be for a few days. Then I'll be back with the family in Lemitar.*

✳✳✳

With the next load of lumber came Manuelito. Melquides taught him how to grade the lumber and stack it so it wouldn't bow with the changes of the weather.

Each day Aurora rushed home from the store at noon to make sure everything was built to order. By the time the evening meal was cleared away and the little family sat on the porch, Aurora was exhausted. She often fell asleep with her head on Manuelito's shoulder.

Josefita hopped off of her chair "I've been talking to Mamá. Maybe we can go back with you to St. Louis." Josefita nudged her dozing mother. "Can we go back with Manuelito? Please Mommy please!"

Aurora half opened her eyes. "We'll see." she muttered.

She squeezed Manuelito's shoulder. "I've started moving the furniture into the new room. It will be done next week. Then we can really have a good visit."

She pulled herself up, brushed a bit of sawdust off Manuelito's sleeve, and waved for Josefita to come inside. "You'll see, things will slow down soon," Aurora promised.

Josefita's room was finished in early July and Aurora invited the family to see the cozy new room. She had made sure the old shade tree behind the house was unharmed during the construction. Tables were set in the backyard and everyone brought their favorite food.

Flavito had learned to play the guitar. With his cousin Adolfo, he played familiar *rancheritas*. Aurora's aunt, Yrinea, brought her daughter, Teresa. Dreamy-eyed, Teresa sat staring at Flavito while he strummed his guitar.

With Josefita's room finished, Aurora finally tried to enjoy her son's visit. After the evening meal, Aurora sat with her arm linked in his. As the sun colored the mesa scarlet, Aurora closed her eyes and memorized Manuelito's voice. She had to keep reminding herself that this was her son talking, not some stranger from back East.

His words painted exciting pictures of St. Louis. Aurora could almost hear the trolley cars. In her dreams, she looked up and up to the tops of buildings that seemed to touch the sky. But every morning Aurora woke with a start. With another day came the reminder that summer was slipping away. As she poured Manuelito his coffee, she wished she could turn back the calendar.

❋❋❋

Manuelito had been recruited to help Melquides deliver lumber. With Melquides so busy in the lumberyard, Aurora couldn't call on him to help in the store. The mercantile was busier than ever. Many people were buying a little extra in case next winter was as harsh as the last.

Melquides' coffee cup sat unused on the kitchen shelf. By the time he got back from his deliveries, he went straight to the ranch. There were fields to be watered and cattle to be fed.

Melquides was grateful that the farm was only four miles north of town. He could be in town at sunrise to help Manuelito load the wagon, then go back to the farm by noon to close the gates in the ditches.

Manuelito delivered lumber to all the ranches between San Antonio and Socorro. Often, he wouldn't come home until his supper was cold and dry. Aurora picked at her food. With her head in her hands, she glanced at the empty chair where Manuelito usually sat. *Will things ever slow down around here?*

On the rare days when Melquides and Manuelito were both at the store, Aurora sat and shared her noon meal with them. Melquides talked about his son and his farm. He said that with the money he earned at the lumberyard he had planned on buying land closer to the river so it would be easier to water his crops. "Now I don't know," he mumbled.

Melquides gulped down a long drink of water. He moved closer and let Aurora in on a secret. Manuel was going to build another lumberyard in Socorro and he wanted Melquides to be in charge of it.

"I told him I would have to think about it. I talked my brother into planting more this year because I would be there to help him. And what about Rafael? He's been with my brother and his wife since Margarita died. If I leave him at the farm, I'll be so far away. If I take him to Socorro, who will take care of him?"

Melquides leaned forward. He put his elbow on his knees and bent his head. He drew in a slow breath and turned to Aurora. "You've had so many changes in your life, and you seem to go through them so easily. Help me decide what to do."

Aurora snorted out a little laugh and shook her head. She couldn't believe this was how people saw her. "Don't you remember how I was after Flavio died? I wasn't able to put one foot in front of the other for almost a year."

"I guess I didn't know too much about that." Melquides touched Aurora's arm. "I was living in Los Lunas at the time."

Melquides sat back. He patted Aurora's arm then whispered, "That was such a long time ago, I'd forgotten. But you went on and married such a big man in Socorro. You had a house built. Now you're running the store. I can't even decide if I should move to Socorro."

Aurora reminded him that summer was almost over and the farm work would soon slow down. She listed all the relatives who lived in Socorro. "I know you can find someone to care for Rafael. "San Antonio is only twelve miles away. You can be at the farm every Saturday. Besides, it will take a while to buy the land and set up the lumberyard. You have time to decide."

Melquides looked past the distant hills. He smiled and nodded. He pressed his hand in hers. Aurora was close enough to see the hazel green eyes that ran through so many families in New Mexico.

She leaned against the door as Melquides left. The dust was blowing down the main street of San Antonio. *Manuelito will be leaving in a few weeks, and if Melquides moves, I'll be all alone again.* A little dust devil swirled through Aurora's mind. *When had Melquides become such an important part of my life?*

91

The week before Manuelito left for St. Louis, Telesfora spent every day in the kitchen. She made all his favorite foods. Telesfora even made a cake from a recipe she had found in the newspaper. She invited the whole family to her house for his good-by dinner.

Telesfora kept dabbing her eyes and staring at Manuelito as if she would never see him again. When the family sat down to eat, Aurora rushed to sit next to her son. She glared at José. He squeezed into a space on the other side of Telesfora.

Aurora had finally started getting to know her son through his adventures and ambitions. Now he was going back to the city she had only dreamed about. Aurora's chest tightened every time she looked at him. Then La Señora's words came back to her. "Everything changes."

Every time Aurora caught Josefita's eyes the twelve-year-old dramatically turned to avoid looking at her mother. Josefita brooded the entire afternoon.

Aurora had expected to travel back with Manuelito, but running the store held her tight. When Aurora told her daughter that they weren't going, Josefita wailed and ran down the street.

"Next spring will be a better time to go. I won't be so busy then." Aurora pleaded.

Josefita twisted her lips into a wad and screamed, "You promised!"

Manuelito rode to the train station with his mother and sister. They had given up trying to pacify Josefita. They rode to the station with Aurora's arm woven into her son's. While they were waiting for the train, Manuelito stood in the little cluster with his Mamá Telesfora, *Tio* José, and his brother Flavito. Telesfora held his hand until the train came into sight. Manuelito hugged everyone before getting on the train. Aurora was the last in line.

Aurora and Josefita rode back to San Antonio in cold silence. Aurora didn't have time to appease her wounded daughter. She could barely keep up with the store and the sales at the lumberyard.

Last year had been good for the farmers. Corrals and hay sheds were going up on their farms. The same wagon that brought lumber to San Antonio took the farmer's wheat to Manuel's grist mill in

Socorro. Then some of the flour was brought back and stored in the rooms behind the mercantile. Aurora learned how to put all of these transactions in the ledger book. She hired Maria's brother, Estevan, to work behind the counter while she bent over the books in the back room.

✳✳✳

When Manuel's wagons brought crates of new treasures, the rift between mother and daughter softened. Josefita opened crates of fine cloth. Ribbons and lace were slowly drawn out and brushed against Joséfita's cheek. Glassware and china were carefully passed to Aurora. Aurora put them on the table and laughed.

"I still get excited when the wagons come. I wasn't much older than you when I helped *Tío* Manuel. I know you're disappointed that we didn't go with Manuelito. I always wanted to see St. Louis too. I promise we'll go get your brother next spring."

✳✳✳

Aurora invited Melquides to stay for supper when he came in late and had deliveries to make the next day. They talked about lumber orders and all the new merchandise the store had to offer. Josefita was a big part of the conversation.

When Manuelito's letters were read, the suppertime conversation revolved around the huge stores in St. Louis.

"I bet what we have in San Antonio would fit in one corner of those big stores." Josefita's eyes danced with imagination.

Melquides shook his head. "I don't think I want to go to a place with so many people."

Aurora and Josefita arched their eyebrows in unison. Aurora sat back. "Next spring we'll see it all for ourselves."

By Christmas, Melquides was a regular guest at Aurora's table. Rafael stayed with Aurora when the weather kept him from going back to the farm. By the time the snow drifts had melted, Rafael was helping Melquides every day after school. The fourteen-year-old was almost as tall as Melquides. With muscles hardened on the farm, Rafael was given the task of carrying the lighter lumber to the wagon. His eyes lit up every time Melquides gave him a pat on the back.

As the children got to know each other, Josefita learned the meaning of all those mysterious Spanish words. With Rafael's help, she practiced her Spanish at the store.

381

As Aurora got to know her customers, she became part of the community. With *Señora* Garcia's help, she organized a benefit dance to raise money for new altar linens. She raised her hand at the Fiesta Committee meetings.

Aurora rearranged her storeroom and invited the women to meet there and discuss more of their ideas. She cleared her throat and sauntered to the middle of the room. Looking around the room, she began to share some of her own ideas.

Aurora had learned from the mistakes the League had made in Socorro. Instead of storming into the mayor's office with demands, the women of San Antonio put their concerns in writing and submitted them. Because of their efforts, new city ordinances were adopted. The people of San Antonio began to feel safer as laws were enforced when rowdy cowboys got out of hand.

When Aurora met with the mayor, she told him about her first-hand experience with the vigilantes in Socorro. "If the sheriff does his job, this won't happen in San Antonio," she said.

The mayor had been ta judge when Socorro was being cleaned up. He assured Aurora that no matter who was on the other side of the law, they would be prosecuted fairly.

Melquides never tired of hearing about what Aurora was doing for San Antonio. He even became a sworn deputy, willing to join a posse if necessary.

Melquides tapped on the back door, then peered inside. He pushed the door shut before the dust swept into the room. When Aurora saw that her visitor was Melquides, her hand automatically flew to her hair. She tucked a curl behind her ear. As she invited him to sit, her fingers touched his arm.

Grinning, he rubbed his hands together. "Good news. . . Manuel said the building of the lumberyard in Socorro won't start until next fall." Melquides twisted the brim of his hat. "I've been wondering about my decision to move to Socorro. Now I have time to make up my mind."

As winter began to loosen its grip, Melquides worked long hours at the lumberyard. Every evening he listened to Aurora read Manuelito's letters. She read the letters with more and more excitement. He would be home in two more months. Josefita wouldn't let her mother forget her promise.

92

As the sun rose above the mountains, the family met Manuelito at the station. This time, Aurora just smiled when Manuel led Manuelito to his buggy. Melquides and Aurora joined the little caravan to La Parida where a banquet was waiting for him. As they bounced along behind Manuel's buggy, a smile kissed Aurora's lips. All three of her children were squeezed into the back seat of their grandfather's buggy. She heard their laughter, and from time to time, snippets of their conversation. *Only one more year and we'll all be together again.*

Arm-in-arm Aurora walked with her son toward Manuel's house. Telesfora and José kept pace just behind them.

Manuelito waved his free hand and talked about all the things he had learned.

"By this time next year, I'll be an engineer," he smiled.

Aurora held his hand. "And you'll be home for good. Tomorrow we'll ride to San Antonio."

Manuelito's smile faded. "I promised Papá Manuel and Papá Esquipula that I would help them."

Aurora dropped his hand and hurried toward the house. Manuelito caught up to her.

"Wait Mamá! Papá Manuel promised that I would spend all next month with you."

Aurora wiped the dampness from her cheeks. "I wish San Antonio wasn't so far away."

Estella's family had been invited to share the homecoming meal. Aurora turned from Manuelito when Estella called to her. When she looked back, he was wrapped in Telesfora's arms.

Estella and Aurora helped Rita clear the table. After the dishes were put away, they sat in the shade of the *plazita*.

"I wish you would come back to Lemitar," said Estella. "San Antonio is too far away."

Rita broke in. "Oh, but Aurora wanted a life of her own. I don't know if she could have that in Lemitar."

A tightness in Aurora's chest erased her smile. "A life of my own? I guess I got what I wanted." She looked back toward Manuelito. "Today, with all my children with me, this is the only life I want."

Rita put her arm around her sister's shoulder. "You can always come back." She patted her swollen middle. "You know I'll always be here," Rita giggled. "Where else would I go?"

Aurora rubbed Rita's tummy. "It was hard when I thought I had lost Manuelito, but I really didn't." Aurora sighed. "He came back, and next year he'll be back for good." Aurora gave her sister a squeeze and the conversation turned to her life in San Antonio.

✳ ✳ ✳

As the morning sun skimmed the sagebrush, Melquides drove the buggy into Esquipula's yard. He warmed up with a cup of coffee while he waited for Aurora to gather her belongings. She wasn't used to getting up so early, but she knew they had to escape the noon day heat. Riding down the rutted road, their shoulders bumped together. Melquides leaned into Aurora and laughed. She nudged back and laughed with him.

They laughed at José who drank too much wine, and *Tia* Guadalupe crying over her scorched tortillas, and Teresa's dreamy-eyed gaze at Flavito. Melquides and Aurora exchanged glances. He slipped his hand over hers.

As they reached Escondida, Aurora's thoughts turned to another time of laughter. She remembered Snake Ranch with Flavio, laughing and talking about what their lives would hold. Instead of the sadness she expected, Aurora realized that she hadn't felt this happy in many, many years.

The next morning Aurora hurried to the store so Estevan could go back to his fields. She only crossed paths with Manuelito when he delivered lumber to San Antonio. She got to keep him to herself for an evening, then it was back to Lemitar.

On his next visit, Manuelito stood at the back door until *Señora* Baca gathered her packages and left. Waiting until his mother was stocking the shelf behind her, Manuelito spoke quickly. "Mamá, *lo siento*, I have to help Papá Manuel."

Aurora turned and faced her son. "What do you mean you have to spend your last week in Lemitar?"

"Mamá, the wheat crop is the biggest in years. Papa Manuel is keeping the mill going day and night. I have to help." Manuelito gave his mother a soft kiss on the cheek. He rushed out of the store without looking back. He didn't want to see that her disappointment had turned her to stone.

The next day Estevan was pulled away to help Manuelito at the grist mill. He assured Aurora that it would only be for a few days.

Without Estevan's help, Aurora was tied to the store. Her hands shook as she scribbled a note to Manuel. She wrote that Josefita would be heartbroken if she didn't get to go to St. Louis.

"Can't you send someone to run the store? It would only be for three weeks."

Manuel sent Aurora a note saying he had been thinking about sending Severo and his wife to St. Louis.

"This would be a good opportunity for him to see where the merchandise comes from. He would also get to meet the sellers. If they agree to go, Josefita could go with them. Don't forget, Flavito is going too. He can help take care of his sister."

Aurora burst through the back door and flung the wadded note across the yard. *He knows I've always wanted to go. What am I, just one of his workers?*

It was too late to ride to La Parida that day, but Aurora planned to make the journey first thing Sunday morning. There had to be someone who could help. Aurora paced. In the end, she closed up the store early and trotted home. With hunched shoulders and downcast eyes, she slipped into her backyard. She hoped Josefita was playing with her friends. She needed time to think.

Her disappointment turned into hot rage. *Maybe I can't go now, but this won't happen again! When Manuelito comes back next spring, Estevan will be ready to mind the store by himself. I'll bring my boy home for good.* When her hands stopped shaking, Aurora went inside.

Aurora chose her words carefully. First, she told Josefita that *Tío* Severo and his wife were going to St. Louis. She explained that with Estevan gone it would be impossible for her to go this time. Josefita started winding up for a rant. Aurora grabbed her arms and blurted, "Wait, you don't understand! You'll still get to go with your *tíos* and brother. Best of all, I'm going back when Manuelito comes home in the spring and you can go again."

Josefita sat with her lips pursed until the news sunk in. Aurora expected her to burst into tears because Aurora wasn't going with her. Instead, she jumped out of the chair and clapped her hands.

"I'll still get to go!" she squealed. She kissed her mother. "And I can go back next year too!" Josefita ran to tell her friends the news.

Aurora sank into the nearest chair. She rubbed her forehead and took a jagged breath. Then she stomped into the kitchen and slammed a pot on the stove.

On the crisp fall day that Aurora's family boarded the train, all the Vigils were in Socorro to share goodbye hugs.

The train took four days to get to St. Louis. Manuel had made arrangements for the family to stay at the Union Station Hotel. He made sure that someone from the hotel was at the station to meet them.

Josefita thought she would be ready for what she saw in the city. After all, she'd been to Albuquerque. But, when she stepped off the train, she stood wide-eyed and mouth agape.

They arrived in St. Louis a week before Manuelito had to start school. The little group from New Mexico held their hats as they craned their heads upward. The buildings touched the sky. They had to dodge buggies, horses, and delivery wagons as they crossed the street.

Manuelito showed them around the university and introduced them to some of his professors. For the first time, Josefita was silent. She peered from behind her brother at the bearded men in dark suits.

When Manuelito led his family up the mahogany staircase, Josefita tugged at his sleeve. "Are those the men who know everything?"

Manuelito laughed. "They think they do, but they wouldn't know how to make grapes into wine or turn wheat into flour."

In the evenings they ate at restaurants with linen covered tables. The tables were set with china and more silverware than they knew what to do with. Their conversations were nonstop comparisons of the houses that looked like castles, and stores stacked one on top of the other.

The day they went to the store that supplied Manuel's mercantile, Severo ran his hand over every item within reach. Dresses, already made, hung on long racks. Glass display cases held little jars of sweet-smelling creams. Soft leather gloves, colored to match the dresses, were draped atop the cases.

Josefita poked Flavito's arm and pointed. Flavito stared mutely at row after row of suits, hats, and even shoes. Josefita covered her mouth to hide her giggles as salespeople scurried around them.

As a young boy walked behind them carrying their packages, Josefita and Flavito began to feel like royalty. They didn't talk about the enormity and splendor of the store until they reached their rooms.

"No wonder you wanted to stay." Flavito said to his brother. "Lemitar must seem like a dirt clod to you."

Manuelito shook his head. "I felt like you did when I first came. But by the time I got on the train to go back home, all I wanted to see were my *abuelo* 's *chili* fields. I could never get used to the smell of this place. When you go back, walk through Papá Esquipula's fields. Then tell me where you would rather live." Manuelito closed his eyes and breathed in deeply.

Every day. Manuelito took them to see another part of the city. Each time, especially at the zoo, Manuelito watched them with a grin. He was so glad he could offer the gift of these sights to his family. When someone mentioned that they wished Aurora was here, Manuelito's smile faded. *Surely next spring I can show Mamá all of this.*

On the last evening, the brothers sat on the hotel veranda. Flavito couldn't stop talking about what he had seen. When Manuelito asked him if he would like to study in St. Louis, Flavito got a distant look in his eyes. He shook his head.

"I don't know if this is for me. There's a mining school in Socorro, but I don't think I'm interested in mining. I might go to the University in Santa Fe." Flavito expected Manuelito to be disappointed, but he slapped his brother on the shoulder and smiled.

❄❄❄

Melquides and Rafael were at the station with Aurora. They stood in front of a gathering of Vigils. Aurora greeted her children with wide embraces. She cupped Flavito's face in her hands. "I'm so glad you're all safe and home."

The family pelted the travelers with questions about St. Louis. Josefita put her arm across her forehead and plodded toward the buggy. "I'm so tired," she whined. "I need some rest. I'll tell you all about it later."

The whole group nodded and drifted toward their wagons. When they reached La Parida, Josefita took Rafael into the room across the *plazita*. This was her room, decorated with wallpaper streamers and one of her mother's old rugs.

She made Rafael close his eyes before she brought out the surprise she had brought him from St. Louis. It was a beautiful glass globe. Inside was a tiny replica of the Union Station Hotel surrounded by swirling, sparkling flakes.

Rafael held the globe in both hands, moving it from side to side.

With an open mouth he studied the towers and the grand staircase. The main tower rose above the sparkling water. Tiny windows blinked from the beneath elaborate archways. He peered up at Josefita, wide eyed.

"Is there really such a place?"

Josefita nodded her head. With her chin uplifted, she announced, "Yes, that's where we stayed. You should see the inside."

The afternoon was spent surrounded by her young cousins held spellbound by Josefita's adventures.

The rest of the family sat at the long wooden table in the *plazita*. All eyes were on the travelers. Severo told about the sky-high buildings and the stores that filled three stories.

Flavito talked about the university. It was just three buildings, but filled with classrooms as big as the whole school at Lemitar. His eyes grew wide. "You can put all of Socorro, and Lemitar, and San Antonio into one part of St. Louis."

Melquides whistled through his teeth. "Don't lie to me." He shook his finger. "There are no buildings that big."

To that, the travelers all spoke at once, swearing that they were telling the truth.

Finally, Melquides yawned and patted Aurora on the shoulder. No one saw him slip away. He rode by moonlight to Lemitar and spent the night in the back room of Manuel's store.

When Aurora noticed that he was gone, she felt a tug at her heart. They hadn't spent a moment alone, and now she hadn't even gotten to say goodbye. Then a little smile crept across her lips. *That's alright, I'll see him tomorrow.*

❋❋❋

Flavito held court in Manuel's store. It seemed that everyone in town stopped by to hear about St. Louis. By the middle of the week, Flavito was tired of telling the same stories. When Melquides came by for a load of flour, Flavito volunteered to go with him to San Antonio.

Melquides hoped he would hear even more about the trip, especially about Manuelito's university. But before they drove onto the main road, Flavito slumped against his shoulder and slept.

When they finally arrived that evening, Aurora had dinner for them. Melquides ate, elbows on the table, with his head cradled in his hands. He said a sleepy goodbye and announced that he would spend the night in the back room of the store. Aurora walked him to

388

his wagon. Melquides glanced toward the house, gave Aurora a soft kiss, and hauled himself onto the wagon.

For the next few days Josefita sat on the counter at the store. She held everyone in San Antonio captive with her stories. She stretched her arms wide as she tried to describe the vastness of St. Louis. The people of the dusty little village gave each other wide-eyed glances, then asked for more.

By the end of the week, the excitement of the trip had faded. Now the people who came in were talking about their crops and new arrivals in their family. The women joined Aurora in the back room to make plans for the *fiesta* of San Antonio.

When they left, Aurora watched Josefita still swimming in memories of the big city, and dreaming of going back. Aurora stepped out the front door and hugged herself. *Next spring I'll get to see it all for myself.*

At the *fiesta* dance, a gust of August wind made Aurora shiver. Melquides stepped behind her and draped his jacket over her shoulders. First, they danced a bouncy *rancherita*. Soon, they dared to sway to a waltz. The *fiesta* dance went on until the morning light faded the stars. Long before that, Melquides and Aurora had stolen away.

The townspeople were used to seeing Melquides coming and going from Aurora's house. The couple was careful to give the appearance that they were never alone in her house. When she sent Dolores home, Aurora made her promise not to mention that Melquides was still there. The times of their secret visits were brief.

The lumberyard in Socorro soon pulled Melquides away. In September, Manuel had broken ground for the Socorro lumberyard. He explained to Melquides that the lumber would be coming from the mill at Magdalena. "Severo will teach you the prices and how to keep the books."

"That won't be hard to learn. I've been at San Antonio for almost two years. Aurora helps me keep the books there." Shifting from one foot to another, he cleared his throat. "Do you think Aurora would like to move back to Socorro?"

Manuel jerked his pipe out of his mouth and coughed. "Aurora! What's this all about? What makes you think Aurora would want to move to Socorro? Isn't she happy in San Antonio? You visit with her a lot. Has she said something?" He arched his brows and waited for Melquides to answer.

Melquides twisted his hands. "Oh, I think she's happy there. It's just that sometimes she misses doing things, you know, to help the town." Melquides moved to the window. *Maybe I've said too much.* He shrugged. "She does a lot in San Antonio, but it's a small town. I just wondered. . ."

Manuel frowned at Severo who raised his shoulders and threw his hands up. Manuel told Melquides that he had sent Aurora to San Antonio to get her away from Socorro.

"After William died, Aurora looked like an old rag. She told me she was torn between the people she had grown up with, and the people in William's world."

Melquides nodded in agreement. "But if she went back now, she wouldn't have to be friends with all those women."

"You're talking in circles," Manuel grunted. He stood and cocked his head. "Besides, what does this have to do with the lumberyard?"

"Well," Melquides stammered, "We've talked, and Aurora doesn't know what she'll do without my help. I just thought she might want to go to Socorro with me, I mean, you know, to help."

Melquides shifted from one foot to the other. "Besides, Rafael will really miss Aurora and Josefita."

Manuel leaned back and crossed his arms. He decided not to push the red-faced Melquides any further. Looking down at the ledger, Manuel said, "I hope Rafael's sadness has lifted. It's been three years since the angels took his mother. My little Margarita was so sweet, but in the end, I was glad her suffering had ended."

Melquides lowered his head. "I'm glad you gave me this job. Keeping busy has helped me get past my loss. Talking to Aurora helps too."

Melquides told Manuel how happy his son was when he stayed with Aurora during the winter. "You know, he's helping me at the lumberyard too."

Manuel stood up. Melquides moved toward the door, but Manuel caught him by the arm. "What are you trying to tell me, Mijo?"

Melquides put up his hands. He wanted to tell Manuel how smart and full of life Aurora was. He wanted to say how much he admired her strength, how much he loved her, but all he could manage was a shy shrug.

※※※

Aurora managed to get away to Socorro as often as she could.

390

She used the excuse of going to the Ladies League meetings to bring back ideas. Instead of attending the meetings, she met Melquides in a secluded room at the Park Hotel. Both agreed that sneaking around like this was for children. "As soon as the lumberyard is finished, I'll talk to Esquipula," Melquides promised.

"I'll talk to him too, so he won't be surprised. With me living so far away, he knows little about my life."

As November's dust storms announced the coming of winter, the lumberyard in Socorro was finished. Melquides loaded his belongings into his wagon. With his son huddled beside him, they rode to Socorro with a promise to Aurora. "We'll be married in the spring."

❉ ❉ ❉

February finally melted into March and Aurora began making plans to move to Socorro. On the first turquoise day of spring, Melquides drove to Lemitar. After the lumber was loaded, he found Esquipula. They walked slowly, inspecting his empty fields.

"March is the worst month," Esquipula said. "I'm ready to plow and plant, but the earth is just waking up."

Melquides listened as Esquipula told him what he was going to plant in each field. He nodded once in a while and twisted the brim of his hat. Finally, on the way back to the house, Melquides put his hand on Esquipula's arm.

"*Tio*, um *Señor* Vigil." Melquides scraped little lines on the ground with the toe of his boot.

Esquipula ducked his head to keep Melquides from seeing his grin.

"Um, Aurora knows how I feel about her. I wanted to ask you first, that is, I want to ask permission to marry your daughter."

"And how does my daughter feel about you?"

A smile spread across Melquides' face. "She loves me. She told me so, and I love her. I think she's the bravest, the smartest, the most beautiful woman I've ever known. I will devote my life to her."

Esquipula kept walking toward home, with Melquides beside him. They walked in silence until they got to a band of willows at the edge of the fields. Esquipula took off his hat and sat on a rickety bench, inviting Melquides to join him. The old man took out his pipe, tapped the tobacco down, and struck a match on the coarse wooden bench.

He laughed a little and shook his head. "I've watched my daughter change like the seasons. She loved Flavio so much. That time in her life was like the spring, with budding plants waiting to grow. Winter came too soon for Aurora. I thought that Flavio's death was going to break her."

"Then came William." Esquipula blew out a slow stream of smoke. "I didn't know what to think of him, but Aurora seemed to bloom. But watching her was like watching my fields in August. My crops weren't quite ready for harvest, so the heat beat them down."

Esquipula grunted. "When Flavio died, Aurora was lost but, when William died, she seemed to put down a basket that was too heavy for her to carry."

Esquipula turned to Melquides. "And what will this season bring? Will she be happy with a simple farmer who runs a lumberyard?"

Esquipula took off his hat and looked across his land. "I remember when she was a girl, begging to go back East with Manuel. Now she's seen something of the world. She's felt what it was like to be part of the things that don't concern most of us."

It was Melquide's turn to light his pipe and look out at the *bosque* . "You know, *Tio*, I've never talked to anyone as much as I talk to Aurora. You're right about the burden she carried when she was married to William. She doesn't have to be torn anymore. You know I'm running the lumberyard in Socorro. She can help me with the business if she wants to, and she can be part of the town without having to leave her people behind."

Melquides went on to tell Esquipula how Rafael got along with Josefita and how welcome his son was in Aurora's house. He blew a ribbon of smoke into the air. "Now that Aurora's sons are grown, my son seems to fill a place in her heart."

Esquipula slapped Melquides on the knee and said, "Aurora has always had a mind of her own. What good would it do to say no?"

Melquides stiffened. "Do you want to say no? Am I not enough for her?"

Esquipula threw his head back and laughed. "From what you say, you will be more than enough. You've grown up in our family and I've watched you become a good man." Esquipula put his hat on and breathed deeply. He pushed himself off the bench with a groan. "Perhaps my daughter is ready to feel the peace of knowing that her storeroom is full."

❅ ❅ ❅

Springtime was gentle. The sun dried the roads quickly, so the whole family was able to attend Aurora's wedding. Josefa pulled Esquipula's good suit from the trunk. She dusted it off with her camel hair brush. Satisfied that it was as fresh as she could get it, she hung it out to air.

On the day of Aurora's wedding, Esquipula slipped the jacket over his shoulders. The fit was a little tighter but, when Josefa saw her husband, she clapped her hands and smiled. Before they went out the door, the old couple hugged, neither saying that this was the same suit Esquipula had worn when Aurora wed Flavio, then William.

Arm-in-arm, Esquipula walked with Aurora down the aisle. He gave her a kiss on the cheek, then handed her to Melquides. Josefita was her *madrina* and Rafael was the groom's *padrino*.

Melquides and Aurora sat at the banquet table at the Garcia Opera House. This time it was filled with a sea of familiar brown faces. The dancing went on past midnight. Melquides slipped his calloused hand into Aurora's and they slipped away to the Windsor Hotel. Their room was lit up with candles. It overflowed with flowers carefully arranged by Josefita.

The next week was a busy one. Manuel traveled to San Antonio to oversee the changing of management at his store. It was left in the capable hands of Aurora's brother, Andres. Her brother's family would be moving into her house as Aurora moved out.

Determined not to take anything she no longer needed, Aurora sat on the parlor floor and began sorting through a box of old papers. Some of the documents were William's. She touched them gently and set them aside. Then she opened a faded envelope. When she unfolded it, Aurora stopped breathing. It was the legal transfer of parental rights to Telesfora and José.

She laid the papers in her lap. *Didn't I have William tear these up? I don't remember really giving up the boys. I got them back, didn't I?* Aurora remembered the day she took them to La Parida. It was when Socorro was being protected by the Committee for Safety. *Just until the celebration of our Santo Nino. That's what I told Telesfora, but when had they come back? Then there were the committees, and the teas, and the dinners.*

Aurora closed her eyes and pinched the bridge of her nose. She remembered a few summer days when the boys were home and underfoot. They came for visits with Mamá Telesfora. Then Papá Manuel needed them at the store.

She tried to remember her sons as small boys. Her memories were like broken glass. She could pick up a few shards, but most were lost to her.

She tried again to remember. The memories of her life with William were more vivid—the excitement of being involved in Socorro's society and the prestige of being married to its first mayor.

She returned to the kitchen, and threw the faded papers in the cook stove. Aurora watched the gossamer flames flicker then turn to ash.

Aurora's furniture was loaded onto a caravan of wagons. She spent the next month settling into the house she bought on Church Street.

Josefita claimed the back room that looked out at the empty garden. Soon there would be hollyhocks framing her window. Her bed was covered with the quilt Josefa had stitched from Aurora's ball gowns. The fifteen-year-old dove onto her bed and laid her head on the cool satin. She rolled over and proclaimed that she felt like a princess. She jumped off her bed, bowed low and burst into giggles.

Rafael took the small room next to his new sister. When Josefita asked if she could decorate it, Rafael jerked and waved his arms. "Get out of here with all your silly girl things." The seventeen-year-old launched a pillow at her.

Josefita crossed her arms and marched to the parlor. As soon as she saw her mother's satin drapes, her pout transformed into a smile. She spent the afternoon helping Aurora hang drapes and arrange furniture.

When Aurora and Melquides finished unpacking, their daughter was enrolled with the Sisters of Loretto. Before going to the lumberyard, Rafael walked his sister to her school. They walked, shoulder to shoulder, down the street and around the corner. Aurora waved goodbye to her fledglings. They didn't notice until she called their names. Then they raise their heads and gave their mother a quick wave.

Rafael strode into the schoolyard. His frown turned into a grin when he spotted Gloria's son Felipe. He invited Felipe to go to the lumberyard with him after school. "Now that I've finished school, I help my papá. Sometimes he lets me drive the wagon when we make deliveries."

Gloria's daughter, Martina, stepped forward and offered to tell Josefita about every boy in the schoolyard. The older girls clustered around the steps. In exchange for information about the boys, they wanted to know about Rafael. By the time the school bell rang Josefita was welcomed into their circle.

✳︎✳︎✳︎

Gloria was the first visitor to Aurora's new home. Aurora took the bone china cups and saucers from her kitchen cupboard. Now they were filled with coffee, cream, and sugar. Gloria set her *bizcochitos* on the kitchen table. The two friends sat on sturdy wooden chairs. As Gloria shared all the gossip, Aurora leaned forward, taking in every word. Gloria asked if she was going to join the Ladies League again.

"I doubt it. I was thinking of starting a little circle of my own. The church always needs help, and so does the school. I have a lot of good ideas. Now that your children are older, maybe you can help."

✳✳✳

Aurora's next visitor was Evelyn. She thought about serving tea, but changed her mind. She let Evelyn know that she was serving the special blend of coffee and chocolate that her uncle imported from Mexico. Evelyn didn't seem to notice. She was caught up in giving Aurora all the news of the various clubs. Aurora sat with her elbow on the table. She listened, with little to say.

The conversation moved toward their families. As Evelyn talked about her husband, Aurora's thoughts drifted for a moment. For a moment she wondered if her old acquaintances could bolster her husband's lumber business. The thought made her stomach tighten.

Aurora didn't offer a second cup of coffee. "Josefita will be home soon," Aurora said.

With that, Aurora ushered Evelyn to the door. They brushed a little kiss across each other's cheeks and promised to visit again soon. As Evelyn's buggy disappeared down the road, Aurora closed her eyes and shook off the idea of using her friends to her advantage. Slipping back into the kitchen, Aurora knew she would see Evelyn from time to time, but it would be Gloria and her old friends that would share her life.

✳✳✳

It wasn't long before Aurora didn't have time for visits. Severo helped her set up the books for the lumberyard. They sipped strong coffee in the back office with its big windows and the scent of newly cut pine.

Severo only had to make two trips from Lemitar. Aurora knew the ledgers and just had to learn the inventory. After she dropped off Josefita at school, Aurora drove her buggy to the lumber yard at the edge of Socorro. She spent her mornings hunched over the lumberyard books.

Every week brought warmer weather and more customers.

396

Aurora opened the door to air out the heavy scent of pine. The aroma that used to welcome her, now made her stomach lurch. Nea, who was now called La Señora, confirmed what Aurora suspected.

Melquides rushed out of the lumberyard. He jumped onto the wagon bed and threw his hat in the air. "I'm going to be a father again!" he shouted to cheers and claps from his men. His work seemed lighter. He told everyone he met that he would be blessed with another child. When Aurora complained about her queasy stomach, Melquides sat her on his lap. He was not one to tell Aurora what to do, but now he insisted that she stay home.

"You don't have to help me take care of the lumberyard. Please, just let me take care of you."

Aurora rested her head on his chest. The scent of pine, mingled with tobacco, clung to his jacket. Aurora pinched her nose and gently pushed away.

When Manuel heard the news, he sent his son, José de Jesus, to take over the office work. Melquides welcomed José with a hearty slap on the back. Their work was often interrupted by stories of their childhood at La Parida. When José turned back to the ledger, Melquides was confident that Severo had taught him well. Aurora's absence was barely noticed.

❋❋❋

"Don't let your fears drive you into darkness again," Nea said as she held Aurora close. "I know you've heard stories of older women giving birth to unhealthy babies." Nea shook Aurora's shoulders firmly. "The Blessed Mother is watching over you. I saw it in a vision. She won't let anything happen to this child."

When Aurora's healthy baby girl arrived, it was Nea who brought Doloritas into the world. Aurora set a pink doily on her corner altar. Every morning she gathered up her baby girl. She made the sign of the cross over her baby's heart, then offered a prayer to the statue of the Blessed Mother.

Doloritas' little round face and plump little legs didn't look at all like Josefita's when she was born. During the two weeks that Nea stayed with Aurora, the baby grew even rounder. On the day Nea left, Aurora had her take the altar out of the room. "I don't think I'll need this anymore."

96

Aurora held Manuelito's letter to her heart. She told Melquides about it then set it aside. When Josefita came home, Aurora pointed to the letter. "Come with me. I don't want you waking up the baby."

"Why, what's the matter?" Josefita stared at her mother.

"Nothing's the matter." Aurora led Josefita to the back porch.

"Manuelito is coming home next month, but now with the baby, I can't go to St. Louis."

"Josefita groaned and sagged onto a chair. Then she straightened. "Is anyone else going? What about Flavito?

Aurora shook her head. "I doubt it. He's so busy helping his *abuelo* that I hardly see him. Besides, I think he has his eye on a girl."

Aurora stood in front of the screen door. The last thing she wanted was for Josefita to slam it as she stormed through the house.

Instead, Josefita walked into the yard. "This is really disappointing, but at least I got to see St. Louis once. I'm sure I'll go back someday." The fifteen-year-old smiled as she brushed past her mother. "Regina is coming over. She's a friend I met at school. We're going to walk to the bakery and meet some friends there. I can go, can't I?"

It was Aurora's turn to sag onto a kitchen chair. She shook her head and wondered out loud. "What happened to the Josefita I used to know?" Then Aurora remembered lengthening the hems of her dresses and of finding her dolls packed away in her trunk. When she walked into her room, Aurora heard Josefita and Regina talking about the dances they would attend. Aurora tiptoed into Doloritas' room. She sat with her hand on the cradle willing her baby girl not to grow up too soon.

❋❋❋

Manuelito's final homecoming was met with both joy and sadness for Aurora. Manuel had nudged Aurora aside and sat Manuelito in the honored chair at the store. The *viejos* sitting around the stove never tired of hearing about the huge buildings and the treasures within them. Manuel sat beside Manuelito assuring the old men that his grandson was telling the truth.

Manuel lifted his chin. "Manuelito is going to build a railroad," he boasted. Manuelito tried to correct him, but his grandfather shushed him. He wagged his finger at the circle of old men. "You wait and see;

I'm going to ride on the first train that travels into Mexico." He patted Manuelito on the knee.

Manuel waved Manuelito's offers to help away. "Don't worry about helping me at the store *Mijo*." He slapped Manuelito on the shoulder. Flavito is still with me, and look at all your big strong cousins. I'll have plenty of help."

❋❋❋

Manuelito's letters were coming from El Paso now. He was an engineer, helping to build the new railroad line connecting the United States to Mexico. Flavito had decided to go with him. A letter came every week. Manuelito wrote about the hardships of building a railroad through the desert. Flavito usually only scribbled a quick note at the end of his brother's letter.

After supper Aurora and the children would each write to Manuelito. Aurora always wrote to Flavito too. She encouraged both of them to come home for a visit, but the *chili* was planted and harvested before Aurora saw her sons again.

Flavito stepped from the train slowly. Then, he slid sideways to reveal his brother. A cheer went up when the family saw the brothers. Aurora barely recognized the sturdy young men that stepped from the train. As always, Telesfora and José were at the train station.

"That was such a long trip. Spend the night with us in Socorro so you can rest." Aurora looked hopefully at her sons.

The brothers exchanged a glance. Manuelito held his breath while Flavito studied his boots. "We promised to go see Papá Manuel as soon as we got back." Manuelito hugged his mother and said, "We'll spend a couple of days in La Parida visiting with the family, then you'll have us for the rest of the week."

It was Aurora's turn to study the ground. Before she had a chance to answer, Telesfora and José surrounded the young men and led them toward their wagon.

Before leaving for La Parida, the family followed Aurora's buggy to her house. The table was laden with all of the foods that Aurora's sons enjoyed.

Aurora nudged Melquides and pointed with her chin. With a quick nod, he sat next to Flavito. Aurora slid into the chair next to Manuelito. With every dish passed around the table came a torrent of questions.

Josefita had been warned not to ask for gifts. When Flavito noticed her wiggling in her chair, he couldn't resist teasing her.

"I might have brought you some little gifts." He rubbed his chin. "Oh, but they're in the bottom of my trunk. I won't be able to get them until we unpack the things we've brought for everyone at La Parida."

Josefita wove her fingers together and squeezed them to her chest. Then she whacked her big brother on the arm. "Can I go with them to La Parida?" she begged.

Aurora shook her head firmly. "I need your help. We have a lot of food to prepare for when your brothers come back. Josefita put her head on Aurora's shoulders. "It'll only be for a couple of days. Then I'll be back to help." Aurora looked up at her daughter, then she thought, *when did Josefita grow taller than me?*

It was Maria's daughter who sweated in the kitchen with Aurora. They cooked more in the next two days than Aurora had in a month. She made empanadas filled with figs and apples, and *piñons*. As she pinched the edges of the little round pies, Aurora smiled. *Tomorrow we'll all be together.*

When Aurora's three children returned to Socorro, all work at the lumberyard was handed off to Melquides' men. The wood box sat empty and the chickens had to fend for themselves. The week was spent embracing Aurora's sons. She clung to every moment. When winter came and her sons were far away, Aurora would have these memories to keep her warm.

❋❋❋

The next Tuesday, Melquides and Aurora took Manuelito back to the train station. Aurora clutched his hand until the porter announced the last call for boarding the train. Telesfora walked him to the train and gave him a farewell kiss. She walked to the end of the platform waving and dabbing her eyes.

He promised to visit again soon, but there was no invitation for his family to visit him. He was often in the middle of the desert, living in a tent, surveying for the best route to run the rails.

Aurora slumped against Melquides. He put his arm around her and reminded her that El Paso wasn't as far as St. Louis. Then he held her close.

"Besides, you have one of your sons in Lemitar."

Aurora drew in a breath. She nodded, remembering that Flavito had announced he would not be going back with Manuelito. Then

400

she remembered the quick hug he gave her as he hurried off to see
his friends. She looked for him in the crowd that was waving goodbye.
He was holding Teresa Pino's hand.

97

Flavito had seen enough of Mexico and El Paso. It was not a grand city like the one back East. The odd tasting food didn't agree with him. Although he spoke the same language, the customs of the Mexicans were foreign to him. He told everyone that he needed to go home and help his aging grandfather. The truth was in the letters he had hidden in his trunk.

They were from Aurora's cousin Teresa Pino. When she first caught his eye, she reminded Flavito that they knew each other when they were children. When Flavito thought back, he could only picture a skinny girl, one of the little kids that the older boys ignored. He wasn't about to ignore her now.

Teresa had come into Manuel's store as often as she could, and soon Flavito was invited to her home to share a meal. Her father met Flavito with a cool welcome. Flavito sat on the edge of his wooden chair while Teresa's father made himself comfortable. The old velveteen chair creaked and sagged, but Elias didn't seem to notice. He leaned toward Teresa. "I'm not sure this is a good match. "He is, after all, your mother's cousin."

❋❋❋

When Flavito told Papá Manuel about his visit with Teresa's father, Manuel just huffed. Manuel didn't mention Teresa again. He just kept talking about Flavito going to the university. "Look how much good it has done for Manuelito."

Flavito's lips tightened into a thin line. "I'm not like Manuelito. I want to stay here with my family."

Manuel turned his back to Flavito and rolled his eyes. "What about the School of Mines? The school is in Socorro. Go for a year. See if you like it." Manuel read him a newspaper article about the Kelly mines. "This is just the beginning. You could be an engineer like your brother—a mining engineer."

Flavito listened, his foot tapping and eyes darting toward the door. He took a long walk to the *bosque* to clear his thoughts. His grandfather had always wanted the best for both of Flavio's sons. He had never done anything to hurt them. Maybe he was right. After all, Socorro wasn't that far away from Lemitar.

When Flavito told Teresa that his grandfather was willing to pay for a year at the School of Mines, he thought she would be happy. Instead, she pulled away and ran toward her house. He ran after her.

"Do you want me to work at my grandfather's store forever? I'm thinking about our future."

Teresa sniffled. "Don't you see what he's trying to do. I heard my father talking to Manuel. Now he's trying to keep us apart. No, Socorro isn't that far, but it's far enough."

Flavito wrapped his arms around her. The seventeen-year-old wiped her eyes when Flavito told her that he would be back every Friday.

Her hands went up in surrender. "And I'll go to Socorro every chance I get." She slapped the air and kissed Flavio's cheek. "They can try to keep us apart, but it won't work."

Flavito squeezed her tight. "Nothing anyone can do will keep us apart."

❋❋❋

When Flavito volunteered to take a load of lumber to Socorro, Aurora wasn't surprised to hear him tapping at the back door.

"Come in, come in. You don't have to knock." She hugged her son and invited him to sit at the kitchen table. She had heard rumors about Flavito and Teresa and the family's concerns. When she thought about this, the corners of her lips turned up. *Flavio and I were planning to run away and get married if my father wouldn't give his consent.* As Flavito sipped strong coffee, Aurora made herself another cup of Nea's chamomile tea.

Flavito asked about the family in Socorro. He said that Manuel was pleased with the way Melquides was running the lumberyard. In a flat voice, he told his mother about going to the mining school in Socorro. He studied the flowers on the tablecloth.

Aurora sat with her hand on her chin waiting for him to build up the courage to talk about Teresa. He rose to get another cup of coffee. With his back to her, Flavito cleared his throat.

"Mamá, you know how much I care for Teresa, uh, we love each other." His voice rose to a high pitch. "It shouldn't matter that she's your cousin." He walked stiffly back to the table. "You and my papá were cousins and me and Manuelito turned out alright. Papá Esquipula said that the family didn't want you to marry, but you didn't listen. You loved each other and that was all that mattered." He sat and stared at his mother.

Aurora put her hand over his. "I want nothing more than for you to be happy. I talked to Melquides about this and he agrees. Don't worry about what anybody else thinks. It's up to me and your stepfather to give you our blessing. You can be sure that we will."

Flavito let out a deep sigh. His shoulders dropped and he dared to smile. Then his smile turned to a frown. "Teresa's parents aren't so sure. Maybe you can talk to them."

Aurora shrugged; her thoughts had drifted backward. "We were so happy, your father and I." Aurora looked deeply into Flavito's hazel green eyes. She drew him close. "You know, I've never told you about your father. I guess life just kept sweeping me away."

Flavito spent the rest of the afternoon listening to his mother's stories about the father that he never knew. He sat with his elbows on the table. A quick smile touched his lips, then faded. "I wished I had known him," he sighed.

Aurora reached for his hand. Flavito clasped her hand, then quickly let go. Aurora swallowed the threat of tears. She hadn't thought about the time she spent with Flavio in years. The pain of losing him had dulled, but the loss of what could have been still stung. After Flavito left, Aurora wondered why she had never spoken about his father before.

Aurora took another sip of Nea's soothing tea and let her stomach settle. The house was quiet and her mind pushed through the fog of the past.

✳✳✳

Cries from the bedroom brought Aurora back into the day. She changed Dolorita's soggy diaper and sighed. She began to rock her one-year-old. "I hope you're out of diapers before the next one comes."

Only Melquides knew she was expecting again. Aurora planned to tell Gloria after Mass and let the news spread to her family.

Nea had assured her that things were going well and she should deliver a healthy baby in the fall. Every time she felt the ache of her muscles stretching, or the smell of food turned her stomach, she went to her room and prayed. She prayed not only for the safety of her unborn child, but that God would take away her fear. She didn't want that fear to mark her child.

✳✳✳

Nea covered her face with her shawl as she hurried across town.

404

A cloudy lavender sky welcomed Aurora's third son into the world. The healthy baby boy was named Antonio. Aurora sent word to La Parida. She hoped that Esquipula could bring Josefa to help her with the baby, but the winds had brought an early snow. Aurora's mother wouldn't get to see her latest grandson until the roads dried out in the spring.

When Maria brought her daughter to cook for Aurora, she found her cousin sitting at the kitchen table. "What do you mean you're not going to stay in your bed for two weeks? Let me send for my sister from Los Lunas to help out." Maria wrapped her shawl around Aurora shoulders.

Aurora waved Maria's offer away. "How can I stay in bed with these two to take care of. Besides, those are the old ways. Joséfita is staying out of school to help me for a while. We'll be alright."

Josefita stayed home from school for two weeks. She brought her mother lumpy porridge for breakfast, then hummed around the kitchen. Running water and clinking dishes put a smile on Aurora's lips. As she laid back against the pillow, Aurora thought about the indulgence of Josefita's father. *Princess, he called her. That's what she was to him*. Aurora listened again and heard the silly voice Josefita used when she talked to her little sister.

Josefita's friend, Angelina, brought her school work every day so Josefita wouldn't fall behind. On Sunday, Josefita's teacher brought Aurora a little bunch of flowers and a soft cotton gown for Antonio. Dolorita played with the rag doll that Josefita had made her as Aurora fed the baby. Josefita sat at the table with her teacher. Slowly she began to understand the arithmetic that had baffled her last week.

As soon as Sister Mary Regina left, the fifteen-year-old announced that she wanted to be a teacher. "I can go to the Normal Institute here in Socorro." She cleared her books away and began setting the table. "I only have a year left with the Sisters. When I go back to school, I'll ask Sister Regina how long it takes to finish at the Normal Institute." Josefita gave Aurora a kiss on the forehead and danced into her room.

Aurora looked down at Antonio. Her thoughts tumbled and her forehead wrinkled. *How is it possible for Josefita to be a year away from going to the Normal Institute?*

❄❄❄

Aurora shoved another stick of wood into the cook stove, then took the letter from the shelf. She scooped up her newborn and be-

405

gin to sway. Tears dropped on little Antonio's head. *I didn't get to see Manuelito get married. He didn't even bring his bride to meet the family and get our blessing. We had to find out about Conchita in a letter.*

Aurora slipped back into her room. *Hopefully they can come to Flavito's wedding.* She started to pull the curtains closed, but the baby squealed. She put Antonio to her breast and peeked out the window. Flavito hadn't visited in weeks. Aurora could only pray that he was still planning on marrying Teresa.

Things hadn't gone as Flavito hoped with Teresa's family. After a year, her father was still reluctant to let her marry him. They had seen as much of each other as they could, but most of the time, Flavito cut their visits short. "I have to go to the laboratory and do my testing before it closes." There was always the promise of a longer visit next week.

Finally, April pushed the cold winds south and the school year was over. Flavito could go back to Lemitar and help Manuel. He and Teresa could start making their wedding plans. Flavito had made up his mind. They would marry in the fall.

❋❋❋

When Manuel took his grandson aside, Flavito's shoulders begin to tighten. Manuel lit his pipe and invited Flavito to sit.

"You've gone to the mining school in Socorro for a year. You tell me you don't think you want to continue." Manuel blew out a cloud of sweet-smelling smoke. "What about going to the university in Santa Fe?"

Flavito's jaws clamped tight and he began to shake his head. He knew that Teresa's father had talked to Manuel, but out of respect, he listened to what his grandfather had to say.

"You want to give Teresa a good life, don't you? A good education will help. Look at what it's done for your brother. You don't have to go clear back East. There's a fine university in Santa Fe and if you really love each other, one more year won't matter. If you're still determined to get married when you come back from Santa Fe, I will gladly bless your union."

"Please let me think about this," Flavito said. Before he went out the door, he turned to Manuel. "How long did you and my *abuelita* have to wait?" Flavito started to slam the door, but caught himself. As he stepped outside, he closed it softly. Then Flavito shrugged. *Santa*

406

Fe, he thought, *where I would be studying law instead of rocks*.

Flavito held Teresa and tried to quiet her sobs. "We'll be together all summer." He cupped her face with his hands and promised he would ride the train home from Santa Fe as often as he could.

"Remember what they promised," Flavito said. "After this year they will give us their blessing. We'll show them just how strong our love is." Flavito gave Teresa a quick kiss. "Besides, this will give you a whole year to plan the big wedding you're always talking about."

98

When Aurora and Melquides arrived at the reception, the tables were surrounded by wedding guests. The family sat at the banquet table, perched on the stage of the Garcia Opera House. Flanking the bride and groom where the *padrinos*, Manuelito and his wife Conchita. Beside Conchita sat Telesfora then José. Flanking each end of the table were Flavito's *abuelos*.

Josefa stood and searched for her daughter in the crowded room. When she spotted Aurora, she waved for her to move closer, but all the seats were taken.

Aurora waved back and mouthed. "It's alright." But when she sank into her chair, she realized how far away she was from her sons.

Esquipula looked from his wife to his daughter. He disappeared into the back room, returning with a small table. The rickety table was set at the edge of the family. Then he ordered two chairs to be brought up to the stage. Still standing, he waved to Aurora with both hands.

Melquides took Antonio from Aurora and led her, head bowed, to the stage. Aurora leaned forward and tried to catch Flavito's eyes. He didn't seem to notice the commotion at the end of the table. With his arms around his bride, Flavito stared, dreamy eyed, past José's long-winded speech.

Josefita strode into the room wearing a beautiful lavender gown. She was with her friends from the teaching school. She floated through the room as if this event had been prepared for her. Aurora's fork stopped in midair. She shook her head and laughed. How many times had she entered a room in the same manner? Josefita waved at her mother then sat with her friends at the far end of the hall.

Aurora passed Doloritas to Josefa. She entertained the toddler by revealing bits of cake that had been wrapped in her folded napkin.

It wasn't long before Antonio began to squirm. Aurora shifted him on her lap. She took the spoon away from him, replacing it with a rattle. Then she smashed bits of food and fed her fussy one-year-old son. He took a few bites, then twisted and reached for his father.

"It's too hot in here." Aurora handed Antonio to Melquides. "I have to get some fresh air."

Outside, she leaned against the wall and took a deep breath. The first person that filled her thoughts was Josefita with her blonde hair and blue eyes. How easily she had folded into a family of brown eyes and ebony locks. But she knew who she was and chose where she wanted to be.

Aurora closed her eyes. Her thoughts turned to Telesfora and José. She balled up her fist and willed herself not to run from the family that hadn't set a place for her at the wedding table.

Aurora wiped her eyes on her gloved hand. *And Flavito,* she thought, *sitting with his La Parida family.* She drew in a long, slow breath. *He too always knew where he belonged.*

Her thoughts settled on the life she had chosen. Socorro's society had pulled her away from her family. How eagerly she had moved into William's world. She had led a gaggle of women to do good works for Socorro. Aurora clicked her tongue. *Señora De Baun, the mayor's wife.*

With her eyes on the ground, Aurora walked along a row of buggies. When she looked up, she found herself in front of William's old office. Aurora remembered how small his place was. There was no room for her sons. She closed her eyes and turned her face toward the fading sun.

Trudging back inside, Aurora leaned on the battered table, hastily placed at the edge of her family. Her sons, surrounded by their family, came into view. Aurora remembered her journey with William and how far she had gone with him.

Then a shiver ran down her spine as she thought about all she had found. . . and all the ones she had lost along the way.

Epilogue

Aurora died in 1904. She was only forty-six years old.
Flavito and Teresa had nine children.
Their third child was a son.
His father named him Flavio.
This gentle child grew up to become
my wise and beloved father.

Acknowledgments

A million thanks to my editor Annette Byrd, I wouldn't have the same book without her.

Many thanks to Zella Alderete and her niece Jeanie Dean, the keepers of our family history.

I would also like to thank the staff of the Genealogy Center at the Albuquerque Library.

Without these amazing people and the records that they keep, I would never have found Aurora's story.

9 780996 313148